BIG DREAMS FOR THE WEST END GIRLS

Elaine Roberts

HEAD
of ZEUS

An Aria Book

This edition first published in the United Kingdom in 2021 by Aria, an imprint of Head of Zeus Ltd

Copyright © Elaine Roberts, 2021

The moral right of Elaine Roberts to be identified as the author of this work has been asserted in accordance with the Copyright, Designs and Patents Act of 1988.

9 7 5 3 1 2 4 6 8

A CIP catalogue record for this book is available from the British Library.

E ISBN: 9781838933517
PB ISBN: 9781800246096

Cover design © CC Book Design

Typeset by Siliconchips Services Ltd UK

Printed and bound in Great Britain
by CPI Group (UK) Ltd, Croydon CR0 4YY

Aria
c/o Head of Zeus
5–8 Hardwick Street
London EC1R 4RG

www.ariafiction.com

To all the wonderful readers and their
continual support.

Joyce Taylor dropped the dirty dishes in the sink at London's Meet and Feast Café. Turning round, her eyes widened as she stared at Simon Hitchin. 'I can't believe this. Why are you telling me now?' She mopped away beads of perspiration. 'What will you do?'

The bell above the café door chimed for what felt like the hundredth time in the last half an hour. Joyce peered through the serving hatch.

Simon shrugged, fighting the urge to wrap his arms around her as he took in how hot and worn out she looked. 'I may not have any choice.'

Two stout grey-haired ladies stepped inside, jostling with their shopping bags. 'Well, Enid, at least 'aving to keep yer 'ead down against that wind yer don't see those blooming Kitchener war posters everywhere.' The bell rang out again as the door slammed shut behind them.

Was he serious about closing the café? She would have no excuse to see him every day. Joyce looked back at the man she loved. He looked as tired as she felt. She tried to batten down the love she felt for him, fighting the urge to wrap her arms around him. Now wasn't the time to show her feelings for him. What would she do if he rejected her?

She would end up losing her job and any chance of them having a future together. 'I can tell you this, Simon: it's your café so you need to decide whether you can just let go of your father's dream. No one can decide for you.'

Her hand automatically rested on the locket she wore around her neck as she found herself repeating her late father's words. 'There's always a choice. You may not like it, but there's always a choice.' Once the words were out she did wonder if that was true; after all look where she had ended up.

She sighed. 'I've got to get back to work. I've got Uncle Arthur clearing tables and making pots of tea, bless him. He only popped in for a cuppa. We're so busy again today. If the last month or so continues then we're going to need to hire some help.'

Simon sighed. 'I know, I just don't know how I'm going to pay the wages. It's hard enough finding the money for the rent and to pay you for the wonderful cakes and bread you make. I don't seem to have time to stop to think about it all.'

Joyce blushed, remembering how he had encouraged her to bring in a cake she had baked so he could try it. 'Thank you, I'm obviously pleased you enjoyed my baking and encouraged it…' She closed her eyes for a second, trying not to think about how her feelings had changed in the years she had worked for him. 'But you just need to make some changes because getting the people through the door isn't the problem.' Forcing herself to smile, Joyce marched back into the café.

Enid scanned the occupied tables and looked over at Joyce. 'Hello, lovey, yer busy again today. Can yer squeeze two small ones in?'

Joyce couldn't help smiling as the woman dropped her shopping bag and unwrapped her woollen scarf. 'I'm sure we can, Enid. Take a seat.' Joyce indicated the chairs standing against the wall. 'It might be five minutes though.' She turned her attention to her order pad, adding cake to an existing bill for the young soldier and his girl sitting at table nine. She crossed it out again, ignoring the guilt that took hold of her – the least she could do was give them free tea and cake.

Enid rubbed her hands together. 'That's all right. At least it's warm in 'ere.' She looked around her before turning to her friend. 'We mustn't forget to tell that young soldier over there that we're proud and they're all doing a good job protecting us. They need to know we're behind 'em every step of the way; after all they're laying their lives on the line for our king and country.' Enid glanced back at Joyce. 'I was reading in the paper about that Zeppelin raid on Sandringham. These are scary times.'

Joyce dropped her pencil on the counter and tucked a stray strand of brown hair behind her ear. 'I've heard customers talking about it.' She paused. 'I'm not sure I even know what a Zeppelin is.'

Enid shrugged before giving Joyce a bleak look. 'I fink it's like a giant hot air balloon, only it carries bombs and people.'

Joyce shook her head. 'It's frightening and you can't help wondering what can come of it, except death and destruction.' She automatically adjusted the frilled straps of the bib to her treasured knee-length white apron. Her slender fingers sought her embroidered name in the corner, which her mother had lovingly stitched before she had unexpectedly passed away with tuberculosis. Would she be disappointed if she knew Joyce was a waitress in a café instead of the great cook she imagined she would be? That dream had died with her mother. Had she made the right decisions? Had she felt she had a choice? Joyce sighed. What did it matter? It all seemed a lifetime ago now. She glanced over where the soldier was sitting, holding his girl's hand. Would Simon finally do what his friends had already done? She hoped not. Shaking her head, she deftly slid the cake knife under the slice of homemade Victoria sponge. A customer caught her attention. 'I won't be a moment, sir.'

The wooden chair creaked as Enid unbuttoned her long black coat. 'You're rushed off yer feet ain't yer, lovey?'

Joyce nodded. After picking up the tea plate and cake fork, she weaved between the tables, and then carefully placing the items in front of the young woman. She walked over to the man who had caught her attention earlier and she pasted on her best smile. 'Yes, sir, I'm sorry about the wait. What can I get you?'

'Just the bill.' The elderly man scowled. 'You should get some help in.'

Nodding, Joyce's tiredness engulfed her. 'I'll do your bill right away, sir.' As she carried on there was a thud of something hitting the floor. Joyce looked down to try to see what it was. It was just visible under a chair. Her throat tightened and tears threatened to make a fool of her as she stooped down and scooped up her locket. She sucked in her breath and examined the gold chain. A link had broken. Joyce blinked quickly. Her chest tightened. She would never be able to afford to get it repaired. Joyce took a couple of breaths before walking over to the counter and carefully placing it on the side where she could see it. Her eyes were sore and red with unshed tears.

The man startled Joyce. 'I'm sorry, I don't mean to interrupt but I need to pay my bill.'

'No, sir, it should be me who's sorry.' She found his ticket and totted up the hot drinks and the egg sandwiches he'd had.

The man studied her for a moment. 'It's obvious you're busy and I shouldn't be taking my bad day out on you.'

Joyce forced a smile. 'Thank you, but I shouldn't have kept you waiting.'

The man handed her a silver florin.

'Thank you, sir, two shillings. I'll just get your change.'

'Keep it – you deserve it.' He turned to walk away but stopped to look back. 'By the way, I don't know where you get your bread from but it's delicious.'

Joyce smiled as pride welled up inside her. She silently gave thanks to her mother. 'Thank you, that's most generous of you.' She watched him as the bell chimed and again when the door closed, bringing her back to reality. There was a chink of coins as Joyce took the change from the till and dropped it in the jar next to it. 'Right, Enid, let me clear the table, then it's all yours.'

'Thank you, lovey.'

Joyce loaded the tray with the used crockery and cutlery. She placed the salt and pepper pots on the chair before giving the table a thorough wipe-over and placing them back in the centre of the table.

'That's lovely, so we'll just 'ave our usual tea and toast please.'

Joyce jerked at Enid's voice behind her. 'Sorry, I didn't realise you were standing behind me. I'll get it ordered now for you.' She picked up the tray and headed back towards the counter.

'Can we have another pot of tea please?'

Joyce nodded as she walked past the young lady who was sitting with someone who looked like a much older version of her. She took the tray of crockery through to the kitchen and placed it on the side near the sink. 'Enid's in. She and her friend want the usual couple of rounds of toast.' Without a backward glance at Simon she rushed out of the kitchen to start making a couple of pots of tea.

The doorbell chimed, indicating the café door had opened. The heat and various cooking smells escaped from inside the café, swallowed up into the cold air invading every corner. The bell rang out again as the door shut.

Joyce couldn't stop the sigh escaping from her as she spooned the tea leaves into the china teapot. She closed the tea caddy and peered over her shoulder at the suited towering dark-haired man. 'Good afternoon, Mr Harris, and what can I do for you?'

'It's Monday, Miss Taylor. I believe you know – as I know – it's rent day.'

Joyce forced a smile. 'You'll need to speak to Simon, er … I mean Mr Hitchin.' She turned and poured boiling water into the teapots.

Mr Harris frowned and sniffed. 'Is something burning?'

Joyce looked through the serving hatch and saw the smoke spiralling into the air. 'Simon, something's burning?' She turned and ran into the kitchen just as Simon pulled some charred bread from the range.

'It's only the toast, no harm done.'

'One of these days you're going to burn the place down.'

'I'm not sure that's fair, Joyce. I've a lot going on at the moment and I was washing up some plates.' Simon shook his head. 'It's not the end of the world. I can start again.'

Joyce immediately looked contrite; she rested her hand on his arm. 'I'm sorry, I'm tired and panicked, and on top of that the landlord is here for his rent.'

Simon, forgetting the trials of the day, let the love he felt shine through as he gently ran his fingers down her soft cheek. 'There's no need to be. I shouldn't try and do two things at once.'

Joyce's lips parted, hungry to feel his lips on hers.

'I'm still here, waiting,' Mr Harris bellowed from the other side of the serving hatch.

Joyce jerked back. She cleared her throat before speaking in a low throaty tone. 'What … what are we going to do about Mr Harris?'

'Are you listening to me or do I have to come in there?'

Simon frowned before rubbing his hand over his face. 'I don't have time for him. Just pay him out of the till, if there's enough, and put a note in there to remind me what the money was used for.'

Joyce ran her hand down Simon's arm. 'I actually think there could be – it's been non-stop today.'

'Just give him what he wants. If there's not enough he'll have to come back.'

Joyce nodded and turned to walk away. She stopped and glanced over her shoulder and smiled at him. 'Keep an eye on the toast this time. We don't need any more accidents.'

'All right, all right.' Simon smiled. 'And you get back to the customers.'

Joyce walked back out to the counter and opened the till. 'How much is it, Mr Harris?'

'Six shillings but it will be going up.'

Joyce stared at him. 'I hope that means you'll come and do some of the repairs we keep asking to be done.'

Mr Harris's mouth sat in a grim, tight line. 'In due course, all in due course.'

Joyce opened the till and took out three silver coins, holding them tight. 'You've been saying that for months. Your father would turn in his grave if he knew how you'd let his property fall into disrepair.'

Mr Harris held out his hand. 'I'm not my father, and you need to stop moaning, otherwise the repairs will be the least of your worries.'

Joyce dropped the three florins into his hand. 'I'm not moaning, I'm just reminding you of your duty as a landlord.'

Simon shouted, 'Enid's toast is ready.'

Joyce turned to take the two tea plates. The bell chimed. She hoped that meant Mr Harris had left.

Arthur stepped forward. 'Let me take them for you.' Reaching out, he took the plates before glancing at Joyce. 'I tell you what you could do with: help clearing the tables, washing up and a nicer landlord.'

Joyce smiled at her uncle. 'Don't I know it. You seem to be here helping out most days now, but the takings don't reflect how busy we are.'

Arthur frowned. 'I'm just keeping an eye on you. You're always so tired when you get home.'

Joyce fiddled with her pencil. 'You've been good to me. I know we've had some rough times together but you've always kept a roof over my head, particularly when my grandmother didn't want me. I'm not sure I've ever thanked you for looking after me.'

'There's no need to thank me, especially when it was more you looking after me. You keep me going.' Arthur looked around the café. 'Anyway, I've been coming here for very selfish reasons.'

Joyce tilted her head slightly. 'That sounds ominous.'

Arthur chuckled. 'Not really, it's since I had that slice of Victoria sponge. It reminded me of when you were a child and I'd visit and your mother would always insist I had a slice. Your mother was always so proud of you. She used to tell everyone how you'd one day be a great cook, and she wasn't wrong.'

Joyce's smile gradually faded. 'I remember, but I don't think either of us thought she meant cooking cake for a café.'

Enid called out. 'Is that our toast?'

Arthur peered over his shoulder. 'Oh yes, I'm sorry.' He patted Joyce's arm before weaving his way to Enid's table.

Ted peered up and down the road. It was early evening but darkness was closing in. The heavy snow that had fallen earlier crunched underfoot on the pavement but was slushy along the busy road as cars chugged past slowly, their drivers leaning forward to see the road.

Ted smiled as two boys squealed with laughter, watching through hooded eyes as they threw snowballs at each other. His smile faded as he remembered playing for hours with his son and daughter, only stopping when the snow had numbed his fingers. He shook his head. There was no point in dwelling on what was lost; he had to stay focused.

The London street lights were no longer lit for fear of

helping the Germans find their way to their targets. Ted blew his warm breath on his hands and rubbed them together, while stamping the snow off his black highly polished shoes, before pushing open the door and walking into the Dog and Duck Public House. It was dark and smoky inside. He wrinkled his nose at the pungent smell of tobacco mingled with the ale. Old men sat nursing their pints of beer. Some played dominoes, while others gave their support to a game of shove ha'penny in the far corner. Ted looked over at the group of men laughing and cheering as they leant over the board. The palm of his hand itched. Should he go over to check out the game? Surely a little bet wouldn't hurt, would it?

He pulled himself up. Not on this day; he had bigger fish to fry. He tipped the brim of his black hat at the barman, who nodded in response. 'Is it all right to go through?'

The barman rubbed a glass with an old rag; he studied him for a moment before nodding. 'I'm surprised to see yer 'ere tonight.'

Ted laughed with more confidence than he truly felt. 'Yer know me, I can't resist a game.' He thrust his hand inside his black trouser pocket and pulled out a wad of pound notes. 'I'll take a bottle of whisky in with me.'

'There's a game of shove ha'penny you could 'ave a bet on.' The barman reached under the bar and grabbed a bottle of Old Highland Whisky and placed it on the counter.

Ted glanced over at the men cheering on the game again. 'No, I'm 'ere for more than that tonight.' He threw a pound note down and took the bottle. 'Thanks, wish me luck.' He turned and walked back towards the backroom door.

'You'll need more than luck.' The barman watched

Ted rap on the heavy wooden door next to the bar before opening it and walking through. The door slammed shut behind him.

'What are yer doing here, Ted?' A man in a dark suit and black tie raised his eyebrows. 'Tonight's game is too rich for yer.'

Ted gave half a smile. 'I've got me money, Slips.' He glanced around into the darkness. The only lights were hanging above four round tables, which were situated around the room; each had six chairs spaced evenly around them.

Slips laughed. 'So, I'm interested; who's the mug that has lent the money this time? I would have thought the word would be out there by now.'

Ted frowned. 'Not everyone has such a low opinion of me as you. With a fifty-pound buy-in it could set me and the family up for life.'

Slips stared at him. 'Well, I need to see the colour of your money. You've a bit of a reputation, as yer well know.'

Ted shook his head. 'That's because of people like you bad-mouthing me. You shouldn't be doing that; after all I've always paid my debts.'

Slips grimaced. 'Only after yer took a bit of a bruising at times, and trust me, I haven't needed to bad-mouth yer.'

'Everyone's so impatient. I've always paid up,' Ted grumbled.

Slips gave a deep, throaty laugh. 'Do yer want to tell the man that? 'E's in tonight.'

Ted thrust his hand inside his suit jacket pocket and pulled out a wad of notes. 'Just count the money and do what the boss tells you.'

Slips's eyes narrowed. 'Yeah, well, I'm going to have to check with the boss to see if he wants yer in the game; after all you've only just paid off your last debt.' He paused, glancing over at the far end of the room as the door that led upstairs slammed shut. 'He may not want to take the money you're about to lose again, or he could be impatient to commit daylight robbery, which yer seem to submit to every day. Either way he's 'ere now so you won't 'ave long to wait.'

Ted looked round and saw Mickey Simmons marching towards them. His heart began to race; perhaps he shouldn't have come. Maybe Slips was right but there was no going back now; there was no running away with his tail between his legs. He had to stand his ground otherwise he'll be a laughing stock, and would never be able to show his face at any game again. Ted thrust out his chest and lifted his chin as he turned back to see Slips lick his finger and flick through the edges of the notes, stacking them in ten-pound piles. 'It's going to be different this time. I'm going to get my money back tonight.'

Slips chuckled. 'You do know gambling is a mug's game don't yer?' He gave Ted a sideways glance before going back to the money. 'I don't think you'll ever learn, Ted. Yer must've had more beatings than anyone else I know and yet yer still come back for more.'

'My luck's got to change sometime.'

'Leave this to me, Slips. It's always impressive to see Mr Taylor at one of my card games.' Mr Simmons screwed up his eyes as he stared at Ted.

Slips opened his mouth to speak, but quickly closed it again when Mr Simmons turned and gave him a killer look.

'Just get on with what you're expected to do this evening,

and it's not turning people like Ted away.' Mr Simmons turned back to Ted. 'I wasn't expecting to see you today. Are you sure you're in the right place? I'm not one for turning anyone away – especially if they have the buy-in – but are you sure you want to do this? I'd hate for you to leave a loser again.'

Ted looked at the bald man, who was as round as he was tall. The buttons on his gold threaded waistcoat were under strain of popping off at any given time. A large cigar rested between his stubby fingers. The grey smoke spiralled up into the darkness of the room. 'That's not going to happen today, Mr Simmons. I can feel it in my bones.'

Mr Simmons chuckled. 'Is that the same bones that have had to be broken on numerous occasions?'

Ted pulled himself up tall, pulling his shoulders back and jutting out his chin. 'It's good that you care so much, Mr Simmons. I've already had Slips telling me I shouldn't be here, but this is my livelihood and I'm going to come good today.'

Mr Simmons looked at him through narrowed eyes. 'You need to know it's not a livelihood you're very good at; maybe you should get a job doing something else.' He sighed. 'But, if you have the buy-in money then I'm happy for you to join us. I just hate to keep taking your money.' He chuckled. 'Mind you, it's easy money. So come on, pull up a chair at any of the tables you like the look of.'

Ted glanced around, weaving between the tables, sizing up the players with their glasses of whisky and their boxes of cigarettes and matches sitting on the edge of the table. The players studied him as he watched them. Perhaps he was in above his head but there was no going back now. He was here to win enough money to get his family back.

*

Annie Cradwell smiled as she remembered they were moving from The Lyric back to The Lyceum Theatre, where she first met the actress Kitty Smythe. Annie had grown up wanting to be just like her, a star of the stage. A chuckle escaped, as she remembered her determination to move from her village to London. She had been so happy when her friend Rose decided to come with her. Her laughter was soon doused with the memories of the last time she saw her mother, which was less than a year ago, but so much had happened in that time.

She sucked in the chilly air inside Kitty's dressing room at the Lyric theatre; thankful their childhood friend, Joyce, had offered them a roof over their heads. When Annie arrived in London and saw Joyce was living in a nightmare with her uncle Arthur's drinking, guilt had swamped her for not being a better friend. She should've kept up the letter writing like Rose had. She shook her head. How their lives had changed since then.

'Afternoon, Annie, it's freezing out there.' Kitty's musical voice rang out. She unbuttoned her ankle-length dark grey coat, revealing a deep blue bell-shaped skirt with a wide floral overskirt and a large collared white blouse.

Annie ran her hands down her plain black serviceable skirt. 'Afternoon, Kitty, you look and smell lovely.'

'Thank you; Stan got the perfume for me. It's Lily of the Valley.'

'Well, it smells lovely. I'll put the kettle on and make you a cup of coffee to warm you up.'

Kitty took a cigarette from its box and tapped down on it before placing it between her reddened lips. She struck a match. The smell of burning sulphur and tobacco wafted towards Annie. 'Are you looking forward to going back to The Lyceum?'

Annie glanced over her shoulder as she placed the kettle on the gas ring. 'Most definitely, The Lyric will always hold a place in my heart but The Lyceum is so grand, almost regal, and it's where I first met you. You were my childhood inspiration that started everything.'

Kitty groaned before sucking hard on her cigarette, clouds of smoke escaping from her nose and mouth. 'The trouble with putting people on pedestals is that they never live up to expectations.'

Annie nodded. 'That's true but your kindness was still in there. It was just buried beneath a whole heap of pain.' She paused as she measured the Camp Coffee into a cup. 'Make no mistake, you have been very kind and thoughtful to me; in fact you probably saved me from making all kinds of mistakes.'

Kitty laughed as she stubbed out her half-smoked cigarette. 'What happens now?'

Annie stopped what she was doing. Frowning, she looked round at Kitty. 'What do you mean?'

'Don't look so worried.' Kitty paused, examining the end of her cigarette. 'I just meant are you happy to continue being my dresser?'

Annie took a deep breath. 'Do you want me to continue being your dresser?'

Kitty groaned before a smile played on her lips.

'Someone, not a million miles from here, once told me you never answer a question with a question unless you have something to hide.'

Annie grinned. 'I can't think who would have said that but I do know I have nothing to hide.'

A smile tugged at the corners of Kitty's lips. 'Then to answer your question, I want for you whatever you want. You have become my family.' She chuckled. 'Whether you want to be or not.'

Annie stared at Kitty before whispering, 'I feel honoured that you see me in that way.'

'See you in what way?'

Both Kitty and Annie swung round to face the doorway. The stage manager come director blocked the doorway as he stared down at a bundle of papers he was carrying.

Kitty beamed at the sight of the man she had unexpectedly grown to love. 'Stan, to what do we owe this pleasure?'

Annie nodded. 'Hello, Mr Tyler.' She reached out and removed the kettle from the heat.

Stan looked up and grinned as he peered over at Annie. 'I know I'm in charge but you can call me Stan – everyone does. Well everyone apart from the delightful Miss Jane Hetherington in the sewing room.'

Kitty's laughter rang out. 'She's a sourpuss that one. Anyway, it's lovely to see you but it's not something that normally happens this time of day, so to what do we owe this pleasure?'

Stan bowed his head slightly. 'Actually, I've come to see Annie.'

Annie frowned. 'Me?'

Kitty glanced at her dresser. 'Well, how things have changed. At one time I was the only thing he worried about.'

Stan walked into the room and kissed Kitty on top of her head. 'Now don't get jealous. You should know by now you're the only one for me.' He looked over at Annie. 'I wondered whether you are coming to The Lyceum with us? We'll be doing a new play.' He looked down at the papers in his hand. '*A Royal Divorce* – it's about Napoleon Bonaparte and his wife Josephine.'

Kitty arched her eyebrows as she studied Stan, wondering where this conversation was going. 'Annie will definitely be coming with us, even if it's only as my dresser.'

Stan's lips tightened for a moment before he forced a smile. 'Of course, Kitty, I do understand, but I suppose I'm asking Annie whether she's going to take her desire to be on the stage further. You know, actively looking for acting roles.'

Kitty's eyes widened. Panic momentarily ran across her face as she stared at Annie. 'She's the best dresser I've ever had.' She paused as she tried to gather her thoughts, her eyes darting left and right. 'I don't want to hold you back from going elsewhere but at the same time I want to keep you with me.'

Annie stepped forward and took Kitty's soft, manicured hand. 'I'm not going anywhere. I love my job here with you.'

Stan cleared his throat. 'Look, Kitty, I'm sorry but this isn't about you and your needs and I can't let you stand in Annie's way.' His glance moved between them both. 'You have proven you have a natural ability and you belong on the stage. Don't get me wrong you have a lot to learn still, but I can teach you.' He coughed. 'There will be no expectations on my part but your talent should be invested in; maybe you could start off by being an understudy for several roles. I would also like to suggest you learn every aspect of the theatre because where we start off is not necessarily where we finish.'

Kitty drummed her long, blood-red fingernails on her dressing table. 'Unfortunately Stan's right. I don't want him to be but he is.'

Annie's heart pounded in her chest. 'Are you saying I have to choose?'

Kitty lowered her eyes and shrugged. 'I suppose you do.'

The rustling of papers caught both of their attention and they stared over at Stan who was separating the papers he was holding. He thrust some at Annie. 'You won't have very long to learn the lines so you'd best start straight away.'

Annie's eyes glistened as she glanced at them. Her hands stayed by her sides. 'You're assuming I will pick the stage over Kitty.'

The confusion on Stan's face was plain. 'I thought you would be jumping for joy at the opportunity.'

'Forgive me for being cautious but since I've been here I've learnt there's no such thing as free help and I owe Kitty; she saved me and I shall never forget that.'

Colour began to rise in Stan's cheeks. 'But I'm not—'

'Stop, Stan. I understand Annie being wary, as you would if you stop to think about it.' Kitty reached out and took Annie's hand. 'You don't owe me anything. It's more likely the other way round. I don't want to stand in your way. As I've already said you're my family now.'

Annie nodded and took a deep breath before giving Stan a determined look. 'Thank you for your kindness and the faith you've shown in me, both of you.' She paused as she looked from one to the other. 'I will gladly take up your kind offer but only if I can still be Kitty's dresser as well.'

Stan raised his eyebrows. 'I'm not sure you can do both roles at the same time. What happens if you're on stage at the same time Kitty has to change her costume?'

Annie shrugged and peered at him with pleading eyes. 'I don't know; maybe Rose will help. I don't know but I would like to try.'

Stan shook his head. 'Whatever we do it has to work seamlessly, and I'm not sure it will as Rose is a seamstress and might be needed to make repairs on any night.'

Annie tightened her lips for a moment. 'You're right, especially as Miss Hetherington doesn't like Rose for some reason.' She sighed. 'I'm afraid I'll have to turn down your offer, but please know I greatly appreciate it.'

Kitty jumped up. 'No, I'm not having this. You can't throw away a great opportunity because of me, or blooming high and mighty Miss Hetherington. I spent many months without a dresser so I'm sure if there is a problem we can all muddle through for one or two performances.'

Stan's glance darted between the two women. He shook his head. 'You drive a hard bargain but we will give it a try and see how it goes, but know, Kitty, I don't want any drama from you when you are minus a dresser.'

Annie jumped up and down clapping her hands at the same time.

Kitty stepped forward and threw her arms around Stan. 'Thank you, thank you.'

Stan chuckled. 'Why do I get a feeling this is all going to end in tears?'

2

Ted looked around the table. All eyes were on him. His eyes were stinging and his throat was dry from the thick smoke-filled air. All the cards had been dealt. His three were laid face down in front of him. Dawn was beginning to let its shafts of light through the window. He took a deep breath and coughed hoarsely as smoke filled his lungs. His gaze darted to the hall full whisky bottle – tempting, but no, he had to keep a clear head.

Someone thumped him on the back. 'Come on, Ted, you can't bail now.'

The betting had risen at great speed in the game. He had been up on his pot of money, but the thrill of the chase had taken hold, allowing him to get carried away. As the money had risen quickly to forty pounds everyone around the table had gradually folded. But not him. As the pot got richer something drove him on.

The only remaining player stopping Ted from walking away with the pot was watching him closely. He counted out a wad of notes and threw them in the middle of the table. 'I'll raise you sixty.' The man smirked, placing the large cigar between his lips and puffing on it, letting the spiral of grey smoke swirl up to the thick mass above their heads.

Ted's hands were damp; he hoped no one noticed him rubbing them down his trouser legs. What had gone wrong? Three hours ago he'd been up on the game, and that's when he should have walked away, yet here he had to decide whether to fold or keep going. His mind delved into its darkest corners, trying to think where he could get some money. He stared at the stack of cash at the centre of the table. He had a lot invested in this game; he couldn't afford to lose it all.

'Come on, Ted, you know you've got to fold. You've got no money left and it's a hundred pound to see me.'

A voice came from behind him. 'I wouldn't mind – you're not even good at three-card brag. I've lost count of how many games I've been in where you've lost staggering amounts of money to someone else.'

Ted flicked up the corners of his three cards face down on the table. He was aware his opponent hadn't looked at his; surely he was due to have a bad hand. Why was he so confident to play blind and try to bluff Ted out of his win? Ted looked at his cards again and saw all clubs looking back at him. It was definitely the winning hand. A running flush, ace, two, three, only a prial could beat him. What were the odds of him having three of a kind? He looked over at his opponent. 'I need some more cash.' He pulled his watch off his wrist. 'I can throw this in the pot or maybe someone wants to buy it.'

The man to the left of him took the watch and turned it over. He examined it. 'You won't get much for this, certainly not enough to keep you in the game.' He handed the watch back. 'You'd be better off keeping it so you're not late getting anywhere, especially paying off your gambling debts.'

The tension around the table broke as the men roared with laughter.

Ted took the watch and slipped it back onto his wrist. 'I'm not gonna fold.' He paused. 'I've got this game, I know I have.'

Ted's opponent stared at him for a while before speaking up. 'Do you know if you didn't gamble so much you could've had your life back on track by now.' He looked around at the men grinning at him. 'Not that I'm complaining, I've bought three pubs and that lousy restaurant, on Great White Lion Street, that's bleeding me dry, on the strength of your losses.'

Again there was a roar of laughter.

Ted stared at him. 'I'm good for it.'

His opponent looked steely-eyed at him. 'Ted, you always say you're good for it but I've lost track of how many times I've had to send my boys out to track you down before you've paid.'

Ted flicked at his cards again. 'Not this time.' He shook his head. 'Not this time.'

'All right, you sound very sure and I don't want to deprive you of a big win. Goodness knows you've earned it with the number of losses you've had. I will lend you the money, but you will only have fourteen days to pay it back.'

Ted looked at the stack of money in the centre of the table. How much was there? It must be at least five hundred pounds. He knew he was in over his head but something niggled at him. It was always the same; he couldn't just walk away.

Men from the other tables had started to gather around.

'You can't lend him the money. You know what it's like trying to get it back.'

'Not at all, it's all about family. Ain't that right, Ted? To my mind there's nothing more important.' Mr Simmons sucked on his cigar, letting the smoke billow out from his nostrils. The air was still. You could hear a pin drop. 'Take yourself for instance; you have a beautiful family, who work so hard. It would be a shame if they weren't able to fulfil their potential because their father hadn't stopped to think when it mattered.'

Gasps went around the room.

Mr Simmons held up his hand. 'But, 'aving said that, it's not for me to deprive Ted of his big win.'

Slips yelled above the groans and murmurs that were gathering momentum as they travelled around. 'Don't do this, Ted, you'll only regret it.'

The room was tense.

Mr Simmons chuckled, breaking the tension. 'You should listen to Slips. He didn't get that name by accident.' He glanced at the money pot before looking over at Ted again. 'I taught him well. He's very successful at collecting money owed from betting slips and games like this; mind you he's a slippery little bugger.'

Low laughter rippled around the table.

Ted didn't look up. His gaze stayed focused on his opponent. A chill ran down his spine. Was he bluffing about his children and his cards? He took a deep breath; it was all part of the game. 'Let's do this then.'

His opponent matched his stare. 'Before we go any further, you need to know I've done my homework since the last loan you had.' He casually drummed the table with his fingers before a smile crept across his face. 'Please don't underestimate how much I know about you, and I certainly know where to find you and your loved ones.'

Ted's gaze didn't waver. 'I'm good for it.' He tried to lick his lips but his mouth was dry.

'It's your last chance to fold.'

Ted smiled. 'That is definitely not happening.' He took a deep breath. 'There's a hundred pounds to raise and see you.'

The room was silent. Tension was high. The man removed his cigar from his lips as a grin crept across his face. He reached out and flicked his cards over. There was a gasp around the room, three threes stared up from the table, mocking Ted yet again.

How was that possible? What were the odds on that?

'Hello, Joyce, I'm back.'

Turning her head, Joyce looked in the direction of the voice and immediately recognised the tall suited man. His trilby hat was nestled between his fingers so she could see his dark hair had been slicked down. 'Mr Simmons, I didn't see you come in.' She took a step towards him.

Frank Simmons looked relaxed lounging on the chair Enid had vacated only minutes before, his long legs crossed at the ankles. 'Please, I know we 'aven't known each other long but call me Frank.' He beamed at her. 'I followed your delightful landlord in.'

Joyce returned his smile. 'Not long, it was only a couple of days ago you came in asking for me.'

'Well, I don't 'ang around yer know.' Frank looked around him. 'I was 'oping we could carry on chatting. I enjoyed finding out about you and this café, but I can see you've been busy. This place must be a little gold mine.'

Joyce frowned as she looked around at the tables that needed clearing. 'It's certainly been a really busy day.' She patted the back of her hair and studied his handsome but hard features for a moment before peering over her shoulder at the customers. 'If I'm honest it isn't a good time; mind you I'm not sure when is these days.' Taking a breath, she looked back at him. 'When does your article have to be finished by?'

Frank loosely linked his fingers together in front of him. 'I don't think there's an immediate rush, although I won't get paid until my editor approves it.'

Joyce nodded. 'I don't want to stop you from being paid. What more do you need?'

Frank flipped open his pad and looked at the scrawling handwriting that filled the page, wishing he could read it. 'Let's see, I know yer've always wanted your own restaurant and spend long days and nights working in this café. Yer single and most importantly yer're a magnificent cook.' He stopped and looked over at the certificate over by the counter. 'As yer winning certificate for cake baking shows, specifically chocolate cake and Victoria sponge, you'll one day make someone a wonderful wife.'

Joyce could feel the heat rising in her face.

Frank stared at her for a moment. 'And, of course yer quite beautiful.'

'Excuse me, can I have another pot of tea please?'

Joyce took a breath before peering over her shoulder and nodding at the customer. 'I'm sorry, Mr Simmons, Frank, as you can see I don't have time to chat now and anyway you should be talking to Simon. It's his café.'

Frank nodded. 'No, it's you I want to talk to, after all yer the award winner. The article is from a woman's point of view, although I might speak to 'im later.' He sighed. 'Yer mentioned yer mother was a great influence on yer love of cooking, and sadly she's now passed away, but I'd like to know what yer father thinks of yer working so hard and trying to achieve yer dream of being a cook.'

Joyce closed her eyes for a second. 'Unfortunately, my father passed away several years ago. He was on the *Titanic*.' She blinked quickly as her eyes welled up.

Frank raised his eyebrows and remained silent for a moment. 'I'm so sorry. I didn't realise.'

'Excuse me…' a customer called out.

Joyce stepped back behind the counter and began spooning tea leaves into a teapot. 'I'm sorry but I must serve the customers.'

Frank nodded as he took in her hunched shoulders. 'I'm sorry, I'll come back another time.'

Joyce gazed over at him. 'Please do.' She glanced up at the clock and sighed – only an hour until they closed. Loading the tray with crockery and the teapot, she weaved her way between the tables to the customer. 'I'm sorry to keep you waiting.'

The hour soon passed with Joyce busy clearing and wiping the tables down. She vigorously ran the damp cloth over the counter in the café as she tried to surreptitiously glance at the only occupied table. The young soldier, and his lady friend, had been sat at that table nearly all afternoon. She didn't have the heart to hurry them outside into the pouring rain. Moving her pad and pencil aside she leant back to admire her work and that's when she noticed something was missing. She spun on her heels and scanned the other worktop before turning round again. She swiftly yanked open all the drawers. There was rustling and clanging as her fingers deftly moved their contents around, but there was no sign of it. Her locket was gone.

The bell at the top of the door jangled as it was pushed open. Joyce groaned as she looked in its direction. A man stood in the open doorway. The cold air swooshed in, bringing the downpour of rain with it. 'Am I too late to get a hot drink and something to eat?'

Joyce wanted to scream yes, she was desperate to find her locket and go home. She jerked round when the girl laughed loudly. The soldier had a sad look about him but a small smile gradually lit up his face. Joyce quickly looked back at the man letting in all the cold air. 'Please come in.' Her voice echoed the tiredness she felt. 'I'm afraid it's too late for hot food but we have cake and sandwiches. What would you like?'

The man beamed at her. 'Thank you so much. I'll have a tea and that last slice of the Victoria sponge please.'

Joyce nodded. 'Please take a seat and I'll bring it over.'

He walked over to the nearest table and removed his coat and flat cap; he shook the rain off them before placing them neatly on the chair next to him and sitting down. 'I thought you might be closing.'

Joyce forced her best smile. 'We are normally but I'm sure we can make an exception on such a cold wet evening.' She glanced through the serving hatch as she reached up for a tea plate. The clean disinfectant smell drifted towards her, mingling with the soap she had used on the counter earlier. Simon was staring down at his kitchen table. She wanted to ask him if he'd seen her locket but now didn't seem to be the right time. Joyce watched as a frown creased his forehead. She wondered what was troubling him. Was it still the café? Was the situation that bad? She shrugged; maybe he was just feeling as tired as she was. They needed help; it was too busy for just the two of them now. Putting the slice of cake on the plate, she began loading her tray with the tea things before walking over to the customer. 'One pot of tea and one slice of Victoria sponge cake. I hope you enjoy it, sir.'

'Thank you, I'm sure I will. I've heard it said that the cake here is lovely.'

Joyce gave a little smile. 'Thank you, that's very kind of you to say so. If there's anything else I can get for you then please let me know.' She slowly weaved her way through the unoccupied tables to her counter. The sound of glass shattering on the tiled kitchen floor had her almost running to the doorway. Joyce called out before she reached it. 'Simon, what happened? Are you all right?'

'Don't worry, I've just knocked over a glass.'

Joyce pushed open the door to see Simon with his hand under the cold water. Crimson drops of blood mingled in with the shards of glass that were shattered across the floor. 'Let me have a look.'

'Mind where you put your feet. I haven't picked it up yet.'

'I'll do it in a minute.' Joyce strode over to the sink, grabbing a clean, dry cloth on the way.

'It's fine. I think it looks worse than it really is.' Simon turned his hand slightly. The blood turned the water red as it ran off his cut and down on to the sink.

'Is there any glass in the cut?'

Simon examined the cut closely before shaking his head. 'I don't think so, at least I can't feel any.'

Joyce took his hand in hers and peered closely at it, catching the smell of fried food that clung to his skin. 'It seems all right but we won't know properly until it's dry.' She turned off the tap and wrapped the cloth around his hand. His fingers wrapped around hers. Her heart jumped in her chest as she looked up at him.

He stared at her for a moment before clearing his throat. 'Thank you for looking after me.'

Heat crept over Joyce's body. She quickly looked away. 'Come and sit in the café where I can keep an eye on you until the customers have all gone. Press down hard on the cut because we need to try to stop it from bleeding.'

Simon nodded and did as she instructed before following her out into the café seating area. 'I'm not sure this is necessary. I'll be all right, and I haven't finished cleaning the kitchen yet.'

'Excuse me, can I pay our bill please.' The soldier stood almost to attention as he waited by the counter.

Joyce and Simon both looked over at the same time. Joyce gathered herself first. 'Yes, sir, I'm so sorry to have kept you waiting. As you can see we've had a minor accident in the kitchen.'

The soldier nodded. 'Don't worry, and thank you for not rushing us out the door. I know we've had that table for a lot longer than we should have.'

Joyce walked over to the counter. 'It hasn't been a problem.'

Simon pushed his uncut hand into his trouser pocket and

his fingers wrapped around the cold metal of Joyce's locket. He hoped she would forgive him one day.

The soldier rolled up two pound notes before placing them in the clean empty jam jar that was on the counter. 'This is a lovely place you have here, very friendly. The sandwiches and cake were wonderful, very fresh. Unfortunately, I won't be back for a while but next time I'm in London I will definitely call in.'

'Thank you, and it's been our pleasure and please don't feel it's necessary to leave such a large tip.'

The soldier gave a wry smile. 'I'll be back on the front line in a matter of hours and trust me there isn't much to spend your money on so it might as well go to a pretty young lady who has worked so hard today.'

Colour crept into Joyce's cheeks. 'Thank you.'

The soldier turned to look at Simon and smiled. 'You want to hang on to this one.'

His girl sidled up to him and tucked her arm through his. 'Are we ready Sam?' The young girl looked at Simon. 'Are you signing up to serve our king and country? I love a man in uniform.'

The soldier shook his head and handed Joyce a pound note. 'Come on, let's get out of here and leave these people in peace.' He guided the girl towards the door.

Joyce shouted after him. 'Wait, this is too much, you need your change.'

'Keep it, one day I might not have any money to pay for a cup of tea and a slice of cake.' The bell rang out and the two of them walked out.

Joyce looked down at the money she was holding. 'We

had better remember him, what with the tip that must be the most expensive cup of tea ever sold.'

The man who'd come in late picked up his cap and his coat, before walking over to pay his bill. 'That young soldier was right: it is a lovely little place you have here. It's a shame it's not open in the evening as well. I would also like to add my thanks for letting me have a cup of tea when you were really closed. You know I would normally have gone for a sandwich, but I have to say the cake was lovely and light, so it's just as well it was your last piece.'

Joyce nodded. 'Thank you for your kind words and it's the least we could do on such a miserable evening.'

The man handed over his money, and nodded before walking towards the door. The bell chimed as he opened it. The cold air and the rain rushed in, carrying the traffic noise along with the chatter of people passing by with it, and then it was gone as the door shut again.

Joyce quickly opened a drawer and picked up a key. She rushed over and locked the door before anyone else tried to come in. She twisted the open sign round before turning and leaning against the door. 'Thank goodness – what a day, it's been so busy.'

Simon watched her throw back her head against the door and close her eyes. 'That soldier was right: I do need to hang on to you.'

Joyce opened her eyes and stared at Simon. 'I'm not going anywhere, unless you make me, so don't start worrying about that.'

Simon looked down at his hand wrapped in the bloodstained cloth. 'It all seems to be a bit frantic these days.' He paused. 'I think it's definitely time to rethink the meals and snacks we sell. But the soldier's right: we're a good team, aren't we?'

Joyce smiled. 'We're an exhausted team. I've still got to make the bread and cakes for tomorrow yet, unless I come in early in the morning. I must admit that has more appeal right now, although it may not do in the morning when I have to get out of bed.'

Simon nodded.

Joyce frowned, and walked over to sit on the chair next to Simon. 'What's going on?'

Simon shook his head but said nothing.

'Something is, you've been in a strange mood all day. You even burnt some toast.'

Simon opened his mouth to speak but quickly closed it again. He studied his hands for a moment. 'Do you think this cut will have stopped bleeding by now?'

Joyce jumped up to walk over to the counter.

Simon grabbed her arm, pulling her back down on to the wooden chair next to him. 'You know I get asked several times a week if I'm going to enlist, if I'm going to fight for king and country.'

Joyce gasped. 'Is that's what's been bothering you? You can't go, you have all this to run.' She waved her arm around to encompass the café, knowing her voice was getting higher but unable to hide the fear that had sprung up inside her. 'Who will look after your ma and sister?'

Simon shrugged. 'I don't know what to do. The war posters everywhere don't help.' He squeezed her arm. 'You could easily run this place, if you had help, and my sister could come and wait tables.'

Joyce stared straight ahead. 'It sounds like you've made up your mind.'

Simon gently turned her face to meet his. 'No, I haven't. None of this matters to me, but you do.' He leant in and lowered his head to let his soft lips brush hers. He opened his eyes and his voice was husky when he whispered, 'You're all that matters to me.'

Joyce's heart pounded in her chest. Butterflies were flying around inside her stomach. She wanted to tell him she loved him but the words wouldn't come.

The chatter and the laughter coming from the corridor of The Lyric Theatre caused Rose Spencer to glance briefly at the open door of the sewing room but no one came in. She studied the empty chair opposite her, where Dot used to sit before she had found the courage to return home and face everyone. She was pleased for her friend but missed their little chats as they sewed. Dot had become a motherly figure to her, listening and encouraging her to have belief in her own abilities.

She shook her head, trying to release herself from the melancholy she had felt most days since coming back to London. Rose stared down at the blouse that was sprawled out on the table in front of her. It was just awaiting six buttons for the front and one each for the sleeve cuff she had created and then it was finished. Reaching over for the button tin, she removed the lid and gazed in at the assortment that greeted her. She moved them from side to side with her fingers, each movement revealing another colour, shape and size. The buttons rattled against each other and the side of the tin. If they could talk she wondered what stories they would tell.

Annie peered round the open door, watching her friend for a few seconds. She looked deep in thought. 'Rose, is everything all right?'

Rose jumped at the sound of her name. 'Of course, come in. I'm just trying to find some matching buttons for this blouse.' She paused. 'I miss Dot's company and advice about buttons.' She smiled and gazed back down at the tin.

Heavy running footsteps and raised voices followed by laughter made Annie turn to look along the corridor before looking back and nodding. She took the couple of steps towards Rose. 'I hate this time of year. Its dark outside already. The days seem so short. And the snow isn't like it is back home. It's quite muddy and slushy.'

'You sound homesick.' Rose smoothed the cotton material at the cuffs of her white blouse. 'Are you missing the snowball fights we used to have? Remember when we used to slide down the hill on a bit of wood?'

Annie chuckled. 'That was a long time ago, but we did have some fun didn't we. Sometimes I wonder if I've made a mistake coming to London. I love working in the theatre but I do miss my family.' She stared straight ahead and shrugged. 'But I try not to think about that side of things too much.' Annie studied the blouse on the table. 'You're so talented, Rose. You might be missing Dot's company but I don't think you need worry about your sewing ability.' She looked up. 'Are they going to replace her?'

Rose shrugged. 'I don't know but Stan, er … Mr Tyler, has asked me to go with them to The Lyceum.' She continued to move the buttons around.

Annie beamed. 'That's excellent news. I think they see us both as part of the team, which means we'll hopefully not have to worry so much about finding work in the future, and we'll get to see Bert again now he's working at The Lyceum.'

Rose laughed. 'Yeah, that's true. I heard he'd moved from the Alwych as well. He was a genuinely caring old bugger wasn't he?'

Annie frowned before giggling. 'I'm not sure I would call him an old bugger, more of a giant teddy bear, but yes he was very caring. We probably should have popped to see him at the stage door. He would have loved that.'

Rose nodded. 'Yes, but I'm sure he'll understand how life can get in the way.' She looked up from the array of shapes and colours in the tin. 'I take it you've been asked to go to The Lyceum with Kitty?'

Annie wanted to squeal with delight but felt now wasn't the right time. 'Yes, I have. It's incredible isn't it? To think all this started when we sneaked in through the stage door of The Lyceum.' She smiled. 'Gosh, I was so scared and sure we were going to be arrested.'

Rose smiled. 'Yes, I remember grabbing your hand and pulling you to hide under the tables in the sewing room.'

Annie looked solemn for a moment. 'All of that was less than a year ago and yet it feels like a lifetime ago. So much has happened in that time.' She forced a smile and chased away the thoughts of her mother passing away, as she glanced around the familiar sewing room. At the shelves heavy with rolls of lace, ribbon and sequins. Rolls of material were stacked on top of each other next to boxes of offcuts. 'At least the sewing room at The Lyceum is bigger – well, it seems larger to me.' Her gaze drifted back to the button tin. 'What are you looking for? And don't say a button.'

'To be honest I'm not sure, but I need eight of them.'

Annie joined in Rose's quest. Flitting some buttons aside she pulled out a small white round button that had a light blue sheen to it. 'This is a lovely one. What do you think?'

'Well, you made that look easy.' Rose took the button from her friend, tilting it from side to side. 'It's certainly a little different to the standard white button.'

'That's because I'm not worrying about it in the same way you are.' Annie smiled. 'Whether there's eight of them is a different matter.'

Rose nodded. 'Hmm, I'll have a look.'

'Good luck. If not I'm sure you'll find something in that tin of treasure.'

Rose bit her lip as she looked up at her friend. 'I do wonder sometimes if we would have come to London had we'd known the country would be at war several weeks later.'

'Probably not, especially if we'd known our brothers were going to join up.'

Rose peered back down into the button tin.

Annie frowned. 'You've been very quiet lately and I've been meaning to ask whether you've heard from any of your brothers.'

'No, I write to them in turn most days but they haven't replied so I hope they're all right.' Rose sucked in her breath. 'I keep telling myself no news is good news.'

'That's all any of us can do.' Annie rested her hand on Rose's. 'Maybe you'll suddenly get a bundle of letters from them. I get the impression they can be a bit slow being delivered, which is hardly surprising.' She sighed. 'I think you need something to lift your spirits.' She paused, tapping her finger against her lips. 'I know, maybe we'll go home via the bicycle shop, and stop there for a chat and a cup of tea.'

Rose's eyes glowed for a moment but then it quickly disappeared. 'It'll be too late by the time we get out of here.'

Annie pursed her lips. 'Hmm, that's probably true; maybe we should leave earlier in the morning and stop off there on our way in. I could chat to Peter for a while.' She laughed. 'Well, if his customers don't mind waiting for their fruit and vegetables that is; mind you if his nephew, Harry, is working it may not be a problem.'

'His barrow does appear to be very popular.' Rose beamed. 'You two will be getting married before you know it.'

Annie blushed. 'I don't think so, and anyway we were talking about you and Charlie Young.'

Blotches of colour settled on Rose's cheeks. 'I shouldn't think that will end up going anywhere.'

'I don't know about that. He gave you a very long and lingering look, which I might add you returned.'

The unmistakable formidable voice of Miss Hetherington rang out in the sewing room. 'Miss Cradwell, are you in this room for a reason?' She stared at the two girls.

Annie blushed under such scrutiny. 'No … I was just checking Rose was all right.'

Miss Hetherington frowned. 'And why wouldn't she be? Let me tell you, in this theatre Miss Spencer's welfare is not your concern.'

Annie placed her hand on top of Rose's. 'Surely everyone's welfare is the concern of all of us, wherever we might be?'

Miss Hetherington scowled. 'Leave the sewing room now, otherwise I shall have to make a complaint about you distracting my staff from their work.'

Rose peered up at Annie. 'Don't worry, I'll be fine – we'll talk later.'

Miss Hetherington stepped to the side of the doorway.

Anger etched itself on Annie's face as she stared at the senior seamstress for a moment.

Rose nudged her friend with her elbow.

Taking a deep breath Annie walked towards the door.

3

Mavis Hitchin peered round the door and watched her son for a moment. She no longer noticed the globular drips that were layered on the floor or the smell of paint that filled the room. She could watch him at his easel all day. Tightening the straps of her apron around slender figure, Mavis cleared her throat. 'Simon, your sister's just laying the table ready for breakfast.'

Simon stared intently at the canvas on his easel. He dabbed the soft paint-laden bristles of his fine brush on to the nearly completed London street scene. It was a view of Shaftesbury Avenue he saw every day and was enjoying the challenge of reproducing his version of it. He leant back against the hard wooden rungs of his chair, tilting his head; he stared critically at his painting before replying absently, 'I won't be a minute. I just wanted to try to get this light and shade right before I go to the café.'

Mavis glanced around at the many painted canvases propped up against the walls, noticing for the first time the outline of a portrait painting. 'I don't know where you get your talent from. It certainly isn't from me, and I don't remember your pa ever doing anything like this.'

Simon chuckled. 'He probably never had a chance to.'

'Anyway, time's getting on. I can't believe it's the start of another week already. I don't want you having to rush your breakfast.' Mavis frowned as she stared at him. 'Is now a good time for me to ask what's been bothering you the last few weeks?'

Simon's gaze didn't move from his painting. 'No, Ma, let me enjoy this time before I have to start my day.'

'Is it Joyce?' Mavis tightened her lips before taking a deep breath. 'I don't want to pry, and, from what you say, she seems like a nice girl, but please know you can talk to me, whatever the problem is.'

Simon sighed and carefully placed his brush down on his wooden palette. He glanced at his mother. 'Joyce is a lovely girl, who hasn't done anything wrong, far from it. In fact, she's baking cakes and making bread for us to sell, and I can tell you it's all delicious.'

Mavis could see Simon's love for Joyce shining from his eyes. He looked so proud when he talked about her.

Simon's eyes clouded over. 'If you must know I'm feeling the pressure from the war posters that are stuck on every wall wherever I go.' He shook his head. 'I get asked practically every day whether I'm going to sign up to fight for king and country. If I'd gone in the beginning I would have been with my friends.' Simon stood up and removed the paint-covered coat he was wearing. 'Then there's the café and Joyce.' Simon shook his head. His shoulders hunched over his chest. 'Painting feels like the only escape from the turmoil.'

Mavis's eyes became watery as she stepped further into the small, well-lit room she had long given up for her son to do his painting in. 'It sounds like your thoughts are going round in circles. It must be difficult for you, especially if I'm right about your feelings for Joyce.'

Simon lowered his eyes. 'I can't help but feel I'm being judged by people who don't even know me for not enlisting. I suppose that's the downside of working in a café.'

'Take no notice of them. I've been asked why you haven't joined up with the rest of the men. I told them it had nothing to do with them.' Mavis scowled. 'People need to mind their own business.' She fought the urge to wrap her arms around her son. He had given up his own dreams to follow in his father's footsteps when he had unexpectedly passed away, and now there was this blooming war. Reaching out, she rested her hand on his arm. His muscles tightened under her touch. 'Simon, it's time to stop torturing yourself and follow what you think is right, not your pa's dream or anyone else's. You should be selling your paintings. It's such a waste to hide your talent away.'

Simon frowned. 'We all know life isn't as simple as that.'

Mavis shook her head. 'If you mean your sister and me, we can work. In fact if what I hear is true they're crying out for women to sign up for work, what with so many men going off to fight.' She paused. 'I hate to see you tying yourself up in knots. You're a good man, so please stop worrying and follow what you think is right. Barbara and I have been lucky to have you still living here and looking after us but it's time for you get on with living your own life, follow your own dreams.'

Simon gave a humourless laugh. 'I think the war will rob many people of any hopes and dreams they had.'

Mavis lowered her eyes, wondering what she could do to help her son. She walked over to the box that was near

Simon's feet. 'What's this then? I don't remember seeing this here before.' She bent down to peer inside it.

Simon got there first and pressed it shut. 'It's nothing, Ma. I've just been having a sort-out that's all.'

Barbara came laughing into the room. 'Come on, you two are always chatting and breakfast is getting cold.'

Mavis scowled at Barbara. 'We were talking.'

Barbara lowered her eyes. 'I'm sorry, I just didn't want the breakfast to be ruined.'

Simon immediately smiled at his sister. 'Don't worry, we're coming.' He put his arm around her. 'I'm ready for something to eat, especially something cooked by someone else.' He squeezed her shoulders into his body. 'Do you fancy coming to work in the café? We were rushed off our feet yesterday and poor Joyce didn't know if she was coming or going.'

Barbara stopped dead in her tracks. 'Can I?' She turned to her mother and gazed at her with wide eyes. 'Can I, Ma?'

Simon smiled as he peered at his mother.

Mavis chuckled. 'Well, I suppose at twenty-one you should be out there earning a crust and supporting your brother.'

Barbara scowled at her mother for a split second before beaming at her. 'Never mind supporting Simon, it will be good to have some of my own money.' She ran at her mother and threw her arms around her. 'Thank you, Ma.' Pulling back, she looked at her brother. 'You won't regret this, Simon.'

Simon shook his head. 'You have to follow Joyce's lead.' He chuckled. 'She's in charge of both of us, but don't tell her I said that.'

Barbara jumped up and down clapping her hands together. 'Can I start today?'

Simon glanced at his mother. 'Only if Ma don't need you here.'

Mavis laughed. 'I don't think I'd have the nerve to say otherwise. Who could take away that beaming smile? But you'd better behave yourself, young lady.' She paused. 'I could do with the extra housekeeping you could bring in.'

Barbara's face dropped. 'Housekeeping?'

Mavis gave her daughter a stern look. 'Money doesn't grow on trees you know.'

Barbara looked sullen.

Simon thrust his hand into his trouser pocket. He pulled out a wad of notes and handed them to his mother. 'Hopefully that will tide you over for a while.'

Mavis looked at the money, her fingers pinning the notes in place. 'Obviously this all helps but I thought the café was struggling.'

'It's busy all the time now and we'll be thankful for Barbara's help and that means I now only need to find someone to help with the washing up. Come on, let's go and have this breakfast otherwise I'm going to be late opening the café.'

The three of them walked down the narrow hallway to the square, warm kitchen. The range that faced the doorway had been lit and was pushing against the cold air. Pots and pans hung from a ceiling pulley maid above a scrubbed wooden table, which had been laid with breakfast things. The aroma of hot toast hung in the air.

'It's a pretty miserable day out there so make sure you wrap up warm when you go to work.' Mavis rested her hand against the teapot. 'This may not be hot enough now but I'll pour a cup and we'll see.'

Simon and Barbara each pulled out a chair. The scraping of the feet against the stone floor tiles made Mavis wince. Slices of toast stood neatly in the toast rack, while the slab of butter sat in a glass dish next to it. Boiled eggs were already placed in the plain white eggcups at each place setting.

The grandfather clock near the front door chimed seven times.

Simon picked up his teaspoon and tapped the top of his egg a couple of times. He peeled back the cracked shell before digging his spoon in and scooping out the bright yellow yolk in the middle. 'Don't worry about tea for me, Ma. I should be on my way by now. I've just enough time to eat this and might get away with taking a slice of buttered toast with me.' He looked across at his sister. 'Don't rush to come in today. Give yourself a chance to eat properly and I'll see you whenever you arrive. I'll let Joyce know you're coming.' He quickly pushed the spoon in his mouth; his teeth chinked against the metal.

Barbara smiled. 'It's quite exciting. I actually get to meet Joyce at long last.'

Simon ran his tongue across his teeth before glaring at his sister. 'I don't want any gossiping. Do you understand what I'm saying?'

Barbara lowered her eyes. 'Of course.'

Mavis looked at her young daughter. 'Remember Simon is the boss so you have to show him some respect in work.'

'Don't worry, I'll behave myself, I promise.' Barbara gave her brother a mischievous sideways glance.

Simon laughed. 'That'll be the day, but Joyce knows what she's doing so please do as she says.' He grabbed a slice of dry toast and jumped up. His chair almost toppled backwards. 'I've got to go.'

Mavis took the toast from his hand. 'Here, take mine. At least it's got a scraping of butter on it.'

'Thanks, Ma, you're a wonderful woman.' Simon bent over and planted a kiss on his mother's soft cheek. 'See you later, Barb. We'll talk hours and money later when I have more time.' The toast crunched as he bit into it.

Before Barbara could answer he was running out the kitchen door.

Mavis shouted to Simon. 'Wrap up warm. It's freezing outside, and take care.'

Simon held the toast between his teeth as he pulled on his winter coat and grabbed a soft woollen scarf his mother had knitted for him. Removing the toast from his mouth, Simon shouted, 'Stop worrying.' He pulled open the door, giving a little shiver as the cold air rushed in, before doing up the buttons of his coat. He stepped outside, pulling the door shut behind him.

The thud of the front door sounded in the kitchen.

Barbara turned to her mother with a glint in her eye. 'I'm quite excited to meet Joyce, to see what it is about her that has him all tied up in knots. Do you think he'll ever ask her to marry him?'

Mavis gave a small smile. 'Who knows, but just remember it's nothing to do with us so don't go causing trouble, even if you do mean well at the time.'

Barbara raised her eyebrows in horror as she stared at her mother. 'As if I would.'

Mavis chuckled. 'Come on, eat your breakfast. You can't go to work on an empty stomach.'

They both began tapping the tops of their boiled eggs, each momentarily lost in their own thoughts.

Joyce moved the three hot individual pies she had made along to the end of the café's kitchen table. After picking up the bowl and cutlery she had used earlier, she moved towards the sink to turn on the tap. The water gushed out, spraying everything within its reach, including Joyce. She jumped back and quickly turned the tap to slow the water down as it filled up the bowl to be washed up. As she put the kettle on the range to boil, the bell above the door chimed, startling her. She put down the kettle and walked towards the kitchen door. 'Simon, is that you?'

'Yes, it is. Something smells nice.' Simon pushed open the door and was suddenly standing in front of Joyce. 'I know I'm late this morning but I didn't think I was that far behind! Or are you particularly early?'

They both glanced up at the wall clock in the kitchen and spoke as one.

'You're late.'

'You're early.'

They both laughed.

Simon glanced at the pies before moving towards two sponge tins sitting on the kitchen side.

Joyce followed his gaze. 'I hope you don't mind but I made another cake this morning. The Victoria sponge sold out quite quick and it's easier for me to make it here rather than at home.'

Simon smiled. 'Of course not. I'm not surprised – it was delicious.' His eyes followed her every move. 'You'll have to teach me how to make them, when we get time.'

'When?' Joyce turned and went back to the sink. 'I'm just putting the kettle on. Do you want a cuppa?'

Simon began unbuttoning his coat and unwrapped the scarf from around his neck. 'Yes, please, it's freezing out there and I didn't have time to have one at home.'

'My, you must have been running late.' Simon's woody scent invaded her senses. Joyce fought the urge to wrap her arms around him, and lose herself in his embrace.

Their eyes locked for a moment. Did they want the same thing?

There were several knocks on the café door.

Simon jumped at the sudden noise, frowning. He looked down at his wristwatch. He hung his coat on a peg and collected his white kitchen coat to put on. His voice was strained when he finally spoke. 'I'm not opening up yet. Customers get earlier and earlier. I know my father wanted a meeting place for the community but I need a bit of breathing space before the mayhem begins.' He fastened the large buttons that ran down the front of his overall before running his fingers through his hair. 'I spent too long painting and chatting. It's my own fault but I'm gasping for a cuppa.' He sniffed the air. 'Is that those pies I can smell?'

Joyce blushed, trying to ignore the ache for him that filled her very being. 'Probably, I hope you don't mind but I made these small pies at home for you to try. I used to make large family pies with my mother so I thought I'd try making small ones for here. If you like them we could perhaps think about adding them for the customers.' Joyce's words tumbled over each other.

Simon smiled as he watched her. 'Slow down.'

Joyce took the step towards the serving hatch to see if someone was waiting outside but there was no one. She turned round to face Simon. 'Sorry, am I getting ahead of myself?'

Simon frowned. 'Not at all, I meant talk slower so I can understand what you're saying.'

Joyce nodded. 'Sorry, please don't think I'm trying to take over.'

Simon stepped forward, shaking his head. 'Why would I think that? We're a team, and a good one at that.' He paused as he studied her. 'Your mother clearly gave you a love of cooking before she passed away.' Simon grinned. 'Now, where's the fork for me to try them? They look and smell wonderful.'

Joyce nodded. 'It's a lasting memory of my childhood. We had such fun cooking together.' Her eyes began to well up; she quickly grabbed a knife and fork to pass to Simon. 'There's a vegetable, a mince and gravy one, and a meat and vegetable pie.' She watched as Simon cut into the first one and dark brown gravy trickled out onto the small plate.

Simon took a forkful of pastry and meat.

Joyce studied him, looking for clues, as he slowly chewed and swallowed.

Simon shook his head.

Joyce bowed her head as her heart and hope sunk.

'That was fabulous.' Simon took another cut of the pie. 'How have I not known before that you can cook as well as bake?'

Joyce's face lit up.

'I know I've only tried one at the moment, but if that's anything to go by then they can all definitely be added to the tariff. The customers are going to love them. They are a feast for the eyes. They smell and taste delicious.'

Joyce's grin spread from ear to ear. 'Really?'

Simon chuckled. 'Really, I can't believe you've kept your cooking hidden for so long. Oh, in all the excitement I nearly forgot, Barbara's coming in today to learn the ropes.'

'Barbara?'

'My sister.'

'Of course. Having heard so much about her it'll be lovely to meet her.'

Simon gave a wry smile. 'She's quite excited but I expect that will soon wear off.' He watched Joyce collecting the crockery together. 'Give her any work you think will help to make life easier for you. Then we've only got to find someone to help with the washing up.' He frowned. 'We can't keep going home so exhausted.'

Joyce nodded. 'I must admit it's been tough going lately so any help is going to be gratefully received; maybe Uncle Arthur will stop feeling like he has to step in every time he comes in for a cuppa.' She spooned the loose tea leaves and boiling water into the teapot. After a few minutes Joyce poured the brewed tea through the tea strainer before passing the cup to Simon. 'Get this down you.' She glanced up at the clock again. 'We'll have to open up in a minute.'

Simon wrapped his fingers around the cup, letting the warmth seep through before sipping the strong dark liquid. 'I'm lucky to have you here, Joyce; in fact I don't know what I'd do without you.'

Joyce fidgeted from one foot to the other as colour rushed into her cheeks. 'You're embarrassing me. You pay me to work hard and do my job properly, which is what I try to do.'

Simon frowned. 'Is that why you come in early and stay late?'

Joyce could feel her skin burning. Her heart was pounding and her stomach somersaulted under his gaze. 'I like to be helpful, besides I don't have much to rush home for, and bread and cakes don't bake themselves.' She spun round and lightly tapped the cooling sponges in their tins. 'I think these are ready to come out now.'

Simon took a step forward and opened his mouth to speak but a loud knock on the café door stopped him in his tracks. 'It sounds like someone wants to come in.' Glancing up at the clock, he groaned softly to himself. 'I'll go and open the door for business.' He shook his head. The moment was gone. Had he imagined the passion of that look just now? Maybe she just didn't love him like he did her. He had spent a long time waiting for this moment; maybe he had left it too long. He walked into the café and tried to ignore the pain that was suddenly coursing through his veins. Simon unlocked the door, turned the closed sign around and pulled open the door. The bell chimed.

Cars chugged past, spluttering their fumes into the grey foggy day. People sped silently along the pavement, shielding themselves against the cold damp air. A couple of dogs were barking somewhere nearby.

'You're late opening this morning, Simon. I didn't know whether to knock or not.' The old man took in Simon's grey pallor. 'I was here earlier. Is everything all right?'

Simon forced himself to smile. 'Of course, Cyril, come in. I was just having a quick cuppa.'

'I'll be glad when this winter is over with; it's horrible out there. Isn't young Joyce here? Are you on your own?'

'No, I'm here, Cyril.' Joyce smiled at the man stooped over his walking stick.

Cyril removed his trilby hat and smiled, showing his brown crooked teeth. 'That's my girl. Your smile brightens my day and makes an old man very happy.'

Simon opened his mouth to speak but changed his mind. No one needed to know she did the same for him, especially if she didn't feel the same about him. Instead he nodded to them both and escaped into the kitchen. The decision of what to do over the questions and the looks that had tormented him for months suddenly seemed very easy. Joyce's voice followed him.

'Take a seat and I'll bring you over a pot of tea while Simon makes your usual breakfast, unless you want something else today.'

Cyril chuckled. 'I'll stick with the usual, thank you.'

'How are you this morning, Cyril?'

The café door opened and closed several more times and Simon was thankful the kitchen door made it harder to hear Cyril's reply along with the bell over the door. He stretched out his arms and leant against the sink for a moment. He lowered his head before shaking it. Standing up straight, he rubbed his hand over his face and took a deep breath.

'The breakfast rush has started.' Joyce paused as she pushed open the kitchen door. 'Simon, is everything all right?'

Simon jumped. 'Of course.'

Joyce eyed him for a moment. 'Cyril will have his usual breakfast.'

'What?'

Joyce studied his wide-eyed expression and wondered what was going on. 'I said, Cyril will have his usual breakfast.'

'Yes, yes of course.'

Joyce frowned. 'You seem preoccupied. Do you want to talk about it?'

Simon gave a humourless laugh. 'Oh to have the time to talk. What's Cyril's usual breakfast?'

Joyce shook her head. 'It's the same you make for him every day: two slices of toast, well done but not burnt.'

'That's right.' Simon reached out for the loaf of bread.

Joyce watched him for a moment, wondering what was going on. Sighing, she turned away, picked up a knife and began liberally spreading jam on the sponge. After topping it with the other half of the cake, she placed it on a cake stand. The bell above the café door rang out several times.

Mr Harris called out. 'Shop.' Sighing, he waited at the counter, his fingers playing with the loose change in his trouser pocket. 'I haven't got all day.'

Joyce sighed. Simon was right: who had time to talk? She picked up the cake stand and turned round to head back into the café. 'Hello, Mr Harris, what can I do for you, a cup of tea maybe?' She forced a smile to her lips.

Chatter filled the café as the door opened and closed again. Joyce glanced around at the tables, which were filling up fast.

'It's rent day.'

Joyce shook her head. 'My goodness, I didn't expect to see you again so soon.'

Mr Harris eyes narrowed. 'I've just come to let you know the rent's going up to nine shillings from this week.'

'What?'

Mr Harris smiled. 'Your café's in a good location here and I have to earn a living too, you know.'

Joyce shook her head. 'That's one hell of an increase from the six shillings I normally pay you.'

'It's the same increase that everyone's putting up rents by.'

'Forgive me if I don't take your word for that.'

Mr Harris smirked. 'Feel free to ask around. You can always move out of here. This is a valuable space that I could rent out for a lot more.'

Joyce glared at him.

A man's voice came from behind Mr Harris. 'I'm sure yer could but not while there's a war on. Yer need to be looking into keeping the tenants yer have.'

Mr Harris turned and glared at the young man. 'I don't see what it has to do with you. This is business.'

Joyce hadn't noticed him come in. She half smiled as she recognised Frank. His lit cigarette was lightly held between his fingers in his left hand, while his trilby hat was sat back on his head at a jaunty angle, showing his black slicked-back hair.

'I will not stand by while you, or anyone else, torment this young lady.'

Joyce's smile wavered. Her brows pulled together as she raised her voice slightly. 'Mr Harris, as you can see we're rather busy in here so I'm afraid there's no time for discussion. I shall give you six shillings and you can discuss the other three bob with Simon, as will I.' Joyce counted three silver coins into her hand and handed them over to Mr Harris. 'Now if you can forgive me I have customers waiting for their tea.' She turned and spooned tea leaves into several teapots.

Simon pushed a plate on to the ledge of the serving hatch. 'Toast for Cyril.'

Mr Harris shouted to Simon. 'We need to talk about your rent.'

Simon frowned. 'Then you'll need to come back later.'

Frank stepped around the counter and picked up the plate laden with toast. 'I'll take these while yer make the tea.'

Mr Harris scowled. 'I shall be back at five o'clock so make sure you're able to talk to me then; otherwise, trust me, you'll be out by yer ear.' He turned and walked over to the door. The bell rang out as he opened it, telling Joyce it was safe to breathe again.

Frank walked back to the customer side of the counter. 'Now, who's Cyril?'

Joyce giggled.

With an expertise that comes with practice, Joyce's cold fingers grabbed the frayed string through the letterbox. The key knocked against the inside of the front door as she tugged it through to unlock the front door. Her feet were killing her and she ached all over as tiredness took hold. The lock grated as she turned the key and pushed on the door, thankful when it swung open. She stepped inside out of the dark wintry evening. Joyce leant against the back of the door as it clicked shut and she closed her eyes.

'Everything all right, Joyce?'

Joyce's eyes flew open. 'Yes, I just feel exhausted today.'

Arthur shook his head and stepped towards her. 'That's not surprising. You were rushed off your feet when I was in the café earlier, though the new girl seemed to be doing all right.'

'That's Simon's sister, Barbara. I'm not sure about her but she worked hard and was friendly enough with the customers so I suppose that's all that matters.'

'Well, best to grab all the help you can get.' Arthur studied her pale features. 'Come in and sit down I'll go and make you a cup of tea.'

Joyce raised her eyebrows and gave half a smile.

'What? That's a look your father would have given me. Sometimes you remind me so much of him. You've got his eyes.' Arthur paused. 'Anyway, I'll have you know I've had a lot of practice recently.' He smiled. 'Come on, take off your hat and coat and let me look after you for a change.'

Joyce was too tired to argue and began unbuttoning the four buttons on her coat.

Arthur reached out and took her coat and threw it across his arm before lifting the hat off her head. He guided Joyce into the dining room and to the black wingback chair next to the crackling fire.

Joyce flopped down and immediately rested her head against the back of the chair. Her gaze was drawn to the flames swaying and flickering in and out between the wood and the coal. Grey smoke swirled up the chimney, disappearing into the night. Pieces of ash sat on the fire's hearth where the flames had spat it out. She should sweep it up, but instead she closed her eyes, allowing herself to enjoy doing nothing for a moment. The fire wrapped her in its warmth while the crackling of the wood gave her comfort.

Cups and saucers chinked together as Arthur's heavy footsteps announced his return.

Joyce opened her heavy eyelids.

'Sorry, did I wake you?'

Joyce smiled. 'No, I was just resting my eyes and enjoying the warmth of the fire.' She watched him take the lid off the teapot and stir the hot brown liquid. The spoon clinked against the inside of the pot. He stopped and replaced the lid before sitting the silver tea strainer on top of one of the cups ready to start pouring the tea. Joyce wanted to tell him how proud she was of him. He had overcome so much and was a different man to the one she had lived with for several years, but it wasn't her place and she didn't want to spoil things. She pulled herself upright and took the cup and saucer he was holding out to her. 'Thank you.'

Arthur smiled. 'It's my pleasure.' He picked up his own cup and saucer and took the couple of steps to the matching chair on the other side of the fireplace. 'I never realised how hard you work in the café. Is it always that busy?'

Joyce sipped the strong tea; the liquid scorched her top lip. 'We're busier than we used to be but I don't think Simon is making much money and now the rent is going up. I'm not sure he'll be able to keep it open for much longer.'

Arthur shook his head. 'I don't understand. You had people waiting for tables when I was in there.'

Joyce yawned. 'I think people are coming in to get out of all this rain and sleet we're having.' She tightened her lips. 'Simon tries to keep the prices down and he's trying to keep it to his father's dream of having somewhere the community can just pop in and meet each other for a chat, which is why we mainly sell things like tea and toast along with breakfasts. The trouble is if the rent keeps going up the idea behind the café is moving further away every day.'

Arthur took a gulp of his tea, not deterred by the heat of it. 'It sounds like the landlord is trying to get Simon out. That café is in a prime location.'

Joyce looked dismayed. 'I hadn't thought of that before, but the landlord has said as much.' She bit her bottom lip. 'Either way I think he needs to find a way of making more money so he can afford to pay it.'

Arthur nodded. 'It's obviously popular, which is always a good starting point. Oh, I nearly forgot a letter arrived for you today.'

'For me? I never get letters.'

Arthur put his cup and saucer down on the small side table next to his chair before pushing himself up out of his seat. 'I left it on the table in the hall.' He promptly walked out of the room and returned a minute later clutching a square envelope. 'Here it is.' He stretched out his hand to pass it to her.

Joyce took the envelope. She turned it over a couple of times, examining it.

Arthur smiled. 'If you want to know who it's from why don't you open it?'

Joyce frowned. 'That would be the sensible thing to do.' She slipped her index finger under the seal and ripped the top of the envelope. Pulling the envelope apart she peered inside at what looked like a single sheet of paper.

Arthur watched her as she pondered whether to actually pull out the letter. 'Shall I leave you to read it in private?'

Joyce opened her mouth to speak but nothing came out. She put her hand to her mouth and coughed. 'Sorry, there's no need. I have nothing to hide.' She pulled out the sheet of paper; it crunched together as it caught on the inside of the envelope. She scanned it quickly before passing it to her uncle.

Arthur took the thin sheet of paper from her and ran his gaze over it. 'It's from a solicitor.'

Joyce stared at the dancing flames of the fire.

'It says they have written to you before and they are waiting to hear from you.'

Joyce nodded, but didn't look away from the fire. 'I don't know why they are writing to me.'

Arthur reached over and clasped her hand in his. 'It says it's something to do with your grandma.'

Joyce turned her head and studied her uncle for a moment. 'Yes, I know, but why should I care? She threw us out remember? And why haven't you had a letter, or have you?'

Arthur's colour began to rise in his face. He leapt to his feet and walked over to put his cup and saucer on the silver tray that was on the dining table. 'That's a long story and one I will tell you when you're not so worn out.' The crockery clattered on to the tray.

'Did you have an argument with her?' Joyce looked down at her clenched hands in her lap. 'My pa did, but I don't know what about.'

'Don't let that spoil any good memories you have of your father, or your grandmother come to that.' Arthur sighed. 'From what I remember they didn't always get on so it was only a matter of time with them living under the same roof.'

'I do know he went off to work on the *Titanic* and never came back so they never had a chance to talk it through.' Joyce blinked quickly before looking up. 'It's all quite sad.'

Arthur fidgeted from one foot to the other. 'It is. We can do a lot of damage to each other in the heat of the moment.' He sighed. 'I know that better than anyone.' He took the couple of steps back to his chair.

Joyce forced herself to smile. 'Whenever he went away to work he always brought me a present when he came home.'

Arthur cleared his throat. 'Yes, I believe he liked to make people happy by giving presents.'

Joyce peered over at him. His expression was dire. 'As I got older, it was no longer a doll or a new dress but jewellery – you know, necklaces and watches.'

Arthur stayed quiet as he stared into the yellow flames licking at the chimney.

Joyce gave a little laugh. 'Thinking about it, I don't think my mother approved of the gifts. Not that I recall her ever saying anything, but I remember the odd look she give him. The money would have been better spent putting food for the table.' She gulped down a mouthful of tea. 'Come to think of it I don't know what happened to all the jewellery he gave us both. I expect it's still at Grandma's.'

Arthur gave her a sideways look. 'I think you need to find out why the solicitors want to see you. It might just be about exactly that.'

A tense silence sat between them.

'I'll come with you if you want me to but I understand

if you would rather go by yourself. Either way you need to make contact with them.'

Joyce nodded. 'Perhaps we'll go together; that's if you don't mind?'

Arthur nodded. 'Of course I don't.'

'I just don't understand why they want to see me. It's probably all a misunderstanding, unless it is about my mother's things and those gifts.'

Arthur frowned. 'Well, the sooner we go the sooner we'll find out.'

4

Annie pulled the blanket up to her chin, trying to ignore the urge to scratch the irritating itch as it brushed against her skin. The bed creaked as she fidgeted. The wind outside battered against the sash window, the wood rattling in its frame as the gale demanded entrance. The closed heavy curtain at the window fluttered as the wind found its way in. The crash of metal bins being blown over carried in the air. It was hard to hear whether it was raining above the wind. The usual barking dogs were silent and there was no sound of cats rummaging for food. She frowned, hoping all the animals were in hiding from the awful weather they were having. The chimes of the clock downstairs could just be heard. Annie's eyes narrowed as she concentrated. Was that ten? She couldn't be sure. The metal bed frame creaked again as Rose sat further back against the footboard of the bed.

'Joyce, Rose and I had some news about our jobs.' Annie paused for only a split second, watching the worry flick across Joyce's face. 'We have been asked to move to The Lyceum Theatre with everyone for the production of *The Royal Divorce.*'

Joyce beamed. 'That's wonderful news. I expect you were

both wondering what to do next. I assume you're both taking up their offer?'

Rose chuckled. 'It would be if Miss Hetherington wasn't coming with us, or if she could stop scowling and sniping at me whenever she gets an opportunity, which seems to be every time she sees me.'

Joyce frowned. 'Is it that bad? Does it put you off moving theatres?'

Rose smiled. 'No, it's nothing I can't handle; it just gets me down. It's always been the same, and I can't see anything changing all the time we're working together. The problem is I don't know what I've done to cause it.'

Annie reached out to her friend and clasped her hand in hers. 'From what I can gather it's not personal to you; she's horrible to everyone.'

Rose raised her eyebrows. 'Why would you want to live your life like that? It's beyond me. Anyway she won't change so let's talk about something happier.'

Annie's eyes sparkled. 'I have more news.'

Rose's smile gradually spread across her face. 'What?'

Joyce giggled. 'Come on, tell us?'

'Stan has asked me to be an understudy.' Annie beamed.

Rose leapt off the edge of the bed and wrapped her arms around Annie. 'That's absolutely wonderful news, and so well deserved.'

Annie smiled as her friend pulled away. 'I'm not sure I'm any more deserving than anyone else but I'm certainly thrilled to be given the opportunity.'

Joyce clapped her hands. 'Don't be so modest; you were wonderful when we saw you on stage and I'm pleased they realise how good you are. It's the best news ever.'

Colour filled Annie's cheeks. 'Thank you, although I still have a lot to learn.' She shifted her gaze heavenward. 'Someone up there loves me, that's for sure.'

The girls nodded.

Joyce whispered, 'Amen to that.'

Rose glanced over at Joyce. 'Talking of that, your uncle Arthur seems happier these days. He was talking about maybe decorating the house.'

Joyce smiled. 'I know. He's like a different person. He even made me a cup of tea when I got home from work today.' She chuckled. 'I don't think I hid my surprise very well.' Her smile faded. 'I have your brother to thank for that, Annie. Whatever words of wisdom he said to Uncle Arthur when he came to see you seemed to work. You two living here has probably made him think about things as well.'

Rose patted Joyce's hand. 'I don't think we can take any credit but I'm pleased we were able to be here for you.'

Annie nodded. 'I think he just told him a few home truths but he's certainly a changed man, that's for certain. I wonder if him and Auntie Dot will ever get back together? They clearly love each other, which just makes it so sad. My father and grandfather were so happy when she returned home after so many years.'

The girls all nodded.

Joyce looked thoughtful. 'I hope they do. I'd like Dot to come back to London. And if Uncle Arthur moves we may not have anywhere to live.'

Annie peered at Joyce from under her lashes. She knew from talking to her father that her aunt didn't want to return to London to live but decided to keep that information to herself. There was no point worrying Joyce when her uncle was still here. She looked pensive and glanced up at Rose. 'Rose, have you had any letters from your brothers recently?'

Rose raised her eyebrows. 'I haven't had any full stop. It's a good job I know they're writing to my mother and she keeps me up to date.' Her eyes screwed up a little. 'From your question I take it you haven't heard from your brother either?'

Annie shook her head.

Joyce leant forward in her chair and patted Annie's arm. 'I expect you will soon. He always writes to you regularly. I expect it's just difficult or the post has got held up. It can't be easy for them to write letters on the front line.'

Annie frowned. 'I know. I just worry, that's all, and I know we're all doing that so it's no different for me than anyone else.'

Joyce took a deep breath. 'Well, I can tell you something that might take your mind off it, even if it's only for half an hour.'

Annie and Rose immediately looked wide-eyed at Joyce, before speaking as one. 'What?'

A slow smile formed on Joyce's lips. 'I have good news and bad news. Which would you like first?'

'Good, bad,' the girls answered in unison.

Joyce's smile got bigger. 'All right, I shall give you the good news.' She paused, taking a breath.

'What?' Rose asked.

'A man, Frank Simmons, has been talking to me about doing an article for a newspaper.'

Annie and Rose stared at each other before quickly looking back at Joyce.

Rose was the first to speak. 'What, you have to write the article?'

Joyce chuckled. 'No, silly, he wants to write about me and cooking.'

Annie beamed. 'That's wonderful. Oh my goodness you could be famous, like Lloyd George or the King.'

The girls giggled.

Joyce couldn't resist smiling as she shook her head. 'I don't think that's going to happen.'

'Is he good-looking?' Rose raised her eyebrows. 'What does Simon think about it?'

Joyce blushed. 'He's quite good-looking and Simon hasn't said anything about it. Why would he?'

Rose glanced at Annie. 'Did I miss something?'

Annie shook her head.

Rose turned to Joyce. 'The last time we saw you two together you looked pretty cosy, so what's gone wrong?'

Joyce shrugged. 'I don't think anything's gone wrong. He's just busy with other things on his mind. I think we will always be very good friends but maybe that's where it will stop.'

Rose rested her hand on Joyce's. 'But you love him don't you?'

Joyce's lips tightened. 'It doesn't matter what I feel if he doesn't feel the same. Although sometimes I catch him watching me and I think he does love me, other things always seem to get in the way.' She took a breath, trying to calm the beating in her chest. After all, she might lose him, like she had everyone she loved. No, she mustn't get carried away. Experience told her she could only rely on herself.

Rose shook her head. 'There's no doubt in my mind he loves you. That evening we saw you through the café window it looked obvious to me, and he's always encouraged you to bake for the café.'

Joyce gave a faint smile. 'He did think my bread and cakes were amazing.' She blushed. 'I think it was after that evening that things changed between us.'

Rose shrugged. 'Maybe you're both frightened of ruining everything. Let's face it, it's not just a good working relationship that's been going for years, but it's also a friendship. Maybe you should be the one to tell him you love him; you know it shouldn't just be up to the men, especially if we want the vote and all that.'

Joyce chuckled as she shook her head. 'That's never going to happen.' She paused. 'Anyway, that was the good news, which I must admit turned out to be not so good.'

Annie smiled. 'Oh I don't know, you're going to be in the newspaper; that sounds quite grand to me.'

Joyce chuckled. 'He even took a photograph of me to go with the article, not that I looked my best.'

Rose clapped her hands together. 'It's an exciting time, so what's the bad news then?'

Joyce clasped her hands together on her lap. 'I received a solicitor's letter today ... actually it's the second one from them.'

The girls waited in silence for Joyce to continue.

Joyce shrugged. 'There's not much more to tell, except it's something to do with my grandma and they want to see me.'

Rose gasped. 'Do you think she's passed away and left you something in her will?'

Joyce shook her head. 'I don't know why they want to see me; you'd think they'd want to see Uncle Arthur rather than me. With my father dying he must be next in line to receive anything. Mind you, I don't suppose Pa would have got anything anyway because my father and grandma argued badly enough for us to move out of her home; that's how I ended up here.'

Annie frowned. 'Have you ever heard from her?'

'I've not spoken to her. I've thought about it but it felt like I was betraying my father so I just left it alone and she's never contacted me.'

Rose shook her head. 'Maybe she didn't know where you and your father had gone.' She paused. 'Do you know what they argued about?'

Joyce's lips tightened. 'I never thought of that; my goodness maybe I should try and contact her or at least go to the solicitor's to find out what's happened to her, if anything.' She paused and glanced over at her friends. 'They were always arguing about money, that was nothing new, but from what I remember the last time was different; they argued over me.'

Annie reached over and rested her hand on Joyce's. 'Why do you think they argued over you?'

Joyce shrugged. 'I just recall my grandmother raising her voice about how it's his responsibility to raise his child, he shouldn't be shirking it and leaving it for others to do.' She blinked quickly trying to stop her tears from falling. 'I must have done something to cause the argument, unless it was about him going to work on the *Titanic*. I don't know and my father never spoke about it. I don't even know if they made up before he died.'

Rose sighed. 'I'm sure it can't be anything you did wrong so I expect it was to do with your father going away to work. I expect it would have been a difficult time for your grandma and your father. The prospect of having the responsibility of a sixteen-year-old in London must have frightened her, and for you not having a mother to guide you.'

Annie squeezed Joyce's hand. 'Do you want someone to go to the solicitor's with you?'

Joyce shook her head. 'Uncle Arthur offered, and I did want to go with him, but the more I think about it the more I feel this is something I need to do by myself, no matter how frightening it feels.'

Rose pulled the front door shut. The key clanged against the inside of it. She pulled at her thick woollen gloves as she turned to glance at Annie. 'I'm sure it's colder in London than it is in our village, especially this early in the morning.'

Annie gave a shiver and pulled her coat collar up and tightened her scarf around her neck. 'That can't be true. We have all that open land for the wind to run through, let alone the rain and snow that drives through it uninterrupted.'

They linked arms and paced along Great Earl Street towards Seven Dials, their breath coming out in grey swirls as they rushed along. A strong aroma of coffee came at them from all sides.

A man carrying a crate of fresh bread on his shoulders walked towards them. The smell of the warm bread immediately transported Annie back home but she said nothing.

'I suppose that's true, although it definitely feels colder to me.' Rose stared ahead, stepping out into the road to avoid the people walking towards her. She glanced across at Annie. 'You know I like Peter. He's a good man, and I'm so pleased you both managed to work things out.'

Annie nodded. 'I couldn't think about not seeing him again. It upset me so much but I thought I had no choice.' She paused. 'When I look back I can't believe he came all the way to Worcester to see me. I'm so grateful I could come back to London. I have a lot to be thankful for, and Dot being my aunt is one of them.'

Rose smiled. 'That's love for you.'

'My family liked him. I think them living on a farm and Peter selling fruit and vegetables on his stall gave them an instant connection.' Annie looked at Rose sheepishly. 'I also think they worked it out we were in love.' She paused. 'What about you and Charlie? You were certainly making eyes at each other. Is there love in the air?'

Rose blushed. 'Oh stop it, I barely know him.' She stepped back so a lady holding a boy's hand could walk past on the pavement. 'I didn't hear Joyce go this morning, which is most unusual.'

Annie gave her friend a knowing look. 'No, nor me. She must have left particularly early.' She frowned. 'I think she's more worried about this solicitor's letter than she's making out.'

'Want some soup, lovey?' a seller shouted. 'It's vegetable, and will set yer up for the day, it will.'

Annie and Rose shook their heads and carried on walking,

peering at the different shop windows as they went past, while trying to avoid people stepping out in front of them.

Rose pulled the sides of her woollen hat down over her blonde hair, attempting to cover her ears. 'It's strange that they haven't asked to see Arthur though; after all he's her uncle and you'd think he would receive any inheritance before Joyce.'

Annie nodded. 'I know but maybe he was disowned because of his drinking.'

Rose studied the pavement as she walked along. 'It's a shame. I know we don't know everything that went on before but he seems to have put it all behind him now.' Rose looked across at Annie. 'He's even talking about painting his son's bedroom, so that means the shrine will also disappear.'

Annie sucked in the cold air. 'The scars will still be there though. I don't know how you get over such a loss.' She stopped to examine the many different items that could be seen through the pawnshop window. 'Look, I've never been in one of these shops but it looks like you can buy anything in there.'

Rose followed Annie and stared wide-eyed. 'There seems to be everything from musical instruments to diamond rings.'

'There's some beautiful ornaments in there. They look expensive, a bit like Dot's.' Annie frowned as she leant in for a closer look. 'I wonder what stories they could tell, maybe of promises of weddings or learning to play an instrument.'

Rose nodded. 'It could be down to just needing the money.' She paused as she studied some of the things in the window. She sighed. 'You'd have a field day in there, making up your stories for everything.'

Annie nodded. 'It's quite sad though don't you think? It's like a shop of broken dreams.'

'Morning, Annie.' Peter's gravelly voice carried over the sellers shouting about their wares. 'Rose.'

'Morning,' the girls turned and called out in unison.

Rose could feel heat rising up her neck. 'I'll leave you to talk to Peter. I'm going to see my bicycle man.'

Annie hugged her friend, all thoughts of the pawnshop forgotten. 'I hope it goes well with Charlie. Don't rush – I'll see you at the theatre.' She pulled back chuckling, letting her hands fall to her sides. 'Don't forget we are back at The Lyceum now with *The Royal Divorce*.'

'Oh yes, thanks for reminding me. I probably would have gone to The Lyric if you hadn't.' Rose giggled. 'If I remember rightly it's about Napoleon and Josephine isn't it?'

'That's right, so very different costumes for this one.'

Rose looked thoughtful for a moment before she shrugged and smiled. 'Well, it's good to have a change.' She gave Annie a last hug. 'I'll see you later. Wish me luck.'

Annie chuckled. 'If the way he looked at you is anything to go by you don't need luck.'

Doubt flitted across Rose's face.

Annie ran her gloved hand down Rose's arm. 'Have faith, you'll be fine.'

Rose nodded. She slowly turned away to walk up the road.

Annie frowned; she had never seen Rose so unsure of herself before.

'Is everything all right?'

Annie jumped. The now familiar earthy smells were caught in the air around her. She peered over her shoulder at

Peter's worried face. His brows drew together while his eyes followed Rose. 'Yes, Rose is going to see Charlie Young, at the bicycle shop in Great White Lion Street.'

'But I'm here.'

Annie jerked round to see Charlie standing next to Peter. Her eyes wide she spun back again and yelled at the top of her voice. 'Rose, Rose...'

Rose glanced over her shoulder and saw Annie waving her to go back.

Annie turned to the two men. 'I'm sorry, that wasn't very ladylike. I can already hear my mother telling me off for such behaviour.'

Peter chuckled. 'Well, it was certainly loud. I suppose that's practising to be heard on the stage.'

Annie blushed. 'Sorry.' She peered back over her shoulder to see Rose almost within touching distance.

Peter nodded, while pulling at the edges of his woollen hat, tugging it further over his ears. 'Listen, I've been thinking yer shouldn't live in London and not visit at least some of the sights it 'as to offer.' He paused. 'Like Buckingham Palace, Westminster Abbey and St Paul's Cathedral.' A smile slowly spread over his face. 'There's different street markets we could go to or maybe we could really push the boat out and have afternoon tea at The Ritz Hotel with the posh folk.'

Annie shook her head. 'That sounds expensive.' She peered over her shoulder. 'Rose, Charlie is here.' She stood aside.

Rose's already rosy cheeks coloured a little bit more. 'Hello, Charlie, I was just coming to see you.'

'I was hoping after our meeting you would have popped

in and had a cup of tea with me, maybe on your way to work or something.' Charlie's gentle voice stopped Rose in her tracks.

Heat rushed into Rose's face, thawing her cheeks against the cold, wintry air. She took a deep breath and lowered her eyes. 'I … I was going to come before today but—'

'But you chickened out—'

'No, yes, yes I did.' Rose sighed, her breath rising in grey swirls and disappearing into the cold air.

Charlie watched embarrassment flit across Rose's face. 'There was no need. I've been looking out for you every day, which is why I'm now hanging around the market, hoping I don't get arrested for loitering or something.' He beamed. 'Come on, let's go and get out of the cold.'

Rose stood there for a moment unsure what to do.

Charlie took a step nearer to her and stretched his arm out in front of him. 'Come on, you were coming to see me anyway, and if nothing else it will give us a break from the cold to have a hot drink.'

Rose looked at the handsome man's outstretched hand for a second before stepping forward and lightly placing her gloved hand in his.

Charlie wrapped his fingers around hers and silently led her away.

Annie watched them both stroll into the growing crowd. 'I think we've just witnessed the start of something wonderful.'

Peter took Annie's hand in his as he watched them go. A sudden rush of jealousy ran through him as he squeezed her hand. 'Love's a wonderful thing with the right person; of that there's no doubt.'

Annie stared up at him. 'Are you all right? It's been a while since we've seen each other properly.'

Peter gazed down at her. 'I would like to spend some time, some proper time, with a beautiful woman, with my beautiful woman.'

Colour flooded Annie's cheeks and her stomach did a somersault. 'Do you have time for a coffee now?'

Peter frowned as he looked across at his nephew, Harry. He looked back at her with smouldering eyes. 'I want to but I can't go too far because it's busy today.'

Annie was lost in his gaze. 'I've missed you.'

Peter pulled her closer, wrapping his arms around her. He lowered his head and gently brushed his lips against hers.

Annie's heart pounded in her chest, her stomach somersaulted, and she didn't want it to end.

There was a crash as boxes and metal hit the ground. Peter pulled back, gazing at Annie before slowly looking over his shoulder. 'I don't want to leave you but I need to get back, before everything ends up battered and bruised.'

Annie forced a smile. 'Don't worry, you go. I'll buy you both a hot drink and bring it over to the barrow and we can talk in between customers.'

'No, please don't worry.' Peter glanced over at his barrow and the queue of customers that was beginning to snake beyond his stall. 'I had better get back to work.' He gazed down at her, fighting the urge to wrap his arms around her again. He gently squeezed her arm before looking back at his barrow. 'I'm sorry, I've got to go.'

Annie nodded. Disappointment washed over her. She forced herself to smile before standing on tiptoes and planting a light kiss on his cheek. 'Of course; don't let me hold you up. Go on, I don't want you losing customers.' She watched him walk towards his barrow and smile at the old lady waiting to be served.

Peter stopped and looked across at Annie. He smiled and yelled over to her, 'Maybe I'll just save The Ritz for a special occasion then.'

The old lady, standing at the barrow, gave a toothless grin as she clapped Peter on the back.

Annie could feel her skin getting hotter but couldn't resist laughing at him.

A woman called out as two boys chased each other in between the barrows.

Annie shook her head and quickly walked away, before she made a fool of herself. She didn't look back as she weaved in and out of the barrows and the people mingling around them.

'Get yer paper 'ere,' a boy's voice rang out.

Annie looked round as a dog barked behind her. Was that Peter's dog? But she couldn't see him. She sighed. Her morning had been planned out in her head and now she was at a loss about what to do.

Joyce stared hard at Barbara. She desperately wanted to like her and, in return, be liked but something was eating away at her and she didn't know what it was. She had felt Barbara's eyes boring into her back several times and when she turned round she had quickly looked away. Joyce forced a smile. 'You've done well today, Barbara. Our regular customers seem to have taken to you.'

Barbara wrinkled her nose as the smell of fried food

hung in the air; she pulled on her heavy winter coat. 'It's been lovely chatting as I served them, and to finally meet you. That brother of mine clearly thinks a lot of you.'

Joyce blushed. 'That's only because he likes that he can just leave me to get on with things.'

Barbara stopped what she was doing and eyed her for a moment. 'Do you like working in the café? With Simon I mean?'

'We work well together, so why wouldn't I?'

'No reason, I'm just asking. Simon's a good man.'

Joyce smiled. 'Of that there's no doubt. Anyway, you've been a tremendous help today, thank you. It's amazing the difference an extra pair of hands can make. Do you think you'll come back tomorrow?'

'Of course. I've enjoyed myself.' Barbara carried on buttoning up her thick winter coat.

Joyce turned towards the sink and dropped the cloth she'd been using to wipe down the kitchen sides into it.

Barbara watched her for a moment. 'Well, I best get home before Mother sends out a search party for me.' She chuckled.

Joyce peered over her shoulder. 'Why don't you wait for Simon?'

'I think he's still got things to do. He's sorting out the black material for the window and door, so I'll see him when he gets home.' Barbara pulled on her gloves. 'Bye, I'll see you in the morning.'

'Goodnight then and take care going home.' Joyce waved as Barbara walked out of the kitchen, the door gliding shut behind her. Simon and Barbara's muffled voices filtered through and Joyce was tempted to try and hear what they were saying but she twisted the tap on instead. The pipes rattled a couple of times before the cold water spluttered and gushed on to her other hand. The bell rang out above the café door and she knew Simon would be turning the key in the lock and turning the open sign to closed. She picked up the bar of carbolic soap and turned it over and over in her hands, letting the soapy lather build up. The bar dropped into the sink and she scrubbed at her hands vigorously. Her thoughts inevitably drifted to why Simon had suddenly decided to bring in his sister to work, and why he wanted her to know he couldn't run the café without her. She shook her head. It was all nonsense; she was easily replaceable.

'What are you shaking your head at?'

Simon's voice made her jump but she didn't look round at him. 'If you must know I was wondering what was behind you bringing in your sister to help?' Joyce picked up the bar of soap and placed it on a dish before rinsing her hands under the cold water.

'She's doing all right isn't she? You have to give her a chance. There's a lot to learn.'

Joyce reached for the towel to dry her hands but Simon stepped forward and handed it to her. 'Thank you, I'm not complaining. I'm just surprised and wondering whether it's connected to you being distracted these last few weeks.'

Simon frowned. 'If you don't have to rush off maybe we could have a cup of tea together.'

A band immediately tightened around Joyce's chest but she forced a smile. 'Of course. My uncle won't mind waiting for his dinner. He's not so demanding these days.'

Simon, wrung his hands together. 'Excellent, I'll put the kettle on then.'

'What is it, Simon? Never mind the tea. I know something's bothering you, and has been for weeks, probably months.'

Simon reached out and took her hand in his; his thumb gently rubbed the soft skin. 'There's not an easy way for me to tell you so I'm just going to say it.'

Joyce's insides fluttered at his touch. She shook her head before frowning as she stepped closer to him. 'Is it the café? Your mother? No it can't be your mother, otherwise Barbara wouldn't have been here today—'

'Stop trying to guess and let me tell you.' Simon gently shook her hand. Without a word he walked her into the café where they sat next to each other at a table for two. He squeezed her hand tight. 'As I said there's no easy way to say this so—'

'For goodness' sake, just say it.'

Simon stared down at their hands clasped together before looking up at her. All colour had drained from her face. Her eyes looked terrified. He sighed, wondering at the wisdom of his actions.

'Simon, you're scaring me. Whatever it is, please just put me out of my misery.'

'I've signed up.'

Joyce's eyes widened. She opened her mouth to speak but nothing came out.

Simon tightened his grip on her hand. 'I don't expect you to understand but I can't take the looks and the comments anymore. I constantly feel guilty knowing my friends are risking their lives while I stay here and fry eggs. It haunts me day and night, to the point I can't sleep.' He paused. 'If I'm honest I don't want to go. I just feel that it's my duty to.' He hesitated. 'I don't want my children knowing I just cooked fried breakfasts throughout the war.'

Joyce's eyes filled with tears. She blinked rapidly. 'I don't know what to say.' She shrugged. 'I never thought you'd sign up, what with this place and your family.' She shook her head and whispered, 'Which is probably daft because lots of men have gone off to war and left their families and jobs behind.'

Simon gazed at her; he choked back his own tears at inflicting pain on the woman he adored. 'I have a few days before I go off for training; maybe we could do something?'

Joyce nodded as she stared at their hands holding on to each other so tightly. 'I don't know what to say. I can't believe you're going.'

Simon gave a hollow laugh. 'No, nor me. It must have been a moment of madness.' He hesitated. 'I want you to take over running this place for me.'

Joyce's eyes widened and her mouth dropped open. 'I don't think I can do that. I don't know how to run a business.'

Simon gave a small smile. 'You do it now; you just don't realise it.'

Joyce closed her eyes for a moment, trying to digest what he was saying. Her eyes flew open. 'What about your mother and sister? They're family; I'm no one.'

Simon's lips tightened as he let go of her hand and jumped up from the chair. He stood still for a second before pacing around the tables. He suddenly stopped dead and stared at Joyce. 'You really have no idea do you?'

'About what?'

Simon shook his head in disbelief. 'How much you mean

to me. You're not no one. You will never be no one; in fact you're everything. Nothing is important if you're not sharing it with me.'

Joyce's eyes widened. 'I … I didn't realise. I thought you just saw me as a friend.'

Simon tightened his lips. 'I should have said something but, I suppose, I was afraid you didn't feel the same. Those words sound so cowardly, but I didn't want to spoil our friendship so I said nothing.'

Joyce's heart was racing, pumping wildly in her ears. She took a couple of deep breaths. *Stay calm. Stay calm.* 'Why are you saying something now?'

Simon lifted his hand and ran the backs of his fingers down her soft cheek. 'Isn't it obvious?' He paused, staring at her. 'I don't want to go away without you knowing how much I love you and that you are everything to me. You're the only reason I keep this café open. It has nothing to do with my father.'

Joyce shook her head. 'What? I don't understand.'

Simon lowered his head before looking up with love shining from his eyes. 'By keeping the café open it has meant I have seen you every day. There, it's out.'

Joyce frowned. 'But … I thought you were keeping your father's dream alive.'

Simon gave her a shameful look. 'I am but that hasn't been the only reason. It's what started it but it's not why I'm still here cooking breakfasts most of the day.'

Joyce lowered her eyes, staring hard at the wooden tabletop. 'I had no idea.'

'No, please don't hate me for it. I just wanted you to understand how much you mean to me.'

Joyce looked up and smiled. 'I don't hate you, Simon. I could never do that ... I'm just shocked.'

Simon lifted her hands, before lowering his head to gently leave kisses as light as butterflies on them. 'Please don't walk away from me or this café.'

Joyce's heart lurched. Tears pricked at her eyes. 'No one could love you more than I do, Simon.' Her tears rolled silently down her cheeks. 'I could never do that. I will try to keep it going until you return.'

Simon gently shook her hand. 'I know you will. I trust you implicitly.' He lifted his hand and, using his thumb, he tenderly wiped away her tears before wrapping his arms around her and pulling her in close. 'I shall tell my family that you are running the place and ask them to give you their support. I have also given my mother some extra money should you need it for rent or anything.' He slowly pulled away.

Joyce remained silent as she gazed up at the man she had loved for so long.

Simon hesitantly lowered his head to taste the sweetness of her lips.

5

Ted stared incredulously at the man who sat in front of him, a desk separating them, letting him know this was business and not friendship. He couldn't believe what he was hearing from the boy he grew up with. The boy who became the man who now spoke on his mother's behalf. 'I don't think you understand how serious this matter is.'

The man shook his head. 'It's always serious.'

Ted scowled and waved his hands around. 'I got turned over but can't prove it, especially not against... Anyway I should have won. It was a big pot and I would have been made for quite some time with that kind of money.'

The man frowned as he sat behind his large oak desk in his book-lined office. 'It's not that I don't understand; you have to understand that I can't help you. I don't work for you, thankfully. I work for your mother and under strict instructions. She is tired of bailing you out. I don't know what's happened to you and why you keep getting into so much debt. Gambling doesn't pay your bills.' He sighed. 'Look, I know you've had a difficult time since your wife died but you're creating your own problems, you must see that. Your mother has always listened and helped where she could. You have benefitted so much from her need to bring the family back together, but she has finally recognised that paying off so many of your gambling debts hasn't worked because you've just found the nearest game and chased the dream all over again.'

The man stood up and thrust his hands in his trouser pockets and gazed out at the rain-spattered window before turning back to Ted. 'It's about time you realised you're never going to win the amount of money you're after.' He shook his head. 'I don't understand, Ted. You could've achieved so much. What's happened to you?'

Ted thumped his fist down on the desk. 'I didn't come here for a lecture from you in your holier than thou position, with your musty old books and certificates. I know I've made mistakes but there are some very dangerous people after me, people I can't just turn my back on. It doesn't work that way.'

'You mean like you did with your family? You just left them for someone else to look after.'

Ted knew he was fighting a losing battle but he couldn't stop trying to get the help he needed. It was different this time. 'It was for their own good; it was for their own safety. Look, Jerry, what you don't understand is that I keep gambling because I want to get them back, because I want to get a home for us.' Ted ran his hands through his hair. 'I don't expect you to understand what it's like for me.'

The man scowled. 'Don't call me that. I hated it when we were younger and nothing has changed; I still hate it.'

Ted forced a faint smile to his lips. 'That's just it, we were friends. Don't you want to help me if only for old times' sake?'

Jerry shook his head. Sighing, he looked up at his

book-lined shelves, evidence of all the work he had put in to get where he is today. There had been no rich parent for him, no one bailing him out.

Was that a chink of light Ted saw in Jerry's armour? 'Please, I shall be forever grateful.'

Jerry straightened his jacket. He studied Ted for a moment before shaking his head. 'You do know if you'd had a regular job you could've kept a very nice roof over your family's heads. I don't know what you expect, but nothing comes for free; there's always a cost. Let's hope the price you're paying is worth it.'

Ted's lips tightened; the moment had gone. 'I wanted to speak to my mother – that's what I expected – and not to have to deal with you.' He scowled. 'Look, I don't want us to fall out but if I don't get this sorted out quickly, at best I shall end up with some broken bones, at worst my body will be found floating in the Thames.'

Jerry sighed at the change of tone. All pretence had disappeared. 'Well, you know your mother isn't available.' He bent down, opened the desk drawer and pulled out an envelope. He handed it to Ted. 'Your mother knew you would end up coming here. She knows you better than you know yourself, and it's about time you started listening to her. I'll leave you for a moment while you read it.'

Ted turned the envelope over in his hands, jerking round as the office door slammed shut behind him, relief spreading through him, as he realised no one had come in. He looked back at the envelope, his name scrawled on the front in his mother's handwriting. He took a deep breath; his mother writing to him wasn't a good sign. Poking his finger under the sealed flap, he ripped it open. He pulled out the single sheet of folded paper.

Dear Edward,

Ted sighed; only his mother ever called him Edward, particularly when he was in trouble.

For you to be reading this letter I am assuming that I am either dead or you are in trouble, again.

As you are fully aware family is very important to me, and I must confess to not coming close to understanding your actions, but I also realise you will not change just because I keep going on. Let's face it, you stopped listening to me years ago. So I've decided to use my money as an incentive to get your family back together and to stop you from ruining people's lives. I don't know how much you owe this time, and I have no desire to know, but there is a substantial amount of money that you can have to clear the path for you to get your house in order. When you have lived together with your family, and have stayed out of trouble then you can have the rest of your inheritance. If this isn't possible then you will get nothing.

Your father, God rest his soul, will be proud of me for finally taking a stand.

Your loving mother xx

Ted stared down at the words on the paper. Nothing had changed, and the only difference was that her disappointment was in writing for all to see. He smiled. At least she was giving him the money to sort out Mickey Simmons. That was all that mattered. Ted turned round at the sound of the door handle creaking. He watched as it turned. He dropped the letter on the desk and stood up, just in case.

The door was pushed open and Jerry walked in.

Ted sighed and sat back down again. He smiled when he noticed Jerry was carrying another envelope, only this one was bulging.

Jerry threw it on the desk. 'This is what your mother is giving you and as I understand it there will be no more until you've sorted yourself out.'

Ted picked up the envelope, squishing the notes down inside. 'You know you could be more help to me. My mother listens to you.'

Jerry scowled. 'You still don't get it do you? Your mother is my client and you are not. It is my job to look after her interests. Now please leave. I have work to do before my next appointment.'

Ted stood up and gathered up his mother's letter and pushed it in his trouser pocket. 'I'm going.' He took the couple of steps to the door and pulled it open, almost bumping into the impeccably dressed secretary with her mousy brown hair neatly rolled into a chignon. He stepped aside for her to walk in. Ted almost ran out of the office, nearly falling over one of the dark oak, red-cushioned chairs that stood lined up against the wall. He pulled open the black front door and stepped out onto the street, trying to avoid the puddles that were getting bigger with every minute that passed. It wasn't long before the rain started to seep through the holes in the soles of his shoes and his feet squelched as he walked along. His grip didn't loosen on the money he had been given; he hadn't even stopped to count it. He knew it didn't matter how much it was; it probably wouldn't be enough. His mind was already chasing round in circles, trying to remember where the next big game was going to be and when.

A car chugged to a standstill and two men dressed in black suits and wearing trilby hats got out. The men were suddenly walking either side of him. 'Hello, Ted, I believe you 'ave something that belongs to us.'

'I don't think so, lads.'

Slips chuckled. 'I admire you, Ted. Yer don't seem to care that you are now playing with the big boys, or that yer playing with fire.'

Beads of perspiration formed on Ted's forehead, and the palms of his hands were damp. 'I'm not, I'm just getting the money together that I owe your father.'

Slips looked around him before grabbing Ted's arm and swinging him round.

Ted lost his balance and slipped to the floor. His suit was instantly soaked and his hat landed in a puddle further along the road.

Slips stood over him. 'Don't take me for a fool. I could give yer a good kicking now.' He snatched the envelope from Ted's hand. 'This was due weeks ago. Don't yer care that Mickey knows everything there is to know about yer? He makes it his job to know. 'Ow do you fink he manages to stay in control of so much? Knowledge is power.' He ripped open the envelope. 'This is a good down payment and may buy yer some time but I'll be looking for the next instalment next week.'

*

Dot's eyes narrowed as she watched her brother reading his letter for the second time. She no longer noticed the fresh outdoor smell that always accompanied him and his patched trousers and check shirt.

Tom sighed as he peered up from the paper he was clutching.

Dot quickly looked down, concentrating hard on the stack of sliced bread that was standing in front of her on the kitchen table.

Tom leant back on the wooden chair he was sitting on. 'Annie still sounds like she's enjoying living her life in London with Rose and Joyce.'

Dot looked up from buttering the stack of sliced bread. 'Be happy for her, Tom. When I worked with Rose and met that niece of mine for the first time in goodness knows how many years they were lovely.' She smiled. 'You should be proud of her.'

The paper rustled as Tom folded up the letter from his daughter. 'I am, I just worry. I don't know Rose like you do. She was always said to be up to no good before she left for London with Annie.'

Dot shook her head. She thrust the end of the knife into the butter. Ran her hands down the front of the blue floral apron she was wearing to protect her plain blue dress. 'I can only speak as I find and she was, is, a wonderful friend and a very talented seamstress.'

Tom turned the letter over a couple of times before thrusting it back into the envelope. 'You sound like you miss it.'

Dot chuckled. 'I suppose I do in a way but still wouldn't change what I have now. It's wonderful to be back with you and Pa, and helping out with the chickens let alone having a family to cook for.' She glanced around her. 'I wouldn't want to be anywhere else, although I do wish Ivy was here. We did have some laughs together.'

Sadness trampled across Tom's weathered face. 'She missed you after you left. I remember thinking at the time she probably only married me because you and her got on so well.'

Dot threw back her head and laughed. 'I shall ignore that Tom because you know as well as I do Ivy totally adored you.'

'I know, I adored her too.' Tom stood up and walked over to the window gazing in wonderment at the new crops growing, despite the awful rain they had been having. There was a time he would have worried about his crops being ruined but not anymore. 'You know everything has changed so much in the last year. I miss them all and I want everything to go back to how it was.' His shoulders hunched over.

'I know.' Dot's lips thinned as she held herself and her tears in check. Staring at his stooped back, she didn't have the heart to tell him Annie would probably always live in London now.

Tom stood silent for a moment, staring hard at the farm he had worked so hard to keep. 'The only thing that remains constant is the land; the crops keep growing no matter what happens in our lives.'

'But it doesn't happen by itself. We have to feed, love and nurture it; otherwise it gets overcome and strangled by weeds.' Dot's eyes welled up with unshed tears. 'That's why I'm here, to give back some of the love and nurturing I casually left behind when I ran away.'

'I know and we're pleased you're here.'

Dot forced a smile. 'Hopefully, that means you're not looking to get rid of me. I have a lot of lost time to make up for.'

Tom turned and smiled at his sister. 'Well, it certainly makes Pa happy to have you back home.'

Dot laughed. 'Only Pa?'

Tom shook his head. 'No, not only Pa, but what about Arthur?'

Dot picked up the knife again and studied the buttered bread in front of her. 'What about Arthur?'

Tom scowled. 'Don't give me the innocent "What about Arthur". He clearly loves you and I believe you love him so what are you going to do about it?'

Dot shrugged.

'If that was one of the girls, you and Ivy would be saying something like: "Don't shrug your shoulders like that." You need to talk it out.'

Dot frowned. 'I know but he's living in London and I'm here so there's not much to talk out.'

Tom walked over to the kitchen table and sat down. He closed his eyes for a moment and took a deep breath. 'You know I've lost Ivy, and far too soon in my opinion, but you still have the love of your life here, Dorothy, and he still wants to be with you. Don't throw it away, sis. It's time you and him had a proper conversation about your futures, even if it means making a compromise somewhere along the line.'

Dot peered under her lashes at her brother. 'It must be serious. You've called me by my full name.'

Tom smiled. 'You may joke but I'm deadly serious. He's visited you here several times since you've been home. He at least deserves an honest conversation before he goes back to London tomorrow.' He paused. 'When he gets back from the village I'll take Margaret and Pa out to give you some space.'

Dot frowned. 'There's no need. We can go out if need be.'

The back door suddenly flew open. The spring sunshine lit up the room. Margaret, wearing an old pair of her brother's overalls, pulled off her muddy farm boots. 'Am I interrupting?'

Dorothy's face lit up at the red cheeks of her young niece. 'No, not at all – you're looking very flushed.' She studied her niece. 'You know you should let me alter those clothes if you're going to keep wearing them.'

'They're not too bad and will do for now.' Margaret gave her father a mischievous smile. 'While Pa's been hiding away I've weeded all around the potatoes and cabbages, and my back is killing me now.'

'Margaret, I'm so sorry, I got caught up talking to your aunt.' Tom smiled. 'It's her fault.'

Dot threw her head back and laughed. 'I haven't heard that since we were children. It's good to know nothing has changed between us.'

Tom laughed.

'What's all the laughter about?' Arthur boomed as he walked through the front door.

Tom smiled at his old friend. 'We've just gone back to

being six years old again.' He turned to Margaret. 'Come on, let's go and find your grandpa.'

Margaret stared at her father before peering down at her boots. 'I've only just left him talking to the chickens.'

Tom chuckled. 'I'd say I'm surprised but everyone seems to talk to the chickens. They're obviously good at keeping secrets.' He walked towards the back door and pulled on his boots. 'Come on.'

Margaret frowned but moved to follow her father. He waited while she bent down to pull on her boots.

Arthur's gaze followed them. 'Was it something I said?'

'What? No, of course not.' Tom looked over at him. 'I'm sure Margaret can confirm I've been idling in here for far too long this morning.'

Margaret's face broke into a smile. 'I would never dare suggest such a thing, even if it is true.'

The sound of laughter followed the pair of them out of the house.

Arthur's laughter faded. He sat down at the kitchen table and began tapping his fingers rhythmically.

Dot watched him for a few seconds. 'I was making Tom a sandwich but as he's gone out again would you like it instead?'

Arthur stopped tapping and ran his hand through his hair. 'No, at least not yet, thank you.'

Dot sighed. 'What's going on?' She placed the buttered slices of bread on top of each other and covered them with a tea plate. 'I know something is, so you might as well tell me and get it over and done with.'

'I thought the same, what with Tom going out as soon as I came in.'

Dot gave a nervous laugh. 'Yes, that brother of mine is not very subtle is he.'

Arthur stood up but his gaze stayed fixed on the grain of the wooden table. 'So what's going on then? It's obviously something to do with me so that means it's something to do with you as well.'

Dot shook her head. 'Nothing is going on. Tom just thinks we should have an honest talk about our futures.'

Arthur sat down again. 'I must admit I agree with him, even though I've been avoiding it.' He reached up and rubbed the back of his neck. 'I wanted to give you a chance to realise I'm not the same man you left in London. It's one of my many regrets that I hurt you so much, but that's something I have to live with. I've never stopped loving you. I, selfishly, got caught up in my own grief, but I'm hoping you could grow to love me again.'

Dot's eyes filled with unshed tears as the memories of their life together bombarded her mind. She reached out and rested her hand on his arm. 'The last few years of our lives together were difficult times but I never stopped loving you. I only left because I needed to mourn our son and try to survive as well. I felt you were slowly, and painfully, killing me.'

Arthur nodded. 'I can't put into words how sorry I am.' His eyes were full of pain. 'I don't expect you to believe me but I've been trying to show you that I want my life to be with you and only you, if you'll have me.'

Tears rolled down Dot's cheeks. She quickly brushed them away with the tips of her fingers. 'It's not as simple as that. You're in London and I'm here. I know it sounds selfish, and it was my decision to leave here in the first place, but I've missed out on a lot of years with my father and brother and I don't want to be left with the regret of not spending time with them. We know better than anyone how precious life is and how quickly it can be ripped away from us.' She sniffed as the tears began to cascade down her cheeks again, leaving their salty residue on her lips. 'I don't want to have to choose.'

Arthur got up from his chair and dropped to his knees at her feet. 'You don't have to choose. Without you there is nothing to keep me in London. I do need to talk to Joyce; I feel I owe her an awful lot.'

Dot nodded.

Arthur took Dot's hands in his. 'Look I don't know whether I'm doing the right thing or not and I want us to be together again but I also want there to be complete honesty between us.' He paused, and swallowed hard. 'I've put an offer on the farm next door. It's a low offer because it needs a lot of work doing to it but perhaps we could live here while we sort it out.' Arthur's words tumbled over each other in their bid to escape. 'That way you are close to your family but we can still live together as man and wife. What do you think?'

Simon stretched his legs out in front of him and rested his head on the back of his late father's prized black leather wingback chair. He stared into the open fireplace. The golden flames danced up the chimney, while occasionally spitting ash out on to the hearth. There was something mesmerising and comforting about an open fire. He shook his head. They would need more money for coal and kindling for the next couple of months. He wondered if his mother and sister would understand if he asked them to light the fire later in the evening, or maybe go to bed earlier. Simon's gaze turned to his mother knitting; he had no idea what she was making but the needles constantly clicked together with every stitch. She pulled at the wool that was wrapped around her fingers and the ball slipped off her lap and rolled across the floor. He leant forward and picked it up and passed it to her.

'Thank you, Simon.' Mavis rested the knitting needles on her lap, creasing the natural folds of her black dress flat. 'Is everything all right? You're very quiet tonight.'

Simon closed his eyes for a moment, instantly forgetting about how the price of coal had shot up recently. He had tried not to think about what he had done, but now his throat tightened as the enormity of it hit him.

'Is it the café? If it is then I don't want you worrying about it. We'll manage one way or another.' She paused but Simon said nothing. 'I don't want you worrying about any of it. I can always get a cleaning job or take in washing.'

Simon's eyes snapped open. 'I don't want you doing no such thing. The café is doing well enough.'

'So what's going on? And don't say nothing because it's clear something is. I can feel it in me water. Are you still worrying about signing up?'

Simon smiled at his mother's words. 'You and your water.'

Mavis chuckled. 'You may laugh but my water isn't very often wrong. So what is it?'

Simon looked grim as he shook his head. 'You'll be pleased to know your water isn't wrong this time either.' He couldn't bring himself to look at his mother. He didn't want to see the pain he was about to inflict on her. 'I've enlisted.' He sighed, glad he had managed to say it.

Silence sat between them for a few minutes.

Mavis sighed. 'I'd say I'm surprised but I've been expecting it since the war began and all your friends joined up.'

Simon opened his eyes and looked over at his mother.

Mavis held his gaze. 'You only have to look around you to know there's a lot of pressure for men to enlist, and let's face it, women whose husbands and sons have gone are asking why others haven't, so I do understand.'

Simon jumped up out of the chair and went to kneel at his mother's feet. 'I'm sorry, Ma'

Mavis scowled at her son. 'You don't think I worry about what others are saying, do you? Where were they when my Bill died all those years ago? I don't care what any of them think; you and Barbara are all I care about. To be honest I'm not sure I even care about that blooming café that was your father's dream. I can't help feeling it's robbed you of yours and now this war is going to wipe away what little hope you had of earning money from your paintings.'

'Ma, my paintings are just my way of relaxing. I don't think I'll ever be good enough to make a living from it, and anyway most painters aren't appreciated until after they're dead.'

Mavis rested the palm of her hand against Simon's bristled cheek. 'In that case I don't want you to do well out of it. I can't deal with thoughts like that, let alone it actually happening, so you just make sure you come back in one piece.'

Simon reached up and kissed his mother's soft cheek. 'Thank you.'

Mavis frowned. 'For what?'

'Making it easy for me to tell you. I've been dreading it.'

Mavis wrapped her arms around her son's shoulders. 'I'm lucky you didn't go straight away like the thousands of other men did.'

Simon breathed in his mother's lavender perfume, trying to commit it to his memory. 'You will write to me won't you?'

'It's not my strongest point but I promise to write to you every day, even if it's only two lines.' Mavis blinked quickly and forced a laugh. 'I'll also knit you lots of socks.'

Simon forced a smile. 'Thank you.' He moved back to perch on the edge of his armchair. The fingertips of both hands came together as he pursed his lips.

The two of them sat in silence, each lost in their own thoughts.

Simon glanced up at his mother. 'I know you said you weren't bothered about the café but you haven't asked about it.'

Mavis tightened her lips. 'I trust you'll do whatever you think is right. As I said, I only really care about you and Barbara.'

Simon nodded. 'I've asked Joyce to keep it going for us but I would appreciate it if you could offer to help out from time to time, and make sure Barbara is kind to her.'

Mavis peered at her son's troubled expression. 'I've never met Joyce and yet I have felt for a long time that you like her a lot.'

Simon looked up and their eyes locked. 'I more than like her, Ma, and I know she likes me. Actually she said, "No one could love you more than I do." But I can't help thinking she sees us as just good friends or brother and sister.'

'Have you told her how you feel?'

'Yes.' Simon paused. 'The trouble is we're always so busy and tired, plus I'm a coward. I've never taken her out somewhere nice, and when we talk it's always about the café.' He frowned, and leant back in his chair. 'What happens if she doesn't like me in the same way?'

'What happens if she does? Tell me about her.'

Simon's face lit up. 'She's wonderful, so shy, kind and thoughtful. She's a great cook. She's not long started making cakes for the café and they're proving to be very popular. We even have three young ladies who have taken to coming in regularly for a slice of her chocolate cake.'

Mavis watched her son's animated features as he talked about the woman he clearly loved. 'I know you can marry whoever you wish but maybe it's time I met her.'

Simon nodded. 'As much as I'd like there to be, I'm not sure it has any future but please be kind to her. I noticed when Barbara was working in the café she kept staring at Joyce and I don't want her to feel so uncomfortable that she leaves altogether.'

Mavis leant forward ran her hand down her son's arm. 'Don't worry, I'll keep an eye on things and if necessary I'll have words with Barbara.'

'Thanks, Ma.'

Mavis took a deep breath. 'When do you go?'

'Tomorrow will be my last day in the café. I have training first before I'm sent off to fight.'

Mavis opened her mouth to speak but fear gripped her as her throat tightened and she tried to hold back the tears that were now ready to fall.

6

Joyce stood outside staring at the gold block lettering of the sign hanging above a shiny black door, which read: Jeremiah King Solicitors. The wind cut through her coat, took hold of a loose tendril of hair, and whipped it across her face. Her fingers quickly grabbed it and tucked it behind her ear. Joyce took a deep breath, fighting the urge to run away, and wishing she'd taken up the offers of someone to come with her. Her stomach churned as she looked around her, not noticing the grand architecture of the Victorian buildings that made up the road.

Voices carried in the air and along the street towards Joyce, making her stop and glance over her shoulder. Thankful the glistening frost on the pavement had melted away, Joyce turned and looked at both sides of the street but couldn't see anyone though the shouting was getting nearer.

The large, round clock hanging from the watchmaker's shop a couple of doors down caught her attention. It was nearly eleven o'clock. She jumped as a single chime came from it. She took a deep breath and mumbled to herself, 'Come on, girl, you can't put it off any longer.' She pushed on the black door and it swung open. As she stepped inside the door swung shut behind her, locking out the sun that was trying to break through the grey clouds.

A woman sat at a large oak desk facing the door, and looked up as Joyce entered. Her mousy brown hair was neatly rolled into a chignon and she looked impeccable in her crease-free white blouse. She gave a faint smile. 'Good morning, what can I do for you?'

Joyce's heart pounded. 'I … I have an appointment … with … with Mr King.'

The lady raised her eyebrows and peered down at a large open book. 'Can I take your name please?'

Joyce fought the urge to giggle; she could hear Peter's voice mimicking the plums in posh people's voices. 'Joyce … Miss Joyce Taylor.'

The lady appeared relaxed as she patted the back of her hair. 'Please take a seat and I'll let Mr King know you are here.'

Joyce nodded and gladly perched on the edge of the nearest red velvet seat of a dark oak chair. She leant forward, straining to look around the dark room. There were many bookshelves lining the wall on one side of the large oak desk. Each shelf was laden with books all standing to attention in size order. A small console table stood underneath a large portrait of a formidable-looking man, which faced the door she came in.

'Mr King will see you now.'

Joyce jerked round at the voice that appeared to come from nowhere; the thick carpet had hushed the woman's footsteps. 'Thank you.' She stood up, pulled back her shoulders and ran her hands down her lightweight coat.

The woman led her into a large smoke-filled office.

Leather-bound books and paper files were scattered over a large oak desk. Books, of various sizes, and paperwork were stacked on the floor next to the desk. A grey-haired man sat behind the desk puffing furiously on his wooden pipe, adding more grey clouds of smoke into the office.

Joyce coughed as the rich, earthy tobacco smoke filled her lungs.

Mr King peered over the top of his glasses as she entered the room behind the secretary.

Joyce placed her hand over her mouth before mumbling, 'Sorry.'

Mr King took the pipe out of his mouth. 'Please come in and sit down.' He waved one hand at her while the other placed his pipe on a glass dish. He stood up and held out his hand. 'Miss Taylor, it's lovely to finally meet you.'

Joyce took in his pristine black three-piece suit before stepping forward to take his fingertips in hers to shake his hand.

'Please sit down.' Jeremiah King indicated a wooden chair in front of his desk. He stared at her for a few minutes, taking in her thin, young features. 'You're not what I expected. You're not much more than a child.'

Joyce felt the hairs on the back of her neck stand on end as she sat down. 'I'm sorry, sir, but I don't actually know why I'm here.'

Jeremiah frowned. 'I assumed you knew.' He took a breath. 'I am acting on behalf of your grandmother, Mrs Edith Taylor.' He picked up some papers and pushed others aside before he looked at her pale features again. 'I take it you do know your grandmother?'

Joyce nodded. 'Not very well though.'

Jeremiah shook his head. 'Well, she's a patient in St Thomas' Hospital.' He paused. 'I'm sorry to tell you she's in a coma, and unlikely to come out of it.'

Joyce gasped, but stayed silent. She became aware that Mr King was waiting for her to say something. 'Thank you for letting me know.' She stood up. 'I'm not sure I needed to come to the office to be told that.'

Jeremiah stood up, just catching the arm of the chair as it swung backwards. 'No, you misunderstand, that's not why you are here; well, it is partly.' He shook his head. 'Please sit down.'

Joyce slowly lowered herself back on to the chair.

'I have represented Mrs Taylor for many years and there was always an agreement that if she became so ill that she was unlikely to survive I was to start putting her instructions into practice, and that's why I wrote to you.'

'I don't understand.'

Mr King took a deep breath. 'Your grandmother claims to have written to you on a number of occasions but has never had any response from you. Consequently I've been given instructions on how to move forward with a certain situation.'

Joyce frowned. 'What situation? And I've never received anything from my grandmother. I would have answered if I had. I didn't think she wanted to see me.'

'Well, that may well be your account of things but I can tell you she was hurt when you didn't reply.' There was a rustling as Mr King put some papers in order. 'There's very little point raking up the past. We need to get down to business.'

Joyce stared at him. Did her grandmother write to her

after all? If she did where were those letters? Does that mean they could have stayed in contact and Joyce wasn't the terrible child she had thought she was when they moved out of her grandmother's house? Her mind had been thrown into turmoil.

Jeremiah King coughed, jolting Joyce out of her thoughts. He looked down at the piece of paper in his hands. 'You are here because I have been unable to find your father—'

'My father died on the *Titanic*.'

The solicitor scowled. 'I'm very sorry to hear that, but I have been unable to find any paperwork on his death.'

Joyce shook her head. 'I don't know about that but, as far as I know, his body was never found. I do have an uncle. His name's Arthur.'

Jeremiah tightened his lips for a moment. 'Not according to your grandmother you don't—'

Joyce's heart was suddenly racing; she could hear it pulsating in her ears. 'What? I don't understand. Are you sure?' She lifted her hand to rest at the base of her neck.

Jeremiah raised his eyebrows. 'I can assure you, Miss Taylor, in my business it doesn't pay to make mistakes like that.'

'No, I'm sure.' Joyce swallowed hard and gave her head a slight shake. 'But … but it can't be true. I've been living with him for years. My father took me there before going off to work on the *Titanic*.'

Jeremiah studied her. 'Maybe we should contact the police if this man is masquerading as your uncle.'

Joyce's head flinched back slightly. 'No, maybe I've misunderstood.' Her eyes narrowed. 'I've always called him uncle so I just assumed…'

'Well, I'm happy to involve the police if there's been any misconduct going on.'

Joyce shook her head. 'Uh no, sir, that won't be necessary. I'm sure everything will be all right when I've spoken to him.' Her thoughts began running around her head out of control. Who was Arthur Bradshaw? Why hadn't he told her he wasn't her uncle? Her hands balled into fists as they lay in the folds of her coat.

Jeremiah studied the young girl in front of him for a moment before pulling a fob watch from his waistcoat and checking the time. 'Well, if that's the case we should get down to business.' He pushed his spectacles further up the bridge of his nose and peered down at the paperwork in front of him.

Joyce jerked and fidgeted on her chair. She pulled herself upright, wondering what she was actually there for.

'Now, as I said your grandmother is in a coma and I have strict instructions to make sure a chest is delivered to you.'

'A chest?'

Jeremiah peered over his glasses at Joyce. 'Yes, a chest. I have no idea what's in it, if anything, but it will be delivered to your home some time over the next week or so.' He cleared his throat. 'Now, there is something much more serious that your grandmother wants you to do.' He paused.

Joyce stared at the solicitor, wondering what he could have to say to her that was more serious than Arthur not being her uncle. 'What?'

Jeremiah cleared his throat. 'She wants you to look after a five-year-old boy who has been left in her care.'

'What?' Joyce's eyes widened. 'You can't be serious?'

He watched what little colour she had drain from her

face. 'Since your grandmother has been in hospital her housekeeper has been looking after him but, long term, that is not possible.'

'A five-year-old boy?' Joyce folded her arms. 'I don't know anything about children, let alone boys. How am I meant to look after him? Surely, there must be someone else who is more suitable to bring up a child?'

'Apparently there isn't.'

'Who is he and why has my grandmother been looking after him?' Anger took hold when she thought about her father being made to leave her house and yet she took in a stray. 'I don't understand, I don't understand why I have been thrown into this problem when it's nothing to do with me.'

Jeremiah stared down at the paper and read the specific instructions not to tell her anything about the boy. He shook his head. 'I can't tell you much, except his name is Philip Edwards, his mother was a family friend and she died. Your grandmother always said there's nothing more important than family, so she took the boy in and now your grandmother is adamant you are the one to look after him.'

Joyce wanted to shout: "Family wasn't important enough for her to keep me," but she didn't. Instead she pulled back her shoulders and lifted her chin. 'What will happen to him if I refuse?'

Jeremiah shrugged. 'I expect he will end up in an orphanage because there's no one else. You are his only hope.'

An uncomfortable silence sat between them. 'I need to think about this, but it does feel like I have no choice.'

'This is a big decision, Miss Taylor, but if you turn your back on him I'm sure you'll regret it.' Jeremiah King forced a smile. 'I'll give you a week or so to think about it but arrangements will need to be made one way or another, and you'll need to sign some paperwork. If you agree to take him I'll arrange for him to be delivered along with his meagre belongings.'

Joyce clenched her hands. 'It's just I've never had any dealings with children. I don't even have any brothers or sisters.'

Jeremiah King stood up and stretched out his hand. 'You'll soon get used to each other, I'm sure.'

Joyce followed suit and shook his hand. Her eyes clouded as she stared at the solicitor. 'I would say it's been a pleasure but you've managed to turn my life upside down in less than an hour.'

Joyce prodded the cabbage with a fork. 'If you two are ready so is the dinner.'

Annie glanced over at Joyce, so at home in the kitchen. 'I love the smell of a roast dinner.' She breathed deeply. 'I don't think you can beat it.'

'Oh I don't know, I've never liked the smell of cabbage boiling on the stove.' Rose pulled at the half-apron Joyce had given her that morning. 'But the smell of bacon frying has to be one of my favourites.'

'Oh, yes, and mine.' Annie laughed.

Joyce grinned. 'Basically anything cooking usually whets your appetite, apart from cabbage.'

'I suppose that's true.' Annie smiled, gathering the cutlery together. 'As there's only us three shall we eat here at the kitchen table?'

Rose picked up a cloth, rinsed and squished it in the warm water that was sitting in a bowl in the sink. 'That makes sense to me. I'll start clearing the things away.'

Joyce peered over her shoulder. 'That's fine, saves all the toing and froing to the dining room.' She gripped the handle of the saucepan and began pouring some of the cabbage water into the baking tray the chicken had been cooked in earlier. 'You might want to take that bowl out of the sink so I can drain the rest of this water away.'

Rose quickly did as she requested. 'My father liked to drink a cup of the cabbage water; he said it was full of goodness.'

'My grandfather does the same but I couldn't think of anything worse.' Annie screwed up her face as the cutlery chinked together in a pile on the table and began moving some of the cooking utensils off it. She sidestepped Joyce to begin making the gravy in the baking tray.

'I wonder if it's true.' Rose wiped the table with the damp cloth.

Annie shrugged. 'Who knows?'

The girls moved like a well-organised formation dance troupe and it wasn't long before the table was laid and the roast chicken sat proudly in the centre of it with a bowl of roast potatoes next to it.

Annie tightened the belt of her apron before looking over at Rose. 'I wish our brothers would write to let us know they are all right. I was reading Arthur's newspaper, about the war, but it doesn't give hope it's going to be over anytime soon – so much for "it'll be over in a few months".'

Rose's eyes welled up with unspent tears. 'It's awful. I've been praying it will be over soon and they'll come back safely.' She blinked rapidly before lowering her eyelashes. 'To be honest I don't read the papers. I can't think about my brothers putting their lives at risk.' She frowned, wiping her hands across her eyes. 'I tell myself they're still at home working on the farm.'

Annie nodded. 'It's a good way of looking at it. My ma used to say all the worrying in the world won't change anything and I suppose she's right but it's all easier said than done.' She sighed. 'I'm going to try and do the same. I'm also going to get on with knitting socks and things for the men. I haven't done any for a while and if the weather here is anything to go by they must be frozen and soaked to the skin on the front line.'

Joyce looked over at her friends, tucking her loose shoulder-length hair behind her ears. She had no desire to talk about the war, not now. She forced a smile. 'Let's talk about something else.' She began to carve the chicken.

Annie licked her lips. 'I don't know if it's the smell or looking at the food but I suddenly feel starving.'

Rose smiled. 'Me too.' Colour rose in her cheeks. 'I have something to tell you...'

The girls turned to look expectantly at her.

Rose's colour deepened. 'Charlie has asked me to go out with him.'

Annie clapped her hands together and beamed at her friend. 'I knew he would. This is the best news ever. I have to admit he's incredibly handsome, in an obvious sort of way that is.'

For a moment Rose had a dreamy faraway look on her face. 'He is, but don't get carried away. It's only a date.'

Joyce chuckled. 'I have a feeling Charlie really likes you.'

Annie giggled. 'And so he should. Any man would be lucky to have any of us.'

Laughter rang around the kitchen as they finally sat down and began putting food on their plates.

Rose stuck the prongs of her fork into a potato and sliced it in half with her knife. 'Now we're sitting down, how did you get on at the solicitor's?'

Joyce shook her head.

Annie caught her look of dismay. 'Did something unexpected happen?'

Joyce made a throaty sound. 'Huh, you could say that.'

Rose gave Annie a troubled look before studying Joyce. 'What happened?'

'Oh nothing too devastating. If I agree to it the solicitors are delivering me a chest that my grandma wants me to have.' She paused, tension etched on her face. 'And a small boy.'

'What?' the girls yelled as one.

Joyce rested her knife and fork on the side of her plate. 'My grandma is in a coma and some time ago the solicitor was instructed to act if she became ill and was unlikely to survive. Apparently, that is where we're at.'

Annie slowly shook her head, putting down the fork, loaded with food, on the side of her plate. 'I can't believe you've known about this and yet you didn't tell us. I don't know how you've kept it to yourself.'

Rose raised her eyebrows and placed her knife and fork on the side of her plate. 'Nor me, who is this boy? Where has he come from and why do you have to look after him? How are you going to do that and work? How old is he?' She shook her head. 'Sorry, my head is awash with questions.'

Joyce stared at her friend. 'Yours is; how do you think I feel?'

Annie looked from one to the other. 'It must have been a terrible shock for you.'

Joyce gave a humourless laugh. 'That's putting it mildly. I don't know anything about this boy.' She paused for a second. 'But there's more; apparently Arthur Bradshaw is not my real uncle, so I don't know who he is.'

Rose shook her head. 'You've had all of that going on and yet you said nothing.'

Joyce picked up her knife and fork. 'That's because I have no idea what to say or how to act. The solicitor implied if I didn't take the boy at best he would end up in an orphanage, at worst he could end up on the streets.'

The girls sat in silence.

'According to the solicitor my grandmother wrote to me several times but I never answered her letters, which apparently hurt her feelings.' Sadness crept across Joyce's face. 'But I never received any letters. I mean why would I not answer them? I don't know, it all feels incredibly unfair, just when things were starting to come together with Simon and getting the opportunity to cook; it makes me think that maybe it's not meant to be.' She paused. 'Although, I don't see why it's my responsibility to bring up a boy I know nothing about.'

Tension joined them at the kitchen table; they sat there stunned at the turn of events.

'I'm also going to have to talk to my uncle ... Arthur ... about the boy staying here. Eat your dinner before it gets cold.' Joyce paused. 'I might have to find somewhere else to live.'

Annie's mouth dropped open. 'Surely it won't come to that, will it?'

Joyce shrugged. 'It might. He may not want a constant reminder of what he's lost living here, especially as he's not long come to terms with life without William.'

Silence reigned.

There was a clatter as Rose dropped her fork on her plate. Her half-eaten dinner had lost its appeal. 'I can't believe your grandma would put you in this position, just when you were getting the chance to bake for the café as well.'

Joyce made a humourless sound. 'None of that matters when you hold it against a young boy's life.' Her knuckles paled as she gripped the handles of her knife and fork.

Rose followed suit. 'It'll be hard on the boy; after all he's being thrust on people he doesn't know. I'd be terrified if I was him.'

The girls stared at Rose for a few seconds but said nothing. The only sound came from the cutlery hitting the plates as they carried on eating.

Annie placed a small piece of the white meat into her mouth and licked the gravy off her lips. She glanced at Joyce's ashen features. 'Looking at you gives me a sense there is more, so spit it out.'

Joyce stared down at the once-appetising dinner. 'Nothing, it's nothing. Let's eat our dinner and talk about something else.'

Rose looked up and nodded. 'Annie's right, we're friends and there's nothing you can't tell us.'

There was a long silence.

Joyce took a deep breath, not knowing if she could

actually say the words out loud. 'Well, it's Simon...' She took another breath and glanced up at her friends. 'He's enlisted.'

The girls sat looking at her open-mouthed.

'I know, it's shocking isn't it. It never occurred to me he would do that. I always thought he'd stay because of the café and his family.' Joyce paused. 'I can't believe it.'

Annie dropped her knife; it clattered on the side of her plate causing gravy to splash on to the table. Shaking her head, she stared at the mess she'd made before reaching over to clasp Joyce's hand. 'I suppose he feels a bit like my brother did and probably Rose's brothers as well. David never had a great urge to fight but when everyone else is enlisting people start to comment if you're not doing the same, and I suppose no man wants to be thought of as a coward.'

Joyce nodded. 'I don't think all the war posters up everywhere help either.'

Rose bit down on her bottom lip. 'It's probably the wrong time to ask but what will happen to the café?'

Joyce shrugged. 'He wants me to run it, which leaves a sour taste in my mouth.'

The girls stared at Joyce, waiting for her to say more.

The tears Joyce had tried to fight off every time she thought about not seeing Simon every day rolled down her cheeks. She had refused to allow her mind to think about the possibility of never seeing him again but suddenly it was there screaming in her head. 'I'd rather have nothing and know he's safe at home smelling of fried breakfasts.'

The girls jumped up, their chairs scraping along the tiled floor. They wrapped their arms around Joyce. Her sobbing and gasping for breath were the only sounds to be heard.

Gradually the tears slowed down and her breathing levelled out. The girls slowly pulled back.

'I'm sorry.' Joyce gulped. 'I don't know what came over me.' She wiped her eyes with the back of her hand. 'I've wanted my own restaurant for as long as I can remember. I wouldn't even sniff at a café or a tea room, but not at the expense of losing the man I love.'

The girls stepped back, all thought of eating long gone.

Joyce stared down at her hands. 'When he told me I did question him about me running it because of his sister, Barbara. She's started working in the café, but he was adamant about me running it.' Her throat made a strange sound. 'I'm not sure how his mother will feel about that.'

Rose tried to swallow past the lump that had formed in her throat. She gave Joyce another squeeze. 'You'd like to think she'd be grateful; after all she won't have to worry about it.'

Joyce gave a half-smile. 'You say that but I've never met Simon's mother so she won't know whether she needs to worry or not. I only met his sister this week and she kept giving me funny looks.'

Annie stared at Joyce. 'Oh my goodness, what are you going to say to Simon? I mean he wanted you to run the café while he was gone, and having a small boy around changes things doesn't it?'

Joyce blinked quickly. 'I don't know what I'm going to say, but I clearly can't do it now.'

Rose shook her head. 'We need to think about this. You can't just give up when something is almost within touching distance.' Her hand rested over her mouth for a moment. 'There must be a solution. There always is.'

Joyce shook her head. 'I don't think there is but thank you for trying to come up with one. Now, please eat your dinner. We definitely can't afford to waste food now.'

Rose nodded as she began slicing a piece of chicken. 'It'll be strange having a child running around.'

'Have you told Simon how you feel?' Annie stroked Joyce's arm. 'You need to tell him before he goes.'

Joyce's red bloodshot eyes had a look of horror in them. 'I sort of told him.'

Rose tightened her lips. 'Annie's right, don't sort of tell him; let him know he has a reason to come back other than that blooming café and supporting his family for the rest of his life.'

Annie nodded. 'Did he say anything about loving you?'

Joyce nodded. 'Yes, he made it clear I was the reason he kept the café open. It had nothing to do with his father; it was so he could see me every day.' She bit down on her lip. Blood seeped through into her mouth. 'I don't think I said enough for him to realise what he means to me.'

Rose sighed. 'You love him don't you?'

'Yes.'

'Then why can't you tell him? What are you afraid of?' Rose shook her head. 'It's obvious by the way he looks at you that he loves you.'

Annie shook her head at Rose. 'Look, Joyce, we watched you and Simon through the café window on our way back from the theatre and you both looked so happy. Isn't it worth a chance?'

Joyce jumped up off the chair and began pacing around the kitchen. 'What you don't realise is I've lost everybody I've ever loved. I can't take the risk of losing Simon as well.'

Annie stood up and grabbed Joyce's arm. 'I'm not having this. You have been without doubt so unlucky to lose both your parents, especially while you were still so young, but none of that was your fault.'

Rose nodded. 'Look, Arthur will be back tomorrow. You've got to think about what you're going to say to him about the whole sorry mess, and remember none of this is of your doing.'

Joyce closed her eyes for a second and took a breath. 'I know. I have no idea what to say to him. I feel exhausted. I'll sleep on it. Things might not look so bad in the morning.'

The early morning grey sky peered through the gap of the closed heavy curtains. Joyce sighed. She should have changed them to the lighter summer drapes by now but time seemed to gallop away from her these days. She opened the curtains wide to see paper and leaves rolling down the street. The sash windows rattled while the rain lashed against the glass. People had their heads down as they almost ran down the street trying to hold on to their umbrellas. She shook her head and yawned. That would be her in about an hour. She was sick of the rain and the greyness of winter.

Tiredness held her still; she had spent the night thinking about the five-year-old boy. Who was he? How she was going to look after him? Why hadn't she received her grandmother's letters, unless she didn't actually write any? Then there was Arthur, the man she had felt obliged to stay with and look after because he was her only family, or so she thought. She shook her head. Who was he? Her mind had been in turmoil all night. Talking to Annie and Rose had made it all real and now she felt she couldn't put one foot in front of the other, never mind go to work. She gave a weary sigh; then there was Simon.

A bedroom door banged shut and heavy footsteps ran down the stairs. Joyce peered over her shoulder just as Arthur stepped into the dining room.

'Good morning, Joyce, I'm glad I've managed to catch you before you go to work. I got home quite late last night.' Arthur's smile faded and for a split second worry took its place. 'I want to have a chat with you.'

Anger chased away the tiredness that had swamped Joyce since she had come downstairs. 'That's good because I also want to talk to you.'

Arthur fidgeted from one foot to the other. 'Really, well, that's good. Shall I make us a cup of tea before we sit down?'

Joyce silently stood aside, revealing a tray of tea things.

Arthur raised his eyebrows. 'Ah, right, you're a step ahead of me.' He took a step nearer. 'Shall I pour?'

Joyce walked away, passing the cabinet that contained the Victorian figurines she loved so much. Not stopping to enjoy them, she sat down by the unlit fireplace. Her thoughts were bouncing around her head. She didn't know how to start this conversation but she did know it had to take place.

Arthur glanced nervously at Joyce. Her shoulders, neck and face were rigid with tension. 'It was lovely going back to the village again; I came home with bags of vegetables and eggs for us all. Annie's family send their love.'

Joyce peered over her shoulder at him. 'That's good of them. I'll write to say thank you.' She took a deep breath. 'I went to see the solicitor, Mr King.'

Arthur bit his lip, concentrating on pouring the tea.

'I was quite nervous.'

A teaspoon clattered onto a saucer. 'Sorry, I dropped the spoon.' Picking up the two cups, Arthur handed Joyce one.

'Thank you.'

'I thought we were going together.' Arthur stumbled on to the seat of the armchair opposite hers.

Joyce picked up her cup and sipped the tea, scorching her top lip. 'I received some shocking news.' She scowled, hoping he would come clean.

Arthur tapped his feet, studying them as if seeing them for the first time. 'You know don't you?' He suddenly looked up at Joyce. 'I wanted to tell you myself; I just didn't know how or when. There never seemed to be a good time.'

Joyce glared. 'So were you never going to tell me? Were you planning on taking your secrets to the grave?'

Shame flitted across Arthur's face as he stared into his hot drink. 'I was too busy feeling sorry for myself.' He put his cup down on the small table next to his chair and clenched his hands together. 'Dot has been on at me to tell you, but I didn't know how or when. The last thing I wanted was you thinking you couldn't stay here when your father died. What was I meant to do, throw you out on the streets? After all, where else would you have gone?'

Lowering her eyelashes, Joyce felt Arthur's eyes boring into her. She looked up and shrugged. 'You could have just been honest with me and let me decide for myself.'

'The state I was in back then you would have left and, selfishly, I didn't want to be on my own. In fact the best thing that could have happened to me was your friends coming to stay, although I didn't know that at the time.' Arthur paused, looking straight at her. 'I'm sorry and I'm glad you now know, but it should have been me who told you.'

Joyce stared at him. 'It was one helluva shock when the solicitor told me I didn't have an uncle. He wanted to report you to the police.'

Arthur gasped. 'He hasn't, has he?'

'No, I told him I must have misunderstood the situation.'

'Thank you, I'm not sure I deserve your protection; after all living with me hasn't exactly been a joy for you.' Arthur hesitated before taking a deep breath. 'Dot and I knew your father for many years. In fact we were childhood friends, but I hadn't seen him for many years when he turned up on my doorstep with you.'

Joyce silently watched the pain of Arthur's memories etch onto his face.

Arthur's knuckles were white as his hands clenched together. He looked up at Joyce. 'The pair of you were only meant to be staying for a couple of weeks but when he didn't come back I was in no fit state to deal with that situation. I'd had the rug pulled out from under me. My world had been complete; I wanted for nothing. Looking back there was probably an arrogance about me. I had everything: money, property and respect. Losing my son was devastating; it was the end of the perfect world I'd worked hard to achieve. It ended any thoughts or caring about life. Material things no longer mattered to me, and I had no desire to live. Then when Dot couldn't live with me anymore, which wasn't surprising, that was the end of my world. I died twice over, or at least I wanted to. I slowly came to realise she wasn't interested in the money, properties and all these fancy ornaments; she had just wanted us to grieve together but instead I shut myself away with alcohol.'

Arthur rubbed his hands over his face. 'I haven't been a good guardian to you; in fact you were more of one to me. All I can say is I'm truly sorry. I have a lot of making up to do and not just with you.'

Joyce didn't know what to say. He had laid out his heart and soul to her. The anger she felt had faded with each word he said. 'It was just a shock.'

Arthur nodded. 'Wait, you said "secrets". I only had the one.'

Joyce looked down at her tea. 'Apparently my grandmother wrote to me on a number of occasions. I told the solicitor the letters were never received by me but I got the feeling he didn't believe me.' She paused; looking up she stared at Arthur. 'During the night it occurred to me they may have arrived and you could have destroyed them.'

Arthur gasped. 'I would never do such a thing; you must think I'm a real monster. I can assure you it's one thing to not tell you about me not being your uncle, but it's something else to keep letters from you.' He shook his head and sat hunched over in the chair.

Joyce shrugged. 'I don't understand why I never received them then.'

Arthur closed his eyes before taking a deep breath and pulling his shoulders back. He opened his eyes; they were dull as they darted from side to side. 'The truth of the matter is, because of the drink, I could have done anything back then.' He flopped his head down. 'I'm ashamed of myself for what I know I've put you through but if I've also kept you away from your grandmother without even being aware of my actions then that's … well it's despicable. I'm not saying I did because I truly don't remember. As you know I was in a very bad way back then. I didn't know which way was up, so anything is possible.'

Joyce took a sip of her lukewarm tea. 'It's no good going over old ground because it won't change anything. Although I would be lying if I didn't say it all hurts and feels like a lot of the heartbreak I've been through was unnecessary.' She shook her head. 'But I had another surprise to come, and if I'm honest I didn't think it could get any worse than finding out you're not my real uncle.'

Arthur nodded. 'I'll never forgive myself. It should have been me who told you about who I was.' He paused. 'If I'm also responsible for the letters too then that's unforgivable, and I'm so sorry, but are you saying there's more?'

Colour drained from Joyce's face, the dark rings under her eyes suddenly emphasised. 'My grandmother is in a coma and is unlikely to come out of it, which is very sad and I don't want to sound cold but I don't really know her.'

'But…'

Joyce stared at Arthur. 'But … she wants me to look after a five-year-old boy, Philip, who she's been looking after.'

Arthur held up his hand. 'Wait, wait, who is this boy?'

Joyce shrugged. 'I have no idea. I just know someone is going to deliver him here in the next week or so unless I tell them otherwise.'

Arthur's eyes narrowed.

'I know it's a lot to take in and goodness knows why I have to be the one to look after him. What do I know about children?'

Arthur bit his lip; his own news would have to wait. 'I'll help you.'

Joyce could feel her eyes welling up. 'How am I meant to earn a living, especially with Simon going off to fight in this blooming war, and look after a child? I don't understand why this has been thrust upon me, and now of all times.'

Arthur raised his eyebrows. 'I don't think there would have been a good time.' He reached out and cupped his hand over hers. 'I will help you. We just need to give it some thought, and we'll find a way between us.'

Joyce felt a tear roll down her cheek. 'This will be too painful for you, I mean to have another child running around the house.'

Arthur shook his head. 'We don't have any choice. What are you going to do? Refuse to take him so he ends up in some godforsaken place or on the streets somewhere?'

'The solicitor said something similar.'

Arthur patted Joyce's hand. 'I know you don't know this child but you can no more turn your back on him than I could you. You were a helpless child just as this boy is. The only difference is you were older.'

7

Joyce walked along slowly. All her usual morning thoughts of getting to work were no longer important. Her mind was still reeling from the conversations with the solicitor and Arthur. So much to digest and think about, she didn't know where to begin. She was oblivious to the smoky grey clouds in the sky and the water running down the back of her neck. Rain had been splattering the pavements for some time. She stared down, watching the raindrops pulling together to form puddles, which were getting larger with each drop that fell. Small rivers were forming along the road. Cars chugged past, their wheels splashing through the water while their windscreen wipers chugged back and forth fighting to clear the windscreens of each drop. People shielded themselves with umbrellas, hiding behind them as the rain drove down, thudding onto them.

A man knocked her sideways as he ran past. She steadied herself, rubbing her arm at the same time as looking back at him.

The man shouted, 'Sorry,' as he glanced over his shoulder and waved.

Joyce shivered. She stared down at her hand, ravaged from working in the café; she watched the globules of water dropping on to it. She should have brought her umbrella, but she had been preoccupied. Her throat tightened, as the lump there grew in size. Her lungs burnt in her chest as she tried to gasp for breath. Her tiny world was getting even smaller. Her uncle wasn't who she thought he was and her grandmother was dying. She had no family at all. She hadn't found the necklace with the locket holding the picture of her mother and father in it. Loneliness swamped her. Her tears mingled with the rain that was falling.

Her childhood dreams had been snatched away; first with the death of her mother and any little remaining hope had died with her father. Her friends and Simon had encouraged and nurtured the dream until it was almost in touching distance, but now she had to choose. She had nothing and no one; she was alone with the feeling of emptiness that she didn't think she could ever fill. How could she hope to raise a boy she didn't know? How could she help someone else when she couldn't help herself? Joyce tried to push a strand of hair from her face, but it was stuck fast. She was soaked to the skin.

'Please, miss, can I have a penny to buy something for my sister to eat?'

Joyce turned to the sound of the soft voice to see a small scruffy boy standing in front of her, as drenched as she was. He was clutching a little girl's hand. The girl's wet curly hair was matted to her head and the rain ran down her cheeks. Joyce wiped her hand across her own cheeks, unable to speak as she took in their dishevelled appearance.

The boy frowned. 'Are yer all right, miss?'

Joyce nodded. Is this what it would be like for Philip if she didn't take him in? Without a second thought she opened her handbag and pulled out a small cloth coin purse that had once belonged to her mother. Opening it, she took out two small silver coins. 'Are you on your own?'

The girl's eyes widened, and she hid herself behind her brother. Her fear was there for all to see.

The boy jutted out his chin. 'We can manage, miss. We just need to eat. Ain't that right, sis?'

The little girl's head bobbed up and down behind her brother's back.

Joyce felt the heavy weight of responsibility sitting on her slender shoulders. 'Where do you live?'

The boy gave her an impish grin. 'We're free, miss, and we're togevva wiv no one beating us.'

Joyce gasped as her eyes narrowed. 'So you live on the streets?'

The boy shrugged. 'Not always. We stay 'ere and there. Wherever we chose every night, and sometimes if we're lucky, people bring us out food or take us in for the night.' He frowned. 'The trouble wiv that is they then wanna get us into a home so we'll be safe, but it ain't safe. We look out for each uffa and they'd never let us stay togevva in an 'ome. None of it matters cos we're got each uffa, and I promised me ma that I'd always look after me sister.'

Joyce gave them both a pensive look.

The boy tugged at her sleeve. 'Don't look so worried. We're all right.'

Joyce shook her head. 'If you need food or anything you come to the Meet and Feast Café on Shaftesbury Avenue and I'll sort you out. Do yer 'ear me?'

The boy's face lit up and the girl came out of hiding.

Joyce stared at them both for a moment. She wanted to give them a big hug and take them home with her. She shook her head again. 'Here's sixpence each. Make sure you get some good food inside you.'

The children's faces lit up.

Joyce smiled. 'Don't forget the Meet and Feast Café on Shaftesbury Avenue.'

The boy nodded. 'Thanks, miss.'

The girl stepped out from behind her brother and wrapped her arms around Joyce's legs.

'Come on.' The boy smiled at his sister as he took her hand. 'Yer know, miss, yer shouldn't get upset about fings cos yer a kind lady. My ma used to say always be 'onest and kind and I fink yer that.'

Joyce wanted to ask about their mother and father but the children were suddenly running up the road. Shaking her head, she knew she shouldn't have let them go. She stared into the throng of people; the children were already out of sight. How brave was that boy to take on the task of looking after his sister. He hadn't turned his back when life got difficult; he was sacrificing everything so they could stay together and he could fulfil his promise to his mother. How could she be so selfish?

Joyce gasped as she saw Simon standing outside a pawnshop; he was carrying a small cardboard box. She frowned. Was he going in? Surely things weren't that bad at the café were they? She took a couple of steps nearer, wanting to see what he was doing, but something stopped her. Simon was a proud man and wouldn't appreciate being caught going into one of those shops.

'Excuse me.' A young woman tried to get past her.

Joyce stepped nearer the entrances of the properties that lined the street. 'I'm sorry.'

The woman nodded and sped up the road.

Joyce eyed up the shop, with its narrow frontage and scruffy door. It wasn't loved; the paint was peeling off the window frame. The temptation to walk over to it and pretend she hadn't seen him was great but suddenly the door opened and Simon stepped outside. The moment was lost.

Simon absently dried his hands on the small blue towel that was hanging off the hook by the café's kitchen sink. He watched Joyce through the serving hatch of the café. She had come in soaking wet, and hadn't said a word. He worried she would catch her death. She moved slower and seemed preoccupied. Her smile wasn't so ready to appear, and when it did it wasn't as full. Was he the cause of that? His heart ached; he leant back and stared at the clock. He had sent his sister home early. Today was the last chance to see Joyce for a while and he couldn't wait for the café to close.

He moved away from the hatch and paced around the kitchen a couple of times before walking over to the kitchen door. He pushed it open, with more courage than he was feeling, and walked into the café, thankful it was empty of customers. 'I think we'll shut five minutes early this evening.' He marched over to the main door and turned the key. He lifted the sign and turned it over to closed.

Joyce stayed silent, and continued to wipe the counter with the damp cloth for about the tenth time.

Simon leant his back against the door. 'Are you going to tell me what's bothering you?'

Joyce continued wiping the counter.

'Joyce?'

Joyce flinched. 'What?'

Simon stepped nearer to her. 'Look, we need to talk—'

'For goodness' sake.' Joyce flung her cloth on to the counter. 'What is it with everyone suddenly wanting to talk to me?' Tension filled her face. 'Do you think I have nothing else to think about but this blooming café?'

'Of course not, it's just…' Simon paused.

'It's just what?'

'It's just that this will be the last time I get to talk to you for some time.'

'And whose fault is that, Simon? Not mine, that's for sure.'

'Please, Joyce, don't do this. I don't want us to part company on an argument. You are more important to me than you know.' Simon reached out for her hand. 'I want us to sit down and spend some time together. I want you to know I've been so torn between my conscience about doing the right thing for our country and leaving you.'

Joyce took his hand before whispering, 'None of it matters because the country won.'

Simon guided her to a table away from the window. 'It does matter, at least to me. I can't go away without letting you know how difficult the decision has been.' He pulled out a chair for Joyce, scraping it along the floor, before sitting down in the one next to it. 'I've heard said that the government are likely to make it law soon so we will all have to go anyway.'

Joyce took his hand and squeezed it tight. 'Please try and stay safe. Don't be a hero.'

Simon forced a smile. 'Does that sound like me?'

Joyce's lips tightened as she shook her head.

Simon ran the edge of his finger down Joyce's cheek. 'Your skin is so soft; you're so beautiful.'

Colour rushed into Joyce's face and she lowered her eyelashes.

'I didn't mean to embarrass you.' Simon paused. 'I want to know what's troubling you today. You don't look like you had any sleep last night.'

Joyce gazed up at him. Once again, and for the umpteenth time, she thought about the brother and sister she met, how she hoped they were all right. Every time the café door had opened she had expected to see them but they hadn't come for anything to eat. She shook her head. 'I had to go and see a solicitor—'

'You're not in trouble, are you?'

Joyce squeezed his hand, staring down at his clean fingernails. 'I wasn't but going forward I might be.'

Simon scowled. 'What does that mean?'

Joyce frowned as she wondered how much to tell him. 'Apparently, my uncle Arthur isn't really my uncle.'

'What? Are you sure?'

Joyce smiled. His reaction mimicked her own. 'Well, according to my grandmother, I don't have any uncles so I suppose that makes it pretty convincing that he isn't one.' She shook her head. 'I have spoken to him about it and he admits he couldn't find the right time or words to tell me, which I suppose I can understand.'

Simon nodded. 'I know life has been hard at times but

at least he kept a roof over your head when he had no obligation to.'

Joyce's smile faded. 'Which brings me neatly on to the other problem that has been laid at my feet. My grandma wants me to look after a five-year-old boy.'

Simon's mouth dropped open but no words came out.

'He could be arriving soon, but I don't know how I can look after him and be here as well.' Joyce put her head in her hands. 'My life has been turned upside down and I can't figure out how to get it the right way up again.'

Simon shook his head. 'I don't know what to say. I'm disappearing when you need me most. I'm so sorry.'

'It's not your fault, Simon. It's my problem and I just have to try to work through it.'

Simon's eyes narrowed as his thoughts ran around his head. 'If it helps, bring him here every day. I don't know what five-year-old boys do but get him some crayons, books and things and he might be all right. There's plenty of food here.'

Joyce gave him a wry smile. 'I can't afford for him to eat out every day.'

Simon shook his head. 'I'm sure we could afford for a little one to have a good meal every day. That can easily be lost in the profits.'

'You're a good man, Simon. I'm going to miss you.' Joyce's eyes became watery.

'Which brings me on to what I want to say, or ask you.' Simon's face began to colour.

'It's all right, Simon, I shall do my best to keep the café running and I understand from Barbara your mother might pop in to offer a hand from time to time.'

Simon nodded. 'Yes, but that's not what I want to ask you.' He paused and looked around him. 'I'm sorry we're not in some fancy restaurant somewhere. I know I'm going away but I want you to know how much I love you.' He took a small blue velvet box out of his trouser pocket and lowered himself down on to one knee. He opened the box and a solitaire ring sparkled at her. 'Will you marry me?'

Tears rolled down Joyce's face. 'Do you know how long I have wanted this to happen?' She sniffed and swiped away the tears. 'You're only asking me because you're going off to war. I don't want you to ask me out of panic or fear.'

Simon lowered his head and flipped the box shut. 'I'm not and it worries me that you think so little of me.'

Joyce shook her head. 'That's just it, I don't. I'm trying to protect you from yourself and I now have this child to worry about. How can I commit to anything until I know how my life is going to be?' She stood up. Wringing her hands, she paced around the café. 'I don't even know if I'm going to be able to keep this café going for you. Do you know how much it hurts me to say all this?' She paused and turned to face Simon. 'My life has been turned upside down and that is exactly why I won't hold you to your proposal. Can't you see we're on separate paths at the moment? I've got to go and tell the solicitors I'm going to look after this boy, and probably sign my life away; goodness knows how that will turn out.' Their eyes locked as they stood in silence. She sighed. 'Maybe when you come back we can talk again; that is, if you still feel the same.'

Simon didn't take his eyes off her. He nodded. 'I'll hold on to the ring because I know my feelings for you won't change, and just so you know, it doesn't matter to me whether you have one or ten children to look after, it doesn't change my feelings for you.'

'Simon, I've loved you for so long, more than you'll ever know, and yet I still feel I'm not in a position to say yes. Please try to understand.'

Simon strode towards her and gripped the top of her arms. He lowered his head, pausing for just a second. Her orange blossom fragrance was at odds with the smell of carbolic soap but he didn't care. He wrapped his arms around her and gently brushed his lips against hers. She pulled him nearer and the pressure of their kiss grew. His arms tightened; he had no desire to let her go.

Unwillingly, Joyce slowly pulled away. She ran her tongue over her swollen lips before whispering, 'I'm sorry but I've got to get to the solicitor's. I don't want to leave you but I must for the child's sake. I couldn't live with myself if something dreadful happened to him.'

The newspaper rustled as Arthur turned the page. 'I don't know why I read the paper. It's all quite depressing. Thank goodness the weather has been so bad the Germans haven't been able to fly their Zeppelins over here anymore.'

'It must have been frightening for those poor people in Sandringham when it happened just after Christmas; they must have been terrified.' Joyce put down her knitting and looked over at Arthur. 'It doesn't bear thinking about.'

Arthur studied Joyce for a moment. 'No, it doesn't. These are certainly worrying times.'

The doorknocker thudded down, startling Joyce. She stared at Arthur, wondering who it could be. Surely they couldn't be dropping the boy off already, not at this time of night. The clock on the mantelpiece chimed seven times. It was too early to be the girls coming home from the theatre, unless Rose had walked out on Miss Hetherington, of course. Surely it couldn't be Peter or Simon; they would never come to the house, would they?

There was another knock and Joyce and Arthur both jumped up at the same time, almost bumping into each other in their haste to get to the front door.

'I'll get it,' Arthur assured Joyce. 'You never know who could be on the other side of the door.' He marched out into the hall, Joyce following closely at his heels. He turned the handle and pulled it open a little and peered out.

It was a dark evening with no streetlights, and no visible stars to pave the way. The wintry air pushed its way in.

An elderly man and woman stood in front of the house; the woman was gripping a boy's hand. He peered up at Arthur, his eyes full of fear. Joyce pulled the door open further and took in the three of them standing there. The boy stared at Joyce; his eyes were dull and lifeless. He pulled his hand away from the woman.

Arthur frowned. 'Yes, can I help you?'

The elderly man cleared his throat. 'We are looking for a Miss Taylor, Miss Joyce Taylor. We've been sent here by Mr Jeremiah King, the solicitor.'

Joyce stared at them. The boy looked as bad as she felt as he stood behind a large leather trunk. 'I'm ... I'm Joyce Taylor.'

The woman gave her a warm smile. 'How do you do?' She reached out to shake Joyce's hand.

Politeness bid that Joyce do the same.

'It's nice to meet you. We're Mr and Mrs Gardner. I work for your grandmother.' Mrs Gardner paused. 'I know this must be a terrible shock for you but this is Philip. He's a good boy, although a little mischievous at times and I'll be sorry to not be looking after him from now on. It's a sorry state of affairs but I'm getting older and with Mrs Taylor unlikely to come round it's important Philip is in a stable home.'

Joyce stared down at the boy for a few minutes. Did he look a little like Arthur's son, William, or was she imagining it? Would Arthur be able to cope with another little boy in the house? She felt sure losing William was still a raw memory for him. Joyce sighed as she looked up at the man she would always regard as her uncle. He was pale and his gaze was fixed on the lad. She didn't have any answers on how to sort out this mess but was suddenly aware that Mr and Mrs Gardner were staring at her. She pulled the door wider. 'Please come in.'

Mr Gardner bent over to pick up the trunk.

The movement seemed to bring Arthur out of his trance and he thrust out his hand. 'No, I'll get that.'

Mr Gardner nodded. 'Thank you, it's quite heavy so be careful.'

Arthur and Joyce moved aside so the three of them could step inside the house.

Joyce led the way into the large dining room. 'Please take a seat on either the sofa or one of the armchairs; it doesn't matter where.'

Mrs Gardner perched herself at one end of the sofa. Philip squashed in tight against her. Putting her arm around his shoulders, she held him close.

Joyce knelt down at Mrs Gardner's feet. 'It's all right, Philip. No one is going to hurt you, I promise.'

Mrs Gardner squeezed his hand. 'He'll be all right once he gets used to you. He has been passed around a bit in his short life, bless him.'

Philip stared at Joyce with wide defiant eyes. 'I can take care of myself.' He pulled away from Mrs Gardner.

Mrs Gardner nodded and pulled him in close again. 'I know, Philip, but what's important is you have a roof over your head and you don't need to worry about anything.'

There was a thud closely followed by the bang of the front door slamming shut. Arthur walked into the room rubbing his hands. 'You weren't kidding when you said that trunk was heavy. I nearly broke me back getting it in the hall.' He stared at the small child. He looked pale and almost undernourished. 'Philip, would you like to come and see your new bedroom?'

The boy shook his head and turned away from Arthur.

'I've painted it blue for you but if you don't like it we can change the colour. I've also put some toy cars on a small stand so you can reach to play with them.'

Philip peered up at Arthur. 'Is there a fire engine?'

Arthur looked thoughtful, tapping his finger on his lips. 'Do you know I can't remember. Shall we go and have a look?' He reached out his hand to the child.

Philip glanced from Arthur to Mrs Gardner.

Joyce felt her heart was going to burst. 'It's all right, Philip. Uncle Arthur won't hurt you; he's a good man.'

Mrs Gardner smiled down at the child and nodded for him to go.

Philip stood upright and slowly walked over and put his small hand in Arthur's.

Arthur grinned at the boy. 'Right, let's go and explore.'

Philip gave a tentative smile as they turned and left the room. Their footsteps could soon be heard on the stairs followed by creaking as they stood on each step.

Joyce stood up and turned her attention to the couple. 'Forgive my manners, I should have offered you a cup of tea but you caught me out. I wasn't expecting you – well, I was – but I didn't know when you would bring Philip to me.'

The woman shook her head. 'I understand, but we can't stay long. I'm not one for being out in the evenings. We've left a small case of Philip's clothes in the hall.'

Joyce nodded. 'What can you tell me about Philip?'

The man and woman quickly glanced at each other.

The man cleared his throat. 'What is it you want to know?'

'Well.' Joyce frowned. 'Who is he and how come he was living with my grandmother? Are there any problems I should know about?'

The woman shook her head. 'His name is Philip Taylor but I'm afraid we haven't been privy to any information about how he came to be living with your grandmother. The only thing I know is he has lived with your grandmother for a few years; in fact he moved in after you moved out. I think it's what your father argued with her about.'

Joyce's eyes widened. 'He has the same name. I thought his last name was Edwards. Did my grandmother adopt him or change his name then?'

Mrs Gardner shrugged. 'I'm your grandmother's

housekeeper and as such was not privy to such information. All I know is Mrs Taylor is a very private person and she doted on Philip.' She paused for a moment. 'I get the impression he has seen more than most at his young age, but I hasten to add it is only an impression and nothing more.'

Joyce nodded. 'Thank you, I'm sorry to ask so many questions. It's all a bit of a shock to me.' She paced around the room wringing her hands. 'I shall try and take things slowly.'

Mr Gardner cleared his throat. 'Philip has more clothes and toys to come. I will arrange for everything else to be delivered by carriage tomorrow. I'm afraid we couldn't manage to bring everything with us today.'

Joyce stopped and looked at the couple who had made an impact on her day. 'I can't pretend all this doesn't terrify me. I don't know where to start.'

Mrs Gardner smiled. 'I can already tell you have a good heart so just follow it.'

Joyce stared at her. 'How do you know that?'

Mrs Gardner stood up and walked over to Joyce and took her hand in hers. 'You have kind but worried eyes, and look how softly you spoke to Philip.' She looked down at their hands clasped together. 'Your hands tell me you work hard. Your uncle Arthur was quick to try and put Philip at ease. You are a good family.'

Joyce opened her mouth to correct her about Arthur being her uncle but she realised it didn't matter so she shut it again.

8

Joyce took a deep breath before knocking on the bedroom door and twisting the brass door handle. It grated as she turned it. She poked her head round the door and waited for her eyes to focus in the dark room that had been given to Philip to sleep in. There was no sound from inside. Fear suddenly gripped Joyce. Had he run away in the night? She ran in and pulled back the heavy green curtains and let the early morning light in. She looked over to the bed. Philip was lying there, very still. Relief spread through her and she forced a smile to her lips. 'Come on, Philip, you should be out of bed by now and eating breakfast.'

Philip stared at her, his eyes wide, but he didn't say a word.

Joyce could see the fear in his eyes. Was she so frightening? Why was he so scared of her? She bent down and kissed the top of his head. 'Don't worry, everything's going to be all right.' Joyce took the edge of the blanket, together with the sheet, and pulled it back, revealing the soaking wet bottom sheet that Philip was lying on.

Philip moved to grab the covers and pull them back over him.

'It's nothing to worry about, Philip.' Joyce's eye caught

the clock on the wall. She had to hurry otherwise she was going to be late for work. She caught Philip watching her and reminded herself the boy was more important than her getting to the café on time. 'I promise you there's nothing to worry about.'

Philip again said nothing; he just gripped on to the bedding.

'Is it living here that's making you wet the bed or is it something you did at Grandma's as well? I'm only asking because I want to help. Do you find this room scary? Is that why you didn't get up to use the pot under the bed?'

Again Philip said nothing.

'Well, we can't leave you lying in it all day otherwise you'll smell and get sore.' Joyce smiled, resisting the urge to wrinkle her nose. 'We can't have that can we, so let's get you out of those wet pyjamas and strip the bed so it can dry for tonight.' She walked over to the window, lifted the latch and pushed it open as wide as it could go. The fresh cold air rushed in. 'That's better. Now, can you start taking your pyjamas off and I will get some hot water and fill up the tin bath.'

Philip nodded.

Joyce smiled. It wasn't much but it was better than nothing. 'Everything's going to be all right. I promise to look after you and no one is going to hurt you.'

Ten minutes later Philip was sat in the old tin bath in the bedroom with a bar of carbolic soap. Joyce was stripping the bed and leaving everything in a pile together with his pyjamas. 'Right, Philip, are you ready to get out of the bath and we'll get you dried?' She picked up a small towel and placed it on the floor in front of the bath, collecting the large grey towel from the chair. She held his hand as he stood up and stepped out of the water onto the towel. She wrapped the large towel around him. 'Right, let's get you dry and I'll see if I can find some lovely talcum powder to put on you. Would you like that?'

Philip nodded.

Joyce liberally sprinkled talcum powder on his back and chest and under his arms; the smooth soft white powder went everywhere. She laughed. 'Look, I'm making a right old mess of this; it's everywhere. I'm going to have to clean up when we've finished.'

Philip's eyes studied her for a moment. 'I don't mind helping.'

Joyce just managed to hold in the gasp of delight that he had actually answered her. 'Well, that will be wonderful, thank you.'

'I used to help my grandma. She let me do the dusting sometimes. It was all part of a game we played.'

Joyce nodded unable to contain her delight at Philip talking to her. 'That sounds like my sort of game. You'll have to teach me.' She picked up the grey short trousers and opened them wide so Philip could step into them.

Philip leant on Joyce's arm as he lifted his leg to step in. 'Do I need to put a vest on today?'

Joyce smiled and nodded. 'I think so, unless you particularly don't want to. My ma used to say it keeps the cold off your chest.'

Philip chuckled. 'Grandma used to say that too.'

Joyce laughed. 'Did she indeed? Well, it must be right then if they both said it.' She hesitated for a moment but decided to continue. 'What about your ma and pa?'

Philip sat with his hands resting on his thighs. 'I don't really remember my ma; she died a long time ago. I used to see my pa all the time but then he just stopped coming to see me.' He shrugged. 'I don't know why because we used to have fun together.'

Joyce's heart lurched in her chest.

Philip giggled. 'He used to tickle me all the time and chase me round the park.'

Joyce nodded. 'He sounds like a good father.'

'My grandma said he probably had to go away for work.' Philip bit down on his lip. 'If he comes back he won't know where I am.'

Joyce could feel the lump forming in her throat as she tried hard not to cry. She took a couple of breaths, exhaling slowly. 'I expect the solicitor has told him, or he'll go back to Grandma's and Mrs Gardner will tell him.'

A smile slowly lit up Philip's face. 'So he can come and play with me then.' He reached over and grabbed his vest and pulled it over his head.

Joyce straightened it. 'That's right, someone will always be here even if you are out with me so you don't have to worry about that.'

'What about if we're all out together?'

Joyce shrugged, holding up his shirt for him to slip his arms into the sleeves. 'Well, he can either put a note through the letterbox or he can come back later. The neighbours know where I work so try not to worry. I'm sure he'll find you because he sounds like a good man, and one who loves his little boy very much.'

Philip nodded. 'I bet he'll bring me a present because he always does when he's been away.'

Joyce pulled the shirt together at the front. 'Ooh, I wonder what he'll bring?'

Philip beamed at her. 'I don't know, maybe some toy soldiers or a toy car. I like both of them.'

Joyce giggled at his excitement. 'Well, we'll just have to wait and see won't we?'

'There's a lot of laughter coming from this room.' Arthur wrinkled his nose as he stepped through the open doorway. 'I thought I'd come and check everything was all right. You're going to be late for work.' He glanced down at his wristwatch. 'Actually, let me correct that statement, you are late for work.'

Joyce sighed. 'I know. I didn't allow enough time this morning for everything. To be honest I didn't realise...' She glanced at Philip before quickly looking back at Arthur. 'Anyway, I need to get up earlier in the mornings for anything unexpected that might happen.' She lifted her hand and ruffled Philip's dark hair. 'At least, once we've done up these shirt buttons, Philip is ready for breakfast and then I only have to sort out these sheets and the bath.'

Arthur nodded. 'Why don't you leave Philip and everything else in here to me and the girls. Just get yourself off to work?' He smiled at the small boy sitting on the edge of the bed, his legs dangling where they couldn't reach the floor. 'We'll have fun won't we?'

Philip nodded.

'We'll go out for a walk because I want to post a letter to Dot, and then we'll play some games.'

Joyce smiled. 'Thank you, appreciate your help, and I'm pleased you and Dot are writing to each other. Make sure you tell her we all say hello and we miss her.'

★

Joyce pulled the collar up to cover her mouth against the sharp wind as she weaved through the street market on the way to the café. Her mind was full of Philip as she huddled inside her coat. His troubled night was probably to be expected. She was grateful Arthur had offered to look after him but she needed a proper plan. Joyce absently pushed hard on the café door but it stayed firmly shut. She frowned as she stared at the door wondering where Simon was. Her heart jumped in her chest. Opening her handbag she fumbled inside for the key he had given her many months ago but never used. Gripping the cold steel she quickly turned the key in the lock of the café door and pushed it open. The silence inside was broken by the bell above the door ringing out.

Simon should have been in by now. Was he not in at all today? Had he really left without saying goodbye? Had she seen him for the very last time? Is that what he meant when he said it would be their last chance to talk? Her throat tightened. If only she hadn't dismissed his marriage proposal. She closed her eyes, her lips parted, and for a moment she could feel his mouth soft and caressing on hers. Her eyes snapped open as the love she felt for him overwhelmed her. She had been a fool, but would he live long enough for her to tell him and for him to forgive her?

The bell chimed as the café door slammed shut, hurtling Joyce back to the job in hand. She had promised to keep the café going for Simon and that was what she was going to do.

The café door burst open and Barbara Hitchin rushed in.

'Oh, I'm so sorry I'm late. I got upset this morning, what with Simon leaving early. He wanted to come here to see you to say goodbye?' She sniffed. 'Did you see him?'

'No.' Joyce blushed. 'I was late myself and didn't realise he wasn't coming to work this morning.'

Barbara scowled at Joyce. She opened her mouth to speak but Simon's words about looking after Joyce and not giving her a hard time rang in her head. She closed her mouth again.

Joyce frowned. 'Was he all right?'

'He seemed distracted, but I expect that's what going off to fight does for you.' Barbara paused. 'My mother and I put on a brave face until he had left and then we cried buckets, but there's nothing we can do except pray he comes back safely.'

Joyce nodded; she couldn't bring herself to think about it. 'It's going to be a tough day with only the two of us so we should start getting ready for the customers; we're already late. Do you think you'll be able to cope?'

Barbara glared at her before answering coldly, 'I'm sure between us we'll manage. My mother has offered to come in and help, even if it's only doing the washing up.'

'That's good of her, and we might have to take her up on that offer but we'll see how it goes.' Joyce marched into the kitchen, lit the range and turned the tap on to fill the kettle. She jumped back, as water sprayed everywhere, soaking everything in its path. She quickly turned it off. The tears came quickly. How was she going to cope with the café and a five-year-old boy? Then there was Simon. Why had she been so stupid?

The kitchen door swung open. 'Is everything all right?'

Barbara's voice held an edge to it. 'Shall I fetch my mother and tell her you can't cope with it today?'

Joyce wiped her eyes before turning to face Simon's sister. 'That won't be necessary, thank you. Do we have customers?' She looked around wondering how to protect her clothes from water, spitting fat and anything that might come her way. She reached out for Simon's white kitchen coat and put it on. The smell of him clung to the material. She breathed in the woody fragrance and fought the urge to cuddle it.

Barbara scowled. 'Not yet.'

'Then why do you think I can't cope? Or perhaps I should say we can't cope?' Joyce's eyes narrowed. 'If we're going to keep this café going while Simon's away then we need to work together as a team because your brother has made it very popular even if he isn't getting rich on it, and I for one don't wish to disappoint him.'

Barbara nodded slowly. 'We can do that, but if it continues to be busy then we will probably need someone to help out.'

The bell chimed.

Joyce forced a smile. 'So it begins.'

Barbara swiftly turned round, opening the kitchen door to greet the customers. 'Good morning, how many would you like a table for?'

Joyce quickly washed her hands, using the carbolic soap Simon kept on the kitchen side.

Barbara's voice rang out from the other side of the serving hatch. 'Joyce, I need two fried breakfasts, one with no tomatoes please.'

Joyce dried her hands before grabbing two large frying pans; there was a clang as she placed them on top of the range. 'Thank you, Barbara. Can you write the orders on tickets? Then put them on the hooks, this side of the hatch; otherwise I'll forget them, or they'll be done out of order when we're busy.'

It wasn't that long before the aroma of frying bacon and eggs filled the kitchen. A few hours later Joyce had found her rhythm, keeping an eye on the many pots and pans that were on a low heat. Joyce mopped away the perspiration from her brow on a clean cloth. Collecting a glass from the cupboard, she filled it with cold water. It was a lovely reprieve from the heat in the kitchen. She had never realised how hard it was working in there. Maybe the tariff needed thinking about.

A deep voice came from the other side of the serving hatch. 'How are you doing?'

Joyce looked up and saw Arthur standing there. 'It's hot and I didn't realise how hard Simon worked in here.' She paused as panic gripped her. 'Wait, where's Philip?'

Arthur laughed. 'Stop worrying, he's here. I brought him here for some lunch and to show him where you worked.' He peered over his shoulder where Philip was sitting on his own. 'He's a good lad, and older than his years would suggest.'

Joyce walked over to the hatch and watched the dark-haired boy drawing on some paper. His shoulders were hunched over. He looked up and gazed around him. There was sadness about him. 'Are you all right looking after him? I mean with losing William?'

Arthur tightened his lips. 'I didn't think I would be but actually it's a delight to have him around.'

Joyce smiled. 'Well, that's good. I need to come up with a plan for looking after him and keeping this place going.'

Arthur nodded. 'Don't forget he'll be at school Monday to Friday.'

'That's true, once I've enrolled him, but then it's about taking him and picking him up.' Joyce shook her head. 'I need to work it out. The trouble is everything has happened at once and I haven't had chance to think about it all properly.'

Arthur leant his elbows on the serving hatch. 'Don't worry, I can at least help out for a little while and I'm sure the girls won't mind taking him to school now and then for you.' He paused. 'Maybe we should all sit down and talk about it.'

Joyce shook her head. 'It seems unfair to ask everyone to help when it's my problem. I just need to think about it.'

Arthur eyed up the growing pile of washing up. 'Look, why don't I get Philip settled and then I'll wash some of those dishes for you.'

The doorbell chiming brought a groan from Joyce. She looked over in time to see Frank walk through the open door. 'Oh no, that's all I need – Frank wanting to carry on with his interview today.'

Arthur frowned and followed Joyce's gaze. 'Frank?'

'Yes, he's interviewing me for an article he's writing for one of the papers but, if I'm honest, I don't really have time for it, especially now.'

Arthur watched the young man push back his trilby and glance around the café. 'Do you want me to talk to him for you?'

Joyce smiled. 'I'd love to say yes but I think this is something I need to do.' She unbuttoned the white coat and placed it on the peg. After patting her hair she pushed open the kitchen door and stepped through to the side she was more used to.

'I'll go and start on those dishes for you.' Arthur took a step through to the kitchen, stopping midway to give Frank one last look as Joyce walked towards him.

'Hello, Frank.'

'Ah, Joyce, I was just looking for yer.' Frank beamed at her. 'You look different out of your waitress uniform.'

Joyce gave him a brief smile. 'Of course, I'd forgotten I wasn't wearing it.' She paused to look over at Philip. 'I'm afraid the situation has changed here and I'm now cooking so I won't have time to sit and chat with you.'

Frank followed Joyce's eyeline. 'Is that yer little boy?'

Joyce snapped her gaze back to him. 'Of course not. What type of girl do you think I am?'

Frank's eyes narrowed. 'I'm sorry, I didn't mean to insult yer. It's just yer were watching him sitting there all alone.' He looked back at the boy. 'In fact he looks quite sad.'

Joyce looked back at Philip. 'He is quite sad. I'm meant to be looking after him while also running this.' She waved her arm around her. 'My uncle is caring for him today but he's currently washing up some dishes to help out.'

Barbara brushed against Joyce. 'Sorry, Joyce, but we need a couple of breakfasts cooked.'

Joyce sighed. 'I'm coming.'

Frank studied Joyce. 'Look, why don't yer introduce me to him and I'll sit and chat with him until yer uncle comes out.'

Joyce shook her head. 'I couldn't do that. That would be a terrible imposition to make.'

'I'm offering.' Frank chuckled. 'Yer can always give me a free cup of tea or something.'

Joyce couldn't stop the smile spreading across her face as he laughed.

Frank put his hand on Joyce's elbow. 'Come on, this is a gift, and yer got breakfasts to cook; 'ungry people get very angry.' He guided Joyce towards Philip and waited for the introductions to be made.

'Morning, Bert.' Annie and Rose chorused as they ran through the stage door of The Lyceum theatre.

'Morning, ladies, it's lovely to see yer smiling faces every day. I missed yer when yer moved to The Lyric.' Bert smiled. 'It's blooming freezing out there innit?'

Annie started to unravel her scarf. 'It certainly is, Bert.'

Rose beamed at him. 'It's good to see you every day too. I'm sorry we can't stop for a chat otherwise we'll be late.'

Bert waved them on. 'Get on wiv yer then. I don't want yer getting into any trouble now.'

The girls smiled and waved as they rushed past him.

Rose dropped her voice to a whisper. 'I heard Kitty and Stan talking last night. I think they have concerns about the lack of male actors, due to them all going off to fight, so I don't know what they will do about it.'

Annie stepped back to let someone pass them and stared at the back of Rose's head. 'I don't want to think about anything to do with the war because then the worry takes over. Like you said I prefer to think David is still working on the farm.'

'I know what you mean. If my brothers survive the war I might kill them myself for not writing to me.' Rose clenched her hands by her sides.

Annie nodded. 'That's brothers for you.'

Rose peered over her shoulder at Annie. 'I was only telling you about the actors because it might mean you'll get a part instead of being an understudy.'

Annie took a deep breath. 'I know, thank you. Changing the subject, but only because I can't dwell on them fighting and risking their lives – it scares me – but we do need to think what we can do to help Joyce.'

Rose glanced back again. 'I know but I'm not sure how.'

Annie upped her pace to walk alongside Rose. 'No, it's difficult. I wonder who he is and why her grandmother was looking after him?'

Rose shrugged. 'I don't know, must be a relation of some sort, don't you think?'

'But according to Joyce she hasn't got any relations, apart from her grandmother that is.'

Rose's eyebrows drew together. 'Not even on her mother's side?'

Joyce shook her head. 'I don't know but you'd assume not; otherwise why did her father leave her with Arthur?'

'That's true.' Rose's lips tightened. 'Arthur might be able to help out with him?'

'Maybe, but that might bring back painful memories for him.' Annie sighed.

'I hadn't thought of that.' Rose paused. 'I don't know, perhaps we need to come up with some sort of system to help out.'

Annie glanced over at her friend. 'I could probably look after him in the mornings because I don't very often have to be here before the early afternoon.'

Rose nodded. 'I could ask old Hetherington if he could

come and sit in the sewing room with me, but I don't think she'd say yes, mainly because it's me asking.'

'I don't understand what her problem is. It's not as though you are not good at your job.' Annie's eyes widened. 'Maybe that's it, perhaps she feels threatened by you because you are so good with a needle.'

Rose laughed. 'I shouldn't think so; she didn't treat Dot the way she treats me. Anyway, I've got to get on. I'm probably going to be here late into the evening.'

'I'll pop in when I'm ready to go and see where you're at.' Annie peered into the empty sewing room. 'I've got to go and listen to the rehearsal.'

Rose nodded. 'I hope it goes well. I'll see you later.'

A couple of minutes later Annie stood hidden in the wings listening to Kitty and the cast reciting their lines. She loved listening to them and smiled as Kitty's voice carried in the theatre as Josephine. Silence suddenly hung in the air. Annie couldn't remember there being such a long gap between lines.

Stan's voice boomed out. 'Come on, come on, haven't you learnt your lines yet? For goodness' sake we're never going to be ready for opening night at this rate.'

Annie followed his line of vision. It was the girl she had almost shut the door on.

The cast began murmuring among themselves.

Stan glanced towards the side of the stage. 'Annie, I know you're waiting in the wings somewhere, listening to this nonsense, so give me the next line.'

Annie stayed silent and didn't move a muscle.

Stan bellowed. 'Come on out and give me the next line.'

Colour rushed into Annie's cheeks as she took a small

step on to the edge of the stage. She cleared her throat but avoided looking at the cast, who she felt sure were staring at her. She walked further on to the stage as though she was carrying a tea tray and mimed placing it on a table. 'Tea, ma'am. Shall I pour?'

Stan grinned at Annie before turning his anger on the young actress. 'And she's not even in the play.' He pointed to Kitty. 'Give me the next line.'

'Yes, of course: then I must rise and write to my love, Napoleon.'

Stan turned to another actress and pointed. 'And the next one.'

Panic ran across the actress's face as she nodded. 'I shall make sure there is ink in the well on the desk, ma'am.'

Stan turned his steel-like gaze to the young actress. 'All of them know every line in this play and you do not even appear to know your own, let alone anyone else's! This is a warning to you: I cannot afford to take a risk on an opening night so you had better know them by tomorrow's rehearsal.' He glanced around the rest of the cast on stage and sighed. 'Let's have a ten-minute break.'

Flushed with colour, Annie disappeared into the wings and rushed back to Kitty's dressing room. She felt sorry for the girl and wondered what she could do to help her. She turned as footsteps came running towards her. The girl was sobbing as she ran past Annie along the corridor. 'Wait, please wait.'

The girl stopped in her tracks and turned slightly. Her tears glistened on her face. She sniffed.

Annie intertwined her hands together in front of her. 'I want to help.'

'Why? From what I hear you're everyone's favourite around here. You can do no wrong. They say everything has been handed to you on a plate because you have Kitty Smythe's ear.'

Bewilderment crashed down on Annie. 'I don't know where this has come from – my guess is from someone who doesn't know what they're talking about. I'm a dresser who happens to love the theatre and there's no denying I've always wanted to be on the stage but never at someone else's expense.'

The girl stared at Annie.

Annie shook her head. 'Let me help you. I don't even know your name.'

'I'm Penny.' She glanced up at the ceiling before looking back at Annie. 'Well, actually, it's Penelope Cooper, but I prefer Penny.'

'I'm Annie, Annie Cradwell.'

Penny frowned. 'I know who you are. You're the talk of the dressing room.'

Annie shook her head. 'That doesn't sound good but I'm not aware that I have done anything to be the subject of gossip, and if people want to know anything they should just ask me.'

Penny wiped away the tears that were drying on her face. 'In my experience you don't always have to do anything.'

Annie could feel herself drawn to her. 'You know, we can read the lines together.'

'Why would you do that? If Mr Tyler sacks me tomorrow you'll probably get the part.'

Annie raised her eyebrows and took a step nearer. 'Maybe,

but as I've already said, I don't want something by hurting or trampling on someone else, and that includes you.'

Penny nodded. 'It might help me to read with someone. I've read the script so many times but I just can't seem to remember it, and it's not as though I have a huge part.'

Annie's heart sang. 'When you've finished on stage we'll sit down somewhere and go through it together.'

Penny took a deep breath. 'Thank you, and I'm sorry for the things that I said.'

'Never be sorry for telling the truth.'

9

Joyce scraped the butter over the thin slice of hot toasted bread and cut it into soldiers before lining them up on a tea plate next to the boiled egg. 'There you go, Philip, get that into yer. We'll have a long day today.' Her mind wandered to the chest that had arrived with him. She had planned to open it before going to work, but it had taken longer to get Philip ready than she thought it would. Joyce thought how silent he'd been when she went into his bedroom that morning. Philip was still lying in bed and didn't get up until she pulled back the bedclothes and discovered he was soaking wet again. She had filled the tin bath with warm water while he stripped his pyjamas off, and then she helped him sit in the bath with a bar of carbolic soap. Joyce stripped the bed and left them soaking in the bath water until she got home later. She had tried to reassure him that everything was going to be all right but he said nothing and his wide eyes had just followed her around the room.

Her shoulders slumped. She would need to make more time in the mornings now she had Philip to get ready as well, especially if his bedwetting was a daily occurrence. It had only been a few days but Joyce had hoped it would stop once he got to know them all. Biting down on her lip, she wondered how she was going to cope with everything, while equally wanting to know what had happened to his family but she knew it would be wrong to ask him. The clanging of the teaspoon against the inside of the teapot pulled Joyce away from her thoughts.

Annie picked up the teapot and began pouring the strong hot tea into the china cups. 'I'll let you all put your own sugar in.' She passed the cups around the kitchen table, starting with Arthur. 'I quite like having breakfast in the kitchen; it reminds me of home.'

Arthur took the cup and saucer and placed it down in front of him. 'Your ma created a lovely welcoming home, Annie, and your father is doing his best to carry on with that.'

Annie smiled. 'Thank goodness Auntie Dot is there looking after them; otherwise I couldn't be here.'

'There's no need to worry. They were fine when I was last up there.' Arthur turned to watch Philip timidly pick up a finger of bread. 'Philip, have you ever been to a farm before, or maybe to a house that's surrounded by fields?'

Philip held his bread mid-air and silently shook his head.

'Maybe, with Joyce's agreement, I could take you to the village and you can experience running free and climbing trees. You could help Annie's father feed the chickens and collect eggs every day.'

Philip's eyes widened but he still remained silent.

Joyce frowned, wondering if he knew what Arthur was talking about. 'It's too soon to be talking about him going somewhere else. He needs to settle in here first and get used to us all.'

Arthur nodded, picking up his cup and taking a sip of tea.

Rose glanced across at Joyce. 'You all right?'

Joyce gave a faint smile. 'Of course, I just have a lot going on. I don't want to be late again today.'

Rose nudged Joyce's arm. 'You should get going then.'

Arthur looked up from his breakfast and opened his mouth to speak but closed it again.

'Of course, I don't want Simon's sister thinking I can't get in on time. Although it's meant to be me running the café, well with his sister, Barbara, helping. She said her mother offered to come in and help with the washing up and clearing the tables.'

Rose smiled. 'That's good isn't it?'

Joyce bit her lip. 'Except, I don't think Barbara likes me very much.'

Arthur reached out and tapped Joyce's hand. 'Well, it's good they are helping; you struggled when it was just you and Simon and you both knew what you were doing.'

Joyce looked at the others. 'Arthur was a great help yesterday, which was appreciated. He did a lot of washing up when he made the mistake of coming in for something to eat.'

Annie held up her hand. 'Hang up, just go back a stage. Are you saying Simon has gone already?'

'Yes.' Joyce could feel the tears stinging in her eyes. She gripped the knife handle. 'He asked me to marry him—'

'That's wonderful news. Why haven't you told us?' Rose clapped her hands together.

Joyce glanced up at the three faces staring at her. 'Because I said no.'

'What?' They all spoke as one.

Philip screwed up his face and stared at them in turn.

Rose clasped Joyce's arm. 'I don't understand. Why? It's not as though you don't love him.'

Joyce shook her head as her tears began to fall. 'I do but everything that has happened lately has caught me by surprise and his proposal was just the last straw, and anyway he probably only proposed to keep me at the café.'

Rose and Annie stared at one another.

Annie shook her head. 'If you think so little of him it's just as well you said no. Does his family know he proposed?'

'Of course I don't; I've regretted it ever since. I didn't know they were going to be practically the last words I said to him, but that's something I have to live with.' Joyce wiped away her tears. 'And if his family do know they're not saying anything to me.' She pushed her uneaten egg to one side. Picking up her cup she gulped down the lukewarm tea. Wrinkling her nose, she replaced the cup on its matching saucer. She peered at Philip. The thud of his feet hitting the rung of the wooden chair irritated her but she resisted saying something to him. 'Come on, eat up.'

Rose shook her head. 'Joyce, this isn't over. We will talk about it later. I can't believe you turned him down.'

Joyce ignored Rose and kept her eyes fixed on Philip. 'Don't you like eggs?'

Philip stared wide-eyed at her.

Joyce suddenly realised she shouldn't be getting upset and discussing these things in front of him. 'Don't be afraid, Philip, I just need to know because I'll give you something else for breakfast tomorrow if you don't like them.'

Philip didn't speak but picked up his teaspoon and dug into the white of his egg.

Joyce nodded; she would have to accept that for the time

being. 'Well, Philip, you've only got a few minutes and then we have to go to the café. Perhaps we'll take some paper and pencils and you can draw some pictures for us.' She stood up and began clearing the table.

Annie reached out to Joyce. 'Leave it, I can do it. I don't have to be at the theatre until lunchtime.' She paused. 'In fact if you want to leave Philip with me I can drop him off to you on my way.'

Joyce stared down at the table and bit her bottom lip. 'No, Philip is my responsibility and I have to make it work.' She picked up her teacup and plate and took them over to the sink.

Annie shook her head. 'But you're not on your own. We need to talk about this because you're surrounded by people who love you and can help.'

'Come on, Philip, I'm already late. I don't want to give Barbara an excuse to report back that I can't manage.'

Rose sighed. 'It's not over, Joyce. We will talk about all this later.'

Philip scraped his chair back on the tiled floor and jumped down from the table.

The clock in the hall chimed eight times. Joyce gasped. 'Come on, Philip, we're going to have to run up the road at this rate.' She frowned at the dirty breakfast dishes. 'I'll have to do them later.'

Annie jumped up. 'Stop fussing, Joyce, we're all quite capable. It's not your place to look after us all. Now get yourself to work.'

Joyce scowled but knew she didn't have time to talk about it and a few minutes later she was pulling the front door closed. The cold March winds cut through her coat and whipped across her face. They turned on to Great Earl Street. The market stalls were already set up, the stallholders trying to sell their wares to every passer-by.

'Hey, Joyce,' a voice rang out over the other stallholders. Joyce stopped and glanced round. She knew that voice anywhere. She rested her hand between Philip's shoulder blades and guided him towards Peter's stall. Peter's dog, Russell, came bounding towards Joyce, but stopped as he got close to Philip, who was hiding behind her skirt.

'I haven't seen you for ages. Have you been going a different route to work? You're not avoiding me are you?'

Joyce gave a faint smile. 'Of course not. I'm just always in a hurry these days.' She half turned to look at the top of Philip's head. 'This is Philip. He has been put into my care for the foreseeable future.'

Peter frowned. His gaze passed between Joyce and Philip. 'My, that's a big responsibility, I have loads of questions but this probably isn't the right time to ask.' Peter stooped down. 'Hello, Philip.' He stretched out his hand. 'It's very nice to meet yer, although I feel sure I've seen yer before.' Peter laughed. 'I don't forget a face so I'm sure it will come to me eventually.'

Philip gingerly placed his hand in Peter's and they shook.

'Let me give you some fruit to take with you. Joyce is always telling me off for giving it away but I think you deserve some.'

Joyce glanced down. 'Say thank you, Philip.'

'Thank you.'

Joyce had the urge to cry at the sound of his little timid voice, and once again she wondered what had happened to him.

Arthur's deep voice carried over the crowds. 'Joyce?'

Joyce spun on her heels; her stomach lurched into her mouth. 'Arthur, what is it? Has something happened?'

Arthur put his hands on his thighs as he bent over gasping for air. After a moment he stood upright. 'Sorry, I'm not as fit as I used to be.' He took a deep breath. 'Leave Philip with me. You're going to have enough to deal with today.'

Annie and Rose ambled along Great Earl Street, stopping to look at some of the flowers that were being thrust at them by a stooped old lady.

Rose pulled her woollen scarf tighter around her neck. 'You should be at home keeping warm in this cold weather.'

The old lady gave them a smile. 'I gotta sell me flowers, lovey, so I can eat tonight.'

Annie stopped to sniff the floral scent of the small bunches of daffodils and heathers. 'They smell lovely but unfortunately we're on our way to work.' She tilted her head one side. 'I'm sorry.'

'I've always loved the spring flowers, the first burst of colour after the greyness of winter.' Rose leant in to examine them. 'Perhaps we should buy a bunch for Joyce.'

'The trouble is we're going to work and they'll be fit for nothing by the time we get them home.'

Rose frowned. 'I suppose. Sorry we can't, not today anyway.'

They carried on strolling down the road until Peter's fruit and vegetable stall came into view. Russell spotted them in the crowd and came running towards them. He nestled his wet nose in the palm of Annie's gloved hand. She promptly made a fuss of him, stroking his soft fur.

Peter's voice carried through the air. 'It seems like ages since I last saw you.'

Annie blushed. 'Sorry, we've just been really busy at work – you know, a new play and Rose has been sewing the new costumes. To be honest, it's all a bit frantic.'

Peter nodded. 'As long as you haven't forgotten me. You two have become indispensable by the sounds of things.' He smiled at Annie before turning to Rose. 'Have you seen Charlie Young lately?'

Rose blushed. 'Not recently, for all the same reasons that Annie has said.' She paused. Panic flew across her face. 'I hope he doesn't think I've gone off him.'

Peter shook his head. 'I shouldn't think so, Rose. I get the impression he's besotted with you.'

Her blush deepened. She fought the urge to fan herself.

Peter chuckled. 'I'll tell you what, why don't we have a double date on Sunday? At least that's one day none of us have to work.'

Rose and Annie both grinned.

'Right, leave it with me and I'll have a chat with Charlie.'

Annie's smiled faded a little. 'Wait, what about Joyce?'

Peter smiled. 'Well, she can come too if she really wants to. I suppose she could invite Simon along.'

Rose's smile disappeared. 'Simon's enlisted, and Joyce—'

'Don't tell everyone Joyce's business. You know she wouldn't like it,' Annie interrupted.

Rose scowled at Annie. 'Peter's her friend. Remember how they hugged in the street when we arrived in London?'

Annie nodded.

Rose returned her attention back to Peter. 'Simon's gone off to war but before he went he proposed and she turned him down.'

Peter looked astounded at them. 'What?'

Annie shook her head. 'I know, it's how we all feel but I think at the time she was overwhelmed with things being laid at her door.'

Rose frowned. 'She hasn't said so but I get the impression she thinks her life is unravelling, and she's not accepting any help from us.'

Peter looked from one to the other. 'What has happened? I met Philip earlier. Where has he appeared from?'

Annie looped her arm through his. 'That's just it – no one knows. All we know is her grandmother is dying and she's told a solicitor that Joyce has to look after him but she doesn't know any more than that.'

Peter scowled. 'Poor Joyce.'

Annie squeezed his arm. 'There's more than that. It seems her uncle Arthur isn't really her uncle; apparently she doesn't have any uncles.'

Peter's eyes widened. 'How did she find that out?'

Someone bumped into Rose, jerking her forward. Frowning, she looked over her shoulder before glancing back at Peter. 'She had to go and see a solicitor. That's when she was told about Philip as well.'

Annie stroked Peter's arm. 'So when Simon decided to tell her he was enlisting and on top of that proposed to her, I don't think she could cope with it all.'

Rose scuffed the toe of her shoe on the road. 'She regrets it now.'

Peter looked stunned. 'I should have checked when I didn't see her.' He shook his head. 'I haven't been much of a friend.'

Annie shook his arm. 'Don't say that. We live with Joyce but she's not very forthcoming with her problems. Even this morning we offered to help with Philip, and the washing up, but she thinks everything is her responsibility, that it's her duty to look after us all. We need to step up because I don't think she looks too good.'

Rose pursed her lips. 'Maybe it's her mother in her.'

'Right.' Peter tapped Annie's hand. 'I'll speak to Charlie later and arrange for us to go out on Sunday and I shall rely on you to bring Joyce and Philip with you.' He smiled. 'Stop on your way to work tomorrow and I'll confirm time and place with you then.'

The girls beamed at him, relieved at having a plan, no matter how small.

'I've got to get back to work but we all need to start being better friends towards her now, when she needs us the most, whether she likes it or not.' Peter peered down at Russell, who was leaning against Annie's leg having his neck scratched. 'Come on, boy, we've got to get back to work before Harry starts complaining about us leaving him to it.' He leant forward and gave Annie a peck on the cheek.

Annie's colour rose. 'I'm looking forward to seeing you properly on Sunday.'

Peter's love was all over his face for her to see. 'Perhaps we should set aside every Sunday; otherwise before you know it a month has gone and then another.'

Annie smiled. 'Let's do that.'

Peter leant in and let his soft lips skim hers.

Annie closed her eyes. Her heart jumped in her chest and her stomach seemed to be doing somersaults as he pulled away.

'I'm sorry, I must go.'

Rose giggled. 'Yeah, get back to work. This is embarrassing for us gooseberries, and we've got to get to work too.'

'I'm sorry, Rose.' Annie's face flushed with colour. 'Come on, let's go.'

An overpowering smell of disinfectant greeted Joyce as she stepped nervously inside St Thomas' Hospital. She was glad to be inside away from the cold air that numbed her face. Removing her woollen hat and scarf, Joyce looked around her. She had been overwhelmed by its size standing outside, but had fought the urge to run away; after all her grandmother won't know whether she'd visited or not. Many people walked past her, some talking in low voices.

'Do you need help?'

Joyce spun on her heels to see a young nurse smiling at her.

'I'm sorry, I didn't mean to alarm you, but you looked lost.'

Joyce nodded, opening her mouth to speak but stopping short as a man caught her eye in the distance. There was something about the way he held himself that looked familiar.

The nurse reached out and touched Joyce's arm. 'Are you all right? You've gone very pale.'

'Sorry.' Joyce moved her head from side to side trying

to peer between the people milling about. 'I thought for a moment I saw … but that's not possible.'

The nurse smiled. 'It's understandable with the number of people coming and going.'

Joyce turned her attention back to the nurse. 'I expect that's so. I've never been inside this hospital before; it's so big.'

The nurse nodded. 'I take it you're here to visit someone?'

'My grandmother, Mrs Taylor, I've been told she's in a coma.' Joyce shrugged. 'I understand she won't know I've visited but thought I'd come and talk to her anyway.'

The nurse clasped her hands in front of her. 'I don't know if that's true or not. I've heard it said that the last thing to go is the hearing so if that's the case she'll know what you're saying.'

Joyce's eyes widened. 'I didn't know that; thank you. Now, I just need to find her.'

The nurse held out her hand, indicating to the left of her. 'If you go over to the reception they'll be able to help you.'

'Thank you again.'

'That's all right. Take care and good luck.' The nurse turned and walked away into the throng of people coming and going.

Joyce watched her, her footsteps silent on the tiled floor.

Half an hour later Joyce had climbed the stairs and was standing outside a side room staring at an elderly grey-haired lady who looked like she was asleep. Suddenly wishing she hadn't come, Joyce wondered what was she going to say to her. What if she woke up and wasn't happy to see her? Joyce turned to walk away.

'Ah, you found your grandmother then? You weren't leaving, were you?'

The nurse from downstairs was standing in front of Joyce. 'No, I just wasn't sure what to do.'

The nurse frowned. 'I know it's scary but don't be afraid to go in. She's just asleep and not in any pain and don't forget she might be able to hear you, so say everything you want to say. You know, let her know you love her, or what you've been doing since you last spoke to her.'

Joyce nodded.

'Would you like me to come in with you?'

'No, no, thank you,' Joyce whispered. 'I appreciate the offer but I'll be fine.' Joyce stepped into the side room, not taking her eyes off the woman lying so still under the bedcovers. The nurse was right. Her grandmother looked like she was in a deep sleep. Slowly lowering herself on to the wooden chair next to the pristine made bed, she wondered what had brought her here. Was it curiosity? She reached out to take her grandmother's thin, bony hand but changed her mind at the last minute.

A nurse popped her head around the open door. 'Is everything all right in here?'

Joyce looked up.

'I'm at the nurses' station should you have any worries about Mrs Taylor. We are keeping her as comfortable as we can.'

Joyce gazed back down at her grandmother. 'She looks peaceful.'

The nurse nodded. 'Mrs Taylor doesn't really get any visitors, although a man has been in a couple of times recently; in fact you've probably only just missed him.'

Joyce frowned as she peered over at the nurse. 'Do you know who the man is?'

The nurse shook her head. 'No, to be honest we were all just happy she had someone talking to her.'

Guilt swamped Joyce and she stared at her grandmother. 'I've only recently found out she was in here.'

The nurse looked contrite. 'I'm sorry, I didn't mean to speak out of turn.'

Joyce shook her head. 'You haven't, I'm just saying.'

The nurse glanced down the corridor. 'I'm sorry, I have to go but don't be afraid to ask if you need anything.'

Joyce glanced up but the nurse was already gone. She fidgeted in her chair. 'Well, Gran, if I'm honest I don't know what to say or actually why I'm here. I don't think we really know each other that well and that saddens me, especially as you're my only family now my father has died.' She frowned. 'Even more so now I know Uncle Arthur isn't really my uncle.' She gently wrapped her hand around her grandmother's cold fingers. 'I wish now I'd come to see you but I thought it would be betraying my father.' She paused. 'Not that I know what you two argued about, and if it was something I said or did then I'm really sorry. It must have been bad for you to kick your son and granddaughter out on to the streets.' Joyce gently ran her thumb over the soft, loose wrinkled skin of her grandmother's hand. 'Especially as Pa always said one of your favourite sayings was: "Family is everything".'

She took a deep breath and sat in silence for a moment. 'None of it makes any sense to me, and then of course there's Philip. Who is he and how did he end up living with you? I have so many questions and no answers.'

Crashes from the hall made Joyce jerk round, wondering if she should offer her assistance but deciding she would probably be in the way.

Joyce turned her attention back to her grandmother. 'I'm grateful to Arthur for keeping a roof over my head after my father died, so I want to give something back, and I will do my best to give Philip a good start in life.' She took a breath and looked around the small room. 'It's quite a nice size room you have here.' Joyce sighed; she had no idea what to talk to her about. 'I suppose I could talk to you about Philip. He chats to me a bit more now. He laughs with Arthur, but it doesn't seem to come so easily with me. I don't know what I'm doing wrong. I suppose it's just about time.' She shook her head. 'I don't know why you thought I could look after him. He was telling me his mother used to entertain a lot so now I find myself wondering what has happened to his mother and father and how he came to be in your care. So many questions and no answers, not that it matters because I want to help Philip but I don't know how. Maybe it will come with time.'

A low moan came from the bed.

Joyce's eyes widened. 'I know the nurse said they thought you could hear me but I wasn't expecting a response.' She looked around and wondered whether to get someone, or whether this was normal. Joyce looked back at her grandmother. Her eyes were firmly shut. She took a deep breath. 'Stop panicking; nothing has changed.' She reached out and took her grandmother's hand in hers again. 'I know it must be hard for Philip because I still miss my mother and father every day. My mother always said I was going to be a wonderful cook in a top restaurant or hotel.' Joyce shook her head. 'I hope she can't see me waitressing and cooking fried breakfasts or making sandwiches all day. That's definitely not what she had in mind. She'd be so disappointed.'

Mrs Taylor's fingers moved in Joyce's hand.

Joyce held her breath. 'Are you trying to tell me something?' Her gaze travelled between the hand she was holding and her grandmother's face but there was nothing; she was still. The nurse's words about her not coming round or her living through this jumped into her mind. She was letting her imagination run riot.

'Would you like a cup of tea?'

Joyce jumped at the voice behind her. She turned to see an orderly standing in the doorway.

The orderly lowered her voice. 'I'm not meant to offer tea to visitors but if you don't tell anyone I can make you one.'

Joyce nodded. 'That would be lovely, thank you, but please don't get yourself into trouble.'

The orderly shrugged. 'It's no bother; it's only a cuppa.' She disappeared back into the hall and came back a minute later carrying the tea.

Joyce smiled. 'Thank you, that's wonderful.'

'It must be hard sitting with Mrs Taylor, especially as there's no response to any conversation.'

Joyce let go of her grandma's hand and took the cup that was offered to her. 'I think she can hear me. She moved her fingers just now and I'm convinced she groaned earlier.'

The orderly raised her eyebrows. 'I'll let the nurse know just in case something has changed.'

'Do you think she might be coming round?'

The orderly rested her hand on Joyce's shoulder. 'I think the doctors should be told of any changes.'

Joyce nodded. Was there a chance her grandmother could come round and give her some of the answers she was searching for?

The orderly turned and walked towards the door. 'I'll let them know.'

Joyce nodded. She wanted to have hope but was sure it was misplaced. She took a deep breath. 'Well, Grandma, I've been given a lovely cup of tea, although no one is meant to know about it, so make sure you don't tell anyone.' She sipped the strong hot tea. 'So what were we talking about before you moved your fingers? I can't remember but I expect it was either my parents or Philip; I can't seem to think about anything else these days. I'm trying not to think about Simon. Oh you don't know about Simon, so I should explain because that's something else I messed up.'

Joyce sighed. 'I love him more than life itself. He asked me to marry him before he went off to war, and guess what, I turned him down. I worry he won't come back and then he will never know how much I love him. There's nothing I wouldn't do for him.' Joyce sat in silence for a few minutes. 'I don't even know why I turned him down. I think I had this messed-up idea he asked me because he was going off to the front line and wanted me to keep his business going.' She sighed. 'And in my defence, I'd just found out about Arthur not being my uncle and about Philip; my head was all over the place.'

A groan came from the bed again.

Joyce's eyes grew wide. 'Can you open your eyes, Grandma? Can you speak?'

Mrs Taylor was as still as ever.

Joyce stared at her, willing her to open her eyes. Did she

blink or was she imagining it? She leant in further as a low noise came from her grandmother. 'What is it? I just know you are trying to tell me something. Is it about Philip or my father?' She watched her intently, fearing she might miss something. Joyce drew back. Was her grandmother trying to speak? She leant in close, her ear almost touching her grandmother's lips, but there was only silence.

Mrs Taylor's finger made a very small movement.

Was her mind playing tricks on her? 'I want you to know that it doesn't matter who Philip is; I will do my best to look after him.' Joyce sucked in her breath. 'It shocks me that you put your faith in me, but I'm proud as well and won't let you down, thank you.' She brushed a grey curl off her grandmother's forehead. 'I'm sorry I didn't keep in touch, I truly am. I miss my family even though I do have good friends, but sometimes I feel quite lonely.'

IO

Joyce mopped her brow with a clean cloth. She glanced up at the clock; the lunchtime rush would begin soon. She sighed wondering what had happened to Barbara. How was she going to manage on her own?

'Is there anyone serving out here?'

Joyce's heart pounded in her ears; her head was thumping. She couldn't be in two places at once. Joyce glanced down at the eggs frying in the pan, her grip tightened on the metal handle. 'Sorry,' she yelled. 'I won't be a moment.' She quickly plated up the two fried breakfasts and sped through the kitchen door and headed towards the elderly couple who had been patiently waiting for over half an hour. 'I am so sorry for the wait but it seems I'm on my own today.'

The lady looked at Joyce's flushed face. 'Don't worry, love, we 'ave plenty of time.'

Joyce nodded. 'Thank you.' She quickly picked up a tray and moved to the nearest table to begin clearing away the used crockery. Damn Simon for burdening her with his unreliable sister. How was she meant to manage? Then it hit her. Her throat tightened. She fought to hold back the tears that were threatening to embarrass her. Maybe Barbara wasn't in because something had happened to Simon.

'Can we have more tea please?' a woman called over to Joyce.

Joyce took a couple of deep breaths before glancing over in the general direction the voice came from and nodded.

A man grumbled, 'I'm still waiting for someone to take my order.'

Joyce pulled herself upright and looked around at the customers who regularly came in for their morning tea and toast with friends. 'I'd just like to say I'm sorry you're all being kept waiting this morning, but I'm on my own at the moment. I'll try and get to you as quickly as I can.' She glanced across at Philip, who was sat quietly in the corner near the kitchen. He looked up and caught her staring at him. She quickly looked down at the table she was clearing, and began vigorously wiping it with a damp cloth.

'Let me help. I can carry things to and from a table.'

Joyce looked round to see Philip standing there.

He reached past her and picked up the tray of empty tea things before taking a step forward to carefully weave his way through the tables.

'No, not the whole tray it will be too heavy; just take one thing at a time. Thank you for helping me.'

Philip nodded. The cups wobbled as he placed the tray back on the table and began making his trips to and from the counter with a cup in one hand and a saucer in another.

Joyce noticed customers smiling at him and pulling their chairs in so he could get past them. She couldn't help the gratitude that threatened to overwhelm her as she finished wiping the table down and placing the condiments back on it. Philip caught her attention as he carried on clearing another table. An abundance of pride washed over her. She took her pad out of her apron pocket and moved to the customer to take their order.

The crash of glass hitting the floor made Joyce spin round on her black serviceable shoes. Shards of glass were like icy fragments on the floor, glistening in the light coming through the window.

Joyce called out as Philip bent down to pick it up. 'Leave it; I'll pick it up.'

Philip's head jerked up to watch her striding towards him.

By the time Joyce reached him she noticed he looked tearful. 'It's all right, accidents happen. I just don't want you cutting yourself on the glass, that's all.' She rested her hand on Philip's shoulder. 'I'll tell you what, you stand guard while I fetch a broom. Can you do that?'

Philip nodded, nervously picking at his off-white shirt.

Joyce disappeared into the kitchen, returning a minute later carrying a broom and a dustpan and brush. She stopped short when she saw Frank talking to Philip.

Frank looked up and smiled at Joyce. ''Ere let me sweep it up, while you get on. Philip's been telling me 'ow he was trying to 'elp when he dropped the glass.'

Philip peered up at Joyce. 'I didn't mean to drop it; it just slipped out of my hand.'

Joyce passed the broom to Frank and stooped down in front of the small, timid lad who had been thrust into her life. 'I know you didn't. It doesn't matter; it's just a glass.' She stood up. 'Thank you, Frank, you always seem to appear when I'm in a mess. You're a godsend.' She smiled. 'I need to take stock of things because I clearly can't do everything.'

The bell chimed as the café door swung open. The cold wind swooshed into every corner of the café as Barbara breezed in through the open door. 'Morning, everyone, it's freezing out there.' Barbara beamed at the customers as they glanced in her direction before scowling at Joyce and Frank. 'My mother's coming in to help with the cooking.'

For the first time, Joyce noticed the grey-haired woman standing behind Barbara. 'Hello, Mrs Hitchin.'

Mavis Hitchin stepped forward. 'Please call me Mavis, and I haven't come here to help with the cooking, unless you particularly want me to. I'm here to do the washing up but I'm happy to do anything you want, as indeed is Barbara.' Mavis glared at her daughter. 'I'm sorry we're late. I will make sure that we're here early tomorrow. You shouldn't have been left on your own. I was misled into believing we weren't needed so early.'

Joyce hadn't realised she had been holding her breath until she gasped to take in air. 'Thank you, Mrs Hitchin … Mavis. I'm sorry but I need to get on. There's customers waiting. Sit down, Frank, and I'll make you a cup of tea and a sandwich to say thank you.' She picked up a loaded tray from the counter and marched towards the kitchen, pushing the door open with her hips. The crockery chinked together as it wobbled on the tray.

Barbara, reaching out to hold the door, smiled at Joyce. 'Here, let me hold it open for you.'

Joyce forced a smile. 'Thank you.' She walked through the doorway with Mavis close behind her. She put the tray on the side and took a breath. Judging from Mavis's smiles Simon must be all right. Joyce gave a silent prayer of thanks for that small mercy. She turned to face his mother. 'I must admit when Barbara was late in I was concerned that everything was not all right.'

Barbara wafted in and frowned at her mother and Joyce. 'Of course everything's all right. Why wouldn't it be? Ah, you're thinking about Simon; no, as far as we know he's fine.' She took a step nearer to Joyce. 'And, for the record, I'm not late. This is my brother's business and I can come and go as I like. I'm only here to look after his interests.'

Joyce stared at her. 'That's not what Simon said before he left.'

Barbara smirked. 'It doesn't matter what Simon said. He's not here is he? And as this business belongs to my family I believe that puts me in charge.' She smiled and walked towards the kitchen door.

Joyce clenched her hands by her sides. 'As you wish. You will need to take over buying the produce and if you're going to start this time every day might I suggest you get someone to either cook or wait on the tables because I can't do both.'

Mavis shouted across the kitchen, 'Simon may not be here but I am, so you need to watch yourself and do as Joyce says. She runs this place not you.' She turned to Joyce. 'Please accept my apologies for my daughter. I think we've spoilt her since her father died but all of that is about to change.'

Joyce shook her head. 'That's all right, Mavis, don't worry. Everything will be all right in the end.'

Mavis shrugged. 'I think Simon knew what she would be like. That's why he asked me to keep an eye on her. Oh, I must tell you Simon brought some of your cake home for us to eat once and it was absolutely wonderful.'

Joyce blushed. 'Thank you, that's very kind of you to say so.'

Barbara reached the door and looked round at them. She scowled before walking into the café.

Joyce shook her head, wondering how long she was going to have to put up with Simon's sister.

'Are you all right, young man?' Barbara's voice carried into the kitchen.

Joyce gently pushed the door ajar and peered round it. She was talking to Philip. Joyce pushed the door wide open and walked over to him, putting her arm across his shoulders. 'Philip is with me.'

Barbara looked from one to the other, and didn't say anything at first. 'That's all fine. I'll keep an eye on him.'

'Thank you, Barbara.'

Philip looked up at Joyce with wide, soulful eyes. 'Can I sit with Frank?'

Joyce's lips tightened for a second. 'Only if he doesn't mind.'

Frank ruffled Philip's hair. 'Of course I don't mind. We can draw pictures and things.'

Philip beamed and ran to make room on his table.

'Thank you, Frank.'

'It's my pleasure.' Frank winked.

Joyce could feel her colour rising in her face. 'Please don't feel you have to sit with him every time you come in here.' She walked over to the table and checked the coloured pencils and the exercise book she'd taken from her shopping bag earlier. 'I'm only through that door if you need anything. You can write me a story if you don't want to draw.'

Barbara took a couple of steps towards them. Her eyes narrowed. She had seen Frank wink at Joyce. 'Philip looks a little like you.' She paused as she eyed him. 'He's only young. Can he read and write?'

Joyce blushed; she had just made herself look such a fool, after all he hadn't started school yet.

The fire crackled in the hearth. The flames danced and licked the coals into shape before disappearing up the chimney. The black coal turned grey and crackled as it fell into place. The dining room was lovely and warm as long as the door was pushed to. Joyce poured a glass of milk from a white stoneware jug for Philip and passed it to him. He stared wide-eyed at her; she could see the tiredness in his eyes. 'I'm sorry it hasn't been much fun for you since you've been here.' Joyce closed her eyes for a second, not knowing how to proceed. 'Thank you for helping me in the café. I would have struggled without it.' He very rarely responded to her no matter what she said or did; at best all she got was a few words and a faint smile most of the time.

She thought of her own mother and father, how she'd always got involved with cooking and making things. She had never felt the need to have many friends. She had been happy at home with her mother; they had always done things together. Her mother could forge a meal out of nothing and often had to because her father didn't always get paid for the work he did. Joyce remembered her father saying how a bad man had robbed him of his wages. He was always off working somewhere, and she wouldn't see him for days but he always brought presents when he came home. Joyce smiled at the thought of some of the dolls and jewellery she had owned.

She shook her head. That was all gone now. How could she get through to Philip? How could she now give him that happy feeling, the good memories? But then she had grown up in the village and there were always things to do. She thought hard; maybe she could try and put something in a pot for him to show him the satisfaction of growing something and then transforming it into something that could be eaten.

'That Barbara pretends to be nice but I don't think she is really.'

Joyce's eyes widened as she fought to hold her happiness inside as she looked across at Philip. 'I don't suppose she's a horrible person; the café is new to her, that's all.'

Philip shrugged. 'My pa used to say some people pretend to be one way but act another.'

Joyce looked at him for a moment before picking up the poker and prodding the grey coals in the fireplace. Sparks crackled as the coals fell and the flames licked and danced up the chimney breast. 'Your pa sounds like a wise man.' She stepped back, wanting to ask him so many questions but something held her back.

Philip stared into his glass of milk. 'We used to have fun together.' He paused. 'When he visited he'd take me out.'

Joyce pushed a plate of biscuits towards him and sat down in the armchair near the open fire. 'Help yourself. Did your father work away a lot then?'

Philip shrugged. 'I don't know. I just know he wasn't always there, but when he came home he played with me and told me all kinds of stories.'

Joyce could feel her eyes welling up. 'It sounds like he loves you very much.'

Philip stared at her before picking a biscuit from the plate. 'He stopped coming.'

Joyce took a couple of breaths, trying to control the tightness that had gripped her throat and chest, wondering if she could rustle up some profound words, but really just wanting to give him a bear hug. 'I don't suppose he meant to stop coming; perhaps he just got caught up with work or something.'

There was no visible emotion on Philip's face when he spoke again. 'Me ma took me to Mrs Taylor's house. She said she would look after me, give me a better life. Ma was crying like, but said she just couldn't look after me anymore, what wiv all 'er entertaining. At least that's what I heard Grandma tell my pa. They were shouting at each other. I don't actually remember me ma.'

Joyce gulped hard. She wanted to ask more questions but she had to fight the urge to cry for what he'd been through.

Arthur pushed the dining room door wide open. 'Hello, Philip, how's it been at the café today with Joyce?'

Philip smiled. 'She was really busy and Barbara wasn't very nice to her although she was very nice to me and Frank drew pictures with me.'

Joyce raised her eyebrows and looked over at Arthur. She didn't realise how much Philip was taking in.

Arthur raised his eyebrows at Joyce. 'So Frank popped in again did he?' He glanced over at Philip and smiled. He moved to stand in front of the fire in the hearth. 'That's because Joyce is in charge. No one likes their bosses.'

Philip looked over Joyce. 'Is that true?'

Joyce looked from one to the other. 'I shouldn't think so; your uncle Arthur has a habit of exaggerating things. I'm only in charge temporarily because it's Barbara's family business not mine, and her brother's away at the moment.'

Philip eyes widened. 'Is he fighting the Germans?'

Joyce immediately looked over at Arthur. How was she going to deal with this? What was she going to say to Philip? She gave a curt nod. 'Philip, tell me what are you interested in. What did you used to do when you lived at Grandma's?'

'We used to go to the park sometimes.' Philip shrugged. 'I've always done what I wanted.'

Joyce scowled at him. 'You know I've never looked after a child before, but I don't think any five-year-old should be able to do exactly what they like.' She smiled. 'I just want to keep you safe.'

Philip folded his arms around his body. 'You don't have to look after me. I can look after myself.'

Joyce nodded. 'Well, I expect that's true but I want to look after you.' She smiled. 'I tell you what, I was going to suggest a visit to the park so maybe we could go on Sunday. How about that?'

Philip grinned and nodded. 'Will Frank come as well?'

'I expect Frank will be busy.' Joyce frowned. 'Look, I know I'm busy all the time and things need to change, but I haven't figured that bit out yet.'

Arthur beamed. 'The park's a lovely idea. You can't beat a run-around.' He took a biscuit from the plate. 'I almost forgot to say, I got a letter from Dot. She's well, and said to say hello to you all.'

Joyce smiled. 'I'm pleased she's happy. I know you want

her to be here but at least you are both talking to each other now.'

Arthur opened his mouth to speak but closed it again. He examined the biscuit before biting into it. Crumbs fell onto the floor. 'Did you make these, Joyce?'

Joyce looked down at the floor and shook her head. 'Yes, I only made them very quickly and by the looks of things they are a bit crumbly.'

'Yes, they are a bit but they are lovely, so make as many as you like.' Arthur picked up another biscuit. 'Philip, would you like a biscuit? You're lucky Joyce makes some beautiful meals and her biscuits are the best.'

Philip grinned at Arthur as he reached for a biscuit.

The audience rose to their feet, cheering and clapping as the red curtains came down for the second time. The cast applauded each other and their excitement spilled over as they patted each other on the back.

Annie clapped her hands together and turned to Kitty. 'Stan must be happy with the way it went tonight. You seemed to love it.' The applause filled the theatre. 'Listen to them; you can hear them cheering and clapping. It's so wonderful.'

Kitty smiled, her eyes lighting up. 'It was wonderful tonight; I think there was something in the air. This is why I love the stage; this is why I love acting.' She grabbed Annie's hand and they rushed across the stage together.

Annie's eyes sparkled and her face flushed with colour. 'It's wonderful, I love being on stage.'

The cast of the play gathered in groups, laughing and joking as they left the stage. Some were in the wings giggling, each enjoying the pleasure of what had happened on stage that evening.

Stan was suddenly in front of them all. 'That went brilliantly. I'm so proud of you. Thank you for all the hard work you've put in.' He turned to a young girl in a maid's costume. 'Penny, you did very well. Congratulations.'

The young girl blushed. 'Thank you, sir, it's thanks to Annie. She helped me to learn my lines.'

Stan grinned as he looked across at Annie before nodding as he glanced back at Penny. 'That doesn't surprise me, but you should take the credit for not giving up.'

Beaming, Annie listened to them both. She caught Penny's gaze and mouthed: 'Well done'.

Stan went up to Kitty and put his arms around her shoulders. 'You were brilliant tonight.'

Kitty smiled at him. 'Of course, darling, aren't I always brilliant?'

Stan chuckled. 'Without a doubt, my darling, without a doubt.'

Kitty turned to Annie. 'Come on, let's get out of these costumes and get our make-up off. Then maybe we can grab a coffee.'

They walked along the corridor to Kitty's dressing room and pushed the door open. A musty smell of stale perfume and make-up greeted them. Kitty wrinkled her nose. 'It's a shame there's no window in here; it gets very stuffy.'

Stan shook his head. 'Maybe next time we can organise it for you; at least a larger dressing room.'

Kitty gave him a sideways look. 'You're not trying to be funny are you, Stan?'

Stan chuckled. 'As if I'd dare.' He sat on the chaise longue and stretched out his legs in front of him. 'You should go out for something to eat. You know, celebrate.'

Annie carried the kettle over to the sink and turned the tap on. 'Would you like a coffee, Mr Tyler?'

Stan chuckled. 'You can call me Stan you know.'

Annie brushed the front of the maid's costume she was wearing with the palm of her hand. 'I know, you've mentioned it before, but I don't want to seem disrespectful at work.'

'I'm sure you won't be. I'm giving you permission so I don't see that as being disrespectful.'

Annie nodded. 'Very well, would you like a coffee, Stan?'

Stan ran his hands through his hair. 'I'd love one, thank you, and make it a strong one please.'

Annie spooned the Camp Coffee into the cups, adding a spoonful of sugar to one of them. 'How's the wedding plans coming along?'

Kitty sighed. 'I haven't done anything yet. I know it's terrible but I'm dreading going out looking for a wedding dress. I'm not even sure what sort of dress I should have at my age.'

Annie shook her head. 'What do you mean at your age? You should have a proper wedding dress just like everyone else does.'

Kitty chuckled. 'I knew you would think that, which is why I haven't spoken to you about it.'

'I don't understand. We can talk about anything can't we? It doesn't matter if we agree or not; it's about how we deal with it.'

Stan laughed. 'Oh, Kitty, that told you didn't it.'

Kitty scowled at Stan. 'You can be quiet. This has nothing to do with you.'

Stan's head jerked back. 'What do you mean it's nothing to do with me? I'm the groom, remember?'

Annie burst out laughing. 'I think Kitty means the wedding dress is nothing to do with you.' She turned to Kitty. 'We should talk about it when Stan isn't in the room. Maybe we could get Rose involved. She might be able to make you something if you prefer it.'

Kitty looked thoughtful at her reflection in the mirror. 'Now that's worth thinking about. I should have thought of that; maybe we should talk to Rose.'

Annie picked up the two cups of coffee and wandered over to Stan and Kitty, placing the drinks on the table.

Stan immediately picked up his cup. 'Well, if you like I could just drink this and then you can talk to Rose, if she's still here.'

Annie nodded. 'I expect she is. She likes to stay in case anything goes wrong with the costumes during the play. She likes being on hand to fix them.'

Kitty frowned. 'Unlike Miss Hetherington.'

Annie shook her head. 'Well, it might be difficult for her. None of us know what goes on in people's lives away from work.'

Kitty laughed. 'You always want to think good of people, and that can get you into trouble as you well know. I don't think Miss Hetherington's got a kind bone in her entire body.'

Annie shrugged. 'I just prefer to think there's not as many bad people out there as we think and, anyway, why would anyone want to keep thinking bad things? It must make for a sad life.'

Kitty smiled. 'You are just too kind for your own good, and Miss Hetherington thinks badly of everybody here so she deserves what she gets.'

'But she could have problems at home that we don't even know about.'

Kitty picked up a cup, took a sip of the hot brown liquid. She licked her lips. 'That's a good cup of coffee, Annie, thank you, and as for Miss Hetherington, if she doesn't share her problems then how are we meant to know?'

Stan put down his empty cup. 'I think this is one of those conversations that you two will never agree on, so I will leave you to it.' He stood up and turned to walk towards the doorway. 'Thanks for the coffee, Annie. You can now talk about wedding dresses, which might be a safer subject for you both.'

Kitty took the damp sponge and gradually wiped the make-up from her face. 'I shouldn't be too long if you want to wait?'

'That's fine. I've got things to do so I'll come back when I'm finished.' Stan walked through the open doorway pulling the door closed behind him.

Annie put down her cup. 'Right, let's get you out of your costume and then you can go and see Stan while I sort myself out.'

Kitty put down her cup. She ran her fingers through her hair, fluffing it out before pushing a brush through it. 'We could get Rose in here while we get changed.'

There was a sharp rap at the door. Annie walked over to open it. 'Oh, Rose, we were just talking about you.'

Rose chuckled. 'That doesn't sound good. Mr Tyler said you wanted to see me.'

Annie stood aside. 'It's nothing to worry about. We've been discussing Kitty's wedding dress. She can't decide what sort to have. I wondered if you could use your talent to make her one?'

Rose gasped. 'I have to say I've never made a wedding dress so it depends what sort of thing you wanted. I don't want to say yes and then do it wrong. After all a wedding dress is something special.'

Kitty turned to look at Rose. 'I have faith in you, Rose. You are an excellent seamstress and it might be good experience for you. You never know where these things can lead to.'

Rose nodded. 'No, I understand that but I don't want you to have a dress that will spoil your day.'

Annie rubbed Rose's arm. 'I can't imagine you would ever allow that to happen.'

Rose's eyes widened. 'All right, I'll do some sketches of what you might like and then we'll see where we go from there.'

Kitty breathed a sigh of relief. 'That just leaves the food and the ring, but Stan can sort the ring out.'

Rose looked at Kitty as she stepped out of her dress. 'Where are you holding the reception?'

'That's something else I haven't decided. To be honest there's not going to be that many people attending so I don't really want a big do. It will be people like us; the theatre is my home and my family so I just want a small place with good food.'

Annie looked tentatively at Rose. Rose looked back at her. Their eyes widened as they stared each other.

'We have a friend who runs a café. It's called Meet and

Feast. We could talk to her about closing early and maybe decorating it for your wedding. What do you think?'

'What is the place like?'

Rose shrugged. 'Well, it's just a café, but put cloths on the tables and small vases of cut flowers in the middle and it can make all the difference. We could even add lace at the windows or something.'

Kitty smiled at the girls. 'I'm so lucky to be surrounded by such creative people. I say we go with the suggestions. It's something different and I like that.'

Annie nodded. 'We'll talk to Joyce, and let you know what she says but know that we won't let you down.'

11

Annie smiled at Rose. 'After all the rain we've been having this feels like a glorious day. You can't beat the feel of the sun on your face, even if it isn't very warm. It just lifts your spirits. It seems ages since I've been out with Peter; we've both been so busy with work. I know he sometimes meets me from the theatre and walks me home but it's not the same as spending a day together.'

Rose looked down at the pavement as she walked along. 'I'm quite nervous; Charlie and I have only been on one date. We've had lots of chats with many cups of tea and coffee in his shop but since then we haven't really managed to find time together until today.'

'I know what you mean, but you'll be all right. Charlie is quite smitten with you.' Annie paused. 'I'm so pleased that we're managing to go out together at last and it's good to have you and Philip with us,' Annie said to Joyce. 'I think we all just need to make more of an effort if we want our relationships to work.'

Rose looked up. 'Do you love Peter?'

Colour began to rise in Annie's face. 'I love being with him, and when he unexpectedly came to my family's home

I was thrilled to see him. It made me suddenly realise how important it was that my family liked him.'

'It worries me that I may not know what love is.'

Annie frowned. 'We're all in that position, Rose. I think if you can truly be yourself around them and can't bear to be apart from them then that must be love, right?'

Joyce nodded. 'Don't make the mistakes I've made. I should've come clean with Simon instead of being so afraid of getting hurt or thinking I wasn't good enough. And now look what's happened. He's gone off to war and I may never see him again.' She shook her head. 'I miss him so much and I'm full of regret at not accepting his proposal. So don't lose sight of what's important.' Joyce reached for Philip's hand as they walked along the road. He wriggled and pulled his hand free before running further ahead along the pavement. Joyce shouted, 'Be careful of the road. I don't want you hurting yourself.'

Annie smiled watching the young boy running along. 'Isn't it wonderful watching a child play? Do you remember when we were that young, running along in the woods and climbing trees? I know we had to do our chores but the freedom we had compared to what they have here in London was wonderful.'

Rose giggled. 'Can you remember when we fell out the tree? I tore my skirt. Did I get into trouble that day!'

Annie chuckled. 'I bet that was your first lesson in sewing and look where that skill has got you.'

Joyce frowned as she watched Philip running along the pavement. 'That's the trouble with being in London; I just don't know what to do with him. We always entertained ourselves, but it was different back home.'

Annie reached out and touched Joyce's arm. 'You have to remember this is all new to you so you're learning as you go along. You haven't given birth to Philip, and know nothing about him. You've been thrown in the deep end.'

Joyce frowned. 'The trouble is I don't think he likes me and don't know what to do about it.'

Rose looked over at her friend. 'I don't think that's necessarily true. He's been uprooted from everything he knows. He's probably frightened. You have to remember you may not know him but equally he doesn't know you; just give him time.'

Annie looked from Rose to Joyce. 'Rose is right. Remember how you would've felt at that age. If my memory serves me right you didn't like meeting anybody that you didn't know. You were very much at home with your parents. Philip has had all that ripped away from him. It's not as if you know what's happened to his parents and he isn't talking about it. Of course he may not know.'

Rose stopped for a moment. 'Have you looked inside the chest yet?'

Joyce shook her head. 'I haven't had the chance. I don't know if I'm coming or going between the café and Philip. I feel like I'm at the end of my tether. Barbara isn't very helpful in work despite what Simon said when she first arrived. She clearly thinks she's in charge and comes and goes as she likes and I'm just run off my feet. Having said that, Mavis, Simon's mother, said it's going to stop so I suppose I've just got to wait and see.'

Rose frowned. 'Maybe you need to get someone else in to help and forget about Barbara.'

'I have thought of that but it's not my business. I can't just override the family and do what I want.'

Annie sighed. 'Maybe if things don't improve have a meeting with them to try and sort out the problems.'

Joyce frowned. 'You could be right but I also need to sort out Philip. It's not fair to expect him to sit in the café all day while I'm working.'

Rose cleared her throat. 'Why don't you ask Arthur to look at the schools, and see about getting Philip enrolled in one. I'm sure Annie won't mind me volunteering her, but we could always take him to school while you're at work and maybe either you or Arthur could pick him up. At least then he's mixing with other children and learning and let's face it he should be at school anyway.'

Joyce nodded. 'I've already thought of that but I just haven't had time.'

Annie sighed. 'And that's definitely true. You've had a lot going on, but that's why you should let us help. It's not all on you. We're your friends, and friends are always there for each other. But you've got to let us help you. Look how you helped us when we first came to London. All the advice you gave us, letting us stay at your home. You've been a wonderful friend to us so let us start repaying some of that by doing the same for you.'

Joyce could feel her eyes welling up. 'You've already made such a difference to my life by coming to London. Look how Arthur has changed and that's down to you two because he certainly didn't change for me.'

Rose laughed. 'I don't think it was anything to do with us. I think it was because Annie looked like Dot, although none of us could see it at the time. He seemed to take on board whatever Annie's brother said when he came to see her. It made him stop and think, and that was obviously a good thing but it wasn't our influence on him in any way. But none of that matters; the fact is he's changed and could be a great help to you if you let him. Think how you looked after him when he was troubled. You've got to let people in, Joyce; you've got to let us help before you sink under the strain of it all. It's not your job to wait on everybody hand and foot. You're not a maid; you're a friend.'

Joyce looked up as Philip ran very close to the edge of the pavement. 'Philip,' she yelled. 'Wait, you're going to get run over if you're not careful.' She ran along the pavement, weaving between people who were standing around chatting and enjoying the sunshine. Joyce caught up with him; she grabbed his hand and shook it. 'You could've been killed. You shouldn't be running so far ahead; you need to stay with me.'

'Annie, Rose.' Peter and Charles shouted in unison as they raced along the road towards them.

The girls slowed down and turned round simultaneously at the sound of their names. Joyce looked up and peered over her shoulder.

Peter tried to smile but he was gasping for breath. 'I didn't think we were going to catch you up; you were racing along.'

Joyce raised her eyebrows. 'I thought we were meeting you at Charlie's bicycle shop. That's where I told Frank to meet us.'

Annie and Rose glanced at each other and raised their eyebrows.

'You never said you'd invited Frank.' Rose tilted her head slightly. 'Does this mean you're getting friendly with him?'

Joyce stared at her in disbelief. 'It means he's good with Philip and I didn't want to play gooseberry to you four.'

Charles took a deep breath and looked around the small group. 'Anyway, we were standing outside talking about the shops that were closing down and how things seem to be getting worse. Even the restaurant over the road is boarded up now, which isn't a great surprise to anyone that's been in there.' He chuckled. 'Sorry, I'm rambling. It was then that we saw you waiting to cross the road, but we can go back to the shop; it doesn't matter.'

Joyce nodded. 'Philip was running ahead and I was frightened I might lose him, or worse, he'd get run over. I'm not used to all this responsibility.'

Peter ruffled Philip's hair. 'He's just doing what boys do. They like to run around. Maybe we should go to the park and not Westminster Bridge. I know you girls like looking at the boats but it might be better for Philip to run round the park and use up some of his energy.'

Joyce smiled. 'Hark at you – when did you become an expert with children?'

Peter grinned. 'I wouldn't say I'm an expert but I 'ave got young nephews and my next-door neighbour has small children so I'm used to being around them.'

Annie looked around. 'I think the park's a good idea. It's getting busy, with traffic and people, and, Joyce, you won't relax if we go to the bridge, as lovely as it is.'

Peter nodded. 'If we go to Hyde Park there's the Serpentine so we could always sit around on the grass and watch the world go by while Philip runs around.'

Rose chuckled. 'Well, I hope you've got lots of energy because he's not going to run around by himself.'

Charles took Rose's hand in his and his thumb caressed the top of it. 'We could get a bicycle from the shop and let Philip ride it. What do you think?'

Annie beamed. 'What a great idea. Are you sure you don't mind us using one of them?'

'Of course not. If Philip doesn't want it after he's learnt how to ride then I'll just sell it as second-hand. It's not a problem and Philip might enjoy it.'

Joyce looked down at Philip. His eyes widened with every word. 'Would you like that, Philip? Would you like to learn how to ride a bicycle?'

Annie laughed. 'I expect he's terrified, but he won't know whether he'll enjoy it until he tries, so I say we go for it.'

Rose clapped her hands together. 'I agree, so let's get the bicycle and then go to Hyde Park. Well, actually, I'd rather it wasn't me who taught him because I'm not very good at that sort of thing.'

Charles laughed. 'I don't mind doing it; after all he's a potential customer.'

Everyone laughed as they all turned to go back to the bicycle shop.

Peter reached out and grasped Annie's hand. He pulled her towards him. 'It's lovely to see you again. It feels like it's been ages since we've spent some real time together.' He leant in and kissed her gently on her lips.

Annie lifted her hand and rested it against Peter's cheek as a soft groan escaped from her.

Philip looked up at Joyce. 'Am I really going to learn how to ride a bicycle?'

Joyce smiled, recognising the excitement written all over

his face. 'Yes, you are, but only if you want to. I think you should try because it's good fun.'

Charles and Rose walked in front, their heads very close together as they were deep in conversation. Joyce felt a surge of jealousy rising in her. How could Simon leave her? She shook her head and clenched her hands together. It was no good thinking about Simon. That moment had passed and she had made her bed. She had to concentrate on Philip now; after all he deserved to have a good life. He was only a child and would enjoy spending time with Frank.

Joyce sat on the bench next to Frank, watching Charlie holding on to the back of the bicycle steering Philip around the footpath. 'Mind the flowers. I don't want us to get into trouble because the flowers have been battered by Philip falling off the bicycle.'

A smile played on Rose's lips as she watched the boys. The blue bike was a great fit. Philip suddenly burst out laughing, and she found herself following suit.

'I'm doing it, I'm doing it.'

Joyce shouted. 'Yes, you are.' She turned and looked at the girls. 'I've never heard him laugh like that.' She found herself smiling at his giggling and couldn't help wondering if they had moved forward and he might be a little happier now.

Annie looked over at Joyce, enjoying the smile that was spreading across her face. 'It's lovely to see you smiling. I don't think I've seen that smile since I've arrived in London. And you have been particularly low since Simon has gone.'

Joyce's smile faded a little.

Frank jumped up from the bench. 'I'm going to 'ave a walk and stretch my legs.'

Joyce nodded. 'Let me just watch Philip a bit longer and then I'll come with you.'

Charlie suddenly let go of the bike and Philip was cycling by himself.

Joyce and the girls clapped their hands and cheered.

'Isn't it wonderful? You forget what it's like to be a young child.' Joyce shook her head. 'That said I think Philip was forgetting what it was like to be a child.'

Peter walked over to the bench. 'You do know you're doing a wonderful job don't you?'

Joyce gave a wry smile. 'There have been times when I thought Philip really didn't like me and I've struggled to know how to cope with him. But as the girls pointed out I've never been much of a mixer. I've always been happy on my own or with my very close friends.'

Charlie looked back at Rose. 'He's a clever boy. It hasn't taken him long to learn how to ride the bicycle.'

Frank was smiling when he strode off to walk next to Philip on his bicycle.

Joyce frowned. 'Now I just have to figure out how I'm going to pay for it.'

Charlie shook his head. 'Don't worry about it, Joyce. Let it be my gift. It's made my day to see a boy so happy on one of my bikes.'

'Thank you so much for the offer but I can't accept it, Charlie. It's your livelihood and, I don't want to sound ungrateful, but I don't want to feel like I owe you or anybody else for that matter.'

Charlie chuckled. 'You won't owe me. We're friends, and you introduced me to Rose and that's priceless to me.'

Rose blushed. 'I never knew you felt like that, Charlie.'

Charlie gave a slight nod. He walked over to Rose and took her hand. 'I've probably said it all too soon, and didn't want to rush things but the more I read about the war, the more I feel time isn't on my side.'

Rose looked from left to right at her friends. 'What are you saying?'

Charlie shrugged. 'I want us to spend more time together. There's things I want to say but now isn't the time or the place.' He paused. 'I've heard there's going to be a push so men will have to enlist whether they want to or not, so I would like us to just make the most of the time that we have before that happens.'

Joyce looked away from Charlie and Rose. He was a good man, as was Peter. Had she been a fool for not pursuing either of them? They were still here and Simon wasn't, but her heart told her she never had a choice. Why did Simon have the urge to go and fight, and Charlie and Peter were still here?

Annie looked round as she heard Charlie talking to Rose. 'Does that mean you will have to go as well, Peter?'

Peter frowned before giving a slight shrug. 'I don't want to go. My family don't want me to go, but if needed or forced I will have to.'

Annie pursed her lips. 'I know from what Joyce has said that Simon and his family had received comments from people because he hadn't signed up. Are you getting the same thing?'

Peter stared straight ahead. 'I get the odd comment but

it doesn't worry me. My family come first and that's all I worry about.'

Annie gazed out at the still waters of the Serpentine.

Joyce bit her lip. 'I don't think Simon felt he had a choice. I just hope he's as safe as he can be.'

Peter nodded. 'I think we need to get back to having fun while we can.'

Annie forced a smile. 'You're right. We shouldn't waste any of the precious time we have.'

Joyce watched the two couples and felt quite alone. Jealousy surged through her. 'I'm going to try and catch up with Philip while he's on his bicycle.'

The four of them sat in silence, each lost in thought, as Joyce moved to catch up with Frank and Philip.

Annie took a deep breath. 'Anyway, this is a beautiful park and I can't believe it's in the middle of London. All this greenery amongst the tall buildings and the busy roads – it's beautiful. The flowers are enjoying the sunshine. You could almost forget we're at war and feel like you're back home in the village.'

Joyce stopped and looked around her, as though seeing it for the first time. 'You're right. It is beautiful. I should come here more often.'

Charlie smiled. 'You should come on Christmas Day when men and women jump into the Serpentine for a swim.'

Rose gasped. 'As much as it looks inviting now, that water must be freezing then.'

Charlie chuckled. 'I expect it's freezing now. Water can be quite deceiving. But we are lucky to have this haven in the middle of London.' He put his arm around Rose's shoulder as they sat together on the grass.

Annie watched Joyce walk away. Her head was low and her shoulders rounded. She looked weighed down. 'Do you think she's all right?'

Rose spoke in a low voice. 'Where does this Frank fit in? Is he replacing Simon?' She turned to follow Annie's gaze. 'We'll have to make sure she's all right.' She jumped up from the grass and brushed the back of her skirt. 'Maybe we need to stop being lovey-dovey because she must feel like she's playing the gooseberry.'

Charlie nodded. 'You're right. It's my fault; I started it.'

Annie turned to him. 'It's no one's fault. We don't spend enough time together so it's obvious we would want to make the most of it. Bringing Joyce with us was a good idea but we didn't think it through – I mean about how she would feel without Simon.'

Peter stood up. 'Well, it's not too late to put it right.'

Everyone gathered and started to follow Joyce.

Joyce grabbed the tea towel and wiped it across her forehead. Thank goodness the day was nearly over, and she was looking forward to going home. Peering out through the serving hatch, she watched Philip flop back in the chair watching everyone around him. She had to sort out his schooling; maybe she'd talk to Arthur tonight. Joyce raised her eyebrows as she watched Barbara march over to him. She leant forward to try to hear what was being said but was too far away. Philip was concentrating on Barbara and suddenly he smiled, lighting up his whole face. Joyce stepped back as Barbara turned and headed for the counter. Once Barbara had moved away again she watched her take a small slice of cake and a glass of milk over to Philip. He smiled and tucked into the cake ravenously and gulped down the milk.

Joyce sighed. 'Well, this isn't going to get the kitchen cleaned.' She turned away from the hatch; her heart was aching. She didn't know how she'd got into this position but was sure she was failing badly.

The kitchen door swung open and Barbara breezed in. She frowned at Joyce. 'I don't think it's right that you bring Philip in here every day. He's bored stiff. You need to make better arrangements for him.'

Joyce threw the tea towel down onto the kitchen worktop. 'Do you not think I don't know that? I'm sick to death of you coming in here feeling like you know everything that's going on when you know nothing, so please just leave me alone.'

'I don't know it all. I'm just trying to help but you clearly don't want any help and that's because *you* think you know it all.'

Philip pushed the door open slightly. 'Joyce, there's a man here to see you.'

Joyce sighed. 'All right, thank you, Philip. I'm coming out.'

'I'm bored,' Philip whined. 'I wish my grandmother was here or maybe we could go out and play hide-and-seek.'

'For goodness' sake, Philip, can't you see I'm busy?' Joyce snapped. 'You can't have your grandmother here, and no amount of whining changes that. You're stuck with me whether you like it or not.'

Philip's shoulders slumped as he quietly stepped back into the café.

Joyce followed Philip out. She stood still when she caught sight of the landlord. 'What can I do for you, Mr Harris?'

'I know Mr Hitchin isn't here, but we need to talk about the rent.' Mr Harris put his hand to his mouth as he coughed a couple of times.

Barbara followed Joyce out into the café. 'That sounds nasty. You might want to get something for it before it gets too deep-rooted.' She stared at the man towering over Joyce. He had a glint in his eye.

Joyce pulled back her shoulders and lifted her chin. 'I'm not in a position to talk about the rent with you. You should've discussed it with Mr Hitchin before he left.'

The landlord glowered at her. When he finally spoke his voice was more hoarse than usual. 'I would've done had I known he was leaving but he kept that a secret, so I'm afraid you'll have to pick up the pieces or I'll have to evict you.'

Joyce took a deep breath, worn down by all the hard work and Simon leaving. 'What do you wish to say to me?'

The landlord smirked. 'The rent is going up. Mr Hitchin didn't pay the extra last time but I'm afraid you now have no choice.'

It was Joyce's turn to smile. 'That's quite interesting because Mr Hitchin left me a copy of his father's contract – the contract his father made with your father putting him on a fixed rent for all the time the family was in business at this property.'

The man clenched his hands by his sides.

'So I think you need to check your facts with your father because you've no right to put the rent up.' Joyce smiled triumphantly.

'Unfortunately, my father is no longer with us so his contract has died with him. That means you will have to pay the increase.'

Joyce again smiled. 'You're not trying to intimidate me are you? I'm not an expert but I'm willing to pay a solicitor to look at the contract, because my interpretation, and indeed Mr Hitchin's, was it says all the time it is open as a café or restaurant. So I think you'll find it is you who doesn't have the power to put up our rent, but I'm happy to get it checked and get it in writing for you.' She paused. 'It's a shame you don't have your father's head for business.'

Barbara gave Joyce a sideways look. 'Do you think we should pay it?'

Mr Harris looked from one to the other. 'I'm sorry I don't think we've met. You are?'

Barbara flushed with colour. 'I'm Miss Hitchin, the café owner's sister.'

Mr Harris smiled and tipped his head slightly, lifting his hat at the same time. 'Well, it's lovely to meet you. I don't believe I've had the honour in the past because I would've remembered.'

Joyce shook her head. 'Miss Hitchin is not in charge of paying the rent. So you can save your charm for somebody else.' She opened a drawer and picked up an envelope and waved it at him. 'I have the contract and I'm happy to show you it, if you don't have a copy, but I can tell you I'll take legal advice rather than pay any more than is written down.'

Barbara lifted her hand and rested it on her chest. 'Simon wouldn't thank us for losing his business for him.'

Joyce pinched her lips together and glanced over at Barbara. 'No, you're right he wouldn't, but he also wouldn't

thank me for spending more of his money than I need to.'
She clenched her jaw as she peered at Mr Harris before
returning to give Barbara her full attention. 'This business
doesn't earn as much as you think, and it needs to keep a
roof over yours and your mother's heads.' She threw the
envelope she was holding back into the drawer and pushed
it shut.

Mr Harris rounded on Joyce. 'You know I can make life
very difficult for you, don't you?'

Joyce clenched her fist down by her side.

Barbara's eyes widened at the underlying threat. 'Maybe
it's something we should discuss together with my mother.'

Mr Harris turned and smiled at Barbara. 'That sounds
like a sensible solution. Perhaps I'll come back tomorrow;
however, if I do, I can assure you I'll not be leaving without
my rent increase.'

Joyce studied him. 'And let me assure you, Mr Harris, I
will not be paying the rent increase and, if need be, I will
take it further. I will not accept any of your bully-boy tactics
so I suggest you leave us alone because if you come back
tomorrow it will be exactly the same answer.'

Mr Harris lifted his hat to them both. 'And let me reassure
you, as the saying goes, there's more than one way to skin
a cat.'

12

The bell chimed behind Mr Harris as he closed the café door behind him. He shivered, and fastened his suit jacket button. He peered back at the café with its steamed-up windows. He was going to have to sort that woman out; she seemed to believe that she had all the answers. Maybe it was time for him to act. What he needed was a plan to take back control. Pulling a handkerchief from his trouser pocket, he mopped the beads of perspiration from his brow; perhaps he should find something for this cold. He squeezed the handkerchief into a ball. He wasn't his father and had no desire to be the easy-going poor person his father was. Everybody had loved him, but growing up they had nothing. His father would always say if you have food on the table and a roof over your head what more could you possibly need.

Mr Harris sighed. Now he was left with all these fixed rents, which meant he would also die with nothing unless he got some of the tenants out. Shaking his head, he pushed his handkerchief back into his trouser pocket, careful not to spoil the crisp line of them. He hated wearing his black suit but he had an image to keep up. Mr Harris moved to step off the pavement when a car horn sounded. He jerked back and waved his apologies at the driver, who shook his head and mouthed something that couldn't be heard. He turned and stepped forward on the pavement, and immediately bumped into a young man wearing a fitted three-piece suit and a trilby hat. He recognised him from somewhere but couldn't remember where.

Two boys ran past pointing their fingers and pretending to shoot each other. One stopped and faced the other. 'It's your turn to be German; it's not fair that it's always me getting shot.'

'Mr 'Arris, we meet again.' The young man pushed his hat back a little and eyed the older man in front of him. 'I hope yer 'aven't bin threatening the young lady in the café.' Frank bent down to stroke the matted fur of a stray dog that had stopped to sniff his leg and shoes. The dog leant into him before licking his hand and moving on down the road.

Mr Harris stared at him. 'I don't know what your interest is in my café but I suggest you don't interfere with my business.'

Frank chuckled. 'That's just it, it's not yer business and yer just trying to bleed them dry.'

Mr Harris shook his head before giving him a condescending smile. 'You youngsters have got a lot to learn, but let me tell you I'm entitled to ask for a rent increase and it has nothing to do with you.'

Frank frowned as he stepped aside to let an old lady get past. He reached and caught her arm as her footing slipped on the pavement. 'Yer all right, lovey?'

The old lady smiled. 'Thank you, yer saved me from an embarrassing fall there.'

Frank beamed. 'As long as yer good, yer too precious to get 'urt so just take care now.'

The lady's eyes lit up. 'Get away wiv yer.' She chuckled, lifting her gnarled hand to stroke his arm. 'Yer've made my day, yer 'ave.' She nodded and carried on walking down Shaftesbury Avenue.

Frank watched her bent figure moving slowly away from him.

Mr Harris watched the younger man, deciding he was all talk with his threats. He moved to walk around him when he found his arm in a vice-like grip.

Frank squeezed his hold of him. 'I 'ave my own fish to fry and I'd 'ate for yer to come unstuck with yer behaviour over a rent increase.'

Mr Harris studied him, only letting his fear show for a split second, before yanking his arm free. 'What is it with you? Do you fancy her or something?'

Frank chuckled. 'She's a pretty little thing, I'll grant yer that.'

Mr Harris shook his head. 'Then ask Joyce Taylor out, but don't get involved in my business or you'll regret it.'

Frank's eyes widened, but only for a second. He had learnt from a young age to think about his reactions. 'Not only will I not allow yer to get in the way of my business but I won't stand by and watch a young girl threatened by someone who's just worrying about pennies. I told yer I've got bigger fish to fry so just make sure yer stay away from her.'

Mr Harris lifted his head slightly and jutted out his chin. Pulling himself upright, he straightened his shoulders. 'I'm not threatening anybody and I will not have someone come in and threaten me, or my business. I don't even know who you are so you're clearly a nobody around here.'

Frank stared at the landlord for a moment. 'No, yer don't know who I am, and that's 'ow I work, but I know exactly who you are. Yer like to dress as though yer a gangster and threaten yer tenants.'

Mr Harris tried to hide his sharp intake of breath. 'I'm not answerable to you.'

Frank smiled. 'No, yer could be though if yer don't watch yer step.'

'I'm a landlord.' Mr Harris lifted his arm in disgust. 'And for your information if I didn't threaten them then most wouldn't pay anything.'

'I'm well aware about threatening people so they'll pay up but not women and children. Yer 'ave to be a low life to do that.' Frank took out a packet of Navy Cut cigarettes from his pocket. He pulled open the lid and removed one of them. He tapped it up and down on the closed box for several seconds, all the time not taking his eyes off Mr Harris. 'I'm sorry, I never offered yer a cigarette. Would yer like one?' Frank didn't open the box or pass it over to him.

Mr Harris caught a glint in Frank's eyes; he didn't know what it meant. Fear suddenly gripped him. Was he out of his depth here? 'No thank you, I prefer cigars.'

'So does my father. Yer may have 'eard of him, Mr Simmons, Mr Mickey Simmons; 'e's a nice guy but 'e don't like to be crossed.'

Mr Harris stepped back slightly. His eyes took in the people who were shopping around them. Were any of them with this young man? He couldn't afford to take a chance.

He'd heard of Mickey Simmons, his reputation definitely went before him, and he had no desires to get mixed up in that circle. 'So *you're* Slips?'

Frank smiled and rested the unlit cigarette between his fingers. 'When we're done 'ere I'm sure 'e'll send yer 'is love – when I tell 'im about yer.'

Joyce leant out of the large dining room window, peering up and down the street to decide when it was best to shake the old piece of soft rag outside. Holding the material in a tight ball, she waited for a grey-haired man to hobble past the house. The light breeze came into the dining room and chased away the overpowering smell of beeswax. Once the man had passed the window she thrust her arm out as far as she could, and shook the rag vigorously, watching the dust particles fly away. She turned back into the room. 'You know, Philip; it's this time of year when we do what we call a spring clean. That means pulling out everything and cleaning in places we don't normally have time for. Would you like to help me?'

Philip nodded.

'Right.' Joyce picked up another smaller rag. 'Would you like to take this cloth and just wipe it over the table. Do it carefully. Then the side tables next to the armchairs and make sure you do the legs as well.'

Philip reached out and took the frayed white material that had seen better days from her.

Joyce watched him vigorously rub it over the tabletop. She smiled, not noticing Arthur stepping into the dining room carrying a handful of papers. 'You've got post.'

'Oh, I didn't hear the postman. He's early this morning.' Joyce started to put some of the porcelain figurines back in the cabinet.

Arthur looked up from the page he was reading. 'Yes, he is.' He paused as he read the letter again. 'I've been thinking about taking Philip with me to the village to see Dot and the rest of her family. What do you think?'

Joyce stopped, clutching a Victorian figurine she was about to place back into the cabinet. 'Oh, I don't know.'

'Well, give it some thought. I was thinking of going in the next day or two and I thought it might be good for Philip, and to give you a break. I get the impression he's never been in the countryside.'

Joyce turned and put the figurine back in the cabinet, adjusting its position slightly.

Arthur watched her. 'You love those figures don't you?'

Joyce tilted her head as she glanced over them. 'I think they're beautiful.'

Arthur smiled. 'I can tell by the way you lovingly dust and handle them. You do know they will all be yours one day, especially when I move away from London and into a smaller house.'

Joyce spun on her heels and stared at Arthur. 'Are you moving then?' Panic ran across her face. 'Are you selling this house? If you are, I need to find somewhere else to live.' Her eyes narrowed. She lowered her head, and slowly dropped down onto the nearest wooden chair. Her mind jumped about as she thought about this new problem that she now faced.

Arthur held his hand up. 'No, no, no, no, I have plans for the future but not yet. Although, even if I was going to move in the foreseeable future you can still live in this house, as you do now. I owe you that much if nothing else.'

Joyce visibly relaxed. 'You don't owe me anything. Life has been hard at times but you've kept a roof over my head. I can't ask for more than that, so if there's something you want to do then please do it. I just need to know so I can make arrangements.' She glanced over at Philip who was vigorously wiping the legs of the table before she looked back at Arthur. 'You know, having Simon's sister at the café has made me think a lot about family. I have a problem with his sister, and I can't pretend to know how to deal with it, but it's made me realise that my hands are tied because she's his family.'

Arthur's eyes narrowed. 'It's always hard working with family, mainly because you have to live with them afterwards.'

Joyce stared at him before once again looking at Philip. 'I shouldn't be selfish about Philip.'

The young lad looked up at the sound of his name.

'It's all right, Philip. Would you like to go with Uncle Arthur to the village where I grew up and see some chickens? Maybe climb some trees, just run free and not worry about the traffic or anything else?'

Philip stared at her wide-eyed before nodding.

Arthur smiled at him before looking back at Joyce. 'What made you decide?'

Joyce shrugged. 'I suppose it's all about his safety. It's not about me, or what I want.'

Arthur frowned. 'It could be good for Philip for lots of reasons but it will let him see another way of life outside of the city, but don't feel he has to go this time because I'll be going again.'

The front door banged shut. Annie and Rose came rushing into the dining room.

Annie beamed at Joyce.

Joyce smiled as they both giggled. 'What are you two looking so happy about? You look like the cat that's got the cream.'

Annie clapped her hands. 'How do you feel about trying to do the food for Kitty's wedding?'

Joyce's eyes widened. 'What? I couldn't do that. I've never done food for a wedding before, let alone getting it to where it's going to be held.'

Rose giggled. 'It could be held at the café. We could put cloths on the tables, some flowers as centrepieces. We might have to move the tables around a little bit, and pretty up the walls in some way, but there's your wedding venue.'

Joyce shook her head. 'You two are mad. How am I going to manage that? It's not like it's my café.'

Annie took a step nearer to Joyce. 'Are you saying that Simon's family would say no?'

'No, I'm not saying that but I've never done a wedding breakfast before. I'm only used to doing everyday meals.'

Rose raised her eyebrows. 'But look how wonderful those meals are. Trust me as someone who eats them every day, they are wonderful.' She looked from Joyce to Annie. 'That's right isn't it?'

Annie nodded. 'You know we've always loved your food. This is a great opportunity for you to have a play and see what you can do.'

Arthur cleared his throat. 'I think the girls are right. We just need to plan it; think through the options.'

Rose clapped her hands together. 'Annie and I can help. You will just need to tell us what to do.'

Annie grinned from ear to ear. 'And that's not all. Rose is going to make her wedding dress.'

Rose paled. 'Well, we don't know that yet. I'm going to come up with some ideas because she doesn't know what she wants.' She turned to Joyce. 'I know it's daunting. I've never made a wedding dress before, so I understand how you're feeling, but sometimes you have to grab the opportunities while they're there and who knows where it could lead to.'

Arthur rested his hand on Joyce's arm. 'It's a good opportunity, Joyce. I will help where I can. I think you need to come up with a menu of some sort, speak to Kitty and find out what she likes, if not what she wants. I'm sure you can make it work, especially with the help from your friends.'

Joyce turned to Rose and Annie. 'When does she get married?'

Annie shrugged. 'I can't remember the exact date but it's going to be at least a few months away. Rose has got a dress to make.'

Philip jumped up and ran towards Joyce. 'I'll help.'

A lump formed in Joyce's throat. She bent down and kneeled in front of him. 'That's so very kind of you, Philip. I might well need your help.'

Philip looked up at her wide-eyed. 'Does that mean I can't go and see the chickens?'

Joyce sucked in her breath. 'No, my sweet, it doesn't. Uncle Arthur can take you, but not this time. I know that when you do go you'll have a wonderful time. It will give me time to think about this wedding breakfast.' She turned to Arthur. 'I think waiting until the next time you go will be best; give you a chance to talk to Dot about it. That's if the offer will still be on then?'

Arthur beamed at her. 'Of course it is. Dot will love Philip.'

Annie frowned. 'You don't think it will be too painful for her, do you?'

Arthur stared at Philip for a moment. 'It might be at first but I think he will give her great pleasure and help ease the pain that I know she still feels.'

Annie nodded. 'Please promise me that you'll bring him back if it gets too much for her?'

Arthur looked towards Annie. 'Of course, I never want to do anything to hurt Dot ever again.'

Annie smiled. 'I know, and I also know that you'd never deliberately hurt her. I don't think you did before; you were just lost.'

Arthur studied the girls in front of him. 'You all changed my life one way or another and I owe you a great deal.'

Joyce shook her head. 'You made the decision. We were just here.'

'Well, one day I hope to pay you back.'

Joyce smiled. 'You're already doing that.'

Mavis stood just outside the ward at St Thomas' Hospital, clutching a telegram tight in her hand. Had she done the right thing in not telling Barbara about it? She was rooted to the spot, not knowing what to do. Fear ran down her spine. Was she right to face this alone? She shook her head. She knew Barbara wouldn't be happy with her, but this was something she had to do on her own. Mavis had to see for herself, without any pretence of being brave for her daughter's sake. No matter how bad it got she had to have a moment with her son. Taking a deep breath, Mavis thrust the telegram back into her jacket pocket. She was luckier than most. At least her son was home and she prayed he felt the same. Stepping forward, Mavis pushed open the double doors of the hospital ward. Wrinkling her nose, she held her breath as the smell of cleaning fluids mingled with urine and blood. Several large windows along each side of the ward let in plenty of light. She glanced at the long wall of beds on either side, each one occupied, wondering which one Simon was in.

'Can I help you?'

Mavis jumped at the sound of the gravelly voice nearby. 'Oh, sorry, you made me jump. I wasn't listening, too busy looking around.'

The nurse intertwined her fingers in front of her. 'No need to apologise. It's probably the flat black shoes we all have to wear. They don't seem to make any noise apart from the odd squeak from time to time.'

Mavis nodded. 'I'm looking for my son, Simon Hitchin. I understand he was brought here last night.'

The nurse pushed a wayward grey curl off her forehead before nodding. 'Come over to the desk and I'll have a look for you.'

Mavis did as she was bid, trying to ignore the sickness

in the pit of her stomach. She concentrated on the ankle-length blue uniform dress and the long white apron the woman was wearing. Her high white collar, long cuffed sleeves and white headdress completed her outfit. There was no mistaking who the nurses were. It was calm on the ward. Men's voices could be heard whispering to each other, respecting the sicker patients among them. Mavis only just avoided a collision with the nurse when she stopped walking. The nurse picked up a wad of crumpled paper from the desk and began to study it, flicking each page over in turn. It rustled as she smoothed it out and turned them over one by one. Mavis clutched the telegram in her pocket, the reminder her son had been sent home injured. He hadn't been gone long but she was so thankful he was home again, no matter how bad he was. She took a deep breath. At least he wasn't dead. She had to remain positive.

The nurse peered over her shoulder before turning round to face her. 'Private Hitchin's injuries are quite serious. It might take him some time to walk unaided again, but the doctor will explain more of that to you when he does his rounds. Your son is obviously feeling low, and as I understand most of his platoon didn't survive the bomb attacks so with that usually comes guilt for the person who is on the road to recovery. In my experience he has difficult times ahead so don't expect joy that he's home because he will be suffering with grief, turmoil and guilt for some time to come. I don't want to make light of this because some never get over it. Of course that's his mental fight. His physical one will be learning to walk with a stick. His appearance seems worse than it is because of all the cuts and bruises, which will heal.'

The nurse paused. 'I'm sorry to be giving you so much information but the more I tell you now than the less of a shock it will be when you see him, and that will be better for him. If I'm honest I'm trying to look after his welfare in the best way I can, so it's important to try and stay positive with him. It's quite common for returning soldiers in this position to feel their life is over, and it isn't.'

Mavis's eyes stung as she fought back her tears. She knew her boy would never be the same again. After taking a deep breath, she exhaled slowly. He was home and that was all that mattered.

'Are you all right to go and see him, or would you rather wait?'

Mavis took another deep breath. 'I'm ready.'

The nurse took a step forward. 'He's in bed six. I'll take you to him.'

Mavis reached out and touched the nurse's arm. 'Thank you … thank you for all the information. It couldn't have been easy for you.'

The nurse looked at Mavis. 'None of this is easy for anybody, but the men are going through much worse!'

Mavis followed the nurse to bed six, keeping her eyes forward. She had no urge to look at other people's suffering, and the groans were enough.

The nurse stopped. She stretched out her arm indicating the appropriate bed before pulling out a wooden chair for Mavis to sit on.

Mavis nodded her thanks and squeezed past her. She sat there for a moment taking in all the red welts and cuts that seemed to cover his arms and part of his face. 'Hello, Simon, it's your ma.'

Simon opened his bloodshot eyes and stared at her, his body still under the bedclothes. He gave a faint smile. 'Am I dreaming, Ma? Is it really you?'

Mavis's chest tightened as she tried desperately to control her emotions. Crying would come later. Her son needed her. 'Yes, Simon, it's me.' She reached out to take his hand but stopped short because she didn't want to hurt him.

Simon closed his eyes again. 'It's good to see you. I wasn't gone long was I?' He opened his eyes again. 'Although it feels like a lifetime.'

Mavis reached out and gently rested her fingertips on the only part of his arm that didn't look sore. 'You're home and that's all that matters.'

Simon scowled at his mother's words. 'No, it isn't, Ma; the number of men and boys dying is unbelievable. Some don't even get out the trenches when we're given the signal to go over. Ma, I've seen things no one should ever witness. I don't know how men that survive months or years of it will ever come back to live a normal life again.' He squeezed his eyes shut but they quickly flew open again.

Mavis didn't know what to say. For the first time in her life she didn't know how to give her son the comfort he so desperately needed. 'Simon, we can only take it one day at a time … maybe an hour at a time. It's small steps. I haven't lived it and can't begin to understand what you're going through. I only have my imagination, but I promise to be with you every step of the way, if you let me.'

Simon gave a slight nod. 'I'm so tired, Ma. Every time I close my eyes I'm back on the front line again. It was terrifying.'

Again Mavis didn't know what to say to bring her son

some peace of mind. 'I know this will sound trite, and don't mean it to, but try to put your mind in a happy place before you close your eyes. When your father died, I prayed for God to help me through that difficult time, to keep my family safe, and to guide me to help others who were grieving.'

Simon raised his eyebrows. 'Having seen what I have I'm not convinced there is a God anymore.'

Mavis nodded. 'I know. It's times like these your faith is tested, but you have to remember this war is manmade. It's greed and power, and that's not the work of the Lord.'

Simon gave her half a smile. 'I know, Ma, I know.' He closed his eyes for a moment. 'Talk to me about anything, anything at all.'

It was Mavis's turn to frown. She had thought his first words would be about Joyce.

Simon slowly opened his eyes. 'Ma, please don't tell anyone I'm here, at least not yet.'

Mavis shook her head. 'Not even Joyce?'

'No one, please.' Simon closed his eyes again.

13

Joyce ran her damp hands down the front of her apron and walked slowly towards the café kitchen door, glad the day was coming to an end. The air was filled with the aroma of coffee and cooked breakfasts. She pushed the door open and peered at the tables. Many of them were unoccupied; laughter suddenly came from three ladies sitting at a table by the window as they each balanced a piece of chocolate cake on their forks. She turned to look where Philip had been sitting and gasped. 'Where's Philip?'

She ran out and looked around café. 'Barbara, where did Philip go? He's not here.'

Barbara frowned as she looked around her. 'I don't know, I didn't see him go. Are you sure he's not in the kitchen?'

Joyce could feel her frustration growing as each second passed. 'Obviously. I've been in the kitchen all day.' Her heart was pounding. The pulse in her temple began to throb. She looked around her in disbelief. Why would he leave? She had thought they were getting somewhere. She thought he was settling in, albeit slowly.

The bell above the café door rang out as it was pushed open.

Joyce spun round with hope in her eyes. 'Oh, Mavis, it's you.'

Mavis smiled. 'You could look happier to see me.' She stood the shopping bags on the floor. 'These bags are heavy today.'

'Have you seen Philip?' Joyce tried to sound calm as she stepped towards Mavis.

Mavis shook her head. 'Maybe he just went for a walk. I expect he'll be back soon. He's a good lad.'

'He's five.' Despite the warmth of the spring sunshine coming through the door Joyce could feel a shiver travel down her spine. 'I need to go. Can you two close up? I'm sorry to leave but I have to go.' She quickly undid her food-stained apron and pulled it over her head.

Mavis stepped forward. The bell chimed as the door closed. She rested her hand on Joyce's arm. 'Of course; don't worry, Barbara and I will close everything up.'

Mavis looked to Barbara, who had remained silent. She nodded.

Joyce followed Mavis's gaze. 'Are you sure he didn't say anything before he left? I don't understand. He's not walked out before.'

Barbara shrugged. 'Maybe he just wanted to get out of here. After all, he's here nearly every day.'

Joyce shook her head. 'He could be anywhere. He's just a child. Anything could have happened to him.' She threw her apron onto a chair and sped towards the door. She had no idea where to start looking but couldn't just stand around waiting to see if he came back or not. For once she didn't hear the bell ring out as the door slammed shut behind her.

Joyce just managed to step back at the last minute, at the same time as a lady moved aside. She brushed the arm of the woman as she rushed past the café, grateful she hadn't bumped into her and knocked her over as she rushed out the door. 'I'm sorry.'

The lady glared at her and carried on pacing along the pavement. The cars sputtered along the road, coughing out clouds of grey smoke as they went, drowning out the thud of her curved heels. She gasped. What if he'd been run over? The hospital wouldn't know who to contact. Joyce bit down on her lip as she looked up and down the road, staring at the throng of people, as she tried to decide which way to go. Where would Philip go? She had to stay calm; otherwise she would never find him. In truth she didn't know where to begin. Would he try to visit her grandmother in hospital? Would he try to go back to where he lived with his mother? Joyce sighed. Where to start? She didn't know where he used to live and had no one who could advise her. Again, she stared up and down the road; maybe she'd go home first. Perhaps that's where he'd gone. She turned and marched along Shaftesbury Avenue as quickly as she could, weaving in and out between people.

'Joyce, Joyce, wait.'

The sound of her name being called finally penetrated Joyce's thoughts; she turned around to see Rose half running towards her.

'You're in a hurry. I've been calling you for ages.'

'I'm so sorry, Rose. Philip has left the café on his own and I don't know where he's gone.'

Rose took in Joyce's pale features, wondering what she could offer to do to help. 'Where are you going to look first?'

Joyce shook her head. Tears gathered in her eyes. 'I don't know where to start. I thought I might go home first and see if he got bored and just went home to see Arthur.'

Rose nodded. 'That's a good place to start. Well, at least it's as good a place as any. I'll come with you and if he's not there then we'll try and figure out where to start looking.'

'Thank you, Rose, I don't know where he's gone and I'm so frightened that something's happened to him. I'll never forgive myself if that's the case. I shouldn't have let him stay in the café all day. It's not a place for a five-year-old. He was probably so bored.'

Rose grabbed Joyce's arm and pulled her round to face her. 'Just stop, you stop that right now. This lad has been thrust upon you and you never really had a choice in the matter, yet you've managed to cope the best you can. I will not have you blaming yourself for this.' Rose let go of her arm. 'Come on, let's get home, and then we'll decide what we're going to do next. Arthur might be able to help.'

Joyce sighed. Her resignation showed in her hunched shoulders and her pale tear-stained face. 'I don't know what else we can do.'

They both sped towards Great Earl Street to see if Arthur had seen Philip. Joyce kept peering all around her, stopping every so often when she heard or saw a child. 'I can't believe he's done this. How could he do this to me? Why didn't he just tell me where he was going? Does he think I would've said no?'

Rose stopped in front of her. 'You know you would've done. You would've said something like: "Wait until I've finished and we'll go together", or "We'll do it tomorrow". Whatever it is he wanted you would've told him to wait because you were at work. That's not wrong, Joyce, but he clearly didn't want to wait.'

Joyce shook her head. 'I'm trying so hard. I wouldn't mind but I don't actually know what I'm doing. I just want him to be happy.' She turned and looked at Rose. 'Do you think he's unhappy?'

Rose shrugged. 'I don't know what goes on in his head, but I'm sure he would rather be with his mother and father than with a group of strangers.'

Joyce nodded. She walked forward with Rose and a sigh escaped. 'Yes, I'm sure you're right. That's what I would want too.'

The girls carried on their journey home, not stopping to talk to anybody but keeping their eyes peeled in case they saw Philip.

Joyce pulled the key through the letterbox, with the usual rattling and banging but no one noticed. She turned the key in the lock and pushed the door open. 'Philip, are you here?' Only silence greeted her and the fragrant smell of the hyacinth by the front door. She ran in and peered in all the rooms. 'Even Arthur isn't home. I wonder if they're together.' Fear gripped Joyce. Her chest tightened as her heart pummelled against her ribcage. Her eyes widened as she turned to look at Rose. 'What are we going to do?' Her voice climbed to a screech as she sobbed. 'What am I going to do? I don't know where to start looking. He could be anywhere.'

Rose grabbed Joyce's arm. 'We need to stop panicking and think. Is he likely to go to the hospital to see your grandma? Does he know your grandma is still alive? Is his mother still alive and if so does he know where she lives?'

Tears rolled down Joyce's face. She threw her arms up in frustration. 'Don't keep asking me all these questions. I don't know the answers to them. I don't know anything about him, except his mother was a friend of the family and she died, and then my grandmother took him in.'

Rose shook her head. 'We need to stay calm and think it through; otherwise we'll never find him.'

Joyce didn't know how she was going to be able to think straight about where he could be when she had no information at all.

Rose looked thoughtful for a moment. 'Did you empty the chest that came with Philip?'

Joyce bit down on her lip in a bid to stop it from trembling. She shook her head. 'No, I haven't got round to it. I've opened it and expected to see clothes and things for Philip, but it appears to be only books and paperwork. He's managed with the case of clothes he came with.'

Rose's face lit up. 'Well, maybe it's time you looked in the chest. It could give you some answers to where he's gone. Of course, he might be at the park. It doesn't necessarily follow he's gone anywhere important. He's a child, remember, and he's probably bored. Remember what we were like as children.'

Joyce raised her eyebrows. 'That's what bothers me. I remember exactly what we were like as children. We did get up to no good sometimes.'

Rose gave a small smile at the memories. 'Well, we have to start somewhere so why don't we look in the chest and then maybe we could split up after that?'

Joyce wrung her hands together. 'No, I'm scared. He's

out by himself and anything could be happening to him. I think we should be out looking for him.'

'But where do we start?'

Joyce sank down onto the bottom step of the stairs in the hallway. She rested her head in her hands. 'I don't know, I truly don't know but I can't just sit here and do nothing.'

The creaking of the front door opening made Joyce look up. 'Uncle Arthur, thank goodness you're here.'

Arthur walked through the front door, pushing it shut with his foot as he put down his heavy shopping bags. 'What on earth's the matter?'

Joyce frowned. 'I take it Philip isn't with you? I don't know where he is. He left the café without anyone noticing. I don't know where to start looking for him.' Tears rolled down her face. 'I'm such a terrible person. I shouldn't have left him sitting in the café all day. It's not right for anybody, let alone a child. It's obvious he was going to get bored.'

'Slow down.' Arthur looked to Rose to get an understanding of what had happened.

Rose shook her head. 'We haven't looked anywhere yet, mainly because we don't know where to look. He didn't say anything about places he used to like to visit to you did he?'

Arthur shrugged. 'Like what? He might have just gone to the park or something.'

Joyce stood up; anger filled her face and her hands clenched in fists by her sides. 'Yes, and he could easily have been run over or be hurt somewhere and I'm sitting here not knowing what to do. I can't do this. I need to do something; I'm going to the hospital.'

Arthur ran his hands through his hair. 'Right, perhaps I'll go to the park and Rose can look through the chest.'

Joyce frowned. 'I'm not sure what you'll find in the chest but it's worth a look. If you have any news I will be at the hospital with Grandma in the hope that Philip turns up there.'

Rose looked at Joyce's pale features. 'We'll find him; we just need to stay calm and think about things properly. Do you think he'd go to the theatre? Because he could be with Annie.'

Joyce rubbed her hands over her face. 'Well, we can't be everywhere; at least if he's with Annie he's safe.'

Rose's eyes widened. 'Perhaps we should let the police know.'

Arthur shook his head. 'They won't do anything yet.'

Joyce wrung her hands together. Her face pinched with tension. 'Has he said anything about where he lived before he moved in with my grandma? He may have gone back there.' She suddenly let out a scream while her eyes looked heavenward. 'I don't know where to look.'

Rose had never seen her friend like this before; she had always coped with whatever life had thrown at her. Rushing over, she put her arm around her shoulder and let her head rest on her shoulders. 'It's going to be all right, Joyce. We will find him, I promise.' She gave her friend an extra squeeze. 'Joyce, we're in this together and we will find him. We've just got to start looking and start thinking about where he might go. Come and help me look in the chest.'

Joyce gulped and gasped for air. 'How can you say that? I feel like I've let him down. I'm not fit to look after him. I don't know what to do.'

Rose stepped away. 'You could help me.' She walked into the dining room and stood in front of the chest that had been sat in the corner of the room since Philip had arrived. She stooped down and unbuckled the worn black leather strap that was wrapped around the chest. Her fingers pressed hard on the cold metal locks until there was a clunk and they sprung open. Gingerly, she lifted the heavy lid. The noise of the front door slamming shut made Rose jump. She peered behind her, expecting someone to walk in but no one did. She stood up and went out into the hall. Her footsteps clipped on the tiled floor, resonating in the hall. There was no sign of Arthur, and Joyce hadn't moved. She was still sitting at the bottom of the stairs sobbing. 'Where did Arthur go?'

Joyce shook her head. 'He's gone to the hospital, just in case that's where Philip is. He said I wasn't in a fit state to go anywhere by myself, and insisted I stayed with you.'

Rose stood up and put her arm under Joyce's and pulled her up. 'Come on, we're not going to find him sitting here.'

Joyce followed Rose into the dining room and stared at the open chest. Joyce wrinkled her nose at the musty smell. 'What is all this stuff?'

Rose looked from Joyce to the brown leather chest. 'I don't know. I haven't looked but it seems to be, as you said, mainly paperwork and books.'

Joyce shook her head. 'That's not going to help us find Philip ... unless there's any clues in there of where he used to live?'

Rose looked at her friend and gave a small smile. 'That's it, Joyce, we got to think logically and then we'll find him.' They both bent down as one and started to look at the paperwork.

Joyce grabbed a wad of papers out of the chest. She

flicked the edges, concentrating as she peered down at the pages, trying to get a quick understanding of what was on each of them. There was no time to read the detail. She had no idea what she was looking for but kept throwing things out of the chest and on to the floor. Some of the papers were thin and fragile when she picked them up. They also held a yellow tinge befitting their age. There appeared to be many books. Some were children's while others were recipe books. She opened one and saw her mother's name carefully written inside. Joyce stopped and took a breath. These had belonged to her mother. The temptation was to examine them but this wasn't the time for a trip down memory lane. She snapped the book shut and put it to one side on the floor. 'Rose, can you see anything that relates to Philip and where he might have gone?' Joyce's voice rose in pitch as her fear took hold again. 'There's just so much paperwork here. I don't even know what most of it is, and we don't have time to sit and read everything.'

Rose kept picking up bits and pieces, glancing at them but everything seem to relate to Joyce and her mother. 'I haven't seen anything yet, but I must admit I'm not reading everything.'

Joyce shook her head. 'I think we're wasting valuable time. Why don't we walk up to the market and see if Peter has seen him go past?'

Rose raised her eyebrows. 'It's better than doing nothing I suppose, but it does feel like we're just going round and round in circles.'

Joyce got to her feet. 'I know but what else can we do? I can't just sit here and do nothing, and this feels like it's a waste of time.' She stepped away from the chest. 'I think I've become more attached to him than I realised. If anything happened to him I'll never forgive myself.'

Rose stood up and put her hand on the small of Joyce's back. 'I know, but we must have faith. He's going to be all right, I know he is. Come on let's go out and have a look. He's quite streetwise.'

Joyce glared at her friend. 'I don't know why you would say that, when he's so young.' Her mind immediately went to the brother and sister she'd given the silver sixpences to. Was he as streetwise as them? Would he know how to survive, and if he did, how did he know? There were so many questions running around her head. It suddenly dawned on her she knew nothing about Philip's life before he came to live with them. She hadn't wanted to push him or upset him, but when he was found she would correct that, tears or no tears.

Rose hesitated for a moment. 'I thought ... I just thought...'

Joyce opened her mouth to say something then closed it again before shaking her head.

Rose frowned. 'I don't know what I thought, but it's best we don't think about it.'

Joyce shuddered. 'Why don't we go to my grandmother's house and see if he's gone there? At least there's some sense to that rather than wandering aimlessly.'

'That's a good idea. Lead the way.' Rose grabbed her handbag. 'Come on then. I'm not leaving you on your own, and I'm sure next door will take Philip in if he comes home.'

Joyce followed Rose out into the hall. 'If we don't have any joy there we could go to the solicitor's. Jeremiah King may know more about Philip than he's told me; at least that might give us some direction.'

Rose turned and studied Joyce. 'See, you're thinking now rather than panicking, so now I know we'll definitely find him.' Rose pulled open the front door and stepped into the sunshine. 'Maybe Philip's gone to Hyde Park to paddle in the Serpentine.'

Joyce gasped. 'Oh my goodness I hadn't thought of that. Would he know the way to Hyde Park?' She shook her head. 'This is an impossible task. Where do we start looking? I wouldn't mind but I don't even know what time he left the café. Has he been gone half an hour, an hour, or two hours? I'm such a bad person. When I find him I'm never going to let him out of my sight ever again.'

Rose put her arm through Joyce's. 'You're not a bad person; you're just juggling so many things. If Simon was here you wouldn't be caught up in the café as much as you are. If you let Arthur and us help then you wouldn't feel so bad and heavy with responsibility. You've got to start letting us in and understand you're not on your own. I know you have no family but you should look on us as your family because we certainly look at you that way.'

Joyce could feel her eyes welling up again. She tried to focus on the people around her. 'I know, I know, you are both very good friends. I suppose I just don't like to put on people.'

A child called out followed by laughter. Rose spun round on her heels to look behind her but it wasn't Philip. 'You're not putting on us if we're offering to help. We offer because we want to.'

'I just hope we find him, Rose. I feel so bad. He's been through so much already and none of it is his fault.'

Rose squeezed her friend's arm. 'It's not your fault either,

Joyce; it's no one's fault. We need to find out what sort of life the little lad has had. He comes across as being very "I can manage on my own and I don't need anyone", but everybody needs somebody and I think that just tells you he's had quite a hard life.'

Arthur wiped the beads of perspiration from his brow with his white handkerchief before they started to trickle down his face. He had almost run to the hospital while trying to keep his eyes peeled for Philip, but now his lungs were on fire and he was ready to collapse in a heap somewhere. He frowned as he stood gazing at the many people coming and going in the foyer of St Thomas' Hospital. The overpowering smell of disinfectant wafted up his nose, along with the distinctive smell of carbolic soap, both hitting the back of his throat at the same time. He coughed in an attempt to clear it away. He looked around him, wondering where Mrs Taylor's room was. His pulse was racing, and he wondered why he had thought it was a good idea to go to the hospital in the first place. Memories of William rushed into his mind; belatedly he realised it shouldn't have been him who came to the hospital.

A boy caught Arthur's attention. Thinking it was Philip, he stepped forward just as the lad turned round to face him. Arthur stopped. It wasn't him. He stood still, looking around the foyer. He had to find Philip. Panic grabbed him. His chest tightened. He wasn't going to lose another child.

He rubbed his hand over his seven o'clock shadow; the bristles were sharp against his fingers. He wished now he hadn't been so lazy that morning and shaved. Would Philip really come here? Would this really be his first place of calling? Arthur walked across the tiled flooring; his soft soles couldn't be heard over the chatter of everyone he passed. He stopped at a desk. 'I'm sorry to bother you but I was wondering if you could tell me where I could find Mrs Taylor.'

'Do you know what she's in for?'

Arthur closed his eyes for a moment before shaking his head. 'All I know is she's in a coma and not likely to come out of it.'

The nurse gave him a pitiful look. 'If you go upstairs someone will point you in the right direction. Take care.'

Arthur strode towards the stairs and then proceeded to climb them two at a time. He pulled open one of the double doors that were in front of him, almost colliding with a young nurse. 'Sorry, I wasn't looking where I was going.'

The nurse smiled as she looked up at him. 'Don't worry, there's no damage done.'

Arthur frowned. 'I'm looking for Mrs Taylor's room. I don't suppose you know where it is by any chance?'

The nurse gave a slight smile. 'It's just along the corridor, the third door on the left.' She paused. 'You do know she's not awake don't you?'

Arthur frowned. 'Yes, I do, but I'm looking for someone and they might be visiting her.'

The nurse nodded. 'There is someone in with her. If you're quick you might just catch them.'

Arthur breathed a sigh of relief; he just wanted to get out of there as quickly as possible. He reached out and touched her arm. 'Thank you, thank you so much.'

Before she could answer he was striding along the corridor to the third door on the left. He stared through the open doorway; it took a while for it to register what he was looking at. He blinked hard. Was it really him? That couldn't be right surely.

A man sat near the bed, his arm outstretched as he held the old lady's hand. He looked up and gasped.

Arthur shook his head in disbelief. 'Tell me I'm not seeing things.'

Ted released his mother's hand as though it was burning his fingers. He jumped up from the chair, almost knocking it over in his haste. Without hesitation, he rushed past Arthur shouldering him against the doorjamb.

Arthur held on to his arm as he slumped against the doorframe, sucking in his breath as the pain took hold.

The man didn't look back. He ran along the corridor to the double doors and the stairs.

Rubbing his arm as he went, Arthur chased the man he thought was his friend. 'Ted, wait, you can't do this. Everybody thinks you're dead.'

A shrill voice called out, 'No running please; this is a hospital.'

Arthur glanced over his shoulder. 'I'm sorry, but I must catch that man.' He looked back to see the double doors slamming shut. He was only seconds behind Ted, but it was imperative he caught him. 'Ted, Ted wait. You can't keep running away.' Arthur stopped gasping for breath. He looked up to see Ted looking back at him, also looking worse for wear. Arthur's lungs were burning but he had to keep going. He weaved in and out between the people in the foyer and ran through the open door of the hospital to find Ted leaning up against the wall gasping for breath.

Ted peered at Arthur before bending over to catch his breath. 'I'm clearly not as young as I used to be.' He pulled himself upright and rested his hands on his hips. 'What are you doing here, Arthur? Why did you come here to see my mother?'

Arthur shook his head. 'I can't believe it, I can't believe I'm looking at you.' He shook his head again, gasping for breath. 'It should be me asking you what you're doing here. You're supposed to be dead!' He kept his eyes firmly fixed on Ted. 'I just can't believe I'm looking at you.'

Ted wiped his damp hands down his trousers; the beads of sweat were forming on his forehead. This wasn't how it was meant to be. 'Arthur, I can explain.'

'Can you? Can you really? Do you have any idea how much your daughter has been grieving for you? Wasn't it enough that she lost her mother? And yet you thought it was all right for her to think you were dead. You thought it was all right to leave her with me, a drunk, at a time when I wasn't capable of looking after anyone, not even myself because of my own grief. Have you no remorse? Did you not think you should come and see her?' Arthur shook his head. 'Joyce isn't going to believe this.' He rubbed his hands over his face. 'I'm not going to be the one to tell her. She's only just found out I'm not her uncle. You've got to come home with me and let her know straight away. She's already in a state because we can't find Philip.'

Ted shook his head. 'Philip? What's happened to Philip? Is he living with you?'

Arthur's eyes widened as he stepped nearer to him, his hands clenched in fists by his sides. He leant in, cutting the air with his hands. 'How and what do you know about Philip, and why are you worrying about him, when you should be thinking about your daughter?'

Ted said nothing. He lowered his eyes, unable to look at Arthur. 'I've made a right old mess of things haven't I?'

14

Drops of rain hit Philip's arms and legs as he sat on the edge of the pavement. His grey woollen socks sat down by his ankles. He wiped his wet arm down the front of his navy blue shirt. The raised slurred voices of men discussing the war could be heard as they came out of the public house over the road. People stared at him as they walked past. He looked too clean and well turned out to be living on the streets begging. Philip looked around him wishing he hadn't left the café. Now he didn't know where he was or how to get home. Should he ask someone? His grandma always told him not to talk to strangers, and if he was lost to find a policeman. Philip looked up and down the road but he couldn't see a policeman so what should he do? A man stopped just in front of him.

'You all right, young man?'

Philip squinted up at him. His eyes suddenly widened with fear. 'Yes, thank you.'

'Are you waiting for someone?'

Philip nodded.

The man stared at him for a moment before walking on. He stopped and looked over his shoulder before walking away.

Philip started crying, his tears free-falling down his face. Once he started he couldn't stop.

'What did that man say to you?'

Philip looked up and saw Frank looking back at him. He gave a little watery smile as relief coursed through him. 'Frank, I'm lost. I don't know how to get back to the café or home.'

Frank shook his head. 'Is that a reason for crying like a baby?'

Philip wiped his eyes with his hands before squinting up at the man who had spent hours chatting to him in the café. 'I can't help it. I'm scared.'

Frank scowled and sat down on the pavement next to him. 'Don't try and get clever with me. It's about time yer grew up. My pa would never 'ave allowed me to sit on the pavement crying like a baby. That would 'ave got me a good 'iding from him; 'e probably would 'ave took his belt to me.' He gingerly put one hand over the other, covering up his red knuckles before looking at Philip. 'I bet you've never 'ad the belt took to yer, 'ave yer?'

'No.' Philip's bottom lip quivered.

Frank leant in nearer to Philip. 'You've got to learn to look after yourself; if I 'ave learnt nothing in my life I've learnt that yer can't trust no one. Everyone wants something. Do yer understand?'

Philip clenched his hands across his knees. He could smell smoke on Frank's suit and his breath, which mingled with the strong smell of ale. It was a smell he recognised but he didn't know where from. 'Is your pa mean to you?'

'Don't ask questions. Do yer understand?' Frank grabbed Philip's arm. 'Yer just a skinny runt ain't yer?'

Fear trampled across Philip's face as he stared at Frank.

Frank sighed. The boy looked terrified as he bit down on his lip. 'Don't look so scared. I draw a line at 'urting kids.' He forced a smile. 'Yer know that's why yer 'ave to look tough, even if yer not. It's all about 'ow people see yer. My pa taught me from an early age to look after myself. He used to make me 'ave fights with uffa kids in front of him and if I lost I got a good 'iding from 'im.' He paused. 'I got scars to prove it, but no one picks on me now, quite the opposite. You need to toughen up; it's an 'ard life. Yer don't get any prizes for being nice or coming second. Yer got to be the best yer can, yer understand?'

Philip nodded. 'My grandma said I should always be polite, always say please and thank you.'

'Yeah well, that's grandmas for yer. I bet yer pa had something different to say about it.'

Philip shrugged. Frank scared him but at least he wasn't on his own now.

'What did he say?'

Philip gripped his knees. 'My pa used to tell me it was a tough world but I had to work hard at school and learn to talk properly. That way I could get a good job; you know, be in charge of the country or something. He said no one would pick on me then because I'd have money, and that's what makes the world go round. That's why my mum used to entertain men, to get money.'

'How do yer know that?'

Philip stared straight ahead. 'I heard someone talking about it once.'

Frank shook his head. 'Anyway, yer won't get streetwise by going to school.' He looked around. A young boy was holding on to a little girl's hand like his life depended upon it. Their clothes were dirty and torn. The lad glanced over; he stared for a moment before taking a step towards the road. Frank watched them but the lad appeared to change his mind. They turned around and walked back the way they'd come from. There were so many old people wandering around, ladies dragging their young children along the road while trying to carry shopping as well. It was a mugger's paradise with all the men away fighting. But there were some things even he wouldn't do and that's where he drew the line. No one should pick on old ladies. That just wasn't right.

Joyce frowned as she looked around her. Her body was tense and her hands were clenched as one held on to the other. 'I don't think we're ever going to find him. Anything could have happened to him.' She could feel the tears pricking at her eyes and blinked quickly.

Rose peered at the many people who were still shopping. Some were milling around chatting. 'I don't know what to say, Joyce. All we can do is keep looking and if we can't find him we'll have to talk to the police.'

Joyce's throat tightened. The pain ran down her neck. 'He could be here but he's so small we wouldn't be able to see him.'

'I know. That's why we have to keep moving.'

A tear dropped on to Joyce's cheek. 'But what happens if we're going the wrong way? He could be out here on his own in the dark.' She immediately thought of the children she had given money to and shook her head. At least they had each other. Philip was on his own, unless of course someone had taken him. A chill ran down her spine as the thought ran riot in her head.

Rose watched as the colour drained from Joyce's face. 'Maybe we should split up but I'm not keen to leave you on your own.'

Joyce pushed down hard on a scream that was rising inside her. 'I don't matter. I have to do whatever I can to find Philip, and if that means walking the streets all night then that's what I'll do.'

Stepping quickly to be closer to Joyce, Rose rested her hand on her friend's arm. 'It won't come to that; we're going to find him. Come on, let's keep going.'

Joyce nodded and sighed as she turned to look around her and yelled. 'Philip.' She waited before yelling his name again. 'Philip.' She raised her head heavenward. *'Please God, if you can hear me, please forgive me for not giving Philip the attention he deserves. I was trying to do the right thing for everyone but none of that matters now. Please, I'm begging you let him be safe. He's just a child. Let us find him safe and sound.'*

Rose watched on through watery eyes. 'He will answer your prayers; you just got to have faith. Come on, let's keep looking.'

Joyce nodded, keeping her eyes fixed on the crowds. She stepped forward slowly, weaving between them.

'Miss, miss, 'ang on.'

Joyce spun round on her heels. Her eyes darted from side to side but she couldn't see Philip. She turned back to Rose. 'Did you hear someone calling out?'

Rose nodded. 'Yes, it was a child's voice but the boy may not have been calling us. He could have been calling anybody.'

Joyce lowered her head. 'I know, I just thought I recognised it.' She felt a tug on the back of her coat and spun round again.

'Miss, are you looking for yer boy? At least I fink it's yer boy. I've only seen 'im around the market wiv yer a couple of times.'

Joyce stooped down in front of the boy she had given money to a few months ago. His hand was clasped round his sister's. 'Have you seen him? He's lost.'

The boy's eyes widened. 'Yeah, in Shaftesbury Avenue. He was wiv a man and none of them looked 'appy but the boy looked scared. I nearly went over to them but I 'ave to fink about me sister, yer know.'

Joyce nodded. 'I understand, thank you for letting me know.' She opened her purse and searched for two silver coins. 'Here, take this and get something to eat.' She stood up. 'Rose, I think we should head back to Shaftesbury Avenue.' She glanced back at the children. 'I can't thank you enough.'

The little girl stepped out from behind her brother. She tucked her hair behind her ear. 'That's all right, miss, you've always been kind to us and we don't want anyfink to 'appen to 'im.'

Frank sighed. 'I suppose you're part right. You should work 'ard at school because then no one can mug yer off; yer know, tell lies about stuff.' He looked down at Philip. 'Yer should always look after yer family, and it's not always blood either. Family's important even in my line of work.' He stood up. 'Come on, let's get yer 'ome. I expect Joyce is going out of 'er mind wiv worry.'

Philip stood up and brushed his hands down the back of his short trousers. 'Do you think she'll be missing me?'

Frank stared down at the boy. 'Why wouldn't she?'

Philip shrugged. 'I'm nothing to her. I'm not family.'

'As I said, family's not just about blood; it's what's in yer 'eart that counts.' Frank stared straight ahead as he stepped forward. 'Where was yer going anyway, I mean when yer left the café?'

Again Philip shrugged, running to keep up. 'I wanted to go and see my grandma but then I got scared.'

Frank chuckled. He thrust his hand inside his trouser pocket and pulled out his packet of cigarettes. 'Well, you've walked quite a way down Shaftesbury Avenue.' Frank pointed in the distance. 'See that big shop sign? Well that's Foyle's Bookshop. We don't want to go down there cos that's Charing Cross Road. We're going to go down Great Earl Street and then yer nearly 'ome.' He opened the packet and pulled one out ready to smoke.

Philip smiled. 'So I didn't have that far to go then?'

Frank smiled down at him, ruffling his hair. 'No, yer were nearly home.' He was quiet while he pulled a match along the side of a matchbox. The rasping sound was repeated when it didn't light. He held it up to the end of the cigarette. Smoke swirled up into the sky.

'Philip? Oh, thank goodness you're safe.' Joyce ran forward. 'I've been going out of my mind with worry.' She wrapped her arms around him before pulling back and having a good look at him. 'Where have you been?'

Rose watched on with relief.

Philip's eyes became watery. Frank nudged him so he blinked quickly. 'I didn't mean to get lost. I just wanted to see Grandma.'

Joyce shook her head; she stooped down in front of him. 'I know and I'm sorry. I will take you but having to work means I can't just drop everything at a moment's notice. I will take you, I promise.' Joyce stood up, beaming at Frank.

Rose wandered over and threw her arms around Philip. 'Thank goodness you're safe. We didn't know where to start looking.'

Frank drew on his cigarette. 'I found him sitting on the pavement.' He dropped his voice to a whisper.

Joyce coughed as the cigarette smoke hit the back of her throat. 'I can't thank you enough. I don't know what I would've done if we hadn't found him. Thank you.'

Frank smiled. 'Well, I'll be on my way and let yer get on wiv yer family reunion.'

Joyce looked at Philip. 'Say thank you to Frank for looking after you.'

Philip looked down at his feet. He scuffed his shoe on the pavement. 'Thank you, Frank.'

Frank nodded before turning to walk away from them.

They stood there for a moment watching him.

Rose frowned. 'He's certainly turning into your knight in shining armour; maybe he likes you more than you think.'

Joyce scowled. 'Of course not.'

Philip peered up at Joyce. 'I'm glad he was bringing me back. I was scared.'

Joyce stooped down in front of the little boy who had crept into her heart. 'I know, I was scared too; you shouldn't leave without telling someone where you're going.'

Philip scowled. 'Frank said it was time I grew up.'

Joyce gasped. 'Why would he say that?'

Philip shrugged. 'He was talking about his father and how he made him tough.' He turned to look at Rose. 'Still, I was glad he sat with me.'

Joyce smiled, while ruffling his hair. 'You must be hungry. I'll make you some food.'

Rose turned to Joyce. 'I'm sorry but I've got to get back to the theatre to speak to Kitty about her wedding dress. I wouldn't have gone if Philip was still missing but—'

'Don't worry, please go. We're all right.' Joyce squeezed Rose's arm. 'Thank you so much for being with me. I don't know what I would have done if I'd been on my own, and don't say panic because I did that anyway.'

Rose chuckled. 'Well, thankfully he's unharmed so all's well that ends well, but I'll only go if you're sure you'll be all right?'

'Of course. Go on, I don't want you to be late. We'll be fine; thanks again.'

Rose took in great gulps of air, trying to level her breathing before going to see Kitty. The rain had held off. It had been threatening for the last couple of hours, and with no umbrella she would have got soaked. Looking for Philip had made it quite a rush not to be late for her appointment. She studied the scrawling lines on the page of her sketchpad. The wedding dress had simple lines but maybe it was too simple for Kitty. She closed the pad before picking it up. The chair scraped across the floor of the sewing room as she pushed it back to stand up.

Rose marched towards Kitty's dressing room and knocked lightly on the door.

'Come in,' Kitty's musical voice rang out.

Rose turned the handle and stepped into the room. 'Good evening, Kitty, I've come to show you some of my ideas for your wedding dress.' Rose could hear the nerves in her own voice.

Kitty put down her lipstick. It was her trademark crimson red, which added a distinct colour to her face. She clapped her hands together. 'Oh good, come in, come in and show me. This is exciting.'

Rose could feel the heat rising in her face. Her hands trembled as she clutched her pad. 'I hope you like them, but remember I'm not an artist so they're pretty rough sketches. Feel free to be honest about them please.' She had never shown them to anyone before; only Annie had come close to seeing them. There were times when Rose knew Annie was itching to know what was in her book. She guessed her friend thought it was a diary and didn't want to pry.

Kitty gave a high-pitched laugh. 'Stop worrying, just show them to me.' Rose closed the door behind her and walked over to Kitty. She noticed her dressing table was littered with make-up, cotton wool and tissues.

Rose looked around but there was no sign of Annie and she fleetingly wondered where she was.

'Pull up a chair and we can discuss the options.' Kitty pushed some of the many pots and make-up brushes to one side to make room for the book on her dressing table. She looked around the room. 'On second thoughts we'll sit on the chaise longue.'

Rose nodded and perched on the edge of the sofa. She

flipped open the pad, turning several pages before she got to her sketches of Kitty's wedding dress. 'I wasn't sure what you wanted; obviously there is the ballroom style or there is a more slim and slender figure-hugging type of dress. And then there's everything in between. It just depends on what you would prefer.'

Kitty sat next to her. 'Can I please have a look?'

Rose took in the orange blossom of Kitty's perfume. She'd noticed before the actress always smelled divine. 'Of course, I could just leave the sketch pad with you if you'd prefer.'

Kitty glanced at Rose. 'Well, if you're in a hurry I don't mind looking and taking my time, but I'd rather we look together if that's all right with you?'

Rose smiled at the forthright actress. 'Of course, it might help if we discussed each one in turn.' She watched silently as Kitty studied each drawing. Her stomach churned as she waited for a response from the actress.

Kitty turned each page slowly, stopping and studying each one but not commenting on any of them.

The rustling of the pages seemed to scream out in the silence. Rose gripped her hands together on her lap; she looked down to see the white of her knuckles peering through the skin. Her mouth was dry; she tried to lick her lips but her tongue stuck fast to the roof of her mouth. She took a deep breath and released her hands, flexing her fingers wide. 'Of course, if you don't like any of them I can go back to the drawing board. They are just ideas.'

Kitty didn't say a word. She turned the pages backwards and forwards as she studied and compared each of them.

Rose fiddled with the ends of her hair, twirling it round

her fingers. 'You look like you're searching for something. Is there something missing that you'd like?'

Kitty's eyes widened as she looked across at Rose. 'You have a real talent. How have you kept it hidden for so long?'

Rose blushed. 'I don't know that I have. You have to remember these are just drawings. I haven't made any of them yet.'

Kitty shook her head. 'No, but you have designed them and they are fabulous.'

Rose decided to try to stay focused on the wedding dress; she didn't want to discuss her drawings with anybody. 'Do you like any of them or do you want me to do something else? Of course you might choose to go and buy one from the shop or get someone else to make you one. I won't be offended.'

Kitty put her arms around Rose. 'Most definitely not. I love these designs. My biggest problem is choosing which one.'

'Well, you don't have to decide right now but, obviously, we need to allow time for me to make it.'

Kitty looked back down at the pad. 'I do like the shape of this one. It's quite simple but I think I'd like some lace on it.'

Rose peered down at her drawings. 'You can have lace or beading or small buttons. I would just have to buy them. Do you want lace sleeves?'

Kitty tapped her fingers across her pursed lips. 'Maybe trumpet sleeves with a tight bodice and a lace overlay on the skirt and some shiny beads or something on the bodice. What do you think?'

Rose looked thoughtful. 'What if I draw another picture for you to look at and then we can see what you think?'

'That sounds like a good idea. You need to let me know how much money you need for it all because I don't expect you to pay for the materials.'

The door burst open and Annie came rushing in. 'Oh, I'm sorry, did you think I wasn't coming back? I don't know what's going on but I had to go to several shops just to get some milk.'

Rose looked up at Annie. 'I'll leave you two to get on.'

Kitty reached out and placed her hand on Rose's arm to stay. 'We were just discussing my wedding dress.'

Annie beamed. 'How exciting. Have you decided on one then?'

Kitty giggled. 'Rose has a fantastic eye for design; I had no idea. She's certainly been hiding her talent away from us all.'

Annie smiled; she hadn't heard Kitty sound so young and girly before. 'Really, Rose, you have been a dark horse for all these years.' She looked down at the book Kitty was holding, recognising it as the one she had assumed was a diary Rose wrote in every day. 'All the times I saw you with that pad I never realised you were sketching in it. Why did you never share it with us?'

Rose shrugged. 'I suppose I just thought nothing would ever come of it and felt silly thinking it might.'

Annie frowned. 'And yet you let me go on and on about wanting to be on the stage without saying anything about your own dreams, even when I asked you.'

Rose shook her head. 'I've told you before the Spencers don't have dreams; they just get on with the things they have to do.'

Kitty's gaze flitted between the two girls. 'Well, I can tell you, Rose, you have a real talent and it shouldn't be kept hidden. I definitely want you to make my wedding dress and, looking at these sketches, I'd say some other dresses as well.'

Fear suddenly appeared on Rose's face. 'I may be good at designing but it doesn't mean I'm good at making.'

Kitty shook head. 'I'm not listening to that. You're a good seamstress and you proved that the very first day I met you. I have faith that you will do a good job.'

Annie nodded. 'You are a good seamstress, Rose, and I'll not hear anything bad said about you or your work.'

The room fell silent.

Annie cleared her throat. 'Anyway, there seems to be a shortage of food. I was talking to a lady who was queuing at the butcher's and she was wearing her larder key around her neck to stop the children from helping themselves to the food.'

Kitty's eyes widened. 'Really, I've not noticed that before. Is that just today?'

Annie shook her head. 'I don't think so. From what I can gather some shops are running short of just about everything. We might have to allow for queuing time from now on or go without.'

Joyce ran downstairs, each step creaking in her wake. She had tucked Philip up in bed, and read him a few pages of *The Wind in the Willows*, as she did every night. He laughed at the funny voices she put on for Mole, Ratty, Badger, and the petulant Toad. It was firmly becoming one of his favourites to read every night, and she would never admit it, but she was having fun reading it to him.

There was a clang of crockery coming from the dining room as Annie stirred the tea in the pot. 'Ah, Joyce, just in time for tea.' She placed the teaspoon onto the saucer and the tea strainer over the first cup. 'I brought up some of those biscuits you made for us to try. I hope you don't mind.'

Joyce smiled. 'Of course I don't. That's why I made them. You're all going to be my guinea pigs for these new dishes I'm trying to make for the café.'

Arthur chuckled. 'That's fine by me. I'm quite happy to be your guinea pig anytime. I don't think I've ever tasted anything you've cooked that I haven't enjoyed.'

Rose laughed. 'I couldn't agree more.'

Annie poured the hot tea into the teacups and placed them on matching saucers. She put a teaspoon on each one before handing them out. 'You can all add your own sugar. I've added a splash of milk but if you want any more you can do it yourself.'

'A splash is normally fine for me, thank you very much.' Arthur took the cup and saucer offered to him. 'I'm glad Philip's home safe and in bed. He doesn't seem any worse for wear for his little adventure.'

Rose frowned as she accepted her cup and saucer. She glanced over at Joyce. 'It was lucky Frank found him the way he did because anything could have happened to him.'

Joyce shuddered. 'It doesn't bear thinking about, does it. I've definitely got more attached to him than I realised.'

Annie sat down in the nearest chair. 'It's not surprising. He's a sweet little lad, and I don't suppose he's had a very easy life.'

Rose looked down at her tea before looking up again at

Joyce. 'I'm sorry, Joyce, but I can't not say anything because it's playing on my mind.'

'What is?'

'I'm more than a little concerned that Frank might know where you live now. Doesn't it bother you?'

Annie's eyes widened. 'Maybe he's been following her because he fancies her.' She giggled but Rose remained straight-faced. 'It's unusual for you to be concerned, Rose. You normally take everything in your stride so why are you worried about that?'

'I don't know. It's just a feeling I have and he wears an expensive-looking suit.' Rose scowled.

Annie chuckled again. 'Is that a crime?'

Rose shook her head. 'I know it probably doesn't make sense but you don't see many men wearing expensive suits like he does.' She looked pensive. 'I don't think it helps he told Philip to stop being a baby and grow up. Is that really something you would say to a five-year-old?'

Arthur and Annie spoke as one. 'What?'

Rose frowned. 'Especially to a child who is lost.'

Joyce tightened her lips. 'I know. It concerns me too; after all, why would someone who writes for a living talk to a child like that? It doesn't make much sense does it?'

Arthur frowned as he studied the girls. 'He's been hanging around a lot. If it wasn't for that article he's writing I would think he probably was attracted to you, but that remark changes everything.'

Joyce fidgeted in her seat 'I know it does, but I don't know what to do about it. After all, if he's dangerous I don't want to upset him.'

Arthur scowled. 'Do you know his full name?'

'Do you know I'm not sure if he's ever told me. If he did I don't remember. I need to think.' Joyce placed her fingers on her lips, tapping them gently as she tried to remember if he'd ever told her. 'He came to see me because I won that cake baking competition, and he wanted to write an article on me for the newspapers, but actually he never mentions it now and I know it was never finished. I could ask him when I see him.'

Arthur frowned. His thoughts immediately turned to Ted. Was this something to do with him? 'No, I don't want you saying or doing anything that might raise an alarm with him, especially if he's dangerous. We need to find out first.'

Joyce's eyes narrowed as she stared Arthur. 'But why would he be hanging around me if that was the case? Oh, do you think he's something to do with the landlord? He's been trying to get me to pay more rent and I've refused. Do you think he's here to put the frighteners on me or something?'

The girls gasped.

Rose almost spat her tea out. She coughed to clear her throat. 'I'm sorry, but are you saying you could be in danger?'

Joyce shrugged. 'I don't know, I only know the landlord wasn't very happy with me for standing up to him.'

Arthur shook his head. 'Leave it with me. I don't like the sound of it but we can't let our imaginations run riot. There's probably a simple explanation. Let me try to make some enquiries.'

Joyce nodded. 'If you don't get anywhere then I'll just ask him outright. You know, now I think about it he always seems to turn up when I need help.'

Rose studied her friend. 'Do you like him?'

Joyce shrugged. 'I don't dislike him and he's always nice to me. He offers to help quite a lot.'

Annie frowned. 'How did he end up coming to Hyde Park with us? Did you ask him? I mean have you given him the wrong idea about your feelings for him?'

Joyce's mouth dropped open for a second before she shut it again. 'Oh, gosh, I hope not. Philip wanted Frank to come with us. I didn't object because at least I wouldn't be playing a gooseberry with you lovey-dovey people. It was as innocent as that.'

Arthur nodded as he finished chewing his biscuit; he licked his lips before brushing the crumbs off his shirt. 'Don't worry, I've still got contacts and something tells me I know exactly where to start.' He paused, his lips tightening. 'I'll find out who he is.'

Annie looked frightened as she stared at Arthur. 'In the meantime what should Joyce do? I don't like the idea of her being in danger every day.'

Joyce chuckled. 'I expect we're just letting our imaginations run away with us. I'll be fine.'

Arthur nodded. 'Joyce is probably right, but I do think you need to be careful and just treat him as you have been. If he's hiding something we don't want him to know you're on to him.' He picked up a biscuit crumb and placed it on the saucer. 'I'll tell you one thing you haven't got to worry about—'

'What?' the girls all chorused together.

'Those biscuits are lovely. I've made a bit of a mess, as the crumbs will testify, but they are very tasty.' Arthur leant forward in his seat. 'In fact I may well have another one.'

15

Mavis stared at each brushstroke of her son's paintings; she stood in front of the London skyline that filled the canvas in front of her. The strong smell of paint had gradually faded from the room. The globules on the floor along with the canvases propped up against the wall were the only evidence of Simon's daily time with his paintbrushes. She sighed, wondering if Simon would ever be able to sit and paint again. The dark circles under her eyes were evidence that she wasn't sleeping. She hated keeping Simon's secret and worried how much his medical treatment was going to tally up to, not that she cared; he was home and that was all that mattered.

'Why do you keep staring at Simon's paintings? You've been stood there since I came down for breakfast half an hour ago,' Barbara asked as she pulled her soft dark hair back into its usual bun.

Mavis jerked round and cleared her throat. 'Sorry, I didn't hear you come in.' Her hand rested at the base of her neck as she turned back to the painting.

Barbara studied her mother. 'Are you all right? You look tired and seem a little jumpy. I know you're worried about

Simon but you can't spend your day and night fretting. Try and keep busy.'

Mavis pulled herself upright and straightened her shoulders. 'Simon is a real artist.' She paused. 'I miss watching him lose himself in his painting.' She blinked rapidly to stop the tears from falling. 'I hope he's going to be all right.' She felt her throat tighten; taking a deep breath she turned round to stare at her daughter. 'Don't you miss him?'

Barbara nodded. 'It's strange him not being here, and the café isn't the same without him there. After all he is Meet and Feast and all that it represents. He's carrying Pa's idea forward.'

Mavis tightened her lips. 'I almost wish he wasn't because he's missed out on his own life by trying to fulfil your father's ambition.' She turned and looked back at the paintings. 'He has such a talent and it's wasted because no one's getting to see these.'

Barbara smiled. 'You would think that, Ma. You're his mother, but I'm not sure everybody else would agree, including Simon.'

Mavis sighed; walking into the hall she grabbed her lightweight coat. 'How are you getting on with Joyce?'

'I don't know, Ma, there's something about her I just don't trust, but I can't tell you what it is.'

Mavis chuckled. 'I can tell you something: the cakes she bakes are to die for. I tried one before Simon left.' She giggled like a naughty schoolgirl. 'Since then I've sneaked a small slice when no one's looking.'

'I agree. I'm not faulting her cooking.' Barbara paused and raised her eyebrows. 'Although, I have to say she stood up to Mr Harris when he came in for extra rent money. She wasn't paying it, and to her credit she stood her ground so there's obviously something about her.'

Mavis nodded. 'She must have something about her for Simon to think so highly of her.'

Barbara shook her head. 'I don't know. I wonder if she's just playing him to get the business while he's away.' She paused. 'And then there's this Frank. He seems to turn up with great regularity.'

Mavis swung round. 'I don't know anything about a Frank. Simon never mentioned him. I shouldn't think she's up to no good. She's worked at the café for a long time and he's never had a bad word to say about her.'

Barbara pulled her hair from the tight bun she had just twirled at the nape of her neck. She ran her fingers through it. 'Perhaps you should keep an eye on things and not be so trusting, then you'll be able to judge for yourself.' She pursed her lips. 'She keeps bringing in the young lad, and I'm not sure he isn't her son. Mind you I think he's too old to be hers.'

Mavis's eyes widened. 'Simon would have said if she had a little boy.'

'Maybe Simon didn't know about him, and she could be older than she lets on.' Barbara paused. 'If Simon is in love he probably wouldn't care.'

Mavis's jaw slackened. 'Have you asked her?'

Barbara shook her head. 'There's something about him, but I can't quite put my finger on that either.'

An hour later in the café, with the smell of frying bacon hanging in the air to whet everyone's appetite, Mavis was up to her elbows in soapsuds. She glanced over at Joyce who was buttering some bread. She had a strong urge to talk to her about Simon being in hospital, but she had promised him, and she could never break a promise. Mavis shook her head; she had to put him out of her mind for now. 'It gets so warm in this kitchen; it's a shame we can't have a door open.'

Joyce peered over at her. 'It does get warm but Simon always said we couldn't have the back door open because of flies. We'll be glad of the heat from the range when the winter comes again.' She went back to buttering her bread before looking up again. 'Is it getting too much for you? Working here I mean?'

Mavis ran her forearm across her brow. 'No, definitely not. I'm pleased to be of use. I'm just not sleeping very well.'

Joyce wanted to ask about Simon but decided she didn't have that right as she'd turned down his proposal. She had fought the urge to write to him, spelling out her regret, because he hadn't waited to say goodbye. Joyce assumed he was embarrassed and regretted his proposal and that's why he wasn't writing to her, but that was her cross to bear and no one else's. She prayed every night for his safe return. 'Why don't you stop and make yourself a cup of tea, maybe cut off a slice of cake or have a sandwich? In fact, I should be giving Philip something to eat.'

Mavis reached for the tea towel and dried her hands with it. 'Have you sorted out a school for him yet?'

'Yes, he starts when the schools go back after the summer. It will be good for him to be occupied and to make new friends. I can't manage to school him, play with him and work at the same time.'

Mavis watched Joyce scraping the butter across the bread before making the sandwiches. She turned to look around the kitchen. 'Wonder if we should look at the main dishes here because you seem to work so hard with very little result, and it just doesn't seem fair on you.'

Joyce stood upright; she stretched her back and tipped her head back before taking a deep breath. 'This is the menu that Simon's father set many years ago and Simon always wanted to follow it. I don't know if I'd be so bold as to change it. I'm not sure he would want me to.'

Mavis held the kettle under the cold tap and turned it on. The rattle of water spraying the inside of the kettle prevented any further talking for a moment. Mavis turned the tap off and put it on the range before turning back to Joyce. She dried her hands on her apron. 'I understand that. You're in a difficult position but you and Simon worked so hard and I think this place could be so much more. I've tried many slices of your cake and you're clearly a good cook so I think we just need to think about it.'

Joyce nodded. 'Well, thank you, Mavis, that's very kind of you to say so but as I said it's not my café.'

Mavis nodded. 'No, I suppose it's mine, although I've never looked at it like that. Simon always wanted to continue with his father's work but I do think Simon's lost himself in trying to do that.'

Joyce put down the knife. 'In what way do you mean?'

Mavis poured milk into two cups, before spooning tea leaves into a pot. 'I don't really know what I mean, but I was looking at his paintings today and he has a real talent and it's all wasted because no one ever sees them.'

Joyce wiped her hands down her apron. 'Yes, I only found out recently he painted and asked if I could see them but it wasn't something we got round to sharing before he left.'

Mavis poured the boiling water into the pot before turning round to face Joyce. 'Maybe it's time we looked at everything; maybe you could cook us something that we could try and then if we're happy we could sell it here.'

Joyce frowned. 'Are you sure that's what Simon would want?'

'Simon isn't here, and I think it's time that his dreams were realised. I know he's not here to enjoy that moment, but hopefully he'll be pleased with the changes when he gets to come back to the café.'

Barbara's voice came from the other side of the serving hatch. 'Are those sandwiches ready yet? They seem to have taken ages.'

Mavis chuckled. 'That's my fault. I've been chatting too much and distracting the cook.'

'That's all very well, Ma, but I've got hungry customers here.'

'Sorry, Barbara, it won't be long.' Joyce quickly popped back to layering the bread with egg.

Joyce moved her hands down the front of her apron. 'We could do a stew in the winter. That would be easy to put on the range and just put so many spoonfuls onto the customer's plates, or we could make some vegetable soup as well.'

'Should we think about summer meals?' Mavis put a finger to her lips and tapped away gently. 'I'm not sure salads would be a good idea. Do you think they would get eaten?'

Joyce shrugged. 'I suppose we could always put one on the tariff and see how it goes. I expect it'll be a case of trying different dishes until we know what's popular.' She paused. 'There's always a meatloaf or meat and vegetable pie; we just need to think about it, but I do agree doing fried breakfasts all day and sandwiches is quite hard work for very little return.'

Mavis nodded. 'We need dishes that can be prepared in advance and that would save you being rushed off your feet. I'm not saying don't do breakfast as well but only until a certain time, say about eleven o'clock, and then move to a lunch tariff or something.'

Joyce smiled. 'This is music to my ears. I did speak to Simon about changing it a little but we never got any further than talking about it. Although he was open to adding other things he really wanted to keep the breakfast as part of the Meet and Feast Café.'

'All right, maybe we can give it some thought and then move forward, as I think it's a good idea.' Mavis walked out into the café and looked around. She stood there for a while watching people eat and looking at the empty walls. Again, she kept her fingers on her lips before returning to the kitchen. 'How would you feel about putting one of Simons paintings on the wall? I think there's room and we could even put a price on it. Wouldn't that be fabulous if he came back and he had an outlet for his paintings?'

'What a wonderful idea. I'm not sure Simon will see it that way but I certainly think it's a good idea.'

Barbara waltzed into the kitchen. 'What's a good idea?'

Mavis smiled. 'I've suggested we put one of Simon's paintings on the wall in the café.'

Barbara shook her head. 'What is it with you and Simon's paintings? I know you think they're good but not everyone would agree.'

Mavis shrugged. 'Well, we won't know until they're put on show and then we'll see who's got the wrong idea.'

Joyce's gaze wandered between mother and daughter and she wondered who would win this discussion. 'Your mother was also talking about changing the tariff a little bit.' She paused, wondering how far to go. 'What do you think?'

Barbara glared at Joyce. 'Is this your doing? Is this your way of trying to take over my father's café, the very thing Simon has worked so hard to keep going in his memory?'

Joyce opened her mouth to speak but Mavis got there first.

'This is my idea so you need to be very careful, my girl. We'll discuss this when we get home, but I can tell you I'll not have you throwing your weight around and undermining all the hard work that has been done in trying to keep this café going for your father.'

Joyce picked up the plate of egg sandwiches and made a hasty exit from the kitchen.

Rose closed one eye as she threaded the sewing needle with the fine white cotton. After running her finger and thumb down the two strands of sewing thread, she tied a small knot at the end. Pinning the needle through the collar of her pale blue blouse, she glanced down at the white material in front of her. Rose ran her hands over it, smoothing out where she had to sew while enjoying the touch of the soft silkiness of it. The Lyceum sewing room table was covered in different-coloured threads, lace, sequins and fine pearl buttons. She picked up a piece of fine lace and began cutting round the flowers that made up its delicate pattern. One by one she layered the flowers flat on the table ready to be sewn onto the white fabric. It was a painstaking job but she had to be careful; this dress was too important to rush.

The sound of heels hitting the tiled floor in the corridor caught Rose's attention. She looked up at the doorway hoping whoever it was would carry on walking by. Instead the door swung open. Rose could feel a sigh gathering momentum, as she expected to see Annie there.

'What are you doing, Miss Spencer?'

Rose panicked as she took in Miss Hetherington's dour expression. She quickly gathered all the sequins and the buttons and put them in a heap, while carefully laying the lace flowers on top of each other. 'I'm just sorting through a few bits and pieces, Miss Hetherington.'

Miss Hetherington glared at Rose. 'Are you indeed? Since when have we needed to have flowers cut out from an already beautiful piece of lace?'

Rose's face paled as she looked down at the sewing table. 'I was just trying something out with this piece that was too short to use for anything.'

Miss Hetherington stepped nearer. 'And the white material?'

Rose cleared her throat as the smell of carbolic soap overwhelmed her. 'All right, I admit to experimenting with something.'

Miss Hetherington walked around the table. 'And is this for the production?'

'No, Miss Hetherington.'

Miss Hetherington's eyes narrowed. 'And yet you are here doing it in The Lyceum's sewing room. Does that sound right to you?'

Rose shook her head. 'No, Miss Hetherington, but I am doing it in my own time.'

'And does that make it right?'

Rose closed her eyes; she knew that Miss Hetherington was not going to let this go. 'No, Miss Hetherington, it doesn't but at least I'm not using the time that is meant for the production.'

'And are you up to date with the costume repairs?' Miss Hetherington leant in and scooped up the white material. 'This feels expensive. I trust this isn't from the theatre; after all, I'd hate to have to sack you for stealing.' Her eyes lit up as she stared at Rose.

Rose stood up, catching a faint whiff of Miss Hetherington's lavender scent. 'How dare you. I have never stolen anything from this theatre.'

Miss Hetherington frowned. 'But if this lace comes from a length that was bought for a costume then you are stealing.'

Rose folded her arms. 'It was in the bin to be thrown out, so I assumed you had put it there.'

'You assumed correctly but until it leaves the theatre it is still stealing.'

Rose shook her head. 'I don't know what I've ever done to you, Miss Hetherington, except work hard – and I wasn't aware that was a crime – and yet you clearly dislike me.'

Jane Hetherington smiled. 'You haven't done anything.' She paused. 'I just don't like you, or the way you have managed to get a job without coming through me. You think you are so clever but you're not.'

Rose let herself fall down onto the chair at the sewing table. 'Is that it? Is that all it took?' She shook her head. 'If I recall you weren't around when you were needed. When

Kitty's outfit needed repairing Annie and I were the only two in here. I know we shouldn't have been but we saved the day, we saved you and your job, and for that you are making my life hell.'

Jane Hetherington pulled back her shoulders and thrust out her chin. 'You need to watch your mouth; otherwise you will be out of a job.'

Rose chuckled as she shook her head. 'Trust me when I say having older brothers I could use much stronger language, but I was brought up to be better behaved than that. You do know that if I left now you would have to remember what it is like to pick up a sewing needle and have sore fingers every day so maybe it should be *you* who thinks about what you say before opening your mouth. Girls don't want to earn what they deem to be a pittance sewing when they can earn five pound a week or more working in the munitions factory.'

Miss Hetherington glared at her. 'And yet you are still here.'

Rose scowled. 'Yes, I am, but you don't make it easy to stay. I'm here because I like to sew and I'm good at it. It's not about the money as long as I've got enough to live on.'

Miss Hetherington dropped the white material back on to the table.

Rose shook her head. 'You know, it's clearly all beyond me. Shouldn't we all be giving thanks that so far we haven't had to deal with the bombs and deaths that other countries have, let alone the poison gas that our own men have been subject to on the front line? Then there's the sinking of the *Lusitania* where over a thousand people died, and yet all you can think to do is tell me off for cutting flowers out of a piece of lace that was in the bin.' She shook her head. 'I don't know what's happened to you in your life but you have no feelings for what people may be going through.' She sighed. 'I do believe you may have actually won. Maybe it is time I moved on.'

Miss Hetherington's eyes widened. 'That won't be necessary, but in future watch your mouth and make sure you ask permission first.' She turned and marched out of the room before Rose could say any more.

Rose rested her head in her hands for a moment.

'How is it going, Rose?' Kitty stopped short. 'Is everything all right?'

Rose smiled. 'Yes, Kitty, just Miss Hetherington. Need I say more?'

Kitty frowned. 'Try not to let the silly old bat get you down. She's not worth it. I'm sure if Stan wasn't as nice as he is she would have got the sack a long time ago.'

Rose shook her head. 'I wouldn't want her to be out of work; I just don't understand her.' She pulled the white fabric nearer to her.

Kitty clapped her hands together and beamed at Rose. 'Ahh, this is what I wanted to see. I'm getting excited about my wedding day now.'

Rose laughed. 'Well, that's good because you are meant to be.' She picked up one of the delicate flowers she had been cutting round. 'I thought I'd see what these looked like sewn on your dress with either a little pearl or sequin sewn in the middle of it. What do you think?' Kitty stared down at it as Rose placed a pearl on one and a sequin on another. 'Or we could have a mixture of them both.'

Kitty giggled. 'I tell you what: I feel like a schoolgirl again. I love them both so I'll leave it to you.'

Simon lay still in his hospital bed, listening to the groans coming from around the ward; they were occasionally drowned out by the nurses and doctors talking to patients. He knew his injuries were minor compared to the poor man in the bed opposite – he had heard talk he may not make it – but Simon wondered what his future would hold. His legs felt quite useless. Every time he tried to move them pain shot through him and the doctor had said it would be a while before he could walk again unaided, if he ever did.

He sighed and looked out of the rain-splattered window, grateful to the nurses who had moved his bed slightly so he could see the quadrangle below. He stared out into the greyness at the comings and goings; so many people were in and out of the hospital. Gasping, Simon watched a brown-haired girl approaching the hospital, clutching the hand of a small boy. His heart jumped in his chest, while his stomach did a somersault. His face screwed up as he tried to move to get a better view, but the pain got too much. He groaned as he slumped back down, thumping the bedcovers with his fists. He felt sure that was Joyce; he needed to get a closer look. Had his mother told her he was at the hospital, despite him saying he didn't want anyone to know? Is that why she was here, to visit him? A surge of excitement ran through him. He frowned, as he immediately chased it away. He wasn't ready to see her.

An old man walked down between the beds, carrying a

bundle of newspapers in his arms. 'Can I interest you in today's paper, sir?'

Simon shook his head.

The old man went to walk away.

'Wait, I'm sorry, my answer should have been no, thank you.'

The old man gave a toothless grin. 'Don't worry, laddie, no one expects you to be on your best behaviour at this time.' The man nodded and walked on to the next bed. 'Can I offer you a newspaper, sir?'

Simon gritted his teeth and pushed himself up a little to peer out of the window again. He regretted not writing to her, but he hadn't known what to say. When she turned down his proposal and wasn't at the café the next morning he had assumed she didn't feel the same after all. He hadn't asked his mother whether Joyce had carried on working, let alone kept the café running. He was too scared. Too frightened to admit he had lost the woman he loved, and without her nothing else mattered. He was now no longer in a position to provide and care for her; he had no desire to be another burden on her time. Spotting her again, Simon watched Joyce stoop down to talk to the child. She kept looking round as though she was waiting for someone. A man came rushing out and almost ran into her.

Simon, tried to get nearer to the window, his face screaming the pain his voice wasn't letting out. He stared intently. Was that the journalist from the café? Was that the man doing the article on Joyce's cooking, on her winning the prize for her cake baking? Simon watched them, wishing he could get a closer look, or better still, go downstairs and find out what was going on. Gasping,

Simon shook his head as the man put his arm around her shoulders. Jealousy travelled through his war-torn body, adding to his helplessness. Had he lost her forever? Had he lost her because of his own inability to write and to say he was sorry for burdening her with his proposal?

His throat tightened as he watched Joyce step away and they both walked into the hospital with the boy. Simon closed his eyes, the tears pricked like sharp needles behind his eyelids. How he wished he hadn't been such a coward and had spoken up sooner before their lives had been turned upside down by war and family events.

'Are you all right, Simon?' A nurse stood to the side of the bed watching him. 'You look a little pale. I thought you looked better this morning, brighter, but I'm not so sure now.'

Simon opened his eyes and turned to look at the nurse. 'I'm fine, thank you. I'm sure things will be better when I can get on my feet again.'

The nurse gave a faint smile. 'I don't suppose they'll keep you in bed for any longer than they have to; just follow their instructions and you'll soon be out of here. And, don't forget the good news.'

Simon frowned. 'The good news?'

The nurse picked up the jug of water on top of the bedside cabinet; she peered inside before putting it back with a thud. 'Yes, it's important to focus on the good news because there isn't much of it around. You'll definitely be able to walk again, especially if you do as you're told and exercise as much as you can. The more you do the quicker you'll improve. It will be painful at first but you have to be strong, and the really good news is you won't have to go off and fight again. You'll be able to pick up your life again. Admittedly, things won't be the same because of the things you've gone through and you'll have a limp. You may even need a walking stick for a while but at least you'll be alive and relatively well.'

Simon turned his head to look back out of the window. 'Doesn't mean much if you can't be with the person you love the most.'

The nurse shook her head. 'Does the person you love the most know you are here?'

Simon stayed silent for a moment. 'No, I don't want her to know yet. She has enough problems without me adding to them.' He paused. 'Besides, she may not want me in her life. I've just seen her out the window with another man.'

The nurse tightened her lips for a second. 'Remember things aren't always as they seem; you need to talk to her, find out from her what's going on. Don't let your imagination lead you astray. Find out the facts before you throw it all away.'

Simon nodded. What he'd seen seemed pretty conclusive to him but he kept his thoughts to himself. He had already said too much.

The nurse pulled the grey blanket straight and tugged in the edges. 'Now, I shall be back soon to change your dressings and give you the medication the doctors said you had to take.'

16

Joyce gripped Philip's hand as they stood outside St Thomas' Hospital, the building towering high above their heads. She stooped down in front of the worried-looking five-year-old. 'I want you to remember what we've talked about, how Grandma is going to look like she's asleep, so she won't be able to answer when we talk to her.' She watched his fear grow. 'It's nothing to worry about and we'll talk to her as though she's wide awake, all right?'

Philip nodded.

Joyce ran her fingers through his soft hair, curling it around her fingers; maybe she'd have to try taking the scissors to it. 'One of the nurses told me they believe she can understand and hear what we're saying; she just can't answer us.'

Philip was watching Joyce with wide eyes. He glanced at the glass doors in front of them. 'How can she hear me but not answer?'

Joyce closed her eyes for a split second. 'I'm not sure, Philip, but it's as though she's in a deep sleep. Anyway, if she can hear us we need to make sure we say all the things we want her to know.' She paused. 'We might want to tell her that we love her or how happy we are, or unhappy, but either way we should just talk to her normally.' She glanced up and down the street; she felt sure someone was watching her. Joyce shook her head. She was just being fanciful. 'I don't want you to worry about it, and I'll be with you so there's nothing to be afraid of.'

Philip frowned. 'I'm not afraid. Frank told me I had to grow up and stop acting like a baby.'

Joyce stooped down and wrapped her arms around Philip. 'Don't you worry about anything Frank says. You're five years old. It's more important that you say what you want and then we can talk about it. That way we can deal with things as they come up.'

Philip nodded.

Joyce stood up. 'Right, are you ready?' She took a deep breath and looked around her, wishing she could get rid of the feeling she was being watched. Her eyes widened. There was that man again. He was rushing out of the hospital almost running down the road by the time she'd gathered herself. 'Pa, is that you?'

The man peered over his shoulder but kept on going.

Joyce looked down at Philip. 'I don't know what's going on, Philip, but I feel like I'm going round the bend. I'm sure that was my father but I don't know how it can be.' She took Philip's hand and turned to go into the hospital.

Frank came out through the double doors, as she was about to walk into the hospital. Joyce did a double take as she took in his flushed appearance. 'Hello, Frank, didn't expect to see you here at the hospital of all places. Are you all right? You look like you're in a hurry.'

Frank took a step back. He scowled and seemed a little

uncertain as he looked up and down the road. 'Yeah, yeah I'm fine.'

Joyce frowned. He looked suspicious. Maybe it was the conversation he'd had with Philip that was embarrassing him. 'What brings you to the hospital?'

Frank fidgeted from one foot to the other. 'Hello, Philip, are yer all right after yer little adventure of roaming the streets?'

Philip gave a little nod but stayed silent.

Frank turned to Joyce. 'What's brought you to the 'ospital? Philip's not 'urt is 'e?'

Joyce raised her eyebrows. 'No, we're visiting my grandmother. And you, what has brought you here?'

Frank looked beyond Joyce, focusing further along the street.

Joyce turned round to see what was holding his attention but couldn't see anything out of the ordinary. 'Well?'

Frank frowned. 'Oh, sorry, I'm a little preoccupied at the moment.' He wiggled his fingers down by his side. 'I 'urt my 'and so I came to get it checked out.'

Joyce nodded. Her eyes narrowed as she looked down at his hand. 'It's wise to get it looked at but it will probably cost you a small fortune.'

Frank coughed. 'What did yer say yer were doing here?'

Joyce momentarily looked down at Philip. 'I've brought Philip to see my grandma; apparently it was where he wanted to go when he left the café.'

Frank sighed. 'Well, I could come with yer if yer don't mind me visiting as well, or perhaps I should say if yer grandma doesn't mind.' He rested his arm across Joyce's shoulders and looked up the road again and gave a smile to anyone who was watching.

Joyce blushed; she didn't take kindly to his overfamiliarity. She stepped aside as the smell of his sweat got too much for her. 'Come on then, let's go in before it starts raining again.'

The three of them walked inside and climbed the stairs, keeping to one side so others could pass by. Joyce led the way to her grandmother's room. They all stood at the foot of the bed staring down at the fragile grey-haired lady. She was lying so still. Nothing had changed since Joyce was there the last time.

Frank didn't take his eyes off the old lady. 'She looks quite vulnerable lying there.'

'She does.' Joyce moved round and sat at her grandmother's bedside, with Philip sitting on her lap. The usual smell of disinfectant was overpowering and made her cough as it reached the back of her throat. She peered at the sleeping woman and wondered what Philip thought about seeing the woman he called grandma lying so still. The nurses had already told her she wasn't likely to come round; she would probably end up just slipping away.

Frank cleared his throat. 'I'm sorry, I've just remembered I 'ave an appointment so I've got to go.'

Joyce gently moved Philip off her knees and stood up. 'That's all right. I don't want to hold you up.'

Frank stared at the bed. 'I expect I'll see yer both at the café sometime over the next few days. I must get the article finished otherwise I'm never going to get paid.' He laughed before raising his hand to wave goodbye and he was gone.

Joyce picked up the small hairbrush and leant in to carefully brush the grey curly hair she could get to. She suddenly remembered doing it for her mother when she was sick. Joyce caught the faint smell of lavender; she picked up the soap dish on the bedside cabinet and sniffed it. She looked over at Philip. 'This must be Grandma's soap. It smells of lavender. Do you want to have a sniff?'

Philip shook his head. 'I know what lavender smells like. Grandma always used it at home.'

Joyce nodded and placed it back on the cabinet. She leant in to brush another soft tendril of hair away from her face. 'Grandma, I think you could do with a haircut.' Joyce put down the hairbrush and gazed at the woman lying so still. 'I look at you and it seems hard to picture you arguing with my father and yet I remember you two shouting at each other before we left.' Her fingers moved a soft stray curl from her grandmother's forehead. 'I wonder what was so bad that you turned your back on your son and if he hadn't died would you have made it up?' Joyce frowned. 'I have so many questions and I suspect I'll never know the answers to them.'

Philip sat quietly looking from the bed to Joyce. 'She used to smile at my father but sometimes she was cross with him as well.'

A nurse coughed from the doorway. 'I'm sorry to disturb you but I wondered if we could come in and change the bedding and her position so she doesn't get bedsores.'

Joyce nodded. 'Of course – we'll get out of your way.'

The nurse picked up sheets and pillowcases from a trolley. 'It should have been done earlier but Mrs Taylor had a visitor so we thought we could do it after he'd gone.' The nurse smiled. 'But you beat us to it.'

Joyce glanced at the nurse. 'I'm sorry, we'll leave while

you get on.' She stepped out of the way. 'I didn't realise Mrs Taylor had any other visitors, which was pretty silly of me really.'

'There's no need to leave. It won't take us long to do.' The nurse placed the bedding on a chair. 'She doesn't really; the man has only been a couple of times, a bit like yourself. Other than that I'm not aware of any visitors.'

Another nurse marched into the side room; glanced at Joyce before turning to the other nurse. 'Ah, good, you've got the sheets.' She looked at the fob watch hanging from the front of her uniform. 'We're running late today. Matron won't be happy with us.'

Joyce and Philip moved aside and watched as they moved expertly around the bed.

'This won't take long.' One of the nurses smiled at Joyce as she squared off the corners of the bedding and tucked it under the mattress.

The nurse turned to Philip. 'Hello, how old are you?'

Philip gave her a serious look. 'I'm nearly six.'

The nurse smiled. 'My goodness you're almost a grown-up.'

Philip giggled.

The nurse nodded. 'Well, that's us done. If you need anything just come to the nurses' station.'

'Thank you.' Joyce sat down on the nearest chair to the bed, staring at the old lady lying so still, while Philip sat on the edge of the bed. Joyce looked up. 'I was just thinking about the man who has been visiting her. Do you know who it was?'

One of the nurses frowned. 'I don't recall hearing his

name, but if it helps he wasn't a young man.' She paused. 'If it's important I can try and find out for you.'

Joyce coloured slightly. 'No, it doesn't matter, I was just curious. It was probably her housekeeper's husband.' She watched the nurses pick up the dirty sheets and carry them out of the room.

Philip stared at the old lady in the bed before peering up at Joyce. 'I liked living with Grandma; it was always fun.'

Joyce forced a smile and tried not to let the jealousy take hold. 'What sort of things did you used to do with her?'

Philip looked sad for a moment before a smile spread across his face. 'We would play games like hide-and-seek. She used to let me help bake cakes, as long as I stayed away from the range.' He looked back at the woman lying so still in the bed.

Joyce could see Philip welling up; she took his hand in hers. 'I didn't know you liked to cook. We could always do that together – that's if you'd like to.'

A grin lit up his face and he quickly nodded. 'Yes, then we can let the others try our food.'

Joyce chuckled. 'Oh don't you worry about that; they will.'

'Did you used to cook with Grandma?'

Joyce shook her head. 'No, but I did with my mother before she died. We used to make all kinds of things together. She taught me how to make bread, pastry, cakes and pies. I've always loved the smell of things baking in the oven.' She paused. 'I can teach you how to make bread first because you have to do what they call kneading and that will be a safe thing for you to do.'

Philip studied her. His eyes screwed up as he pulled a face. 'What's that?'

Joyce laughed. 'It's where you pull the dough around and fold it back in on itself.' She smiled. 'My ma used to say, "Learn how to make good bread and you'll never go hungry," and she wasn't wrong.'

Philip didn't take his eyes off her.

'Also, if you enjoy it, and make wonderful bread, you could become a master baker. Then you'll never be out of work either.'

Philip nodded. 'And then your family will never go hungry. That's important because Grandma said family was everything, and nothing was more important than that.'

'And Grandma's right.' Joyce could feel the tears pricking at her eyes. 'You know, Philip, people talk about breaking bread and that's about family and friends coming together.' Her voice dropped to a whisper as she remembered her mother's words. 'It's spending time with each other, moving forward, overcoming problems and letting go of them.' She stopped talking and peered at Philip. She forced herself to smile. 'So you see why spending time with family and friends is so important.'

Joyce slammed the till shut. The May sunshine had seemingly brought everybody outside and into The Meet and Feast Café. She watched Barbara talking and laughing with a customer and waited for her to come over to place the order. Every now and then the raised voices of the anti-German demonstrators travelled through the air and could be heard inside the café. Joyce frowned as she glanced at the café door, wishing Mavis would arrive so she knew Simon's mother was safe. From what the newspapers were reporting some of the demonstrations had turned into riots and people were being arrested.

'Table six would like to try some of your meat and potato pie. I've offered it at a discounted rate to get people to try it.' Barbara wrote on the docket and put it through the serving hatch on to the hook.

Startled, Joyce forced a smile. 'That's a good idea. Sometimes people are wary of trying something new so it's good to encourage them. How much of a discount did you offer?'

Barbara fidgeted from one foot to the other before lifting her head defiantly. 'I said they could have it at half price for today only.'

Joyce raised her eyebrows. 'Well, hopefully, we'll still break even with the cost of making it.'

Barbara pursed her lips together. 'Sometimes you have to lose a bit to gain some. Hopefully tomorrow more people will want it and then we won't have to use a discount.'

Joyce smoothed her hand over the pile of crisp white napkins. 'I'm sure you're right.'

Barbara gave her a wry smile. 'I often am. The difference is not many people listen to me. I'm just the little girl who everyone thinks knows nothing.'

Joyce's eyes narrowed. 'I don't think that's necessarily the case. Sometimes it's more about the way things are done.' She turned to walk back into the kitchen but stopped and looked over her shoulder. 'I'd just like to mention when I cashed up last night the till was short so we need to be careful. We should count the coins into the customers' hands. That acts as a double check, and ensures we give the right change.'

'I always count the money out. I don't know what you're getting it.' Barbara's cheeks reddened and her eyes widened. 'I hope you're not accusing me of anything.'

Joyce held her hands together in front of her. 'I'm not accusing anybody; we all use the till. I'm just saying it was short so we all need to be careful. It never used to be wrong at all. Simon was always particular that if we took any money out to pay for goods we put a ticket in the till to remind us how much we'd taken out and what it was for. So it's important that we carry on how Simon wanted it.'

Barbara's lip curled. 'This is worse than being at home. All I hear about is Simon there and now here. No one notices what I do or even what I don't do.'

Joyce shook her head. 'This isn't about Simon. This is about your family trying to keep your father's dream alive and Simon has worked hard to do that. Unfortunately, you seem to be the only person who can't see that.' Joyce turned and went back into the kitchen. She pulled the docket off the hook and set about slicing a piece of meat and potato pie and putting it on a plate with a little salad next to it. Her blood raced through her veins at Barbara's insinuations that only Simon mattered. Joyce put the plate on the ledge of the serving hatch together with the docket. 'Barbara, the order for table six is ready.' She turned away and took another order off the hook. She found no pleasure in coming to work anymore.

Joyce wondered how Philip was getting on with Arthur. He was quite chatty with her these days, but at times she caught glimpses of him looking pensive. Joyce shook her head, and started to butter some bread. She didn't have time for all of this. She didn't know how or why her life had become so complicated. She had always dreamt of having her own restaurant, cooking her own dishes. She should be enjoying this instead of wondering if this was how it was going to be. Her throat began to close. She gulped, trying to stop the tears from flowing. 'Come on, girl, stop feeling sorry for yourself. You've got work to do.'

Barbara thrust another docket onto the hook. 'We've another meat and potato pie order.' She didn't wait for a response.

Joyce leant against the hard edge of the café's kitchen table. She absentmindedly picked up her lukewarm cup of tea as she glanced out through the serving hatch. She watched Barbara standing at the counter, wondering if they would ever get on with each other. Joyce wanted to but there was clearly a problem. She put the cup back on the table; there was no time to let her thoughts meander about these things. The café was busy. 'Is everything all right out there, Barbara?'

Barbara didn't look round. Her head appeared to be fixed, gazing straight ahead. 'Of course. Why wouldn't it be? I'm quite capable of serving a few cups of tea and coffee.'

'I just thought I'd check with you because I know you're on your own. If there's any problems then please let me know.'

Barbara turned and glared at Joyce. 'I can assure you I am more than capable of looking after my brother's business. You have to remember this is my family's café and not yours.'

Joyce's hands clenched down by her sides. 'Let me assure

you, Barbara, that I am aware this is not my business but your brother asked me to look after it and I have no desire to let him down. When he returns it will be me he will look to when things haven't gone right.'

'Of course, and it will be you who gets the credit when we have all worked hard to make it a better business.' Barbara turned away before Joyce had a chance to respond.

Joyce's jaw tightened. Her neck tensed as she fought the urge to go after Barbara. It would've been a lot easier if it hadn't been family helping her in the café. She shook her head. No good would come of telling Mavis about Barbara's attitude; after all they were family and families stick together.

The doorbell chimed as it opened and shut. 'Morning, everyone,' Mavis's cheery voice rang through the café.

'Morning, Mavis.' The café customers spoke as one.

Joyce breathed a sigh of relief; at least Barbara would behave better with her mother here.

The kitchen door swung open and Mavis breezed through. 'Morning, Joyce, it's busy in the café this morning.' She removed her hat and coat and hung them on the clothes stand in the corner. 'Right, what would you like me to do first?'

Joyce smiled at her. 'How do you feel about peeling some potatoes and maybe some carrots? I've had the meat in the stew going all morning on a very low heat but I think it's time I did the vegetables – if we just cut it up into small pieces. What do you think?'

Mavis slipped her apron on over her head and began tying it around her back. 'That sounds like a great idea. I'll do it straight away.'

Joyce grinned at Mavis. 'I hope it's not proving too much coming in here every day. I don't want Simon thinking I'm working you into the ground.'

Mavis gave a little chuckle. 'You must be joking. I feel like I've got a new lease of life. It's lovely to have a purpose. Simon and his father have both tried to protect me and, don't get me wrong, it's lovely of them but there have been times when it's been quite suffocating. So it feels like I've been set free. I am the butterfly gracefully flapping its wings.' Mavis threw her head back and laughed. 'Not that anyone would look at me and think butterfly; there is nothing delicate or fragile about me.' Her laughter filled the kitchen.

Joyce couldn't help laughing along with her. 'I don't think any of us are as delicate as a butterfly but I get your meaning. You've been a great help to me. I'm glad we finally met.' Joyce wanted to ask if she'd heard from Simon but she didn't want to spoil the mood for Mavis.

Joyce ran up the now familiar stairs in the hospital and thrust open one of the double doors, just stopping it from hitting the nurses and visitors coming from the opposite direction.

'Please no running; otherwise someone will end up getting hurt.'

Joyce lowered her eyes as everyone stared at her. 'I'm sorry.' She bit her lip. 'It won't happen again.' Turning away, she unbuttoned her lightweight coat as she marched along the corridor. The tap of her curved heels on the tiled floor gave away she was almost running, but fear of being told off by the nursing staff slowed her down a little. All her rushing had made her too hot to notice the chill of the evening air against her skin. Something had prodded her to visit this evening; the urge to come on her own had been overwhelming. Joyce hadn't stopped to try and make sense of it. Her whole being was shouting at her to be at the hospital, and she had no idea why, especially as it wasn't that long ago she and Philip had been at her grandmother's bedside. She hadn't been in the hospital so late in the evening before and there was an eerie feel to it. There was minimum light while the windows were blacked out for the night. There was more of a hush to it. People whispered in the corridors, while some of the patients were already asleep.

Joyce ran into her grandmother's room expecting to see the old lady lying in her bed, as still as always. She stopped short. Her hands reached out to clutch the doorjamb for support. Was her eyes deceiving her? Was she seeing things? Was she actually seeing the man she thought she'd seen over the last few weeks or was her mind playing tricks on her? Was it really him sitting there? That was impossible, wasn't it? She stood rooted to the spot, unable to speak. Her mouth was dry. Her eyes became watery. What was happening to her? Joyce had the urge to run away but also to strike out. How could this be him. How? His head was low almost touching the bed.

He suddenly looked up and his eyes widened with shock as he saw her.

Joyce's grip tightened on the doorjamb. She wasn't sure her legs would be able to keep her upright. The room became blurry. She blinked quickly. She tried to stare at the man sitting beside the bed, the man who was so familiar to her. The man who she had thought was dead. A groan escaped as she dropped to the floor. Hands grabbed on to her arms as she was scooped up.

'I've got you, Joyce.' The familiar deep voice slowly penetrated the fog that had engulfed her brain.

Joyce whimpered and her eyelashes fluttered. The hard wood of a chair supported her back and legs.

'Thank you for the water.' The man's voice continued. 'I'll stay and look after her.'

'And you are?' a woman's voice almost whispered.

'I'm Mr Taylor, her father.'

So it was true. The room fell silent. Joyce was aware of cold liquid being pressed against her lips but she had no desire to open her eyes.

'Joyce,' Ted urged her to respond. 'Joyce, I'm so sorry, please try and drink this water.'

'I've brought some smelling salts.' A woman spoke matter-of-factly. 'This will bring her round.'

Joyce knew she couldn't feign being unconscious for any longer. It was time to face her father. She slowly opened her eyes to see his anxious face staring down at her.

'Thank goodness. I'm so sorry I frightened you like that.' Ted turned to the nurse. 'Thank you for your help. I think she's going to be all right now.'

The nurse reached out and pressed the tips of her fingers on the inside of Joyce's wrist. She gave Joyce a concerned look as she dropped her arm on to her lap. 'Stay sitting for a while, and no sudden movements.' She looked over at Ted. 'If anything changes come and get me from the nurses' station.' She gave Joyce one last look before turning and leaving the room.

Ted nodded. 'Thank you.' He turned and stared down at Joyce. 'How are you feeling?'

Joyce gave him a withering look as her emotions swung like a pendulum between wanting to hit out and hurt him, and wrapping her arms around him. She couldn't believe what she was seeing and hearing.

Ted nervously licked his dry lips. 'Look, I know this is a shock for you, and I'm really sorry; this wasn't how I wanted you to find out.'

Joyce shook her head. 'You are unbelievable. How did you think this was going to end? I thought you were dead for goodness' sake. I thought you went down with the *Titanic*.' Her voice got higher with every word. 'You let me think that. What sort of father are you?'

Ted dropped his head in his hands but said nothing.

Joyce's eyes widened. 'Don't you have anything to say? Are you not even going to defend yourself?'

Ted rubbed his hand over his face before looking up at her. 'I was always going to come and get you. I've always dreamed we would live in a great house together.'

Joyce frowned. 'Live in a great house together – how about we just live together? I've been mourning the death of my mother and father, which I now find out wasn't the big loss I thought it was, while you left me living with a drunk who was grieving for his young son. Not to mention Dot leaving him, and Arthur having no idea where she had gone. Are you so wrapped up in yourself that you have no compassion at all?'

Ted began to pace up and down the small room, unable to meet her look of horror and disappointment. 'Look, Joyce, I don't expect you to understand but you need to know I can't explain it to you. Is it not enough to know that it was just something I had to do?'

'Had to do?' Joyce shook her head. 'Have you any idea what it's been like for me? Are you just so wrapped up in yourself that you can't see beyond that? I'm surprised you're even here seeing your own mother.' Joyce jumped up; she grabbed the edge of the chair as the room began to spin.

'Sit down, Joyce.' Ted quickly stepped nearer as he barked at her. 'Do as you're told.'

Joyce's mouth dropped open for a moment before she gathered herself again. 'You lost the right tell me what to do a long time ago.'

Ted looked shamefaced as he faced his daughter. 'Look, I knew it was never going to be easy when we finally got together again, but you heard the nurse say you've got to sit still for a little while.'

Joyce's anger grew with each passing minute. 'Oh, so you planned to see me again then, and yet every time I thought I'd seen you here you ran away. I started to believe I was imagining things. I mean, after all, who does that? Who actually pretends they are dead?' Joyce opened her mouth to say more, but shook her head instead. 'I just can't believe it.' She took a breath. 'I remember you saying once there's always a choice; you may not like it, but there's always a choice. Well, you certainly made yours and it didn't involve me.'

Ted stood next to the bed; he couldn't bring himself to look at his daughter. 'I'm sorry, but I thought I was protecting you.'

'Protecting me? Protecting me from what exactly?'

'It's too complicated. You wouldn't understand.'

Joyce clasped her hands on her lap. 'Wouldn't understand? You have no idea about what I've had to learn to understand in the last few years. You have no idea what I've been through. And where were you? What were you going through that was so big that you couldn't be there to support your daughter? I can tell you where you weren't on the *Titanic*.'

Ted moved towards the window to stare out into the darkness, before noticing the black material blocking it. 'I have no words to tell you what I've been going through.' He rubbed his hands over his face. 'Isn't it enough that I was in trouble and had to stay away for a while?'

'A while? It's been three years.' Joyce stood up. 'Again it's all about you. You're so busy thinking about you there's no room for anybody else. You just don't get it do you? You knew you weren't coming back but you didn't even have the backbone to tell the truth. You've never contacted me to let me know you're alive.' She sighed. 'You haven't even asked me how I am. I need to get out of here. If you weren't dead to me before you certainly are now.'

She forced herself to leave the room. There was nothing to be gained by staying. Tears ran down her face as she marched out of the hospital.

17

The house was quiet, the silence only broken by the ticking of the clock on the mantelpiece; there were a couple of hours still before the girls were due back from the theatre. Joyce sunk down on the carpet and sat cross-legged in front of the leather chest. She moved her long crimson skirt around her stockinged feet. Arthur was out and Philip was in bed. She had thought about doing housework or baking for the café tomorrow but had decided to do nothing instead. Joyce hadn't been able to concentrate on anything since seeing her father; even now it felt strange to know he was still alive. She lost track of how many times she had wished he hadn't gone to work on the *Titanic*, crying herself to sleep most nights, hoping it was all a mistake and he would come back.

She leant forward and unbuckled the worn leather strap that wrapped around the chest. As she pushed the locks to one side, the metal catches sprung up, and she lifted the lid before pushing it back on its hinges, letting it fall as she gazed at the contents. Everything inside was a bit haphazard from when she and Rose had pulled almost everything out to search through it. When they had returned with Philip she'd just thrown it back in. She took a deep breath; it was time to find out what else had been kept hidden away, if anything. Joyce pulled out some papers. They looked official and a little complicated to her. She turned the pages and continued to study them, and realised they seemed to be about the house they had in the village before they moved to London. Maybe Arthur would give them the once-over.

Joyce sighed. Living in the village seemed like a lifetime ago. Her eyes welled up. Folding her arms around her, she gripped the soft material of her blouse. As the tears fell she rocked back and forth sobbing. *"Dear Lord, please help me, I can't take any more. I miss my ma so much. She would know what to do. What was my pa up to that he could just abandon me without giving it a thought? Please help me and show me how to recover from all of this."* Her cries sounded around the room, her tears leaving a salty taste on her lips. Joyce dropped the papers she was holding and took a couple of deep breaths. She wiped her hands over her face. Her throat was tight and her eyes felt raw. Exhaustion washed over her. She reached out and picked up the recipe book that she'd found earlier. The corners of the hard cover were worn with use, as was the spine. Joyce stroked it before opening the front cover where she saw her mother's name written on the inside. Her eyes welled up again. She ran her fingertips over her name. 'Oh, Ma, I miss you so much. I can't begin to explain what things have been like since you left us. I hope God is looking after you because there's not much happening down here that would make you proud. Pa is alive; yes that's right you heard me correctly. Just saying it shocks me.'

Joyce squeezed her eyes tight and snapped the recipe book shut. 'I'll have a good read of that when I'm in bed.

I'm sure it will bring back some great memories of our time together in the kitchen.' She wiped her eyes with the back of her hand and put the book down on the floor. A silver-framed photograph of her mother and father caught her eye. Picking it up, she stared at it for what seemed like an eternity before putting it on the floor. She glanced across at it again. 'You look so in love, Ma, and I always thought we were a happy family so where did it all go wrong? Or maybe it didn't. Perhaps Pa wasn't as strong as I remember him being, and you were the one who kept us all together as a family.'

A small gift box had been placed under her parents' photograph; it was calling her to open it. Joyce gingerly lifted it out and opened the lid. A small gold band sat in the middle of it. A sob escaped. Joyce realised it was her mother's wedding ring. She snapped the box shut and placed it on the table. She would need to put it somewhere safe. Maybe one day she'd wear it, if she ever got married. Sighing, she realised that wasn't likely to happen now. Gazing into the trunk, she already felt drained by it all. Joyce shook her head. She thought it would all be connected to Philip, and hadn't expected to see anything that belonged to her mother and father.

Joyce heard the click of the front door locking shut, and immediately looked at the clock. It was only half past eight so it was too early for the girls to be home from the theatre. Arthur strolled into the dining room and took in Joyce sitting cross-legged on the floor. 'Ah, you're finally emptying the trunk are you?'

Joyce jerked her head round at the sound of his voice. She nodded. 'It seems to be mainly my stuff in here or things to do with my family, not that I've got anywhere near to the bottom of it yet, but I assumed it would be all to do with Philip.'

'So did I.' Arthur frowned. He stared at her red eyes and the dark lines that sat beneath them. 'Well, you should go through it then because there could be something important in there – or some treasured possession that belonged to your mother.'

Joy stood up, and ran her hands down the front of her skirt. 'I've already found this.' She picked up the small box that was on the table. 'It's my mother's wedding ring; at least I think it's hers.' Opening the lid of the box, she passed it to Arthur. 'There's also a picture of my mother and father in the trunk. They looked so happy together.' Joy shook her head. She watched as Arthur put the box back on the table. She blinked quickly before taking a breath. Her eyes widened as she stared at Arthur. It took all her energy to stay calm. 'Did you know my father was still alive? Is that another secret you've been keeping from me?'

Arthur paled. He lowered his eyes.

'Well, that tells me the answer is yes. How many more secrets do you have? Do you not understand what it's like for me? I keep discovering lie after lie and now it's beginning to feel like my whole life has been a lie.'

Arthur stepped forward and held his hand up in front of him. 'Wait, I didn't know your father was alive until I went to the hospital looking for Philip, and that's when I saw him for the first time. I was as shocked as you are and told him he had to come and see you because I couldn't carry that burden. I thought he would once I knew, but was clearly wrong. Please understand, I didn't want to be the one who hurt you all over again.'

Joyce walked over to the armchair and lowered herself slowly onto the soft cushions. She shook her head. 'I can't believe it, and every time I think about it I find myself shaking my head in disbelief.'

'I'm exactly the same, and I'm not his daughter, so it must be a hundred times harder for you. Can I ask, how did you find out?'

Joyce sat very still in the chair, staring into the grate of the unlit fire. 'There have been a few times when I've thought I caught glimpses of him around the hospital, but I assumed my mind was playing tricks on me. He was always too far away for me to be certain.' She paused, looking down at her hands gripped on her lap. 'Something drove me to the hospital earlier today and when I got there he was sitting at my grandma's bedside.'

Arthur shook his head. 'It must have been one helluva shock for you.'

Joyce looked up at him. 'That's putting it mildly. I passed out.'

Arthur stared at her; his eyes were full of sadness. 'I don't know what to say. I trust he stayed and looked after you?'

'Yes, he did.' Joyce's eyes became watery.

'Did he offer you any explanation?'

Joyce shook her head. 'None that I heard, but I must admit I wasn't listening very much. I was too busy telling him what I thought. He did say he was trying to protect me and I wouldn't understand.'

Arthur remained silent as he watched the raw emotion etched on Joyce's face.

Joyce pulled her lips into a tight line, before a sob managed to escape. 'What I don't understand, is why he would want to abandon me like that, especially so soon after my mother's death. Why he would want me to think he was dead? I'm his daughter. Was I such a bad daughter that he wanted to get away from me? I just don't understand and unless he can explain it to me I'm not sure I ever will.'

Arthur walked over to the chair she was sitting on. He knelt down in front of her and clasped her hands in his. 'I have no idea what your father was thinking, and I certainly don't know where he's been or what he's been up to, but I can tell you this: from my experience, you are a wonderful person and I would've been grateful and proud to have you as my daughter.'

Tears ran down Joyce's cheeks. She didn't know how much more of this she could take.

Arthur pulled her into his arms while she sobbed.

Arthur closed and folded his newspaper, the rustling carrying in the silence. He placed it on the table next to his armchair. Looking up at the clock on the mantelpiece, he saw it was quarter past five. Joyce and Philip should be home soon. He stood up and ran his hands through his hair, wishing he knew where to find Ted. He hadn't been able to stop thinking about Joyce and what she said. He had been to the hospital a couple of times, hoping he would find him visiting his mother but he had either stopped going or Arthur had picked the wrong times to go.

Arthur paced around the room, wondering what he could do to help Joyce. He couldn't stop worrying about her. Her life had been turned upside down in the last few months and now to discover her father was alive? He shook his head. Would it be the last straw and tip her over the edge? Would she survive the shock of it all? 'I think I'll go and put the kettle on,' he said into the empty room. 'Gosh, never mind Joyce going mad; I'm talking to myself.' He shook his head, picked up his newspaper and walked out into the hall. There were a couple of thuds at the front door as the doorknocker dropped in quick succession, making him jump. They didn't get many visitors and he assumed it wouldn't be any of the girls because they would've let themselves in. His footsteps were silent as he strolled over to the door. The doorknocker thudded again. He reached out and turned the handle to open it. It groaned under the pressure. A warm gust of wind blew into the hall, almost taking the door out of Arthur's hand. He tightened his hold on it and shook his head, not believing what he was seeing. 'You've got a nerve coming here.'

Ted stared Arthur straight in the eye. 'You know I wouldn't have come if I wasn't desperate.'

Arthur stepped over the threshold and glanced up and down the road, the ends of his grey hair taking flight. 'You've been desperate since you've arrived in London. What makes today any different?'

Ted watched Arthur closely. 'You're all right, no one knows I'm here.'

Arthur stepped back inside, running his fingers through his hair. 'Well, you best get inside before anybody sees you. I don't want no trouble being brought to my doorstep. I have the feeling that's exactly what you would bring. Joyce deserves better, as indeed they all do.'

Ted shook his head as he stepped over the threshold,

removed his trilby, and closed the door behind him. 'We were friends once.'

Arthur stared at him, taking in his dishevelled appearance and the bruising on his face. 'You're right, but looking at you right now I find that quite hard to believe. I can't imagine what we ever had in common to form that friendship. I can't believe how badly you've treated Joyce. You should be ashamed of yourself.'

'You've got a nerve; you were a drunk!'

Arthur's mouth tightened. 'That's right I was, but mine was caused by grief. What's your excuse? And, before you say anything, it's not an excuse I'm proud of, but trust me I lost everything that was important to me.'

Ted shrugged. 'I didn't come here for a lecture. I know what I've done but no one knows what I've been going through.'

Arthur could feel anger raging through him as he stared at Ted. 'And what about your daughter? What about Joyce? What about what she's been going through? Don't you care at all?'

'As I said, I didn't come here for a lecture.'

Arthur shook his head. 'No, you could never be told. If I had to guess what brought you to my doorstep I would say it was money. It's always been about money. You have no idea what it's like to lose a child, and yet you've just thrown yours away with no thought. One day you'll wake up to the fact that life isn't about money; it's about caring for the people around you and the ones you love. Let me tell you something, when you lose everyone you love none of it means anything anymore because you have no one to share it with.'

Ted glared at Arthur before brushing past him and striding into the dining room. 'I don't have long.' He stood next to the window and pulled back the edge of the curtain. He peered round it, looking on to the street. 'I have a debt to pay and I don't have the money.'

'Then get a job and stop gambling.' Arthur stared at Ted. 'Have you not learnt anything from when you left your family short, your wife working miracles to put food on the table? Do you seriously think that when you had a win the presents you brought back made up for that?'

'Look, Arthur, do you think I wanted to come here? Do you not recognise desperation when you see it?'

'I'll tell you what I think, shall I? I think it's about time you got yourself together and had a proper conversation with Joyce.' Arthur paused, and stared at Ted. 'Don't you care you could lose your daughter to a German bomb?' He waved his newspaper in the air and it rustled as Arthur turned its pages. 'According to the newspaper those bombs we heard the other night were around Stoke Newington, Dalston, Hoxton, Shoreditch, Whitechapel, Stepney and Leytonstone. They're getting nearer and people are dying.'

'Of course I care. Those poor people must have been terrified.' Ted glanced over at Arthur, but didn't look down at the newspaper. 'I hope they were all taking shelter in their basements.'

Arthur studied Ted for a moment. 'The homes were bombed to the ground and people were killed and you can't even bring yourself to look at the paper – never mind read about it.'

Ted turned away and gave a troubled sigh. 'Look, I don't

want to bring trouble to Joyce, or to you, but I have a feeling it could already be too late for me to change that.'

Arthur took a sharp intake of breath. 'What does that mean? Is she in danger?'

'Not if I can pay my bill.'

Arthur's eyes widened as he suddenly made the connection. 'Is that who Frank is?' He dropped his paper and clenched his fists down by his sides. 'I've been trying to find out about him because he keeps turning up and I'm not convinced he's the guardian angel he professes to be.'

Ted didn't answer. He looked at the floor before looking up again and letting his eyes roam around the room.

'Don't even think about taking something that's not yours; believe me I won't hesitate to contact the police.'

Ted shook his head and bit his lip before pleading with Arthur. 'I have to pay this debt. I was cheated out of a big win and now they're after me. I've paid some of it but I still owe quite a bit. As I said I wouldn't come here if I wasn't desperate.'

Arthur didn't know what to do. He had no desire to help Ted but also wanted to protect Joyce at all costs. 'Wait here and I'll get you some money but don't ever darken my doorstep again unless it's with Joyce's blessing.' He turned and walked out of the room.

Ted wandered round picking up figurines, examining them before returning them into the cabinet. He noticed the small box on the side and opened it. He gasped as he stared down at the thin gold band that sat in the middle of it. Ted looked up as heavy footsteps thudded along the hall. He looked down at the ring one last time and thrust the box into his jacket pocket.

Arthur waved the notes around. 'You can have this and I don't want it back but there is a stipulation to this deal: you make sure Frank is called off and you talk to Joyce. She has been in a right old state since she saw you at the hospital.'

Ted nodded and reached out to take the money.

Arthur scowled at him and pulled his arm back. 'No nodding, I want to actually hear the words. I want to see if I can believe you.'

Ted's lips tightened. 'I want to make it up to her, I promise. I didn't mean to just leave her but my life went from bad to worse, and I got into a right old mess. In the end I thought it was safer for her if I wasn't in her life.'

Arthur stared at Ted. 'And yet you've still brought trouble to her door so that hasn't quite worked out, has it?' He shook his head and threw the money on the table. 'Take this and get out.'

Ted reached out to seize the money before Arthur changed his mind. 'I will sort it, I promise.'

Ted stood outside the pawnshop in Victoria Road. He had purposely travelled away from Arthur's house so he wouldn't bump into Joyce. He peered up and down the busy street. The fumes from the coughing exhaust pipes filled the air while the clouds of smoke drifted up and disappeared into the grey sky. The sun was trying to break through, although, at the same time he felt a couple of spots of rain. He looked around him. The last thing he needed was to bump into Arthur or Joyce. He turned to stare in the pawnshop window at the many items of jewellery and watches trying to entice the customers in. He could see the shop was full to the rafters with many different things that people had sold on.

Ted tapped the outside of his trouser pocket to check the folded notes Arthur had given him were still there. He didn't want to part with the money he had been given; it felt like a gift. He had the idea of trying to find another card game where he could double it again, but not one of the Simmons games. He smiled. It was good to have a plan, and this one would work. He could pay off his debt and then talk to Joyce about them living together as a family. His fingers clasped around the small box in his jacket pocket. He pulled it out and opened it. His eyes glazed over as he stared down at his wife's wedding ring. Could he do this? Could he really sell his wife's wedding ring? A voice yelled in his head, telling him he could always buy it back again when he'd had his win. His conscience thought otherwise and argued back. What if he didn't have the win? His wife's ring would be lost forever.

'Well, fancy seeing you here, Ted.'

Ted looked up, trying to hide his misery from the man standing in front of him.

'Is the ring worth anything do you think? Could it pay off your debt once and for all?'

Ted shook his head. 'Look, Slips, I'm doing the best I can to raise the money. If I hadn't been stitched up in that game it would never have come to this.'

Slips sneered at him. 'Do yer want me to pass that on to my father?'

Teds eyes widened and panic trampled across his face. 'No, of course I don't, but you know as well as I do I had a great hand there, and it's strange that he had the only hand that could beat me.' Ted paused for a second. 'Let's face it he was supposedly playing blind as well, so how else could he have known? I was convinced that money was mine; otherwise I would've stopped.'

Slips threw back his head and roared with laughter, drawing attention to them from people walking by. 'No, yer wouldn't of, yer can't help yerself. There's your daughter working so hard and yer just throw away yer money. I wouldn't mind but yer not even any good at it. I told yer not to play when I met yer on the door but would yer listen? No. So when yer say yer shouldn't be in this position and were cheated out of yer winnings: yer right yer shouldn't be in this position, because yer should've listened to me before yer joined the game. But as always, Ted Taylor, yer know better than everybody else so yer reap what yer sow.'

Ted stared at the ring. 'This was my wife's wedding ring. I've just stolen it from my daughter. That's what I've come down to.'

Slips shook his head. 'That makes yer worse than me, because I'd never steal from someone I loved, or maybe yer don't love 'er so that makes it easier. Were yer not brought up to believe family is family and nothing else matters?'

'Of course I was, but difficult times call for desperate action.'

Slips snatched the box out of Ted's hand. 'Let's have a look, see if it's worth anything.'

Ted snatched it back. 'You can't just take this; it belongs to my daughter.'

Slips leant forward and grabbed Ted's jacket with both fists and pulled him in close. 'Don't push yer luck wiv me because I've tried to be nice, but now yer just plain taking advantage of my good nature. Don't make me 'ave to remind yer what the taste of yer own blood is like.' He stared at Ted's terrified expression. 'Yer need to understand yer no good to me dead but if I 'ave to send a message then I will; after all I can always get the money from yer daughter, Joyce, now she's a lovely girl and a great cook.'

Ted's arms were limp as they hung by his sides. He tried hard to hide his fear by turning his head away.

Slips shook Ted. 'Look at me.'

Ted turned his face to look at him. The smell of onion on Slips's breath was strong; he tried to hold his breath.

Slips slammed his forehead against Ted's, knocking off his trilby hat. 'I'm not messing.' He pushed Ted away and snatched the ring back.

Ted frowned. 'Please, you can't take it. It was my wife's and now my daughter should have it. Look, Slips, I just need a bit more time. I'm getting there.'

'I'm not heartless. You can keep the ring, but yer must give me the money that your friend Arthur has given you.'

Ted shrugged. 'What makes you think Arthur has given me any money? And how do you know about him?'

Slips smiled. 'Trust me when I say I know everything about you. I even know what room your mother is in at the hospital. So it's up to you; do yer wanna play clean or dirty because I can do either as yer well know?'

Ted fidgeted as he looked around him.

Slips took a step nearer. 'No one is coming to your rescue so hand it over.'

Ted took a deep breath. 'What makes you think I have any money?'

Slips chuckled. 'It's one of the oldest signs in the book,

Ted; you keep touching your pocket to make sure it's still there.'

Ted sighed, his shoulders hunched over.

Slips shook his head. 'Please don't tell me you were going to gamble it away?'

Ted shook his head. 'Of course not, what do you take me for?'

'Ted, one thing you're not is a very good liar so I'm saving yer from yourself.' Slips paused and held out his hand. 'Hand it over. Don't make me hurt yer again because I will. It's better yer get a beating than me.' He lifted his chin. 'Yer know, snapping your arm in half will be easy, then there will definitely be no card playing for yer.'

Ted's heart was pounding. He thrust his hand inside his pocket and pulled out the wad of notes and handed it to Slips.

'It's good to see you're finally learning.' Slips flicked through the notes before handing back the wedding ring. 'As I said, I'm not heartless, but it's not enough, although it will buy yer some time.' He turned to walk away, stopping to pick up his hat, and looking thoughtfully at Ted. 'Think carefully about what yer do with that ring.' He turned away and carried on walking.

Ted frowned. 'Please, Slips; leave my family out of this mess. I beg you not to involve them in it.'

Slips put his hat on his head at a jaunty angle. 'Ted, I didn't involve them; yer did that when yer didn't pay. Yer know 'ow it works; everything is fair game.'

18

There was something about hospitals, the smells and the quiet stilted atmosphere of people whispering. Doctors and nurses moved silently around the ward; only the uniforms rustling together as they moved gave their presence away. The trolley wheels squeaked as it made its way down the ward, carrying books and newspapers for the patients.

Mavis sat very still in the chair next to Simon's bed. For the first time there was tension between them. She wasn't sure if it was her age or the heat of the June sunshine beating through the window but beads of perspiration formed on her forehead. Opening her black handbag, she retrieved her white lace-edged handkerchief and dabbed it on her face. How she now longed for the rain they'd had in April. 'Don't you think it's time I told Joyce and Barbara you are here?'

Simon was still in the same position; he had one pillow and was lying flat on his back. He scowled. 'No, Barbara can't be trusted to keep anything to herself and Joyce has probably moved on.'

Mavis's lips tightened. She couldn't argue about Barbara but Joyce…

A doctor was suddenly standing at the foot of Simon's bed flanked by two nurses. 'Good morning, Mr Hitchin, how are you feeling today?' The doctor picked up Simon's notes and took a pen from the top pocket of his white coat and began writing on them. He walked round to the side of the bed and placed the notes on the bedside cabinet. 'Have you tried to get out of bed yet?'

Simon frowned. 'No, Doctor, I haven't. It's quite painful to move any part of my body.' He took a breath. 'Actually, it hurts just to lie here.'

The doctor picked up Simon's notes again and started to read them. 'It looks like you are doing well so there's no reason why we shouldn't get you out of bed.' His lips twisted a little. 'Of course before we do try I expect you realise it's going to hurt like hell. That's partly stiffness, where you've been so still, and also your body has started healing. The skin needs to have movement, as indeed do your joints as they can all stiffen through lack of use. As far as we can tell we managed to get all the shrapnel out of your back so it's just about letting it heal now. You're lucky with where it hit your body; it could have been much worse.'

Mavis cleared her throat. 'Would you like me to leave?'

The doctor looked up and smiled. 'Not on our account; your son might be glad to have you here by the time we've finished with him.'

Mavis stood up. She clasped her hand round the top rung of the heavy wooden chair, and set it down a little further away from the bed. It went down with a thud and nearly toppled over. She glanced across at the doctor and nurses. 'Sorry, I was trying too hard to be quiet.'

The doctor nodded.

One of the nurses stepped round the bed and stood nearby. 'Don't worry, it's all right.'

The doctor cleared his throat.

Each of the nurses eyed him before moving into position, one either side of the bed.

The doctor watched as Simon prepared himself for the pain. His breathing was already coming in short bursts. 'Mr Hitchin, you're not expected to do it all yourself this time; the nurses and I will push and pull you into position to sit you up, but first they will bend and stretch your legs a little and then your arms. If it really gets too much then please let us know and we'll stop for a moment for you to catch your breath.'

Simon nodded, bracing himself for the pain that was going to assault him from every angle.

Mavis watched as they pushed and pulled Simon about. His face screwed up in agony, his hands gripped the side of the bed, but he never screamed out.

'You're doing very well, Simon. Keep going and you will get there.' The doctor watched Simon's every move while offering words of encouragement. 'If you do this every day it won't take long before you'll be relatively pain-free. Your leg will take a few of months to heal so you'll need a walking stick going forward.' The doctor paused. 'I know it's painful and I'm sorry to push you so hard but you'll thank me in the long run.'

Simon's face screwed up in pain. 'I know.' He gasped. 'I've got to get better, no matter what.'

Mavis welled up as she watched the pain etched on Simon's face. She felt so helpless. She wanted to do what every mother wanted to do, protect and cradle him from harm, but she didn't. She sat in silence watching and praying he was going to be all right. She sent up silent prayers hoping they would be answered. Mavis couldn't help but think it would've been a good thing if Joyce could have been there. She would have lifted his spirits rather than him thinking their relationship was no more.

The doctor helped Simon sit in an armchair and propped his leg up. 'I know you're feeling extremely uncomfortable right now; hopefully the painkillers will soon start to take effect, and as exhausting as it is, it will do you good to get out of bed and start moving around. You've been in here for a while and it's not a good thing for you to still be in bed. The more you move the quicker you'll be released from the pain and the easier moving will become, but it will take some time for it all to go.'

Simon flopped his head against the back of the chair. Beads of perspiration ran down his face. He took several breaths before nodding. 'Thank you, Doctor, I promise I shall try and do all the stretching movements and exercises that you suggested. I have no desire to end up in a wheelchair.'

Annie marched purposefully along the corridor, her heels clicking. She was hot and sticky but her excitement was growing with each step as she headed towards Kitty's dressing room. She loved the theatre's smell of make-up mingling with the paint the stage team used to patch up any knocks on the scenery as it came on and off stage. There was always something going on; it was a hive of excitement and activity, hammers banging on wood somewhere, instruments being tuned, and actors reading their lines or music playing.

Walking past an open doorway, Annie thought she heard someone sniffing. Stopping for a moment to listen, she turned to walk back and peer around the doorway. 'I'm sorry to intrude, but are you all right? I couldn't help but hear you crying from down the corridor.'

The young girl looked up. Her eyes were red and blurry. 'You can't help me. From what I hear you're the last person I'd want to help me.'

Annie jerked her head back. Her face didn't sting and yet she felt as though she'd been slapped. 'Well, I'm not trying to intrude. I just wanted to help if I could. You know a problem shared is a problem halved and all that, but if you don't need or want my help that's fine.'

The girl clenched her hands as she folded her arms. 'What you mean is you want to tell the director, or worse Miss Hetherington, that I'm not fit to do the work.'

Again Annie looked shocked. 'I don't know where this is coming from. I don't even know your name.'

'Exactly.' The girl wiped her hands over her face. 'So why would you want to help me, if not to tell the people in charge that I'm no good as a seamstress because I'm too busy crying?'

Annie shook her head. 'I don't understand why you think I would do that. I've never purposely got anyone into trouble.'

The young girl glared at her.

'Do you want to talk about it? After all I might be able to help.'

The girl dropped like a stone onto a chair. 'No one can help me.'

Annie shook her head. 'If you don't mind my saying so that sounds very dramatic; sometimes by working together you can solve these things but first I need to know what the problem is.'

The girl sniffed. 'You really don't know who I am do you? Not that you should but you've been in the sewing room talking to Miss Spencer most afternoons and yet you just haven't noticed me sitting in the corner.'

Annie's eyes widened. 'I'm sorry you did say earlier about Miss Hetherington, I really should pay more attention. What's your name?'

The girl eyed her suspiciously.

Annie sighed. 'You do know it won't be hard for me to find out who you are, don't you?'

The girl bit her lip for a moment before a sigh escaped. 'It's Lizzie Turnbull.'

'Well, Lizzie, if I may call you by your first name, Rose isn't a problem for you is she?'

The young girl shook her head. 'No, it's Miss Hetherington; I don't think she likes me very much. She says some awful things to me.'

Annie couldn't help laughing. 'Miss Hetherington is horrible to everybody so don't take it personally. She even tries to be horrible to Kitty and Mr Tyler so you're in good company.' She stepped further into the room. She tentatively reached out and put her arms around her. 'Come on, let me take you back to Rose. She will look after you; she is one of the nicest people I know. If she saw how upset you are she would be upset herself. Miss Hetherington treats Rose terrible as well so she'll know exactly what you are going through.'

Lizzie looked taken aback. 'Thank you, I wasn't expecting you to be nice to me.'

Annie sucked in her breath. 'I don't know what's being said, and don't really want to know, but no one here has ever spent any time with me – apart from my friend Rose and Kitty, but that's because I'm her dresser – so how could they possibly know me at all?'

Lizzie nodded. 'I will make sure they know that you're actually a very caring person.'

Annie smiled. 'I'm sorry for not noticing you in the sewing room. I've had a lot on my mind and always seem to be in a hurry but that's no excuse.' She paused for a moment and, looking at Lizzie, decided she didn't look much older than fifteen or sixteen. 'You know I come from a small village; Rose and I came down here together. I wanted to be on the stage and Rose supported me. I don't know what I would do without her. I've learnt since being here that there are some lovely people who are prepared to give you a chance but there are also some who want to take advantage of a trusting and innocent young girl. Someone tried to take advantage of my need to learn and improve my singing. I was warned but didn't want to listen. Anyway, the upshot of it is I got into a terrible situation, and was fortunate Kitty was there for me. I'm lucky to have found a family here and would never throw that away. If you ever need anything you just need to ask because I know what it's like to be somewhere strange.'

Lizzie looked at her wide-eyed. 'Was that Matthew? He was the pianist here wasn't he?'

Annie raised her eyebrows. 'My! Gossips have been talking. Let me just say it was a very unpleasant time. I am curious though as to how you know so much when you haven't been here very long?'

Lizzie squirmed on her chair. She lowered her eyelashes. 'I haven't been here very long but my friend has worked here for years and she used to come home and tell me all the gossip. I'm sorry I listened to it now and made judgements based around it.'

Annie shook her head. 'You're no different to anybody else so don't be hard on yourself.' She put her arm through Lizzie's. 'Come on, let's get you back to Rose before Miss Hetherington does sack you.'

Lizzie smiled at Annie and followed her lead out into the corridor.

Rose stepped out of a side room looking pensive. She looked up and down the corridor. Her face immediately broke into a smile as she walked towards them. 'Ahh, I've been wondering where you were. Is everything all right?'

Lizzie nodded.

Annie looked from one to the other. 'I think Miss Hetherington has been at it again.' Her lips tightened. 'That's all I'm saying.'

Rose smiled at her friend. 'Trust me you don't need to say anything else.' Frowning, she looked towards Lizzie. 'Are you all right?'

Lizzie nodded. 'I'm sorry, I should've known better.'

Rose shook her head. 'It happens to the best of us so

don't worry about it; however, you do need to talk to me about these things because I've been there as well.'

'I promise I will in future.'

'Well, you should. You're excellent with a needle and I don't want to lose you as a seamstress.' Rose smiled as Lizzie's face lit up. She turned to Annie. 'Thanks for looking after Lizzie.'

Annie smiled. 'Any time, it was quite enlightening actually. I hope you have a good day, Lizzie, and don't listen to the gossip.' She turned to walk away, before stopping to peer over her shoulder. 'I'll catch up with you for a break in about an hour, Rose. That's if you get a chance.'

Rose nodded. 'Most definitely.'

The hour soon passed and Annie strolled into the sewing room to see Rose on her own but tugging a drawer from its runners and turning it upside down to empty it on to the large sewing table. She watched her fervently move threads and pieces of material out the way. Her hand moving swiftly between the items that had been inside before scooping them up and dropping them back in to the drawer. 'What on earth is going on? What have you lost, Rose? I'm assuming you've lost something from the way you're frantically tipping up the drawers.'

Rose didn't look up; she carried on pulling out drawers and banging them shut.

'Rose.' Annie walked over and rested her hand on her arm. 'What on earth is the matter? Talk to me.'

Rose shook her head. 'You wouldn't understand.'

'How can you say that?' Annie stared at her friend, with disbelief running across her face. 'What do you mean

I wouldn't understand? You're my friend; if something is bothering you then it bothers me, so tell me what the problem is.'

Rose stood up straight. Her eyes were red as they darted around the room. She sighed. 'It's my sketchpad; I have a few of them. Most of them are at home, but the one I'm looking for is meant to be here.'

Annie waited, remembering the number of times she saw Rose hide a pad under her pillow when Annie had walked into her bedroom. 'I always thought the ones at home were diaries you were keeping. That's why I never asked about them; I didn't want to pry.'

'This particular one had Kitty's wedding dress in it; it's what I was using to make sure the dress was made as we both talked about.'

Annie tried to hide her dismay from her friend. Wondering what she could do to help, she glanced around the room, which had already been turned upside down. 'It must be here somewhere, or else it's at home. There's nowhere else it can be.'

Rose jerked her head round and stared at her friend before snapping, 'Don't you think I know that?'

'I'm sorry, Rose; I'm just trying to help. Where do you want me to look?'

Rose shook her head. 'I don't think it's here.' She flopped down onto the wooden chair; her shoulders slumped as the tears started to roll down her face. 'I don't understand. I don't let it out of my sight.'

Annie put a hand on her friend's shoulders. 'Maybe somebody's picked it up by mistake. Has anybody been in here today? Or perhaps we should start with where did you last see it and when? Perhaps Lizzie picked it up to have a look at? Maybe we can retrace your steps.'

Rose shrugged. She put her head in her hands.

'Come on, Rose, think because we have to start somewhere.'

Rose let her hands fall, banging down on to the desk. She let out a sigh. 'I am almost certain I had it this morning.'

'Well, have you left the room at all? You know, did you go and talk to Bert or Kitty or even go to the ladies room? Has there been any time when you and the sketchpad have been parted?'

Rose glanced around the room before standing up and picking up rolls of material that had been left on the table and looking underneath them. 'I've been in here the whole morning, apart from when I met you and Lizzie in the hall, which is why I've turned the place upside down looking for it.' Rose's eyes widened. 'What am I going to tell Kitty? I shouldn't have started this dress; it was always above me, and my capabilities. And now I have to tell Kitty she won't have it. She's going to love me doing this so late in the day. A bride without a wedding dress.'

Annie stared at her friend, wanting to help but not knowing where to start. She put her arm around her shoulders. 'No, we just have to think and if we can't find it then we'll have to do it from memory. After all you've already done so much of it.'

Rose sighed. 'I know but it's not just about Kitty's dress; I have lots of thoughts in there, ideas for future outfits, all my dreams are in that pad.'

Annie squeezed her friend tight. 'We'll find it. I promise we'll keep looking until it's found.'

Joyce stood upright and stretched her aching back. She ran her forearm across her face as she turned to see Barbara sweeping the floor and Philip filling up the salt cellars. He shook the paper funnel she had made earlier to avoid the salt granules going all over the table, and was twisting round the salt cellar, admiring his handiwork.

Philip smiled; he sat back down on the wooden chair waiting for Joyce to finish work.

Joyce sighed and moved the condiments to one side of the café table, wiping the available space vigorously with a damp cloth.

Philip called out, 'Is there anything else I can do?'

Joyce smiled at the young lad she had become quite attached to. 'I don't think so, we're nearly finished now, so we shouldn't be long.' She went back to cleaning the tables ready for the morning.

The bell chimed above the café door as it swung open. Joyce didn't look up. 'Sorry, we're closed.'

Barbara stopped sweeping and looked up. The grey-haired man looked familiar to her.

'I know.'

Philip's excited voice suddenly rang out in the café. 'Pa!' His chair scraped over the tiled floor as he pushed it back. His footsteps were hardly noticeable as he ran across to his father.

Barbara smiled as she watched the boy's excitement.

Joyce stopped dead. She knew that voice, but was sure she had misheard. She looked up, intrigued to see who Philip's father was. Her eyes widened while her mouth dropped open in surprise. Philip had already wrapped his arms around his father's legs. She was stunned as she took in the scene in front of her. There was no mistake.

'Hello, Philip, I'm sorry I haven't seen you for a little while.' Ted scooped him up into his arms and held the boy tight.

Philip threw his arms around his father's neck and squeezed him tight. 'That's all right, Pa, I expect you've been busy working.'

Ted tickled him. 'That I have, that I have.'

Philip giggled.

Barbara started to laugh. She glanced over at Joyce but there was no happiness in her face; she looked ashen.

Joyce stood rooted to the spot. She stared at them both, unable to take in what she was seeing. She hadn't misheard Philip. He was her half-brother. How was that even possible? How did she not know? Her mind immediately jumped back to 1910. Her brother was born before the *Titanic* sunk, before her father disappeared and yet he hadn't told her. Why not? She shook her head. Her mother had passed away many years ago so there was no shame in it, or maybe there was, if Philip's mother was a streetwalker?

Philip turned to Joyce. His smile lit up his face. 'Look, Joyce, my pa is here. Isn't that wonderful?'

Heat swamped Joyce. She held on to the edge of the table, closed her eyes for a moment while she took a couple of deep breaths. She opened her eyes again, hoping the scene in front of her might be different but it wasn't. 'Yes it is, Philip, yes it is.' Joyce took a breath before turning to Ted. 'What are you doing here?'

'Why do you look so sad? This is a good day. Pa is here; it's a good day.' Philip stroked his father's cheek. He looked very serious when he spoke. 'Your face is all prickly and hot. If grandma was here she'd tell you off for not shaving.'

Joyce couldn't take her eyes off them both. It suddenly hit her that her grandma was also Philip's. All this time she thought he'd called her that because he didn't know what else to call her. Her legs felt like jelly as they tried to support her.

'I know, I promise I'll shave as soon as I get a minute.' Ted looked over Joyce before looking back at Philip; who wrapped his arms around his neck again and gave him another squeeze.

'Are you going to stay for a while?'

Ted nodded. 'Yes I am, son, and I'll definitely be making more time for you in the future, I promise. I just have a few things to sort out.' He held Philip close, squeezing him tight. Their love for each other was there for all to see. 'Philip, I need you to give me a minute with Joyce. Can you do that for me?'

Philip studied his father, holding his prickly face in his small hands. 'You're not going now are you?'

Ted shook his head. 'No, my little man, I'm not going anywhere.' He lowered Philip to the floor. 'Maybe we'll go out and have some tea and cake, or in your case a cold drink and cake.' He laughed. 'If Joyce doesn't mind that is.'

Philip grinned. 'You can have that here. Joyce makes wonderful cakes and it's not just me who says so, everybody does. Look, she's even got something on the wall that says so too. Frank read it to me and said I should be proud living with someone so clever.'

Ted's eyes narrowed and his mouth tightened at the sound of Slips's name. He stepped forward and glanced at the certificate. So Slips had made friends with his family. He suddenly knew what he had to do. He turned and smiled at his son. 'So she has, well, I clearly need to try some of her cake. It's a good job I came to see her.'

Philip nodded. 'You could come home with us and have dinner. Joyce won't mind, will you, Joyce?'

Joyce was suddenly aware that Philip was staring at her. What could she say? Did she break this little boy's heart because she couldn't forgive her father? She forced a smile to her lips. 'Of course he can, if he wants to.' She paused, looking at her father. 'Although, I'm sure he has other things to do.'

'Oh no, it would be lovely to come home with you both.'

Joyce stared at her father, her anger simmering and only just being held in check. She wondered what his game was. The doorbell chimed, as it swung open again. 'We're closed.'

The bell sounded again as the door clicked shut. 'Nothing is ever closed to me.'

Ted turned quickly, and pushed Philip behind him. 'Go and sit down for a minute, Philip. Sit over in the far corner.'

Joyce swivelled on the heels of her shoes and stared at Frank. 'This is not a good time, Frank.'

Philip didn't move. 'Hello, Frank.'

Ted scowled at Philip. 'Please do as I say.'

'Hello, Philip.' Frank smiled before turning to Joyce and shaking his head. 'Actually, I don't think there could be a

better time than a long-awaited family reunion, do you? It's
all quite touching.' He took a step forward and sniffed the
air. 'I don't know what you've been cooking today but it
smells delicious.'

Joyce scowled at him. 'What do you want, Frank?
You're clearly not writing any article because you haven't
mentioned it for a while, not even when we were in Hyde
Park. So what is it you want?'

Ted gave Philip a little nudge. Philip gazed up at his
father. 'Go and sit down.'

Philip screwed up his face but did as he was told.

Frank sneered at Joyce. 'Yer smarter than yer father I'll
say that for yer.'

Ted pulled himself upright and puffed out his chest.
'Leave them alone; this is my problem not theirs.'

Frank pulled out a box of cigarettes from his jacket
pocket. 'Yer don't get it do yer, Ted; yer don't understand
that they could be the means to getting what I want.'

Joyce stepped forward. 'The means?'

Frank said nothing, just smiled and winked at her.

Something was happening here but she didn't understand
what; she only knew she had to protect Philip and Barbara.
She gave Barbara a sideways glance. 'Barbara, why don't
you go home and I'll lock up.'

Barbara frowned and held her wooden broom handle
tight with both hands. 'No, Joyce, I shall stay with you and
Philip.'

Joyce didn't know whether to be pleased that Barbara
was staying or not, but it was obvious Barbara had the
same feeling as her about the situation. She was thankful
Mavis had gone early, and wasn't here to witness what was

possibly unfolding in front of them. 'Thank you, Barbara, I appreciate it, but I think it would be wiser if you left.'

Barbara gave a nervous laugh. 'I think that is probably quite true but we are in this together, whatever this is, and I'm staying put.'

Slips looked between the two girls before gazing over at Philip. 'Philip, why don't yer come over 'ere and chat to me?'

Philip stood up. The rattling and scraping of the chair against the table and floor echoed in the silence of the café.

'No,' Joyce shouted as she walked over to stand next to Philip. 'I don't know what's going on here but I will not allow my little brother to be part of this.' She turned to Ted. 'Whatever trouble you've brought to our doorstep you need to sort it out, and quick.'

Ted lowered his eyes. 'I'm sorry, Joyce, I'm sorry you have become a target through my actions. It's the last thing I wanted.'

Joyce shook her head. 'You've had a rough time, we've all had a rough time, but do you see any of us bringing trouble to someone else's front door? I don't know how many times I have to tell you, stop feeling sorry for yourself and realise it's not just about you. It's about Philip, it's about Barbara, and it's about Simon's café. Now sort out your mess instead of bringing it to other people's doorsteps.'

Ted glanced across at Slips before looking back at Joyce. He nodded. 'It's also about you.' He sighed. 'I can't sort it out because, as always, it's about money. I owe Slips's family quite a bit.'

Slips stared intently at Joyce. 'Yer know it doesn't give me any pleasure to be 'ere but yer father has lost a lot of money through 'is gambling and I'm 'ere to collect the debt.'

Joyce could feel her cheeks getting redder as her anger took hold. She stepped forward and placed herself in front of Philip. 'How much money do you think we make selling tea and cake? It's beyond me how you think that coming here can pay the rest of the debt, regardless of how much it is.'

The doorbell chimed again. Joyce sighed; she should remember to lock the door the minute they close down for the day. 'We're closed.'

'What's going on here?'

Joyce didn't know whether to laugh or cry at the sound of Simon's voice.

Barbara ran forward, almost colliding with Joyce, and wrapped her arms around him. 'This is wonderful. I can't believe you're here.'

Simon winced.

Barbara pulled back. 'Sorry, I didn't mean to hurt you.'

Joyce had also stepped forward but stopped short when she saw he was on crutches. 'Sit down. You don't look very secure on them.'

Mavis followed Simon in through the door. 'No, he isn't. This is the first time he's used them; there's a wheelchair outside. I wasn't sure I'd get it through the doorway and I didn't want to batter him by trying.' She laughed as she helped Simon onto a chair. Suddenly she noticed the men who were standing in the café. 'Hello, what's going on here?' She paused before stretching out her hand. 'How do you do, gentlemen. I'm the owner of this establishment so what can we do for you?'

Joyce couldn't take her eyes off Simon.

19

Joyce reluctantly drew her gaze away from Simon to glance at his mother. 'Mavis, I don't mean to be rude, but I think you, Simon and Barbara should leave.'

Simon studied Joyce for some time, caught up with his desire to sweep her into his arms and protect her. Anger surged through him as it dawned on him he was unable to do either. 'I don't think we're going anywhere. I know you're running this place for me, Joyce, but it is still my café.'

Joyce stepped back, suddenly flushed with colour. He might as well have slapped her round the face; the pain and humiliation wouldn't have felt any worse. She had been firmly put back in her place as the hired help. 'I know it's still your café; I was just trying to protect you all.'

Simon tilted his head. 'Protect us from what, Joyce?'

Joyce studied him for a moment. Something had changed. Now he'd had time to think about it was he glad she'd turned down his marriage proposal? Did he feel humiliated and that was why he was putting her in her place?

Barbara took a deep breath as she watched the pain flick across Joyce's face. 'Simon, this is Frank, or perhaps I should say Slips, and he's been coming to the café quite regularly. I originally thought he had taken a shine to Joyce and it was my job to look after your interests, especially as I thought Joyce was responsible for you enlisting, but I was clearly wrong about that. I made that assumption because you were so sad when you left and I've known for ages that you were in love with her.'

Joyce gasped.

Simon opened his mouth to speak but Barbara held up a hand. 'No, let me finish. Joyce has done a good job running this place, standing up to the landlord, coming in cooking while trying to look after young Philip. She had never encouraged any friendship with Frank, but he just kept turning up. I do believe Joyce had no idea that Frank – Slips – was some kind of gangster with little regard for life.'

Frank stepped forward, his hands curled into fists by his sides. 'That's not true, I'll not 'ave yer spread malicious lies about me, do yer understand?'

Joyce stepped in between Frank and Barbara. 'Thank you, Barbara.' She gently squeezed her arm.

Frank stared at Joyce, but she didn't waver. He looked at Ted. 'Look, I'm not 'ere for anything other than the money Ted owes. Now we can do this the easy way or the 'ard way. Which is it to be?'

Joyce shook her head. 'What else are these good people going to think when you come in here with your threats? I've already told you; we don't have the kind of money you're looking for. Pa, you need to leave here and sort it out with Frank and leave us all alone in peace.'

Simon frowned. 'Pa?'

Joyce tightened her lips. 'Oh yes, Simon, let me introduce you to my father.'

Simon shook his head. 'But I thought your father was dead. Didn't you say he went down with the *Titanic*? Are you sure it's him?'

Joyce gave a humourless laugh. Perspiration was trickling down from her forehead. She ran the palms of her damp hands down Simon's white kitchen coat. 'Unfortunately I am sure. I did think he was dead but it seems he's back. He's risen from the dead to bring trouble; however, there's some good news. It seems I also have a little brother who I didn't know I had.'

Simon opened his mouth to speak but shut it again.

Slips looked around the room at the shocked faces that were staring at Ted and Philip. 'Right, let's get on with this. I came 'ere for money, not an 'istory lesson, and I'm not going until I get what I need. Once I 'ave that yer can all get on with your lives. I'm not interested in them; I'm not interested in any of yer. I just want the money that's owed.'

Simon frowned; a pulse throbbed at the side of his temple. 'How much is it?'

Joyce shook her head. 'No, Simon, I have purposely not asked because I don't want to know. I'm not going to help my father. He has made no apology for leaving me to deal with my own grief and to look after a man who's not my uncle. I have no forgiveness and I will not be helping him.'

Simon stared at the pain on Joyce's face. 'Trust me, Joyce, from what I've seen over the last few months life is very precious and can be ripped away without notice. Forgiveness helps us to find peace within ourselves and in others; it moves us forward. It helps to heal the agony that rips us all apart and it's a heavy burden for any one of us to carry, and we all need to be forgiven at some time in our lives because we all make mistakes. None of us are perfect.'

'Yeah, all very nice and touching; who doesn't love a reunion?' Frank stepped forward and spread his hand over both her soft cheeks and squeezed them tight. 'I think yer don't 'ave any choice. Trust me when I say I don't wanna 'urt yer but I will.'

Ted ran forward and pulled Frank away from his daughter. 'No, I'm not having this, Slips. This is my fault not hers, not Philip's, not Simon's.'

Like lightning, Frank thrust his hand around Ted's throat and squeezed it. 'Be careful, Ted, be very careful. Just remember who yer dealing wiv. Yer shouldn't need reminding I'm in control 'ere, not you, and don't yer forget it.' He thrust him backwards, watching Ted stumble before brushing his hands down each of his suit jacket sleeves in turn. 'Don't push your luck, Ted. I've been very patient with yer for quite some time, but yer need to know my father's patience is running out, and I'm not going to take a beating on yer behalf.' A smile crept across his face. 'Perhaps it's time we bought this little family reunion to an end.' He glanced over at Joyce before turning to Ted. 'Have yer told 'er yet? Have yer told 'er what yer stole? Did yer pawn it in the end?'

Ted fidgeted from one foot to the other while shaking his head. He caught Joyce staring at him.

Frank chuckled. 'Obviously not. Don't yer fink yer should?'

Joyce's tone was cold when she finally spoke. 'What did you take?'

Ted shook his head. He lowered his eyes and stared hard

at the floor. 'My reason for coming here tonight was to return it, I should never have taken it.' He looked up and met her gaze. Thrusting his hand in his jacket pocket, he pulled out a small box. He took a deep breath. 'I should never have taken it, and I'm sorry.' He stretched out his arm to give Joyce the box.

'You took Ma's wedding ring?' Joyce took the box from him. Her eyes widened. 'That means you've been to the house. Is there nothing sacred to you?' Tears pricked at her eyes and she blinked quickly in a bid to stop them from falling.

Ted took a step forward and reached out to Joyce.

Joyce backed away, shaking her head. 'Ma's wedding ring?'

'If it helps I couldn't do it. I loved your ma and couldn't sell it.' Ted paused. 'I came here to return it and to own up to what I'd done. I didn't want to sneak it back into the house.'

Barbara moved closer and put her arm around Joyce.

Simon watched everybody in the room. His sister Barbara had a new bravado about her; even his mother didn't look frightened. Everything had changed while he'd been away, including him. 'How much does he owe?'

Frank eyed the injured soldier sitting on the chair. 'Sixty pounds will call it quits.'

Simon shook his head. 'I don't have sixty pounds. What about if we say forty pounds and call it quits?'

Frank stared at the man; he had no desire to cause him any problems. He looked like he had enough on his plate. 'Fifty.'

Simon nodded. 'You need to come back for it tomorrow.'

Slips scowled. 'And what if I don't wanna to come back tomorrow? 'Ow do I know yer can be trusted to 'ave the money then?'

Simon stared at Frank. 'You don't, you'll just have to take my word for it. It's not like I can go far.'

Slips turned to Ted. 'It looks like it's your lucky day.'

Joyce shook her head. 'Pa, how can you stand by and watch Simon bail you out?'

Ted flopped down on to a wooden chair. 'I'm sorry.'

Frank chuckled. 'Course yer are, Ted, but yer'll be back because yer'll never learn.' He turned to look at Simon. 'I'll come back tomorrow at around 'alf past four. That'll give yer some time, but trust me if the money's not 'ere I'll come looking for each and every one of yer. Do I make myself clear?'

They all stared at him.

'I said, do I make myself clear?'

'Yes,' they all chorused, not taking their eyes off him.

Frank arched his eyebrow as he stared at them all in turn. Without a word, he turned and walked towards the door. The bell rang out as he opened it, deafening in the silence. He stepped outside letting the door slam shut behind him.

Ted lowered his eyes before staring across at Philip, who had gone very pale. 'I'm sorry, but I'd run out of choices. None of this is what I would choose but I didn't know what else to do.'

Joyce fought the urge to strike out, as she screamed at him. 'Stop gambling, that's something you could do. Get a proper job, like most people do. Here's something else you could do: start thinking about somebody else other than yourself. I'm not sure you've ever done that. There's no easy solution. Nothing comes for free in this world; we all pay one way or another.' She looked at Simon. All happiness at seeing him disappeared as her anger took over. 'How could you, Simon? The last thing I wanted to do was bail him out.'

Simon stayed calm and focused as he looked at Joyce. 'But it's not you bailing out your father; I'm doing it.'

Joyce picked up her cloth and began vigorously wiping the nearest table. She suddenly stopped and spun round to face him. 'But it will be me who has to pay it back and I don't like owing anybody anything.'

Simon's eyes narrowed. 'What you don't seem to understand is my family's lives are now at risk as well.'

The room fell silent.

Joyce shook her head. 'You're right of course. I'm sorry, I wasn't thinking straight.'

Ted stepped forward and rested his hand on Joyce's arm. 'Thank you, Simon, I know you don't know me, but it's appreciated, and I promise to pay it back.'

Joyce scowled. 'Hah, why do I feel that's just a lie, like everything else around you is?'

Philip ran over to his father and slipped his hand in his before looking up at Joyce. 'Don't be angry with Pa. We haven't seen him for ages.'

Joyce sighed as she stooped down in front of him. 'I'm sorry, Philip, but I feel like your pa has a lot of making up to do.'

Philip stared wide-eyed at her. 'Isn't he your pa too? Didn't you say we're brother and sister now?'

Joyce nodded, struggling to come to terms with everything that had just happened.

Philip slipped his other hand in hers. 'I'm glad you're my sister.'

Joyce could feel her tears pricking at her eyes. 'I'm glad you're my brother too.'

Philip gave a little smile. 'So can Pa come back to the house then?'

Joyce wanted to scream but knew she couldn't do that to him. 'Of course he can. I tell you what, why don't you go back home with Pa while I finish up here?'

Philip jumped up and down clapping his hands.

Ted nodded at Simon. 'Thank you, Simon, and I'm sorry I've put you and your family at risk.'

Simon shook his head at Ted. 'You didn't just put us at risk; you put your daughter and your son at risk, although they don't seem to matter to you.'

'Of course they do.' Ted turned and walked towards the door. 'I should go. Joyce is furious with me and I'm just making it worse by being here.'

Simon stared at him. 'Don't run away from her a second time. You don't seem to have thought about how Joyce was coping with that first lie you told, or the subsequent lies you've told to cover up that first one, let alone the grief that followed it. She has a right to be angry with you and you need to face it, talk about it, and take it on the chin because nothing will move forward until you do.'

Ted pulled open the door and the bell chimed.

Joyce stared at her father. 'I'm trusting you with Philip. You go to Arthur's house and nowhere else. Let's just see if you can do that.'

Ted nodded. The bell rang out as he slammed the door shut behind him and Philip.

Mavis took a step nearer to Joyce, opening her mouth to speak but then closing it again.

Joyce tightened her lips and lowered her eyes. She took a breath trying to calm herself before looking over at Mavis and the family. 'I'm sorry you've all had to witness the mess that is my life; I've never felt more ashamed.'

Barbara and Mavis both moved closer and threw their arms around her.

Barbara sniffed and wiped away a tear as she pulled back to look at Joyce. 'There's no need to be ashamed; you're like family and if we can help you in any way we will.'

Mavis nodded, giving Joyce an extra squeeze. 'Barbara's right.'

Joyce sat on the old worn armchair, next to the open fireplace in the dining room, her head propped up by the wings of the armchair. She closed her eyes as exhaustion took over. Simon jumped front and centre in her mind as she relived the moment he unexpectedly came into the café on his crutches. She had been so happy to see him and yet something about him told her he didn't feel the same. *He is injured*, she thought, but instantly shook her head. That wasn't it. How she regretted turning down his marriage proposal. Her tears were ready to fall; everything seem to be going wrong.

Her mother's words rang out in her head. *"Misery breeds misery."* Is that what she was doing, breeding her own misery? She should've been happy. Her father was alive. She should be happy she had a little brother, and she definitely should be happy that the man she loved with all her heart was back, albeit injured, but at least he was home and safe. And yet here she was sitting around wanting to cry, fighting back the tears that told her she'd made mistakes. Simon's words rushed into her head. *"Forgiveness helps us to find peace within ourselves and in others; it moves us forward."* She ran her hands over her face and took a deep breath. 'Come on, girl, there's no point feeling sorry for yourself. You've just gotta get on with it, and maybe it's time to let go of a few things.'

She looked back at the chest and realised it was time she emptied it once and for all. Weeks had passed and it still was in the same position as the day she had last opened it. Joyce sat down in front of it and closed her eyes, feeling emotionally drained at seeing her father again. Having to show restraint in front of Philip, and discovering he was her brother. She opened her eyes. Remembering the wedding ring she had left on the table she stood up and picked up the box. After opening it she took the small gold band out of it. Her mother had been so small and thin; she placed the ring on one of the fingers of her right hand and stared down at it. 'Oh, Ma, I miss you so much.'

The front door slammed shut. 'Sorry, I didn't mean to slam it,' Arthur called out.

Arthur's footsteps thudded along the hall and into the dining room, the smell of fresh air coming in on his clothes. 'I wondered if you'd be sitting in here.'

'You look better for your walk. I'll make you some tea.'

'There's no rush; stay where you are.' Arthur sat down in the chair Joyce had just vacated.

Joyce watched him. 'Do you feel better for escaping?'

Arthur looked thoughtful. 'I do. I needed to give myself time to think. I was in danger of just exploding.'

Joyce grimaced. 'You don't have to explain. I understand.'

'I can't believe you agreed to him being here for dinner.'

Joyce shrugged. 'I didn't really have any choice. Philip was beside himself with excitement, so how could I say no?'

Arthur nodded. 'Yes, I can see that. He was so happy, like a different child.'

Joyce stared over at Arthur. 'Does it sadden you to know that his father will always come first?'

Arthur gave a little smile. 'No, well yes a little, but it is the right way round.' He paused as he looked at Joyce. 'He's your father too.'

Joyce frowned. 'I know, I do want to forgive him for all the upset he's caused but I can't deny I'm struggling with it all. One minute I had no one.' Her head jerked up. 'Sorry, I didn't mean that the way it came out.'

Arthur's hands were clenched on his lap. 'Don't worry, I understand; carry on.'

'Well, I was just going to say one minute I had no family, then suddenly, I had a father and a brother.' Joyce paused as anger flitted across her face. 'Simon is paying off the rest of his debt. How embarrassing is that? I was resentful that he offered to do it, no matter how much he was trying to help. In fact I'm not sure who I was more annoyed with. I was outraged at my father for bringing all his troubles to my place of work, I was offended at Simon for offering to pay off his debt and I was angry with Frank for pretending to be something he wasn't. I feel like everybody has lied to me, yet again! Everybody's pretending to be something they're not. Simon doesn't have the means to pay that bill, so I'll have to pay it back, and I can't afford it either.'

Arthur stared at her for a moment. She looked so tired, and her shoulders were hunched over as she slowly lifted her hand to take something else out of the chest.

'I don't understand how I can have a little brother and have not known about him.'

Arthur sighed. 'Your father has always been a rule unto himself, but at least you know he didn't cheat on your mother.'

Joyce looked up at the ceiling as she heard movement upstairs, forgetting that Ted was still in the house reading Philip a story. She had watched them closely together; she didn't understand what had gone on but it was obvious he loved Philip.

There were several sharp bangs at the front door, causing both Arthur and Joyce to automatically look at the clock on the mantelpiece. It was eight o'clock in the evening.

Joyce frowned at Arthur. 'Who could that be knocking on the door at this time of night?'

After pushing himself up out of the armchair, Arthur walked towards the hall. 'There's only one way to find out.'

The floorboards creaked in places as he stepped towards the hall. Joyce heard the front door creak open. She leant sideways, straining to hear the mumbled voices, wondering who it could be. Should she go and see, in case Arthur needed help? The voices grew louder as they got nearer. The dining room door was suddenly pushed open and Arthur walked in, quickly followed by Jeremiah King.

Joyce's eyes widened. She shook her head, wondering what the problem could be now. 'Mr King, what brings you here this evening?' She took a breath. 'I'm sorry, please forgive my manners. I will make us some tea.'

'Good evening, Miss Taylor, tea won't be necessary, thank you. I've come to tell you your grandmother has come round and wondered if you and Philip would like to go and see her?'

'Oh my goodness, of course we would; just give me a minute to go and get Philip. He's in bed. You need to know my father, her son, is here as well.'

Mr King nodded. 'So I understand. I am happy to take you all to the hospital if you wish to go. I'm sure your grandmother would love to see you. I don't think there's time to hang around because though she's awake they seem to think she won't make it through the night.'

Joyce gripped Philip's hand as they walked along the hospital corridor. Her brow wrinkled as she bit down on her lip. Her heart was pounding. It was one thing to see her grandmother when she was in a coma, but another when she could tell her what terrible things she had done to be thrown out of her house. She held back, letting everyone else enter the room first, Jeremiah King leading the way. Philip let go of her hand and ran to be next to their father inside. She wiped her damp palms down the side of her skirt and took a deep breath.

A young nurse was sat next to the bed, holding the patient's hand. She looked up as they all trundled in. 'Mrs Taylor, your family are here now so I'll leave you all to chat.' She released her hand and stood up. 'If you need anything then please come and see me. I'll be at the nurses' station further along the ward.' She nodded and walked towards the doorway, only the squeaking of the shoes on the tiled floor and the rustling of her uniform broke the silence.

Joyce turned to the nurse. 'Thank you.'

The nurse nodded and left the room.

Philip rushed forward to sit on his father's lap.

Edith Taylor kept her eyes shut as she lay still under the bedcovers. Joyce watched her chest for movement; she wasn't convinced she wasn't unconscious again.

Without a word, they all sat down around the bed on the extra wooden chairs that had been brought into the room in preparation for their visit. The only noise was the chairs groaning as they were each sat on. They all stared at the frail, grey-haired lady in the bed.

Joyce held her breath. She would normally have said hello when she walked in but not tonight.

After a few minutes Ted broke the silence. 'Jerry, I thought you said she was awake?'

Jeremiah King stared at his client lying in the bed. She was so thin, and she didn't look at all how he remembered her. He glanced round everyone's pale, still faces before letting his gaze rest on Ted. He stared at him for a few minutes, wondering whether to speak up or not, but something inside him wouldn't let it go. 'Don't call me Jerry.'

'It's good to see you all.' The low whispering voice caught all their attention.

'Grandma.'

'Ma.'

The family all spoke as one.

Edith Taylor slowly opened her eyes and gave a thin smile.

'You always were impatient, Ted, a bit like your father.' She closed her eyes for a moment. 'It can't be long now,' She peered at each of them from under her lashes. 'I don't think they were expecting me to wake up.' She took a breath. 'And, as you're all here it must be just a matter of time now.'

Ted leant forward. 'Don't say that, Ma, you're going to pull through I know you are. You're a strong woman, who has been tested many times over by me. I'm sorry.'

Edith gave a weak smile. 'Is that genuine sadness I see on your face, Ted?' She tried to laugh but it came out as a cackle. 'You certainly kept me on my toes. I'm amazed I've lasted as long as I have.' She moved her gaze to Joyce. 'It's good to see you here. Jeremiah tells me you have turned into a fine young woman. How have you enjoyed looking after Philip?'

Joyce glanced at Philip. 'I wouldn't be without him.'

Philip smiled. 'I love having a sister; she's a good cook, Grandma.'

Everyone chuckled.

'That's good – at least you won't go hungry.' Edith turned her head slowly to look at Jeremiah. 'It looks like I've won our little bet. It looks like I was right.'

Jeremiah gave a boyish smile. 'Yes, you were right and your plan seems to have worked. Philip and Joyce know they are brother and sister now. There's a bond between them, which they formed without knowing anything about each other.' Jeremiah paused before looking over at Ted. 'And Ted, well, he appears to be changing his ways, but don't hold your breath on that one.'

Edith gave a faint smile. 'Rome wasn't built in a day and at least everyone knows who everybody is.' She paused to take a breath. 'I can die happy. Joyce now knows she has a brother and her father is still alive and that's all that matters for now.'

Joyce took a couple of deep breaths, trying to calm the anguish that was coursing through her body. She leant forward. It was now or never. 'Grandma, I'm sorry for what happened, although, I don't know what I did, but it must've been bad for you to kick us out of your home.'

Edith reached out her scrawny arm to take Joyce's hand in hers. 'You did nothing, my child; don't waste your time worrying about such things. I argued with your father over looking after Philip, it was definitely nothing you had done.'

Joyce shook her head in confusion. She squeezed her grandmother's surprisingly soft hand and leant in further, picking up her lavender scent. Joyce gave her a kiss on the cheek. 'All that time I thought it was something I'd done wrong. We have wasted so much time. I'm so sorry I didn't come to see you to find out, to ask the question.'

Edith tried to smile but didn't quite make it. 'I did write to you a few times but when you didn't reply I thought you didn't want to know.'

Joyce laid her hand flat on her chest. 'Grandma, I didn't get any of your letters. I promise I would have replied.'

'None of it matters now.' Edith gasped, fighting for her breath. 'What matters is that you're all together, which is all that I've ever wanted. There's nothing more important than family, whether they are blood or people you've let into your life and value as family.'

Joyce nodded, remembering her friends who encouraged her and helped her with Arthur, who also let her live under his roof as family. 'You're right, Grandma. I'm sorry I wasn't there for you though.'

Edith squeezed her hand tight. 'You weren't to know.' She turned her head slightly to Jeremiah. 'It's time, Jeremiah. You know what you have to do and I'm happy for you to do it.' She let her eyes roam over her family. 'I'm not going to be here for much longer but let me tell you just seeing you all sitting here together brings me so much happiness. Ted, I want you to promise me you'll keep your family together now and do your best to put food on the table for them but not by gambling.'

Ted peered at his children before looking across at his mother. 'I will do the best I can, Ma, and you can rest assured that Joyce will keep me in check. She has your way with words, and she doesn't mince them either.'

Edith turned to Joyce. 'That's good – that's the Taylor way. Keep it up! He needs to be held in check… Your mum was always good at that. You have your mother's beauty and love of cooking, but you also have the backbone to achieve so much; you just don't realise it.' Edith paused to take a breath. 'Keep working towards your dream. I know it seems impossible right now but if your father does his bit it won't be.' She closed her eyes and the room was silent as they all stared at her.

20

J oyce stepped alongside her father as they ambled along Shaftesbury Avenue towards the Meet and Feast Café. The normality of the cars coughing and spluttering along the road, or the warmth of the evening along with the wonderful aromas that escaped from the restaurants as they walked past, did nothing to ease the growing numbness she felt inside. Her grandmother had passed away with them all gathered at her bedside; she had looked peaceful, almost asleep. They had all sat in silence for some time, but Joyce couldn't recall how long; no one wanted to say what everyone was thinking.

A nurse came in to check on her grandma and told them she had passed away. No one said a word. They each stood up and kissed her soft face in turn before going home, where Philip had sobbed in Joyce's arms. She had stroked his back and wiped his tears before he finally settled down for the night. It had broken her heart listening to him and she had shed her own tears at the same time, but wasn't sure who she was crying for. He had experienced so much loss in his young life.

Joyce struggled to put one foot in front of the other, but her mind wouldn't stop jumping around. She had decided to try to walk it off. Her father insisted on joining her, and she was too tired to argue. Her thoughts were going round in circles, fretting about the wasted years away from her grandmother and her father. How she never knew it wasn't her who had done something wrong; the argument had been about her father not looking after his son. How she wished she'd known that years ago.

'You know, I still can't believe you're alive, here walking and talking with me. Every time I think about it I get so cross with you for hiding away, leaving me on my own and not telling me I had a brother. Now, on top of that, I've discovered the argument you had with Grandma was nothing to do with me. It was always about Philip. I feel sick just thinking about the pain she must have felt when she thought I didn't want to know her.' She shook her head. 'I don't understand what happened to those letters.'

Ted frowned. 'At least your grandma knows different now. We were lucky to have those final conversations, but there's no doubt I should have told you everything instead of running away.' He glanced down at her pale features. 'I can understand you being angry with me. I deserve it. If I ever get to see your mother again she'll never forgive me, but I'm not sure I'll be going upstairs when I leave this world. I'm more likely to be downstairs.' He paused, shaking his head. 'I haven't been a very good husband or father. When your mother died I took comfort in another woman's arms. That's one thing, but keeping Philip a secret from you is unforgiveable.'

Joyce suddenly felt sorry for him. She shook her head and glanced up at her father, studying him for a moment. Where she remembered him always looking smart he now had an unkept look about him. There was now sadness where the bravado had been. 'It's never too late to make amends, but you have to work at it and mean it. It's not just about saying the words it's doing the deeds. It's about meaning it; after all we all make mistakes.' Thoughts of Simon immediately jumped into her head. She bit down hard on her bottom lip. 'You know before Simon enlisted he asked me to marry him, and I turned him down.'

Ted looked straight ahead, too afraid to meet her gaze. 'Why did you turn him down? Did you not love him?'

Joyce shrugged.

'You obviously don't have to tell me but you've started to share with me so I'd like to know why you turned him down. I'd like to get to know the woman you've become.'

Joyce welled up. The tears were pricking at her eyes, but once again she didn't know who they were for. She took a deep breath. 'I don't expect you to understand. I don't think Annie and Rose did.'

Ted nodded. 'Try me.'

Joyce hesitated. She wasn't sure if she could say the words out loud again. 'It crossed my mind that I was bad luck for people to get too close to.'

Ted shook his head, rubbing his hand over the back of his neck. 'I'm so sorry. Look at the damage I have done without even realising it. Please never feel you are bad luck; you deserve to be loved.'

Joyce shrugged. 'At the time I had lost everyone I ever loved, and as much as I loved Simon I struggled to say yes and then let him go off to fight for king and country in case he didn't come back.'

Ted felt the sorrow oozing from his daughter.

Joyce closed her eyes for a moment before shaking her head. 'That was quickly followed by the thought he was only asking me so I would look after the café for him.'

Ted moved to wrap his arms around her and give her comfort like a father should, but he stopped before she noticed. He didn't feel he had that right. He had a long way to go yet. 'That doesn't make him sound like a very nice man.' He tightened his lips. 'Do you still feel like that?'

Joyce raised her eyebrows and sighed. 'It doesn't matter what I think or feel; the moment has passed and I will never get it back again. It's important that I now concentrate on Philip because I can't do it all.'

Ted felt his heart had been ripped out of his chest as he listened to her words. 'I've made a right old mess of things, and all I was trying to do was to protect you from the mess I'd made after your mother died. She tried hard to keep me on the right road as much as she could. Looking back, I kept her short of money all the time, just so I could gamble a little bit here and a little bit there. I loved her so much and wanted to give her everything, and yet she died not having the one thing that was probably the most important to her, besides you of course.'

Joyce's eyes narrowed as she tried to figure out what he was talking about. 'What was it?'

Ted shook his head. 'She loved me dearly, and I know that it never diminished but I didn't appreciate that love and let her down. I let it go in a bid to keep winning money to make our lives more comfortable. She kept telling me that she wasn't bothered about any of that; she just wanted us to be happy, and to have more children. If I'm honest I wanted to give her the life Arthur and Dot had but Arthur was right: I had it all and didn't look after it, and that's something I have to live with.'

Joyce felt her anger ebbing away as she thought about his words. 'I suppose pride gets in our way. I wonder if that's the biggest sin of all because it holds you in a place, and not a very good one at that. I expect Simon's injuries are coming between us right now, for very different reasons, and the pride that goes with it. Neither of us are mentioning it, partly because of his injuries, but also because of how it was left between us. The trouble was, at the time, I had so much on my plate. I had just found out about Philip, and before that I'd agreed to run the café. I couldn't cope and didn't want a sympathy marriage proposal.'

Ted frowned as he looked down at her. 'You do know he still loves you, don't you? That hasn't gone away.'

Joyce laughed, but it wasn't humorous sound. 'And, pray tell, how do you know? You've only met him the once.'

It was Ted's turn to give a gentle laugh. 'I love it; you're so innocent.' He paused. 'You're right, I have only met him once and yet he bailed me out so what does that tell you?'

Joyce's lips tightened. 'And that's something else that makes me angry because none of us can afford to pay it back and I don't want to be beholden to him or anybody else.'

'You won't be, don't you worry about that.'

'All right, Pa, tell me: how are you going to pay it back?'

'That's my concern but a married couple shouldn't start off their life together with money problems between them.'

Joyce stopped walking and stood rooted to the spot. 'What?'

'I have the money here in my pocket.' Ted looked around

before patting his trouser pocket. 'Jeremiah, or Jerry as I like to call him.' He chuckled. 'Anyway, he gave it to me when your grandmother passed away, and before you say anything I'm not going to gamble it. I'm going to pay off my debts and make a home for Philip, you, and me; if you want to come that is. I understand if you want to carry on living with your friends but I would like to take Philip home, if you'd let me.'

Joyce stared. 'I don't know what to say. He's your son so you're entitled to do whatever you see fit.'

Ted nodded. 'I know that, but whatever I do, I want to do with your blessing. I want to know that I have my daughter back and that you will visit me and Philip. I want you to stop being a mother and start being a daughter.' He laughed. 'Of course, you might start being a wife before that happens.'

Joyce stared straight ahead. 'Will you stop saying that? There's no marriage going to happen here. I might even have to find another job.'

'That's never going to happen.' Ted shook his head. 'I tell you, Simon loves you, and he won't want you to leave the café or him. I think a bigger problem is that he'll think he can't look after you because of his injuries. But you could address that if you were just honest about your feelings and opened up to him.'

'And what if he doesn't want me? What if he rejects me like I rejected him?'

Ted took a chance and put his arm around her shoulders. 'He won't. I know you don't believe me, but he loves you and that's obvious to me. One thing I've learnt, between your ma dying and the war, is that life's short and we have to grab it while it's there to be grabbed. You know in some cases there's no warning; everything you hold dear is suddenly whipped away from you.'

Shaking her head, Joyce looked up at him before staring back at the road ahead. She wrinkled her nose as smoke wafted in their direction. 'Is that a fire?'

Ted looked up and sped up as he walked along the path. Joyce was almost running beside him. She almost screamed when she realised it was the Meet and Feast Café. Mavis was outside screaming for someone to get Simon out.

Joyce went running towards the fire but Ted grabbed at her arm, pulling her back. 'This is something I have to do.' He pulled his jacket over his head and ran forward.

Time stood still as Joyce heard her father coughing in between shouting Simon's name over and over again. The stench of smoke and dust filled the air. A blood-curdling shriek rang out, jerking Joyce out of her trance. She ran towards the screaming and put her arm around Mavis's shoulders, holding her tight, squeezing her soft woollen jacket. 'It's going to be all right. My father will get Simon out.' She held her breath, too scared to speak or move her gaze away from the café doorway.

'How do you know that? He could be dead already.' Mavis sniffed. 'Oh my goodness I hope your father does find him and pull him out.'

They both jerked and stooped down as the shards of glass blew out on to the pavement from the window, quickly followed by billowing clouds of black smoke. They kept their heads down as the heat and the dust rained down on them.

Joyce wondered if she was going to lose her father all over again, before she had chance to let him know she loved him and didn't want to be angry anymore. Then there was Simon. She wanted to tell him how much she loved him. Was she going to be given that chance? She looked heavenward, hoping God was listening to her low tones. *'Please forgive me as I must learn to forgive others. Please don't take them from me; please let me tell them how much I love them.'*

Mavis sobbed. 'He's only just come back. He can't walk so your father will have to drag him out.' A yelp escaped. 'I can't bear the thought of him dying in that rotten café.'

'Don't think like that. You've got to have faith.' Joyce hugged her tight. 'If my father can get him out he will; we just have to pray that he's going to be all right.' A tear ran down her cheek, its saltiness resting on her lips as she fought the urge to run in after her father. She frantically looked around for someone to help. 'Mr Harris?' Was that the landlord she saw standing there with a strange look on his face? She raised her voice. 'Mr Harris, is that you?'

The man turned her way before quickly looking away and striding down the road.

Joyce shook her head; she couldn't be certain in this light but felt sure it was him. Did he start the fire? Why? And what was Simon doing in there? He was meant to be resting.

Coughing and spluttering came from the café, getting louder as it got nearer to the door. Ted suddenly appeared carrying Simon in his arms.

The women both ran forward as Ted laid Simon on the ground. Mavis was sobbing as she dropped to the ground beside her son. Ted was bent over double, gasping for air. Dust and smoke oozed from him. The sleeve to his once-white shirt was torn with scorch marks on it.

Joyce immediately stepped back from Simon and moved towards her father. 'Thank you, you probably saved his life.' She suddenly glanced up at him. 'My goodness, are you all right? Did you get hurt?' She pulled at his sleeve. 'You shirt obviously got burnt but did you? You might have to go to the hospital to get checked out.'

Ted shook his head. 'I'll be fine; I could do with some water to take the smoke out of my mouth. Go and look after Simon. He needs it more than I do.'

An ambulance and fire engine suddenly came rattling down the road and the area became a hive of activity as the fire was doused with water.

A young woman stepped out of the ambulance and ran over to Simon. 'Lie still for a moment. My name is Alice. What's yours?'

Simon licked his dry, scorched lips. 'Simon, Simon Hitchin.'

Alice nodded. 'That's good, Simon. Were you in the café when it caught fire?'

Simon nodded.

Alice pulled his tie lose and undid his top button. 'Do you know whether there was anyone else in there?'

Simon shook his head. When he tried to speak it was a croaking sound. 'No, the fire started in the kitchen.'

'Don't worry about the fire; just lie still for a moment. I want to listen to your breathing and see if you have any burns that need treating.' Alice carefully and silently checked Simon's body. 'You seem to have been very lucky;

there's only what appears to be minor burns on your legs but your hands will need treating.'

'You won't be doing any baking in the café tonight.' Ted sighed and wrapped his arms around his daughter and hugged her tight. 'I wonder how the fire started, and what was Simon doing here at this time in the evening?'

Alice looked up and spoke to Mavis. 'I'll take him to St Thomas' just to get him looked at. They might want to keep him in overnight.' She turned to Ted. 'How are you?'

'You mean apart from burnt clothes and stinking of smoke?' Ted smiled. 'I'm unharmed, thank you.'

Simon tried to prop himself up. 'No, I'm not going to hospital. I don't need to waste valuable bed space.'

Alice peered over her shoulder at Simon and frowned. 'Will you at least let me take you so they can give you a thorough check.'

Simon scowled. 'I'm not staying in though.'

Alice turned back to Ted.

'Don't worry about me, I'm fine, although I'm not sure my jacket is.' Ted hooked up his jacket that had fallen to the ground, its woollen sleeves still smoking where they had been singed by the fire. 'I'd better get you home,' he said to Joyce.

Joyce turned to Mavis. 'What are you going to do? I don't think you should be on your own.'

Mavis rested her hand at the base of her neck. 'I don't know. I want to go with Simon.'

Joyce nodded. So did she but she hadn't earned that right. 'What about Barbara? Do you want me to go and tell her while you go to the hospital?'

Mavis's eyes darted around for a moment. 'Barbara isn't

in. She's gone to the theatre with a friend. I walked with them to this point.' She took a deep breath. 'It's only because I stopped to admire some material in the haberdasher's window that I'm unharmed; otherwise I would have been in the café as well.' She shuddered. 'When I turned round that's when I saw the smoke and the flames.' Mavis clung on to Joyce. 'It was then you and your father came along, and I can't tell you how grateful I am.'

Joyce patted Mavis's arm. 'Thankfully, it looks like Simon won't have any lasting damage from it.'

They both watched Simon being put into the back of the ambulance. Joyce could feel her tears pricking at her eyes, as it dawned on her they would no longer have an excuse to see each other. It was definitely over, what little hope she thought there was had gone up in flames with the fire.

Everyone sat in silence in the dining room. Joyce closed her eyes as she tried to take in the events of the day. Her throat tightened as the lump formed, making it hard to swallow. Her eyes snapped open; she couldn't allow herself to wallow in self-pity.

Annie frowned as she looked over at Joyce. She looked grey in colour. Her eyes were red and bloodshot. She had no words, but then no one did.

Rose looked up as people passed by outside the house, their loud voices screaming in the silence of the dining room.

Joyce felt numb, having lost her grandmother earlier, and now her place of work was gone. She shook her head. She had been finally realising her dream along with the man she loved, but she had to forget it all now. It had gone up in smoke with café. She had no idea what the future held for her. She had heard how much could be earned in the munitions factories; if they were true it was definitely well-paid work. Joyce had heard women with yellow streaks in their hair talking about it, but she'd also heard rumours of the many deaths from working there too.

She remembered the horse and cart funeral procession going slowly past the café and the women walking either side of it. Someone had said it was one of the canary girls. It was explained to her they were called that because working there turned their hair yellow. Prior to finding Philip and her father that might not have bothered her, but her friends had arrived with their encouragement to live her dream, and Simon had offered the means when he found out about it. There had been hope, but now that had all been ripped away; it was no more. Maybe she was never meant to cook; maybe her calling was to work in a munitions factory.

She closed her eyes and rested her head against the back of the armchair. Her mind was in turmoil as she tried to figure out what to do. The nearest munitions factory was either over the river in Woolwich or she'd have to travel to the docks in Silvertown, which wasn't a short journey. When Joyce spoke her voice was barely a whisper. 'I think I saw the landlord watching the fire, but I can't be certain it was him.'

Arthur tightened his lips. 'It wouldn't surprise me; he wanted you and Simon out of there. Although, I would like to think he didn't know Simon was inside the café at the time.'

Joyce's face contorted with anger. 'It's people's livelihoods;

it was Simon's father's dream. How can anybody think that was the right thing to do?'

Everyone looked at each other, hoping for some words of wisdom from someone, but there were none.

Joyce cleared her throat. 'The fire looked bad so I've obviously lost my job now.'

Arthur looked at the young girl he regarded as his own daughter and wondered what words he could offer. 'Try not to worry. Tonight is not the time to be thinking about what you do next.'

Ted sat there in silence; he didn't know how his daughter was still breathing. He knew instinctively it wasn't the café she was pining for, it was Simon. All contact was now lost. Could he help in some small way? His mind jumped about wondering what he could do. Maybe, he should go and talk to Slips. He wasn't sure that was wise but he would know where Simon lived. He would know where everybody lived when it came to his business, or Ted's. Then he could go and talk to Simon and see what plan they could come up with. He kept his thoughts to himself. Joyce wouldn't thank him for interfering, and rightly so. He knew he couldn't stand by and do nothing. His daughter looked broken; they clearly loved each other. It was his time to prove to Joyce how much she meant to him.

Arthur frowned as he looked over at Ted before looking back at Joyce. 'Maybe this is the time for you to start again. I mean maybe it's your turn to open your own restaurant, tea room or café, whatever you want.'

Rose's eyes widened as she looked at Arthur. 'That's a good idea. That way out of something awful something good will happen.'

Joyce looked from one to the other. Tiredness seeped from every orifice. 'I don't have the money to set up a restaurant or anything else for that matter.' She turned to Annie. 'You need to tell Kitty and Stan that I won't be able to do the food and they won't be able to use the café for their wedding.' A tear slowly trickled down Joyce's cheeks.

Annie nodded. 'I'll tell her about the café, but we'll just have to think of another place she can hold it. I think you can still do the food; we just need to put our thinking caps on and see what we can come up with.'

Ted studied his daughter. 'Let me help you, Joyce. I know I've been a rotten father to you over the years but please let me make amends.'

Joyce looked at her father. 'That's all in the past and I'm too tired to have a fight about things that have already happened. We need to move on, if only for Philip's sake.' She looked thoughtful for a moment. 'I'm really doing you an injustice; you probably saved Simon's life tonight so you have nothing to prove to me. What were we saying earlier about pride? Well, the past is the past and that's where it should stay. We need to try and look forward; only at this precise moment I'm not sure I can do that.'

Ted lifted one side of his mouth. 'We were, but let me also remind you what I said earlier this evening, about how much Simon loves you. I know you don't believe it but I think the way he's been acting since he's been back is all to do with his injuries so a conversation needs to be had.'

Annie and Rose both nodded in agreement.

'I hate to say this, Joyce, but I think your father's right.' Arthur glanced over at Ted before looking back at Joyce. 'Some of the things I've seen and heard, and from what

Annie and Rose have said, everyone is in agreement that you two are meant to be together. It just means you have to have an honest conversation with each other. Life is too short to throw your love away, as your father and I both know.' He turned and studied Ted for a moment. 'We're lucky to have been given a second chance with the people we love but you have to grab it with both hands and look after it.'

Ted nodded.

Joyce shook her head. 'I can't put myself out there; it would be too painful if Simon disagreed.'

Ted watched her closely. There was no emotion. She had shut herself down to cope. He had seen her do it before when life got too difficult to deal with.

21

Joyce pushed open the heavy street door of Jeremiah King's office. The heat hit her as she walked into the dark, hushed surroundings. It took a moment for her eyes to adjust after being outside. The prim and proper lady was sitting in the same position at the large desk; she smiled as Joyce walked in. Joyce's heart was pounding as she took in the book-lined walls and the red velvet seated chairs, reminding her of the last time she was there. She peered over her shoulder at her father who had followed her in.

Suddenly she remembered Mr King's strange expression when she mentioned her father was dead. She hadn't thought anything of it at the time, but it dawned on her now that he knew he wasn't but hadn't told her. She had left the office with her life turned upside down, having been told that Arthur wasn't her uncle and she could have a five-year-old boy to look after. Joyce had fretted that morning about leaving Philip with Arthur. He had been close to their grandma and took a while to settle after seeing her. Joyce didn't want him to think she was leaving him too. She had promised him she wouldn't be long.

Without preamble, the lady at the desk showed them into Mr King's office.

'Good morning, I wasn't sure we would make the meeting today what with the severe thunderstorms that are travelling across the country. Apparently, they've done quite a lot of damage uprooting trees in some areas.' Mr King paused. 'Anyway, it's good to see you both so please take a seat.'

The door thudded shut behind them.

Joyce sat down on the nearest chair, opposite Mr King. She gripped her hands tight on her lap.

Ted raised his eyebrows, looking around at the dark oak walls lined with leather-bound books. 'Thank you, although it's very formal, isn't it?' He nodded to the pile of papers sitting on the end of the large desk. 'I take it business is thriving, although I don't know how you work in this place. It's quite dark, even a little austere, wouldn't you say?' He wrinkled his nose. 'You need to open a window and let some fresh air in here.'

Mr King said nothing. He sat down at his desk and waited for Ted to comply with his wishes.

Ted sighed and sat down next to Joyce, in front of the desk.

Not for the first time that morning Joyce wondered why she was having to come back to this office. She assumed her father was the next of kin. She truly hoped there were no more surprises, or shocks, in store for her.

'Now, I just wanted to talk to you about Mrs Taylor's situation.'

Ted smirked at Jeremiah. 'Situation, is there a situation?'

Jeremiah closed his eyes for a second. 'I'd appreciate it if you could just for once stop and listen. Let me say what I have to say. Then you can leave, and hopefully, I won't have to see you again.'

Joyce looked across at her father. 'Stop it, Pa, Mr King was obviously close to Grandma so this is difficult for him too.'

Mr King nodded at Joyce. 'Thank you, Miss Taylor, please do not worry; your father and I go back a long way.' He paused. 'It's always been his hobby to try and bait me into a reaction.'

Ted chuckled. 'That's true, Jeremiah, but I'm going to try to stop what is after all just a life-long habit with no substance.'

Jeremiah arched an eyebrow and nodded. He looked down at the pile of papers that were sitting in front of him. He took a breath. 'As her next of kin, Mr Taylor, I need to inform you that there will be no need for you to worry about funeral arrangements because Mrs Taylor had already made and paid for them.'

Ted raised his eyebrows. 'Is that because she didn't trust me to do it correctly?'

Jeremiah stared at Ted for a moment. 'No, I think she was trying to be helpful to you. You may find this hard to believe but your mother was never against you, Ted. She just wanted you to take control of your life again. Believe it or not she worried about you all the time, and your brother, Luke.'

Ted glared at Jeremiah. 'He's not my brother. We had different mothers and I don't even know where he is these days. I'm afraid he disappeared when our father died, and I haven't seen him since then.'

Jeremiah nodded. 'Your mother always wanted to do the right thing by him but there's been a distinct lack of response from his last known address. It's been many years since I heard he was in Norfolk and, despite my many letters, there hasn't been any news of him.'

Joyce gripped her hands in her lap, not knowing whether she should say something or not. 'So, I do have an uncle then?'

Ted stared at his daughter. His lips curled. 'Yes, but he turned his back on us for his own ends and probably spun some story about his childhood to some unsuspecting soul.'

Joyce stared at her father not knowing what else to say because nothing was going to change the situation. She turned back to the solicitor and forced a smile. 'Is that all you wanted us for, Mr King?'

Mr King looked at her kindly. 'I also wanted to say to you, Miss Taylor, that you have done very well with Philip. I know it was quite a challenge for you, particularly with the café as well.'

Joyce nodded. 'It was certainly a shock to look after a five-year-old, and then to find out he was my brother was quite unbelievable. However, I'm grateful to have him in my life and I thank you for that.'

Jeremiah smiled. 'It's your grandmother you should be thanking. To be honest I didn't think you'd be able to cope.'

Ted sneered at him. 'Obviously you know nothing about my daughter; she's quite resilient.'

Jeremiah frowned as he straightened some papers. 'I think your daughter has had to be resilient. She has had a lot to put up with.'

Joyce stood up. 'Well, if that is everything I'll be going.'

Ted shook his head. 'No, while I'm here I'd like to talk about my mother's estate.'

Jeremiah's eyes narrowed. 'I thought you might.'

Ted turned to his daughter. 'Perhaps you could just sit outside for a moment.'

Joyce nodded and left the room.

Jeremiah studied Ted for a moment. 'Your mother left you several thousand pounds and the house. Personally, I think she should have left it to Joyce and Philip. However, I genuinely hope she proves me wrong again, or maybe I should say you prove me wrong. That would give me great happiness.'

Ted raised his eyebrows. 'Well, if that's the case I have some business to attend to, which I would like to talk to you about.'

Jeremiah shook his head and fiddled with some papers on his desk. 'I can't imagine there is any sort of business that you have to attend to that could possibly involve a solicitor, at least not one of my standing.'

Ted raised his eyebrows. 'You could hear me out before you pass judgement.'

Ted stood outside Simon's terrace home wondering how he would be greeted. He didn't know him and yet he had given Ted the money to pay off his debts. He patted his jacket pocket. The money to pay Simon back was still there; nothing was going to come between Joyce and Simon – not if he had anything to do with it. His palms were damp and beads of perspiration ran down the sides of his eyes. A pulse throbbed in his temple. He pulled out a handkerchief and rubbed it over his face. The July heat was draining him of energy, or was it his nerves playing up? He had to look confident and sure of himself. This was too important for him to mess things up.

Ted took a deep breath; the money was his excuse to see Simon. Ted had never had such a personal conversation before but he had to be brave enough to say what he thought about their relationship, and remember he was doing it for Joyce.

The front door suddenly opened, catching Ted by surprise. Simon's sister stared at him. 'Do you want something?'

Ted pulled himself upright and pushed back his shoulders. He thrust out his chin. He now only had to find the courage that always evaded him in his own life. 'Good morning.' Ted removed his hat. 'I'm sorry to come unannounced, but I would like to see Simon, please.'

Barbara studied him for a moment. 'I understand you saved my brother's life, and I would like to thank you. I thought when Simon went off to war we may not see him again but when he came home I never envisaged he would almost die in a fire at the café, so thank you. Although, that doesn't seem enough.'

Ted fidgeted from one foot to the other. 'Thank you for saying that. It's very kind of you, but I didn't do anything that someone else wouldn't have done. Is it possible to see Simon please?'

Barbara stood aside, pulling the door wide so Ted could walk in. 'He's painting.' There was a thud as the front door shut behind him. 'Sorry, you probably don't know, but he likes to paint to relax. He hasn't been doing any since he got back, but Mother practically locked him in the room this morning.' Barbara gave a small smile. 'Mainly because he wouldn't get out of bed to do anything.'

Ted breathed in the familiar smell of beeswax and took heart from her words. Does that mean Simon was suffering the same way Joyce was? 'I've no desire to disturb him if he's busy but it's important that I see him. For both him and Joyce.'

Barbara sighed. 'Good luck with that. I have been trying to talk to him about Joyce but he won't entertain anything I say. He thinks that's over with but you can see it's eating him alive.'

Ted nodded. 'If it's any consolation Joyce thinks the same, which is why I'm here. I'm also here to pay Simon back the money that he paid Frank.'

Barbara nodded. 'I'll take you to him and then I'll make you a cup of tea.' She paused. 'Maybe I should go and see Joyce, especially if she isn't listening to anybody either, not that she should listen to me.' She shook her head. 'I'm ashamed to say I wasn't very nice to her when I first went to the café. He's my brother and I thought she didn't return his love, but I was wrong and they should be together.'

Ted nodded. He was pleased to have an ally. 'It's all worth a shot and thank you, I'll appreciate the tea. I know we didn't meet in the best of circumstances and that's something I'll always regret.'

'A lot has happened since then so it's no good us worrying about all of that. My concern is Simon; I'm not even bothered about the café anymore. I thought it was important to keep my father's dream alive but my mother was right. We've all been held in a place instead of moving on, particularly Simon, and my goodness it's such hard work. I can't imagine

Joyce would have stayed there if she didn't love him.'
Barbara pushed open the door into a small, well-lit room.
The smell of paint filled the room. Paintings, large and small,
were propped up around the room. Simon was staring at a
practically blank canvas that was on his easel.

'I haven't started yet, just leave me alone.'

Barbara looked up at Ted. Her lips tightened as she
shrugged. 'Joyce's father has come to see you.'

Simon half turned on his chair. His eyes widened. 'Is
Joyce all right?'

Ted nodded. 'She's probably about the same as you are.'

Simon turned and gazed back at this canvas.

'I didn't know you had a talent for painting; Joyce never
mentioned it.' Ted chuckled. 'Mind you we've been too busy
arguing to discuss the finer things in life.'

Simon didn't look at him; he kept his eyes fixed ahead.
'I'm not surprised – you certainly made an entrance. You
have to remember she's been mourning you for years and
then you suddenly pop up without any explanation but
wanting money.'

Ted nodded. He pulled up a wooden chair and sat down
closer to Simon. 'I deserve that; in fact I deserve everything
that she throws at me. I've been a terrible father but I'm
now here trying to make up for it.' He paused, unsure
whether to continue or not. 'Joyce doesn't know I'm here.
She'd probably kill me if she did.'

They both chuckled.

'Of that there is no doubt.' Simon turned to look at
Ted again. 'So what brings you here? What makes you
risk the wrath of your daughter? And trust me I have been
on the end of it and it's not a nice experience.'

'And yet you still love her despite her temper.'

Simon looked back at his canvas. 'Your daughter is a kind and gentle soul who will do anything for anybody. She does have a temper but it doesn't come to the forefront very often.' Simon looked around for a means to escape this conversation.

Ted watched him knowing only too well what was going on in his head. 'I want you to listen to me, Simon. I don't deserve you to but I'm here because I'm concerned about Joyce. She's talking about not cooking anymore and yet that was her love, her dream. It was her mother's dream for her.' Ted looked down at the different globules of paint on the floor before taking a deep breath. 'She's a broken woman. I believe it's the thought of not seeing you anymore that's breaking her heart.' Ted paused. 'I think you love her as much as she loves you and I'm not going to sit back and let you both throw it all away just because you're too stubborn to talk to each other. Trust me as someone who has been there: it's not the right thing to do, not if you really love her.'

Simon shook his head. 'I have nothing to offer her; I don't even have a business anymore. Joyce turned down my hand in marriage when I had everything so I picked up the message loud and clear.'

Ted stood up and walked around the room. 'She may well have done, but at the time she had a lot going on, and I know that's something she has always regretted. It's breaking her heart not seeing you every day, just like it's breaking yours.'

Simon lifted his head. 'I thought Frank was stepping into my shoes.'

Ted threw his head back and laughed. 'Slips used Joyce to get at me – nothing more, nothing less. Joyce didn't care for him. He just kept turning up but I think that's because he was following her or following me. How do you think I found out where you lived?'

Simon's face reddened as rage bubbled inside him. 'What, you mean he knew where I lived? So my mother and sister were put at risk as well as Joyce?'

Ted frowned before nodding. 'I've made a right old mess of things and I can't apologise enough. I never thought for one moment it would come to that. It was always my problem but it's not going to be repeated and to prove that to you I've bought the money that you paid to get me out of debt.' Ted put his hand inside his pocket and pulled out a wad of notes and passed them to Simon. 'That's how I know you love Joyce as much as she loves you. You didn't hesitate to pay off my debt even though you didn't know me. How much more proof does anyone need?'

Joyce stood outside the café with Rose and Annie. She was steeling herself to go inside and see how bad it was. Was there anything that could be taken away? After all, Simon might want to start again with his mother and sister. A lump formed in her throat.

Rose did the buttons up on her jacket. 'I think that thunderstorm that lit up the sky last night has definitely left it cooler today.' Her gaze moved from the café to Joyce.

'It's the first time I've seen it.' Annie stared at the café, studying where the flames had scorched the wood. The broken window had been boarded up.

'It's the first time for both of us.' Rose shook her head. 'Do you think it's safe to go in?'

Joyce shrugged. 'I don't know, but I got the impression it wasn't a massive fire in the front of the café, although it did spread there. I think it was mainly in the kitchen, which is where Simon was.' She hesitated for a moment; the cold steel of the café key was stuck to her hand in her jacket pocket. 'I am going in, if I can open the door; but I don't want you both to feel that you have to follow me. I understand you have to go to work.'

The girls glanced at each other.

'I don't think you understand, Joyce. Where possible, wherever you go we go.' Rose stepped forward so she was in line with Joyce.

Annie nodded. 'We need to get out of the café what we can.'

They all move forward as one.

Joyce's heart was racing; fear gripped her as she wondered what they would find. She felt sure Simon wouldn't have been back, and assumed he would be resting. Once this was done she had plans to take everything to his house and have a talk with him. Her father was right; she just couldn't throw it all away. She pulled the key out of her pocket and put it in the lock. The key wouldn't turn to unlock it but she rattled the handle and the door opened. The bell above it chimed as always.

The girls gasped.

Joyce looked at them. 'Do you think anyone is in there?'

The girls shrugged.

Rose looked towards Joyce. 'There's only one way to find out.'

Joyce nodded. 'I bet it's Mr Harris, the landlord. I'm sure he had something to do with the fire.'

Joyce stepped into the café and looked around, running her fingers over the counter. She left a trail where her fingers had been; it was thick with dust from the fire. She wrinkled her nose as the smell of the fire damage wafted around her.

Rose looked at the tablecloths that were as they would've been left when the café was last open. 'I think we could wash these because it doesn't look like there are any marks on them. They might take several washes but we could reuse them. Maybe we could embroider something on them, like your initials.'

Joyce frowned. 'They aren't mine; they're Simon's.'

Annie started wandering from table to table. 'I think most of this stuff could be used elsewhere, especially if we can get the smell of the fire out of it all.' She looked around her. 'It's not as bad as I thought it would be.'

Joyce swallowed hard, trying to move the lump that was forming in her throat. 'If you don't mind I'd like to just have a bit of time on my own.'

Rose stared at her. 'Are you all right?'

Joyce nodded. 'I just want a bit of time. I'll probably never come here again after today.'

The girls nodded. Each walked over and gave Joyce a hug.

Annie stepped back from Joyce. 'Are you sure?'

Joyce's lips tightened as she nodded.

'I don't mind waiting outside for you,' Rose whispered. 'I don't want to leave you.'

Joyce forced herself to smile. 'I'll be fine, just go and I'll see you later.' She waved as she watched them leave before sitting down at one of the tables. A tear rolled down her cheek as she looked around her. Everything was gone. She had gained a father and a brother but lost the man she loved along with her dream. 'Why does it have to be one or the other? Why couldn't I have it all?' Her sobs echoed in the damp smoky room she had loved so much.

'It doesn't.'

Joyce jerked round at the sound of Barbara's voice, quickly rubbing her hands across her blotchy face. 'I ... I didn't know you were here.'

Barbara stepped nearer. 'I didn't mean to startle you. I was looking at the damage in the kitchen.' She picked up a burnt piece of paper and handed it over to Joyce. 'I'm sorry, it got ruined.'

Joyce stared down at her certificate for baking cakes. 'It doesn't matter now. None of it does.'

Barbara pulled out a chair and sat next to Joyce at the table. She rested her hand on hers. 'It does matter. You are a fabulous cook and you need to carry on. This place was my father's dream, but you made it popular with your cakes and pies. We didn't have anything to do with it. Simon tried but none of us were up to it. You were the star here.'

Joyce sat in silence staring at her burnt certificate.

Barbara squeezed Joyce's hand. 'Coming here every day taught me a lot, even if it was only how hard Simon and you worked to keep it going. I think he hated it. He only kept it so he could see you every day. My mother was right when she said keeping it going had robbed him of his dreams, although I couldn't see it at the time.'

Joyce gave a wry smile. 'He told me that before he went off to do his training.'

Barbara watched as a tear slowly rolled down Joyce's cheek. 'You and Simon can start again. He loves you and I know you love him; otherwise you wouldn't be sitting here like this.'

Joyce shook her head. 'Simon and I have hardly spoken since he's been back. He never wrote to me and he didn't tell me he was back so I think that moment has gone.'

Barbara sighed. 'I've never seen two more miserable people who are determined to stay apart.'

Joyce couldn't look at Barbara. 'It was clearly not meant to be.'

Barbara shook her head. 'Well, regardless of Simon, you need to pick yourself up and start again, as indeed will Simon when he's ready.'

Joyce looked up. 'I don't have the money to start again. I just need to find other work.'

Barbara stood up. 'We just need to put our thinking caps on; I'm sure between us we can come up with something. I'm not going to let you throw everything away.'

Joyce watched as Barbara started to pace around the room. 'Why? I thought you didn't like me.'

Barbara smiled. 'I admit I wasn't sure at first. I didn't know anything about you and I must admit I thought you were probably using Simon.'

Joyce gasped. 'I wouldn't do that to anybody, let alone Simon.'

'I know. It wasn't based on anything, except my immaturity and maybe being protective of my brother.' Barbara paused.

'I'm ashamed to say I went out of my way to make life difficult for you when you should have had my support.' She smiled. 'You truly got my respect when you stood up to our lovely landlord, Mr Harris. You're a brave woman and I'm sorry for not being a better person, especially as I do believe I'm going to end up as your sister-in-law.'

Joyce twisted her hands in her lap. 'Thank you, but that's never going to happen. I appreciate your honesty, especially as I've had so many lies told to me. None of it matters now; it's all in the past.'

Barbara threw her arms around her. 'Thank you; now, we just need to figure out how you can move forward with your cooking.'

'Are you girls planning on robbing the place?'

Joyce froze on the spot. Fear ran down her spine. Her chest tightened. She took a breath before looking round towards the open door. 'Mr Harris, we've come to see how bad it is and what can be rescued.'

Mr Harris remained silent. He didn't take his eyes off Joyce. 'Well, make the most of the next couple of days because I'll be round to change the locks after that.'

Joyce stood up. 'What? Aren't you going to repair it so it can reopen?'

Mr Harris laughed. 'I told you once I'm not my father. It will not be reopening as a café.'

Joyce glared at him. 'But we have a contract—'

'Do you? Would you like to find it for me so we can read it together?'

Joyce marched over to the counter to the drawer where she had placed the contract. The scorched wood scratched as she pulled it open, splintering in places. Gasping, she moved her hand from side to side, lifting bits up, but it wasn't there. She looked up at Mr Harris, her eyes blazing with anger. 'Have you taken it?'

Mr Harris sneered. 'I told you I'm not like my father. I'm tired of being a landlord and trying to manage my father's ridiculous contracts.' He clapped his hands together. 'Now that you can't open the café, any contract you might have had has been broken so I'm selling. What's more I have a few interested parties lined up so you only have a few days to pack up your things and vacate the premises.'

Joyce's anger raged through her body. 'Did you start the fire?'

Mr Harris laughed. 'Oh dear, what a question to ask your landlord.' He turned and walked towards the door looking like the cat that got the cream. He didn't look back.

Joyce screamed after him. 'We're not finished.'

22

Joyce put the last of the washing-up onto the wooden draining board and emptied the water out of the bowl before rinsing her hands under the cold tap.

Rose and Annie took it in turns to dry the breakfast dishes.

Annie picked up a tea plate and rubbed it vigorously before placing it on the plate rack. 'I know this might be a delicate question, Joyce, but have you decided what you're going to do now the café is shut?'

Rose frowned at Annie before glancing across at Joyce. 'What?'

Annie grabbed another tea plate. 'We can't pretend everything is all right when it isn't.'

Joyce chuckled as she glanced over at her friends. 'Annie's been mixing with you too much, Rose. I suppose decisions will have to be made.'

'Charming.' Rose feigned a hurt expression. 'Well, insults aside, you'll have to make some decisions if only because you don't wanna be stuck in here all day.'

Joyce smiled at the girls. 'I'm so pleased you two are here. I'm very lucky. Although I must admit I haven't felt like that lately.' She grabbed the nearby towel and dried her hands on the rough cotton. 'But you're right I do need to start thinking about it.' She paused. 'Barbara was in the café while I was sitting there looking at everything.'

'And, getting upset, I bet,' Rose piped up.

Joyce ignored her quip. 'She thinks I should start again, with Simon.' Her lips tightened. She lowered her eyes. 'I don't know where Simon's head is at the moment. It might be best if I just try to move on by myself for now, and maybe with time, we could sort ourselves out.'

Annie nodded. 'I can see why Barbara thinks that, because you're clearly in love with each other. It would seem everybody can see it except you two. But if we shelve that for a moment, we need to work out what you are going to do next. Perhaps we should all sit down and write down some ideas.'

Rose's face lit up. 'Oh I love that idea, we can all just shout out whatever we think and then cross out what doesn't work. This could be fun.'

Joyce laughed at her friend. 'You best keep it clean. Remember there's a five-year-old in the house.'

The girls filed out of the kitchen and walked along the hall to the dining room. They each pulled out a wooden chair and sat at the table. There was suddenly a sound of ripping paper as Rose tore a page out of one of her sketchpads and grabbed a pencil. 'Right, where shall we start?'

Joyce stared down at the blank page. 'I don't know. I'm not even sure what we need to write down. I don't actually know what I'm going to be doing.'

Arthur walked into the room and looked at the girls staring blankly at the table. 'What are you all up to?'

Joyce looked up with relief at seeing him. 'That's a very

good question, and if I knew the answer I would tell you.'
She laughed. 'No, I do know what we're doing: we're trying
to make a list of jobs that need to be done.'

'What sort of jobs?' Arthur frowned. 'Are you talking
about jobs around the house?'

Annie laughed. 'No, you're all right. You're quite safe.
We're trying to think what Joyce could do to start again.'

Arthur pulled out a chair and sat down at the table. He
waved Philip over as he walked into the room. 'Come and
sit on my knee. We're trying to sort your sister out.'

Philip giggled. 'What do you mean sort her out?'

Joyce smiled at him. 'I can no longer work at the café
because it's closed so I have to find something else to do.'

Philip's mouth opened wide. 'You're not going to stop
cooking, are you?'

Laughter filled the room.

Rose looked at Joyce. 'Out of the mouths of babes.'

'All right, all right, but how am I going to start again? I
can't afford to open a shop or café, so how am I going to
manage?'

Joyce ran her damp palms down the sides of her black
dress, wishing she hadn't been practical and had instead
worn something more colourful. She stood outside Simon's
house with Barbara firmly by her side.

'Are you ready?' Barbara glanced across at Joyce.

Beads of perspiration started to form on Joyce's forehead.
Her eyes widened as she turned to stare at her. 'I'm not sure
I'll ever be ready; I think this was a bad idea. He probably
won't want to see me.'

'You two need to talk to each other, and both of you are letting pride get in the way. Well, I can tell you I'm not going to stand by and watch you both throw it all away.' Barbara shook her head. 'I know he won't be able to take his eyes off you. Trust me, I have to live with him.' She stooped down and picked up the two large shopping bags.

Joyce closed her eyes and took a deep breath. She had prayed for God to give her this chance so now she had to put her fear behind her. She opened her eyes before stooping down to pick up the two heavy bags at her feet.

Barbara nodded and stepped nearer the front door, with Joyce close behind her.

Joyce gasped as the door flew open; she was terrified Simon was going to be on the other side of it.

'Joyce, how wonderful to see you. Please come in.' Mavis beamed at the girl she was convinced would be her daughter-in-law one day. She just needed to bang their heads together. She chuckled. Hmm, maybe locking them in a room together might be a better idea.

Joyce forced herself to smile. 'Hello, Mavis, it's lovely to see you again.'

Mavis moved aside so the girls could step inside. 'My goodness, what have you got there?'

Barbara grinned at Joyce. 'It was everything we could carry from the café. Mr Harris is selling it or something so we went back and stripped it bare.'

'There's more but we couldn't carry it.' Joyce dropped the bags at her feet. 'Simon might want to start again one day. I know his father's dream was important to him.'

Mavis shook her head. 'It was important to his father

but I want Simon to let go of it. He's wasted too many years living his father's life.'

Joyce's heart sunk. She was on her own.

Mavis shut the door behind the girls. 'Anyway, I'll let Simon know you are here then Barbara and I will go and prepare dinner so you two can catch up.'

Joyce's heart was pounding in her chest. She wrung her hands together. 'Please don't worry. I should go really.' She turned to face the door.

Barbara reached out and tucked her arm in Joyce's. 'It would be rude not to have a cup of tea with us.'

Mavis raised her eyebrows as the corner of her mouth lifted. 'Let's go into the sitting room.'

Barbara clung on to Joyce and guided her through an open doorway further along the hall. 'Simon, look who's popped in. Take a seat, Joyce, and I'll help my mother with the tea.'

Colour flooded Joyce's cheeks. 'Thank you.' She perched on the edge of an armchair close to the fireplace. She felt Simon's eyes on her. 'Hello, Simon, I'm sorry to spoil your peace and quiet. Barbara and I have been clearing out the café so I helped bring some of it home. How are you feeling now?' Her words tripped over each other in the haste to break the silence.

Simon smiled. 'Slow down, you talk so fast when you're nervous.'

Joyce pulled back her shoulders. 'I'm not nervous; it's just we haven't really talked since the day you asked... Anyway, how are you? I hope there was no lasting damage from being in that fire.' She hesitated for a second. 'I think

Mr Harris caused the fire. I'm almost certain I saw him outside the café that night.'

Simon frowned. 'If he did the police couldn't find any evidence of it. They have already been to see me and said it looked like an accident.'

Joyce's eyes widened. 'I find that hard to believe. I know it was him. He wanted us out of there.'

Simon gazed at her. 'I've missed you.' He looked down at his burnt hands. 'In fact I miss seeing you every day.'

Joyce opened her mouth to speak but no words came out. It was now or never. She looked anxiously at the door that Barbara had pulled to when she left the room.

Simon laughed. 'Don't worry, they won't be back for ages. They're as subtle as someone hitting you on the head with a house brick.'

Joyce nervously glanced around the room, barely noticing the plush deep green curtains or the many family photographs that stood on every surface. 'You have a lovely home.'

Simon's lips tightened. 'Is that what we're going to do? Make polite small talk and ignore what's sitting between us. I made that mistake before and I'm not going to make it again—'

'No, wait, it's me who should clear the air between us.' Joyce peered down at her hands clasped together on her lap. 'It's me who ruined everything. It's me who said no when I should have said yes. It's me who prayed you would come out of that fire so I could tell you what you mean to me.' She looked across the room at Simon and took a deep breath. 'It's me who wanted you to know how much I love you, and how I regretted saying no to your proposal.' Heat flooded her cheeks. She looked back down at her hands, not wanting to see his embarrassment at her words. The silence seemed to hang in the air between them. She stood up. 'Anyway, I should go.'

'No, wait, please sit back down.' Simon stared at her. 'Please.'

Joyce slowly lowered herself back on to the armchair.

Grimacing, Simon flexed his fingers. 'I've never stopped loving you; in fact I've loved you since the first day we met. That was not long after your father died. Well, maybe I should say not long after the news of the *Titanic* sinking. I thought I'd left it too long and lost you for good when I proposed. It's something I regretted after.'

Joyce's heart sunk. She felt sick about what had she done. 'I can understand that after the way I spoke to you.'

Simon tried to edge forward in his seat. His mouth tightened as the pain of his injuries gripped him.

'Don't.' Joyce jumped up. 'Please don't try and get up, I don't want you to hurt yourself anymore.'

Simon sucked in his breath. 'Please come and sit nearer to me.'

Joyce walked over and sat at his feet, careful not to touch his injured legs.

Simon took a breath. 'You smell lovely.'

Joyce looked up and smiled. 'It's orange blossom. I no longer smell of fried food.'

Simon gently rested his hand on her shoulder. 'When I said I regretted it, you must know I don't regret proposing to you; it was my timing. I've had years to ask you and I waited until your life was turned upside down. I couldn't have got it more wrong.'

Joyce's eyes became watery as she looked up at him. 'If it's any consolation to you I've waited years too, and I regretted it after you'd gone. I thought you'd changed your mind because you didn't come and say goodbye so I could tell you I was sorry.'

Simon shook his head. 'It's all such a mess. I did go to the café that morning but you weren't there.' He took a breath. 'I thought you were so angry with me that I was never going to see you again.'

Joyce tightened her lips. 'You're right, it is a mess. I was late that morning because Philip had wet the bed. When I realiscd you had gone I couldn't believe you had just left me without saying goodbye.' Her throat tightened as she looked up at Simon and moved onto her knees. 'I love you with all my heart.'

Simon lowered his head and let his lips brush hers. 'I love you too but the problem is I no longer have a future, or a business to offer—'

'Sshhh.' Joyce placed her fingers on his lips before lifting herself up to softly press her lips against his.

Ted pushed open the black door of the Dog and Duck Public House and stepped inside and out of the muggy weather the summer had brought. It took a few minutes for his eyes to adjust to the darkness. The barman looked towards the door. The stench of stale alcohol and cigarette smoke immediately hit him and the soles of his shoes stuck to the floor, making walking noisier and slower. He looked around. He had never been in here at lunchtime before. A couple of old men sat in the corner nursing their pints of beer. It looked and felt different to him. It was shabby and run-down with its sawdust sprinkled on the floor. He nodded at the barman who was using a grey piece of rag to wipe down the drinking glasses while reading a newspaper that was laid out across the bar.

The barman nodded back.

'Is it all right to go through to the back room?' Ted took a packet of cigarettes out of his pocket. He fidgeted with the box, suddenly riddled with doubt. He was out of his depth and he knew it. 'Is Mickey Simmons in?'

The barman nodded. 'I don't know if he's seeing anybody, but just knock and go through. I'm sure they'll soon throw you out if they don't want you in there.'

Ted smiled, although he didn't know what he was smiling at. He certainly didn't want to get on the bad side of Mickey Simmons again. He took a couple of breaths before striding forward and giving a sharp rap on the door with his knuckles. Immediately he twisted the handle, opened the door and walked in.

Slips marched over towards Ted. 'Oh my goodness, Ted, what are yer doing here? Haven't you had enough? I didn't think I'd see yer for a while.'

'Slips, I'm here to see your father.'

Slips smiled. 'And what business could you possibly have with my father when there is no game going on?'

Ted smiled. 'I don't wish to be rude, Slips, but I want to talk to Mickey. I have money and I want to talk business.'

Slips shook his head. 'Well, I can tell you when the next game is going to be if that's what yer want to know, although I had hoped you'd learnt yer lesson this time and wouldn't be back again.'

'Thank you for your concern Slips, but as I've already said, I have money and wish to talk to your father.'

There was a scraping of a chair across the tiled floor. Slips looked behind him and saw his father walking towards them. The smell of cigar smoke got stronger as Mickey Simmons got nearer. 'Well, to what do I owe this honour, Ted? Don't usually see you during the day. I heard you say you wanted to see me.'

Ted pulled himself upright pushed his shoulders back and mumbled, 'I mustn't show fear.' He took a breath. 'I have some business to discuss with you.'

Mickey Simmons laughed. 'And what possible business could you and I have to talk about? Apart from you losing at cards to me what else is there? Or maybe you just wanna list of where the games are? You should know better than anyone that I never reveal when and where games are going to be held until a day or two beforehand.'

Ted studied Mickey Simmons for a second. 'I am expecting someone to join us shortly, but I wanted to get some preliminary talks out of the way first.'

Mickey put his cigar to his lips and puffed vigorously on it, sending swirls of smoke into the air. 'Now you have me intrigued.'

Ted nodded. 'That's good. I just want five minutes of your time to discuss some business.' He peered over his shoulder at Slips standing there waiting to chuck him out, before looking back at Mickey. 'I have money in my pocket and this bit of business will be to your advantage. You just need to sit down with me for five minutes.'

Mickey's eyes darted from side to side. 'All right, come over here and we'll take a seat and discuss your business proposal. Do you wanna whisky?'

'No thanks, I need to keep a clear head and make sure my decision is sound for once in my life.'

Mickey chuckled. 'I think this is a side of you I haven't seen before.'

Ted looked over his shoulder at Slips. 'I am expecting a Jeremiah King to join us shortly so can you please let him in when he knocks on the door?'

Slips looked over at his father, who gave him the nod.

Mickey walked Ted over to a nearby table. 'So, I can't pretend I'm not surprised to see you.' He indicated for him to sit down.

Ted nodded. 'No one is more surprised than me.' He walked round the table and pulled out a chair where he could see the room and the door.

Mickey smiled but said nothing.

Ted didn't take his eyes off him. 'I have some money in my pocket here and I want to buy something you own.'

Mickey's eyes narrowed as he once again drew on his cigar. 'Show me the colour of it, and then we'll discuss detail.'

Ted pulled a wad of notes out of his pocket and placed them on the table in front of him.

Mickey studied the notes for a moment. 'There's quite a sum there, Ted.' He paused, then reached out and picked up a pack of cards and confidently started shuffling them. 'You can tell me what you want in a moment but why don't we have some fun first.'

Ted watched the cards closely, almost mesmerised by the movement.

'Why don't we cut the deck and say ace high and the highest card wins?'

Ted sat in silence for a moment. 'Wins what?'

Mickey smiled, his cigar balancing in the corner of his mouth. 'If you win you can have what you want for nothing, but if I win I get that pile of money for nothing.'

Ted stayed silent.

Mickey stopped shuffling. 'Come on, there's a fifty-fifty chance you'll win, that's not bad odds is it?'

Ted's lips tightened. 'No, Mickey, I'm not gambling this money away. It has to be done all legal and above board. The person I've asked to join me here is a solicitor, who will draw up papers if you agree, which I think you will.'

Mickey raised his eyebrows. 'What is it you want to buy?'

Ted smiled. 'It's the place my wife and I had some good times in whenever we were in London together, and as you said it's bleeding you dry I thought I'd take it off your hands.'

Mickey threw back his head and roared with laughter. 'You most certainly can.'

Ted's heart pounded in his chest. 'First, we have to agree a figure.'

23

Rose stopped and put the two shopping bags down by her feet. She sighed, looking over her shoulder. 'Remind me why we volunteered to do this?'

Annie followed suit. She smiled at her friend. 'Because Joyce is our friend and she's trying to earn a crust and cooking is all she knows; at least until she works out what she's going to do.'

Rose chuckled. 'Oh yeah, that was it. Well, next time we have the urge to help just remind me it's hard work being nice to people.'

Annie giggled. 'You know you don't mean that. You'd do anything for Joyce, as indeed would I.'

Rose waved her hand in the air. 'I know, but where's her father when he's needed? He seems to have disappeared again.'

Annie moved aside to let someone pass her on the pavement. 'I've had similar thoughts but haven't liked to mention it. Do you think despite everything Joyce has been through, and him, he's gambling away his mother's money?'

Rose shrugged. 'It wouldn't surprise me. It's a shame because he could be helping her to build something good, but, I suppose, he's not that sort of father. I mean he's even left Philip. It's a good job Arthur is so great with him.'

Annie nodded. 'I was hoping that once she discovered he was alive they would be able to have a good relationship. It's a shame, especially as she had such a good one with her mother.' She picked up her shopping bags. 'Come on, let's get going. We're nearly at the theatre.'

Rose sighed before doing the same. 'I hope he doesn't keep hurting her because I may not be able to keep my mouth shut.'

Annie smiled at her friend. 'You will. You're not as tough as you make out. Look how kind and careful you were with Arthur when we first arrived and he was drinking all the time.'

Rose stared straight ahead. 'That was different. It wasn't right, but he was grieving whereas Ted just doesn't seem to care about anybody but himself.'

They stepped forward together, the sun warm on their faces.

Annie looked across at her friend. 'He did save Simon's life, so maybe he's not as selfish as we think.'

Rose nodded. 'Maybe, I hope I'm proved wrong, for Joyce's sake, but time will tell.'

They walked on in silence, each locked into their own thoughts.

'Thank goodness we've got here.' Annie pushed the stage door of The Lyceum open with her elbow and hips. She almost fell in when it flew open, and dropped the bags at her feet. Gasping for breath, she mopped her forehead. 'It doesn't feel like it's getting any cooler out there.'

Rose quickly followed. 'Let me get in out of this heat.' She squeezed past the bags Annie had dropped and followed suit.

'Sorry, I shouldn't have just left them there.'

Bert pulled his ample body up from his chair. 'It's not likely to end anytime soon; after all it is August.' He took a step nearer. 'Those bags look heavy. What yer girls got in there?'

Annie rubbed the palms of her hands together, the red welts confirming Bert's observations. 'They are heavy. We bought some food that our friend Joyce has cooked to sell. We thought we'd try and get the word out that she's a great cook. We're hoping that one day she'll have her own restaurant, but until then…'

Rose sighed. 'She's certainly had her life turned upside down lately so we're just trying to help where we can.'

Annie leant against the wall. 'I don't know if you met Joyce. She was cooking at the Meet and Feast Café in Shaftesbury Avenue, but it's closed down because there was a fire.' She raised her eyebrows. 'And before you say anything – no, she didn't cause it.'

Bert chuckled. 'I wasn't going to say anything.'

Rose laughed. 'Knowing you, Bert, I expect you were. Anyway, we bought in some food to see if the staff would like to buy any of it. Joyce was up all night cooking so it's very fresh and hopefully we can get her back on her feet.'

Bert tapped his lips with his finger. 'I don't know if yer need permission from Mr Tyler to do that.'

Annie lowered her head and her shoulders hunched over. 'Oh, I hadn't thought of that. It seemed like a good idea at the time but we obviously didn't think it through.'

Bert stepped forward and picked up the bags. 'Don't let it get yer down. I'm sure he'll say yes to yer. Where do yer wanna put it all and I'll carry them for yer?'

'I'm not sure; they need to be out of the way.'

'Look why don't yer just leave them 'ere with me while yer speak to Mr Tyler and see what he says.'

Rose stood up on tiptoes and kissed his cheek. 'Thank you, hopefully we won't be long.'

Kitty swung open the stage door and stepped inside. 'What's this? Are you two leaving home?' She laughed.

Annie smiled. 'It certainly looks that way doesn't it, but actually we bought some food in. We're hoping to sell to the cast for lunch or whenever they're hungry. I thought if I put a jar out then people could just leave the money for what they take. I trust them.'

Kitty gave her melodious laugh. 'That could be your first mistake.'

Annie looked crestfallen. 'Don't you think it's a good idea then?'

Kitty laughed again. 'I'm only playing with you. Who has made this food?'

Annie opened one of the bags and the smell of fresh bread wafted up. 'Our friend Joyce did. The one meant to be doing the food for your wedding. Actually, that's something we need to discuss with you now that the café's not available, but now isn't the right time or place.'

Rose nodded. 'Do you think Stan will allow us to lay a table out?'

'It smells lovely. I don't see why not! Leave him to me. We've just got to figure out where to put it where it won't be in the way.'

Bert opened one of the bags. 'Everything smells delicious. Can I have a pie? I'll give yer the money for it.'

Annie laughed. 'Of course. I have no desire to carry it all home again.'

There was a rustle of paper as Bert pulled out a meat and potato pie. He looked up to see three sets of eyes staring at him. 'I don't know if I can eat it with yer all staring at me.'

The girls laughed at his awkwardness.

Annie was the first to look away. 'Sorry, Bert, we were just waiting to see what you thought of it.'

Bert bit down on the edge of the pastry; he raised his eyebrows as he silently chewed and licked his lips.

Rose stared at the doorman, trying to second-guess what he was thinking. 'Well?'

Bert smiled. 'It's the best pie I've ever tasted. It's wonderful. The pastry almost melts in yer mouth. I'll tell everyone I see, don't yer worry about that.'

The girls stepped further along the corridor, ready to talk about laying out the food when Rose rushed back to one of the shopping bags. 'I almost forgot my material.' There was a rustling noise as she pulled out a brown paper bag, which had some white cotton peeking out the end.

Simon sat in front of the canvas tilting his head one way then the other. He'd never painted portraits before, and he wasn't sure if his attempt was good or bad, but he decided to persist. It hadn't taken long for it to take shape; he was enjoying the challenge of painting something different.

Mavis poked her head round the door, not saying a word;

she stood there almost holding her breath while watching her son. He appeared quite relaxed and relatively happy sat with his paintbrushes poised mid-air. He had always made no secret that painting was his way to lose himself. She no longer moaned about the smell of the paints or the drips from his brushes that formed shapes on the floor. Every morning she heard the groans coming from his bedroom as he did the exercises the hospital had given him. She worried he pushed himself too hard but had to admit she could see an improvement in the way he moved. He suddenly seemed to have purpose again.

Simon looked down at something in his hand and smiled.

Mavis craned her neck but couldn't see what he was holding, only the thin gold chain dangling from his hand. She stopped worrying about it and smiled, happy that he seemed more content, but she knew he was missing Joyce and couldn't understand why he wasn't doing more to contact her. However, she had to step back and let him make his own decisions. He appeared to have come to terms with everything that had happened, which somewhat surprised her.

Barbara sidled up to her mother. Mavis moved sideways in the doorway, leaning against the doorjamb, so her daughter could see in the small room. Barbara opened her mouth to speak but Mavis nudged her with her elbow. They both stood there in silence watching Simon at work.

There was a faint clicking noise before Simon suddenly turned round, his eyes narrowed. 'I thought someone was watching me, and assumed I was imagining it.' He put what he was holding into his painting coat pocket, away from prying eyes. He wasn't ready to share yet.

Mavis gave a nervous laugh. 'I'm sorry, Simon, but I could watch you paint all day long. It fascinates me.'

Simon gave half a smile. 'Well, maybe you should try doing it yourself.'

Mavis threw back her head and gave a hearty laugh. 'Oh no, I could never do what you do. I keep telling you you're the one with the real talent.'

Barbara stepped further into the room. 'How are you feeling, Simon? Are you still doing the exercises you were told to do?'

Simon chuckled at her. 'You're getting as bad as Mother. Keep fussing.'

Barbara sighed. 'I don't know whether to be pleased or insulted by that comment. However, I do want to make sure you're improving, and according to Mother, the doctor said you would. Mind you, after the pair of you keeping the fact you were back a secret for several weeks, I'm amazed I'm even talking to either of you.'

Simon put down his paintbrush. He took his sister's hand in his and squeezed it tight. 'Please try to understand I wasn't really in a fit state for visitors, and still needed to get my head around a few things. Even now I'm not sure I have. I still have a long way to go.'

Barbara nodded. 'I do understand. You're lucky I love you, but I can't help feeling a little hurt. And if I feel that I hate to think what Joyce must feel. You know she worked her socks off in that café every single day, early mornings to late evenings, even bringing that poor little mite in every day. She stood up to the landlord and wasn't going to pay any more rent, even though I thought we should, and he was scary.' She paused. 'I wasn't sure I liked her at first but

I was wrong. You need to pay her a visit and sort it all out before I really become right motherly and bang both your heads together.'

Mavis and Simon burst out laughing.

Simon turned to Mavis. 'See, Ma, she's turning into you. God help me with two of you in the house.'

Mavis winked at her daughter. 'And, that's without Joyce being here, to boss you around.'

Barbara run her hands down Simon's back; the coarse material of his painting coat was rough to the touch. 'In all seriousness, Simon, Peter is selling Joyce's baking on his stall. I've seen it, and everything is selling very well, which isn't that surprising. Are you going to help her? Are you going to be a part of it?'

Simon glanced back at his canvas and said nothing for a moment. 'Don't you worry about what I'm doing; you should just try and do your bit, if that's what you want.'

Mavis looked at her daughter and shook her head.

Barbara frowned. 'I'm sorry, Simon, I can't stand by and watch you and Joyce throw everything away.'

Simon stared straight ahead. 'Don't worry, I'm not throwing anything away.'

Barbara clenched her hands down by her sides. 'I don't know if you're interested or not, but all her friends are trying to help her one way or another, and you could be doing the same, especially considering how hard she worked for you.'

Simon rested his hand on the back of a nearby chair and pulled himself upright, grabbing his walking stick, which was leaning up against it. He peered up at the clock sitting on the solid oak mantelpiece: nearly ten o'clock. 'It's time I ventured out for a walk.'

Mavis frowned. 'I'll come with you.'

'No, Ma, I have to learn to get on with things and you have to let me.'

A tight band of fear gripped Mavis's chest. 'What if you fall or get tired?'

Simon frowned and his lips tightened for a moment. 'I'm not going to live my life as an invalid, Ma. If I get tired I'll find somewhere to sit and if I fall I will get up again, with or without someone's help.'

Mavis had anxiety etched on her face.

Barbara looked from one to the other. 'Ma, Simon's right, you have to let him go. You can't mollycoddle him for the rest of your days.'

Mavis lowered her eyes. 'I can try.'

Simon limped over to his mother. 'Ma, I'll be all right, have faith. This is something I have to do to start making everything right again.' He began undoing the buttons of his coat and smiled. 'See, I'm getting quite good at undoing buttons with one hand.'

Barbara smiled. 'Or you could have undone them while you were still sitting down.'

Simon chuckled. 'Yes, that's true, but who said I was organised enough to think things through properly?' Wincing, he took a step nearer to Barbara. 'Thank you for bringing me clarity.' He smiled at her serious expression. 'I'm a lucky man, and I'd be even luckier if you helped me out of this so I can get out of this house.'

24

Joyce glanced across at Peter. She was bursting to tell everyone about her conversation with Simon but there never seemed to be a good time. Annie and Rose hadn't been in the house at the same time lately so she had hugged her secret to herself. She watched as Peter weighed potatoes to put into his customer's shopping bag. Saturday was the busiest day of the week for the market. She was exhausted. Getting up early to do some baking to earn a living was taking its toll. She was grateful to Annie and Rose for asking Peter to sell her goods on his stall and for taking pies and bread to the theatre but she didn't know how long she could keep managing on just a few hours' sleep.

Peter smiled at the old lady. 'I 'ope you're going to be able to carry all these. They're going to be quite 'eavy.'

The old lady beamed at him. 'I'm stronger than I look.'

Peter chuckled. 'I'm sure that's true – most women are.'

The lady cackled. 'Anyway, that's what I've got the baby's pram for. Yer didn't fink I 'ad a baby in there, did yer?'

Peter looked over to the large wheeled carriage. 'Well, yer never know, I reckon yer young enough to.'

The old lady threw back her head and gave a loud cackle.

People strolling past stopped to glance in their direction, smiling before moving on. 'Get on wiv yer.'

Peter tipped the potatoes into the bag before picking up a couple of extra ones and throwing them in. 'I've given yer extra to make up for all the dirt that's on them.'

The old lady nodded. 'That's very generous of yer, dearie, thank you.'

Peter smiled. 'Anytime, we got ta look after yer now ain't we.'

The old lady handed over a couple of copper coins and Peter walked round the barrow with the bag. 'Now try it, if it's too 'eavy I'll bring it to yer 'ome for yer.'

The old lady took the handles of the bag. 'That's very kind of yer but I've been carrying potatoes for as long as I can remember so don't yer go worrying now.'

Peter nodded. 'I'll lift them into the pram as long as yer can get them out again.'

The woman peered at Peter. 'I will, even if it's only one potato at a time, I shall get them out.'

Joyce watched the woman as she walked away. 'You're very good with the customers – you even speak like them sometimes – no wonder you're so popular.'

Peter chuckled. 'If they don't like you then they'll go somewhere else and soon word gets about.' He nodded to a stall further up the road. 'Old Fred up there is a miserable so and so and I'm convinced that's why he doesn't sell much.'

Joyce followed Peter's gaze. 'Do you mean the flower seller?'

Peter nodded. 'Yep, I would imagine when people buy flowers they're usually for some kind of occasion or other, or maybe a centrepiece at home, but you're also selling the fragrance and happiness.'

Joyce glanced at him and laughed. 'Hark at you, getting all poetic.'

Peter gave her a sideways glance. 'Are you saying I'm wrong?'

'No.' Joyce looked up the road again. 'I must admit he doesn't seem very busy.' She gasped as she noticed a little boy holding a girl's hand just up the road. She took a step to run up the road but stopped suddenly. 'Sorry, Peter, I won't be a minute.' She sped up the road, muttering as she went. 'Excuse me, sorry, excuse me.' She kept focused on the children as she weaved in and out between people strolling along.

The little boy peered over his shoulder and saw Joyce running towards them. He stopped and stepped aside.

Joyce stopped in front of them gasping for breath. 'I've … I've been keeping an eye out for you two.'

The little girl stepped forward, but stayed close to her brother. 'Are you all right, miss?'

Joyce took several deep breaths. 'I've been worrying about you both. You never came to the café.'

The boy gave her a wide-eyed stare. 'We don't like to get to know people because they always want to split us up.'

Joyce nodded. 'I remember you saying that before. I have no desire to split you up; I just want to make sure you're all right.' She paused. 'My friend has a stall. Do you want to come and get some food?'

The children looked at each other for a moment before looking back at Joyce and nodding.

Joyce held her hand out to them then thought better of it. 'Follow me and I'll bag you up some bits.' She started walking away from them but kept glancing over her shoulder. 'Do you like pies?'

'Yes, we both do.' The boy hesitated. 'Not that we've eaten anything like that since our ma died.'

Joyce stopped at the stall. 'Thank you, Peter, I'm sorry for dashing off but I had to catch these two.'

Peter frowned as he tried to understand what was going on.

Joyce put some pies in one bag and bread rolls in another. She passed them to the boy. 'Come here every day and I'll get Peter to give you some food. There's extra in the bags for tomorrow.'

Peter watched her and started bagging up some fruit. He handed it over to the little girl.

'Thank you,' the children said as one.

The little boy stared at Joyce. 'Thank you, but why are you doing this for us?'

Joyce smiled. 'You shouldn't be living on the streets, but I do understand your reasons, so all I can do is make sure you don't starve.' She paused and gave them both a smile. 'Besides, you helped me to find my brother so I owe you a big thank you.'

The boy looked at his sister. She shrugged. He looked up at Joyce. 'I don't understand but thank you.' He took his sister's hand and they both walked up the road.

They both turned, smiled and gave her a wave.

Joyce smiled. 'That was a good thing you did, Peter.'

Peter reached out and wrapped his arms around her. He pulled back and smiled. 'And, you, I expect to hear that story when we're not so busy.'

Joyce nodded; she cleared her throat as she began filling the gaps that had emerged because of sales. 'You know I never expected to be this busy. It's been quite a week.'

Peter moved back to his own barrow and shook his head. 'I don't really know why. You're always being told what a good cook you are.'

Joyce looked wide-eyed at him. 'I know, but I suppose it's one thing to be told it and another thing to believe it.'

'Well, now you have the proof and when things settle down I'll carry on selling your bread and pies for a price.'

Joyce laughed. 'You mean I'd have to pay you?'

Peter chuckled. 'Business is business. You're the one who's always told me I had to stop giving everything away.'

Joyce looked at the ever-growing crowd wandering up and down between the stalls. 'Well, joking aside, if it continues you might have to get help.'

Peter nodded.

Joyce smiled. 'Yes, I'll muddle through with my baking for now. Mornings seem to be the busiest time for me so once Rose and Annie have finished organising things for Kitty's wedding I might be able to ask for their help. I don't know what Rose is making. I thought she was only doing the wedding dress, but she appears to be always sewing and embroidering things. Maybe her sewing business has grown and she hasn't told us. I hope so; she's very talented.'

Peter smiled. 'I'm sure she'll tell you when she's ready. Just as I'm sure they will help and be there when you need them.'

Joyce nodded. She looked at the queue that was forming and realised why Peter had to have help.

The breeze caught the front door out of Joyce's fingers, causing it to slam shut, making the key bang and rattle against the back of the door. 'Sorry, that wasn't meant to happen, despite how hot it is, it's a lot windier than I thought it was.' She turned to Rose and Annie. 'I wonder where everyone is? I'm a little concerned that Arthur took Philip out ages ago and he hasn't returned yet. Maybe I shouldn't leave the house. I mean, what if something has happened to them?'

Rose pushed her arm through Joyce's and gently tugged her down the front door step. 'Stop worrying, though I know you're not happy unless you're fretting about something.'

Annie waved a fly away from her face. 'Rose is right: it's a lovely day, the sun is shining, maybe Arthur has taken Philip to Hyde Park or something, letting him run around to tire him out. He's in safe hands so stop letting your imagination run all over the place.'

Joyce swung her handbag gently down by her side. 'I'm so glad you two came to London, and stayed with me. It feels like so much has happened in, what, just over a year. I couldn't have got through any of it without you.'

Rose squeezed Joyce's arm. 'You would've done because you're made of stern stuff, and let's face it, the reality of these things is that you don't really have much of a choice, but I'm glad we were here for you. But let's not forget you were here for us too.'

'It's what friends do, and we must promise to always be there for each other regardless of what's going on.' Annie straightened the line of buttons down the front of her pink blouse.

Joyce watched Annie tugging at her top. 'I love that blouse; it's a pretty colour.'

'Thank you.' Annie smiled. 'It's a hand-me-down from

Kitty. She has some beautiful clothes, but I suppose when you're in that position you always have to look good.'

Rose chuckled. 'That will be you one day.'

Annie threw back her head and laughed. 'I have a long way to go before that happens but I've been fortunate and had some wonderful support already.'

Rose nodded. 'Well, we all need help along the way, sometimes more than others but that's life.'

Joyce looked thoughtful for a moment. 'I can't believe how everyone has pulled together to help me get back on my feet after the café caught fire. I haven't told you but I went to see Simon, well, Barbara dragged me along to carry bags full of things from the café.' She took a deep breath. 'Anyway, I told him I was wrong in how I acted when he proposed to me. I even told him I love him. It's lovely that we finally got to talk. He told me he loves me and has done for a long time.' Joyce sighed. 'But he didn't propose again.' She shook her head. 'I should never have said no when he asked me, and now I'm frightened the moment has been lost forever.'

The girls remained silent for a few moments.

Annie stepped out into the road to avoid an older lady who was walking towards her. She glanced across at Joyce. 'I don't think for one minute it is over with. When we saw you and Simon through the café window it was obvious, even all those months ago, that you both loved each other. I cannot believe that either of you will just walk away from that.'

'Do you think he still wants me?'

Rose shook her head. 'I can't believe you're even asking that question. Do you still want him?'

'Of course I do. I've just said that I love him.'

'Then why wouldn't he want you?'

Joyce looked down at the pavement and took a deep breath. 'Rose, I had my opportunity and I threw it back at him, so why would he want me?'

Annie stepped back onto the pavement. 'Joyce, what you have to remember is he knew you were going through a difficult time. Do you not think he would forgive you for that? If he can't find that in his heart would you want to be married to him? Everyone makes mistakes, but your life has been turned upside down in the last few months, so I would think anybody would forgive you anything right now.'

Joyce nodded, but her frown told them she didn't really agree. Her thoughts immediately went to Simon's words in the café. *"None of us are perfect."* So would he forgive her for the pain she had caused him? 'Right, let's change the subject. Remind me why Kitty wants to see me this late in the afternoon?'

Annie forced herself to get excited about the up-and-coming conversation. 'She wants to talk to you about the food for the wedding. She and Stan are eating the food we've been taking in every day, and they've loved it all. So they probably want to talk about having something similar. They don't want anything too fancy. They've talked about it being wrong with the war still going on.'

Joyce pursed her lips. 'I'm not even sure I should be doing the food; I mean where am I going to cook it? The range at home is almost permanently in use just keeping up with the barrow and theatre sales. There's a need for a proper café kitchen because then there's more than one oven. Have they decided where they going to hold their wedding breakfast now the café has gone?'

Annie's face lit up. 'You have no worries there; it's all being taken care of.'

Joyce shook her head. 'What does that mean, "I have no worries there"? I have to know where to take the food and the people who run the venue where they're holding it might want to do it themselves.' She paused. 'Where are they holding it?'

Annie quickly peered under her eyelashes at Rose, who was smiling, clearly finding Annie's awkwardness amusing. 'I can't remember the name of the place now, but I'm sure Kitty will tell you when you see her. Has she mentioned it to you, Rose?'

Rose's smile vanished as she scowled at Annie. 'I'm not sure I've ever been told, and if I have I don't remember.'

Joyce glanced from one friend to the other. 'It all sounds a bit strange to me.' She looked around her, thankful it was quiet, but a Sunday wasn't really a day off for her. Guilt swamped her; she'd probably regret this outing in the morning when she didn't have enough produce to sell for the Monday morning customers. She suddenly realised they were walking down Great White Lion Street. 'Are we popping in to see Charlie?'

Rose shook her head. 'As much as I would love to, we don't really have time to stop for a cup of tea.'

Joyce scowled. 'It's a shame some of these businesses have closed down; hopefully when the men come back they'll reopen. My father was telling me that he and Ma enjoyed a couple of lovely meals in a restaurant down this road but I think it's all boarded up now.'

Rose felt her body temperature rise. 'Yes, Charlie

mentioned it had a change of ownership a few years ago, and the food wasn't so good after that.'

Joyce frowned. 'It's a shame when that happens. Mind you if the café was anything to go by it's hard work. I do miss it though, all the characters who liked to stop by and have a chat.'

They all walked on in silence for a moment.

Joyce glanced at Rose. 'You do know this isn't the quickest route to the theatre, don't you?'

Rose smiled. 'We're going the long way round, especially as it's got all the makings of a lovely day.'

Joyce gazed up at white clouds blowing across the blue sky. 'Hmm, it does look good at the moment.'

Annie cleared her throat, giving Rose the sign that she had seen Simon limping out of a doorway just up the road.

Rose nodded.

Joyce turned her head to look at Annie but stopped halfway. 'I … I hope … you're not…' She stopped walking and stared straight ahead, her voice barely a whisper. 'Simon?'

The girls turned to watch Joyce. Her eyes were shiny and damp; the tears didn't look far away.

Rose took Joyce's hand. 'Come and talk to him.'

Joyce slowly took a step. What was she going to say to him? Hadn't they already said everything that had to be said? A voice screamed in her head, *"Tell him you want to marry him. Tell him it doesn't matter about his injuries or what you'll do for money, just don't let him go again."* She nodded, stepping up her pace. 'Simon.' She beamed as she got nearer.

Simon's face broke into a broad smile. 'Joyce.'

Tears rolled down her cheeks. 'I really wanted to come

and see you again but I wasn't sure what to do. If I'm honest I was frightened of messing things up again. There was so much I didn't say when I came to your house…'

Simon dropped his walking stick and wrapped both arms around her, squeezing her tight. He pulled back before slowly lowering his head to lightly kiss her lips.

Joyce's stomach immediately did a somersault as she pulled him closer to passionately return his kiss. Her fingers moved up his back, feeling every muscle through his white shirt.

They were breathless when they pulled away from each other.

Joyce's lips felt swollen with passion.

Simon traced her lips with his fingers. 'We need to talk. There are things I should have said but I was too afraid. I was too worried I'd send you running out of my life.'

Joyce nodded. She didn't want to talk; she just wanted to be held in his arms forever.

'Hello, Simon, Joyce.'

Joyce couldn't help the groan from escaping from her. She peered over her shoulder. Her father looked tense as he held Simon's walking stick. 'Hello, Pa, you never were very good with your timing.'

Simon tucked his hand under her chin. 'Give your father a chance; please just listen to what he has to say.'

Joyce stared into his eyes. 'But we need to talk. There's things I want to say, which I should have said before.'

Simon nodded; the love he felt was shining bright from his eyes. 'Don't worry, I'll step back for a moment but I'm not going anywhere, not ever again.'

Joyce nodded.

Simon lifted his hand and gently thumbed away the lone tear rolling down her cheek. 'Go on, you can do this, and I'll be waiting.' He nodded to Ted as he reached out and took his walking stick from him.

Joyce took a deep breath before turning to her father. 'Is this how it's going to be now, you just popping up when you feel like it?'

Ted tightened his lips. 'I deserve everything you say or think about me but please just let me explain.'

Joyce shook her head. 'Explain what? You've obviously already gambled your mother's money away. I'm afraid I'd worked that bit out when you disappeared as soon as you got it.'

Ted nodded. 'I have gambled with the money, but I'd rather think of it as a sound investment and I did win this time.'

Joyce looked down at the pavement, wishing she was alone with Simon and not having this conversation. 'Pa, there's no such thing as a sound investment. You have to work hard to get anywhere in this life. I was hoping after everything that's happened you would have left the gambling behind.'

'I have, come with me.' Ted held out his hand for his daughter to take.

Joyce looked back up the road at Simon leaning heavily on his stick. 'Pa, I can't do this now; you must understand I need to talk to Simon. I can't let this happen a second time.'

Ted nodded; the pain was etched on his daughter's face. 'Simon is coming with us.'

Joyce's eyes widened. 'Where are we going?' She placed her hand in his.

Ted clasped it tight; he never wanted to let her go again.

'I have a lot of making up to do, and I hope what I have done will show you that I've turned over a new leaf and can be trusted.'

Joyce opened her mouth to speak but closed it again.

Ted smiled. 'Don't worry I know it's a big ask, but I'll keep trying until I get there.' He stepped forward and guided her to an open doorway. 'You first.'

Joyce stepped in and gasped. 'This is beautiful.' She looked around at the linen on the tables; church candles placed on small ceramic stands were the centrepieces. She spun round and looked at her father. 'I don't understand why we're here. I thought this had closed down. I was only just telling Rose and Annie about this place.' Her face lit up. 'Have you got me a job here?'

Ted beamed at her and nodded.

'Oh my goodness, this is exciting.' She looked around and noticed there was a certificate on the wall by the till. There was also a chalkboard to write on. The other walls had paintings of London on them, in various sizes; one in particularly caught her eye. She walked over and studied it for a moment. 'I do believe that's Shaftesbury Avenue.'

'It's the view we saw every day from the café.'

Joyce spun round at the sound of Simon's voice. 'This is fabulous. When do I meet the owner?'

Simon laughed. 'I think you may already know the owner.'

Joyce raised her eyebrows. 'Don't tell me it's you?'

Simon shook his head.

Jeremiah King pushed open the kitchen door just then and stepped out into the front of the restaurant, quickly followed by Joyce's friends as well as Philip, Kitty and Stan, Mavis and Barbara.

Joyce covered her head with her hands when she saw him. 'Hello, Mr King, forgive me but I don't connect you with good news so please tell me you are not here for me.' Her mouth dropped open when she noticed everyone had gathered around her. 'What's going on?'

Simon stepped forward and put his arm around Joyce's waist. 'Everything is all right.'

Ted glanced over at the solicitor. 'Do the honours, Jeremiah, before Joyce collapses.'

Jeremiah grinned as he stepped forward. He held some folded paper in his hands and an envelope and reached out to give it to Joyce.

Joyce stared at it, hesitant to take it from him.

Jeremiah waved it at her. 'Go on, I promise it's good news. Your grandmother left your father a substantial amount of money.'

'Always a solicitor, you're so officious.' Ted turned to Joyce and waved his arms around. 'This was the gamble. All of this is yours, and those papers prove it. For once in my life I did things right; I bet on my family.'

Joyce took the papers but didn't look at them. 'I don't know what to say.'

Ted walked over and wrapped his arms around his daughter. 'You can tell us what you're going to call it.'

Joyce shook her head. 'I can't believe it, but if it's really mine then it will be called Breaking Bread.'

The whole room broke into applause.

Philip turned and gave Arthur a huge smile. 'That's cos it's about coming together and sharing.'

Arthur ruffled his hair. 'Joyce has given it a good name then.'

Philip turned back, grinning and clapping his hands together as hard as he could.

Rose beamed. 'Good, now I can embroider the initials on the table linen.'

Joyce looked over at her and the penny suddenly dropped. 'Was that what all the sewing was?'

Rose nodded. 'But we've all had a part to play; Annie, Peter, Charlie and Barbara have been busy painting everything in sight, while Mavis taught your father how to clean everything in sight.' Everybody laughed and cheered.

Mavis giggled. 'The paintings on the walls are Simon's, although he would never tell you that.'

Simon smiled and shook his head. 'Peter also got all the plants you can see. Barbara picked out the mirror on the wall so it all looks bigger and brighter in here.'

Joyce shook her head. 'I can't believe it. I don't know what to say, except thank you but that doesn't seem enough.'

Ted glanced at Simon. 'Are you going to do it now?'

The room went quiet.

Simon took a deep breath before taking Joyce's hand. He led her over to the other side of the room. 'Ted, I'm going to need a hand.'

Ted stepped forward so that they stood either side of a covered frame on the wall.

Joyce's heart was pounding as she stood with her hands in a prayer position in front of her mouth.

Simon took a deep breath and nodded at Ted. The covering dropped. Everyone in the room gasped; silence reigned for a moment.

Tears rolled down Joyce's face.

Simon stepped forward. He frowned as his worry took

over. 'You don't have to keep it. I've never done a painting like this before.'

Joyce shook her head. 'It's beautiful.' She couldn't take her eyes off the family portrait. 'How, I mean, how did you know what my mother looked like?'

Simon thrust his hand in his trouser pocket and pulled out her gold locket. 'I've had the chain fixed. I'm sorry. It was never lost but I couldn't tell you without spoiling the surprise.'

Joyce threw her arms around him and hugged him tight.

The restaurant was high with excitement; laughter and clapping filled the room.

Joyce pulled back and looked at the portrait of her mother, father, Philip and herself. She frowned. 'It can't stay up there. It will have to come down.'

Simon turned to look at the painting and pursed his lips. 'I did say it wasn't good enough to go up on the wall.'

Joyce moved her gaze from the painting to Simon. 'That's not the reason. It's wonderful, but you've left a very important person off.'

Simon frowned as he looked at her.

Joyce smiled. 'You're the one who's missing.'

Annie and Rose gasped. They jerked round to stare at each other with wide eyes. They gripped each other's hands as they turned back to watch what was unfolding in front of them.

Simon passed his walking stick to Ted. He thrust his hand into his jacket pocket and pulled out a square blue velvet box. His eyes didn't leave Joyce's as he struggled to get down on one knee. 'Joyce, you are the love of my life. Will you marry me?'

Acknowledgements

As I write this most of the world is still in some level of Coronavirus lockdown, but we're all hopeful the vaccination is going to bring back a level of normality, like hugging each other; that's what I miss more than anything. It's a strange time we're living in, with people working from home and having to find new ways to entertain themselves. As always there have been some splendid heroes/heroines sprinkled with villains, but I hope everyone stays safe and keeps well. I can honestly say I'm grateful technology has enabled me to see my children and grandchildren over the Internet. I would like to thank my wonderful family for being so encouraging and supportive, their guidance is always appreciated.

A big thank you, and a lot of love, must go to the people I have never met, the virtual friends on social media and readers who have sent me messages, saying how much they have enjoyed my writing and are looking forward to the next book. I have had huge support from them, both in my writing and personal life, and that means the world to me.

I almost feel it goes without saying that I thank all the writing community and friends for their encouragement in the last year. I'd like to thank the Aria team, with special thanks going to Rhea Kurien, for her patience, understanding, and for giving me time and space. You were a pleasure to work with. I'd also like to thank my new editor, Hannah Todd, for fine-tuning my novel.

I truly hope everyone who reads this novel enjoys the second instalment of The West End Girls.

Thank you.
Elaine xx

If you wish to talk to me, here are my details:

Facebook: https://www.facebook.com/ElaineRoberts Author/
Twitter: https://twitter.com/RobertsElaine11
Website: https://www.elaineroberts.co.uk

About the Author

ELAINE ROBERTS had a dream to write for a living. She completed her first novel in her twenties and received her first very nice rejection. Life then got in the way again until she picked up her dream again in 2010. She joined a creative writing class, The Write Place, in 2012 and shortly afterwards had her first short story published. Elaine and her extended family live in and around Dartford, Kent and her home is always busy with visiting children, grandchildren, grand dogs and cats.

Hello from Aria

We hope you enjoyed this book! If you did, let us know – we'd love to hear from you.

We are Aria, a dynamic fiction imprint from award-winning publishers Head of Zeus. At heart, we're committed to publishing fantastic commercial fiction – from romance to sagas to historical fiction. Visit us online and discover a community of like-minded fiction fans!

You can find us at:
www.ariafiction.com
f @ariafiction
🐦 @Aria_Fiction
📷 @ariafiction

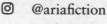